The complete Tales *and* Trifles *of* *Jean de la Fontaine*

Cover: From ‘The Stolen Kiss’ by Jean-Honoré Fragonard

Printed on acid-free ANSI archival quality paper.

Jean de la Fontaine,
de l'Academie Françoise

Contents

Illustrations

Life of
Jean de la Fontaine

Jean de La Fontaine was born on the 8th of July, 1621, at Château-Thierry, and his family held a respectable position there.

His education was neglected, but he had received that genius which makes amends for all. While still young the tedium of society led him into retirement, from which a taste for independence afterwards withdrew him.

He had reached the age of twenty-two, when a few sounds from the lyre of Malherbe, heard by accident, awoke in him the muse which slept.

He soon became acquainted with the best models: Phaedrus, Virgil, Horace and Terence amongst the Latins; Plutarch, Homer and Plato, amongst the Greeks; Rabelais, Marot and d'Urfe, amongst the French; Tasso, Ariosto and Boccaccio, amongst the Italians.

He married, in compliance with the wishes of his family, a beautiful, witty and chaste woman, who drove him to despair.

He was sought after and cherished by all distinguished men of letters. But it was two Ladies who kept him from experiencing the pangs of poverty.

La Fontaine, if there remain anything of thee, and if it be permitted to thee for a moment to soar above all time; see the names of La Sablière and of Hervard pass with thine to the ages to come!

The life of La Fontaine was, so to speak, only one of continual distraction. In the midst of society, he was absent from it. Regarded almost as an imbecile by the crowd, this clever author, this amiable man, only permitted himself to be seen at intervals and by friends.

He had few books and few friends.

Amongst a large number of works that he has left, everyone knows his fables and his tales, and the circumstances of his life are written in a hundred places.

He died on the 16th of March, 1695.

Let us keep silence about his last moments, for fear of irritating those who never forgive.

His fellow-citizens honour him in his posterity to this day.

Long after his death, foreigners went to visit the room which he had occupied.

Once a year, I shall go to visit his tomb.

On that day, I shall tear up a fable of La Mothe, a tale of Vergier, or several of the best pages of Grécourt.

He was buried in the cemetery of Saint-Joseph, by the side of Molière.

That spot will always be held sacred by poets and people of taste.

Tales
and
Trifles
of
Jean de la Fontaine

Volume I

The Author's Preface to the First Volume of these Tales

I had resolved not to consent to the printing of these Tales, until after I had joined to them those of Boccaccio, which are those most to my taste; but several persons have advised me to produce at once what I have remaining of these trifles, in order to prevent from cooling the curiosity to see them, which is still in its first ardour. I gave way to this advice without much difficulty, and I have thought well to profit by the occasion. Not only is that permitted me, but it would be vanity on my part to despise such an advantage. It has sufficed me to wish that no one should be imposed upon in my favour, and to follow a road contrary to that of certain persons, who only make friends in order to gain voices in their favour by their means; creatures of the Cabal, very different from that Spaniard who prided himself on being the son of his own works. Although I may still be as much in want of these artifices as any other person, I cannot bring myself to resolve to employ them; however I shall accommodate myself if possible to the taste of the times, instructed as I am by my own experience, that there is nothing which is more necessary. Indeed one cannot say that all seasons are suitable for all classes of books. We have seen the Roundelays, the Metamorphoses, the Crambos, reign one after another. At present, these gallantries are out of date and nobody cares about them: so certain is it that what pleases at one time may not please at another! It only belongs to works of truly solid merit and sovereign beauty, to be well received by all minds and in all ages, without possessing any other passport than the sole merit with which they are filled. As mine are so far distant from such a high degree of perfection, prudence advises that I should keep them in my cabinet unless I choose well my own time for producing them. This is what I have done, or what I have tried to do in this edition, in which I have only added new Tales, because it seemed to me that people were prepared to take pleasure in them. There are some which I have extended, and others which I have abridged, only for the sake of diversifying them and making them less tedious. But I am occupying myself over matters about which perhaps people will take no notice, whilst I have reason to apprehend much more important objections. There are only two principal ones which can be made against me; the one that this book is licentious; the other that it does not sufficiently spare the fair sex. With regard to the first, I say boldly that the nature of what is understood as a tale decided that it should be so, it being an indispensable law according to Horace, or rather according to reason and common sense, that one must conform one's self to the nature of the things about which one writes. Now, that I should be permitted to write about these as so many others have done and with success I do not believe it can be doubted; and people cannot condemn me for so doing, without also condemning Ariosto before me and the Ancients before Ariosto. It may be said that I should have done better to have suppressed certain details, or at least to have disguised them. Nothing was more easy, but it would have weakened the tale and taken away some of its charm: So much circumspection is only necessary in works which promise great discretion from the beginning, either by their subject or by the manner in which they are treated. I confess that it is necessary to keep within certain limits, and that the narrowest are the best; also it must be allowed me that to be too scrupulous would spoil all. He who would wish to reduce Boccaccio to the same modesty as Virgil, would assuredly produce nothing worth having, and would sin against the laws of propriety by setting himself the task to observe them. For in order that one may not make a mistake in matters of verse and prose, extreme modesty and propriety are two very different things. Cicero makes the latter consist in saying what is appropriate one should say, considering the place, the time, and the persons to whom one is speaking. This principle once admitted, it is not a fault of judgment to entertain the people of to-day with Tales which are a little broad. Neither do I sin in that against morality. If there is anything in our writings which is capable of making an impression on the mind, it is by no means the gaiety of these Tales; it passes off lightly; I should rather fear a tranquil melancholy, into which the most chaste and modest novels are very capable of plunging us, and which is a great preparation for love. As to the second objection, by which people reproach me that this book does wrong to womankind, they would be right if I were speaking seriously: but who does not see that this is all in jest, and consequently cannot injure? We must not be afraid on that account that marriages in the future will be less frequent, and husbands more on their guard. It may still be objected that these Tales are unfounded or that they have everywhere a foundation easy to destroy; in short that they are absurdities and have not the least tinge of probability. I reply in a few words that I have my authorities: and besides it is neither truth nor probability which makes the beauty and the charm of these Tales: it is only the manner of telling them. These are the principal points on which I have thought it necessary to defend myself. I abandon the rest to the censors; the more so as it would be an infinite undertaking to pretend to reply to all. Criticism never stops short nor ever wants for subjects on which to exercise itself: even if those I am able to foresee were taken from it, it would soon have discovered others.

Joconde

IN Lombardy's fair land, in days of yore,
Once dwelt a prince, of youthful charms, a store;
Each FAIR, with anxious look, his favours sought,
And ev'ry heart within his net was caught.
Quite proud of beauteous form and smart address,
In which the world was led to acquiesce,
He cried one day, while ALL attention paid,
I'll bet a million, Nature never made
Beneath the sun, another man like me,
Whose symmetry with mine can well agree.
If such exist, and here will come, I swear
I'll show him ev'ry lib'ral princely care.

A NOBLE Roman, who the challenge heard,
This answer gave the king his soul preferr'd
—Great prince, if you would see a handsome man,
To have my brother here should be your plan;
A frame more perfect Nature never gave;
But this to prove, your courtly dames I crave;
May judge the fact, when I'm convinc'd they'll find:
Like you, the youth will please all womankind;
And since so many sweets at once may cloy,
'Twere well to have a partner in your joy.

THE king, surpris'd, expressed a wish to view
This brother, form'd by lines so very true;
We'll see, said he, if here his charms divine
Attract the heart of ev'ry nymph, like mine;
And should success attend our am'rous lord,
To you, my friend, full credit we'll accord.

AWAY the Roman flew, Joconde to get,
(So nam'd was he in whom these features met;)
'Midst woods and lawns, retir'd from city strife,
And lately wedded to a beauteous wife;
If bless'd, I know not; but with such a fair,
On him must rest the folly to despair.

THE Roman courtier came, his business told
The brilliant offers from the monarch bold;
His mission had success, but still the youth
Distraction felt, which 'gan to shake his truth;
A pow'rful monarch's favour there he view'd;
A partner here, with melting tears bedew'd;
And while he wavered on the painful choice,
She thus address'd her spouse with plaintive voice:

CAN you, Joconde, so truly cruel prove,
To quit my fervent love in courts to move?
The promises of kings are airy dreams,
And scarcely last beyond the day's extremes
By watchful, anxious care alone retain'd,
And lost, through mere caprice, as soon as gain'd.
If weary of my charms, alas! you feel,
Still think, my love, what joys these woods conceal;

Here dwell around tranquillity and ease;
The streams' soft murmurs, and the balmy breeze,
Invite to sleep; these vales where breathe the doves,
All, all, my dear Joconde, renew our loves;
You laugh!—Ah! cruel, go, expose thy charms,
Grim death will quickly spare me these alarms!

JOCONDE'S reply our records ne'er relate,
Nor what he did, nor how he left his mate;
And since contemp'raries decline the task;
'Twere folly, such details of me to ask.
We're told, howe'er, when ready to depart,
With flowing tears she press'd him to her heart;
And on his arm a brilliant bracelet plac'd,
With hair around her picture nicely trac'd;
This guard in full remembrance of my love,
She cried;—then clasped her hands to pow'rs above.

TO see such dire distress, and poignant grief,
Might lead to think, soon death would bring relief;
But I, who know full well the female mind,
At best oft doubt affliction of the kind.

JOCONDE set out at length; but that same morn;
As on he mov'd, his soul with anguish torn,
He found the picture he had quite forgot,
Then turn'd his steed, and back began to trot.
While musing what excuse to make his mate,
At home he soon arriv'd, and op'd the gate;
Alighted unobserv'd, ran up the stairs;
And ent'ring to the lady unawares,

He found this darling rib, so full of charms;
Intwin'd within a valet's brawny arms!

'MIDST first emotions of the husband's ire;
To stab them while asleep he felt desire;
Howe'er, he nothing did; the courteous wight;
In this dilemma, clearly acted right;
The less of such misfortunes said is best;
'Twere well the soul of feeling to divest;
Their lives, through pity, or prudential care;
With much reluctance, he was led to spare;
Asleep he left the pair, for if awake,
In honour, he a diff'rent step would take.—
Had any smart gallant supplied my place,
Said he, I might put up with this disgrace;
But naught consoles the thought of such a beast;
Dan Cupid wantons, or is blind at least;
A bet, or some such whim, induc'd the god,
To give his sanction to amours so odd.

THIS perfidy Joconde so much dismay'd;
His spirits droop'd, his lilies 'gan to fade;
No more he look'd the charmer he had been;
And when the court's gay dames his face had seen;
They cried, Is this the beauty, we were told,
Would captivate each heart, or young or old?
Why, he's the jaundice; ev'ry view displays
The mien of one,—just fasted forty days!

WITH secret pleasure, this, Astolphus learn'd;
The Roman, for his brother, risks discern'd,

Whose secret griefs were carefully conceal'd,
(And these Joconde could never wish reveal'd;)
Yet, spite of gloomy looks and hollow eyes,
His graceful features pierc'd the wan disguise,
Which fail'd to please, alone through want of life,
Destroy'd by thinking on a guilty wife.

THE god of love, in pity to our swain,
At last revok'd BLACK CARE'S corroding reign;
For, doubtless, in his views he oft was cross'd,
While such a lover to the world was lost.

THE hero of our tale, at length, we find
Was well rewarded: LOVE again proved kind;
For, musing as he walk'd alone one day,
And pass'd a gall'ry, (held a secret way,)
A voice in plaintive accents caught his ear,
And from the neighb'ring closet came, 'twas clear:
My dear Curtade, my only hope below,
In vain I love;—you colder, colder grow;
While round no fair can boast so fine a face,
And numbers wish they might supply thy place,
Whilst thou with some gay page prefer'st a bet,
Or game of dice with some low, vulgar set,
To meeting me alone; and when just now
To thee I sent, with rage thou knit'st thy brow,
And Dorimene, with ev'ry curse abus'd
Then played again, since better that amus'd,
And left me here, as if not worth a thought,
Or thou didst scorn what I so fondly sought.

ASTONISHMENT, at once, our Roman seiz'd;
But who's the fair that thus her bosom eas'd?
Or, who's the gay Adonis, form'd to bless?
You'd try a day, and not the secret guess,
The queen's the belle:—and, doubtless you will stare,
The king's own dwarf the idol of her care!

THE Roman saw a crevice in the wood,
Through which he took a peep from where he stood;
To Dorimene our lovers left the key,
Which she had dropt when lately forc'd to flee,
And this Joconde pick'd up, a lucky hit,
Since he could use it when he best thought fit.
It seems, said he, I'm not alone in name,
And since a prince so handsome is the same,
Although a valet has supplied my place,
Yet see, the queen prefers a dwarf's embrace.

THIS thought consol'd so well,—his youthful rays
Returned, and e'en excelled his former days;
And those who lately ridicul'd his charms,
Now anxious seem'd to revel in his arms
'Twas who could have him,—even prudes grew kind;—
By many belles Astolphus was resign'd;
Though still the king retain'd enough, 'twas seen;—
But now let us resume the dwarf and queen.

OUR Roman, having satisfied his eyes,
At length withdrew, confounded by surprise.
Who follows courts, must oft with care conceal,
And scarcely know what sight and ears reveal.

YET, by Joconde the king was lov'd so well,
What now he'd seen he greatly wish'd to tell;
But, since to princes full respect is due,
And what concerns them, howsoever true,
If thought displeasing, should not be dispos'd
In terms direct, but obviously dispos'd,
To catch the mind, Joconde at ease detail'd,
From days of yore to those he now bewail'd,
The names of emp'rors and of kings, whose brows,
By wily wives, were crown'd with leafless boughs!
And who, without repining, view'd their lot,
Nor bad made worse, but thought things best forgot.
E'en I, who now your majesty address,
Continued he, am sorry to confess,
The very day I left my native earth,

To wait upon a prince of royal birth,
Was forced t'acknowledge cuckoldom among
The gods who rule the matrimonial throng,
And sacrifice thereto with aching heart
Cornuted heads dire torments oft impart:

THE tale he then detail'd, that rais'd his spleen;
And what within the closet he had seen;
The king replied, I will not be so rude,
To question what so clearly you have view'd;
Yet, since 'twere better full belief to gain,
A glimpse of such a fact I should obtain,
Pray bring me thither; instantly our wight;
Astolphus led, where both his ears and sight
Full proof receiv'd, which struck the prince with awe;

Who stood amaz'd at what he heard and saw.
But soon reflection's all-convincing pow'r
Induced the king vexation to devour;
True courtier-like, who dire misfortunes braves,
Feels sprouting horns, yet smiles at fools and knaves:
Our wives, said he, a pretty trick have play'd,
And shamefully the marriage bed betray'd;
Let us the compliment return, my friend,
And round the country our amours extend;
But, in our plan the better to succeed,
Our names we'll change; no servants we shall need;—
For your relation I desire to pass,
So you'll true freedom use; then with a lass
We more at ease shall feel, more pleasure gain;
Than if attended by my usual train.

JOCONDE with joy the king's proposal heard;
On which the latter with his friend conferr'd;
Said he, 'twere surely right to have a book,
In which to place the names of those we hook,
The whole arrang'd according to their rank,
And I'll engage no page remains a blank,
But ere we leave the range of our design,
E'en scrup'lous dames shall to our wish incline,
Our persons handsome, with engaging air,
And sprightly, brilliant wit no trifling share,—
'Twere strange, possessing such engaging charms,
They should not tumble freely in our arms.

THE baggage ready, and the paper-book,
our smart gallants the road together took,

But ‘twould be vain to number their amours;
With beauties, Cupid favoured them by scores;
Blessed, if only seen by either swain,
And doubly bless’d who could attention gain:
Nor wife of alderman, nor wife of mayor,
Of justice, nor of governor was there,
Who did not anxiously desire her name
Might straight be entered in the book of fame!
Hearts, which before were thought as cold as ice,
Now warm’d at once and melted in a trice.

SOME infidel, I fancy, in my ear
Would whisper-probabilities, I fear,
Are rather wanting to support the fact;
However perfectly gallants may act,
To gain a heart requires full many a day
If more be requisite I cannot say;
‘Tis not my plan to dupe or young or old,
But such to me, howe’er the tale is told,
And Ariosto never truth forsakes;
Yet, if at ev’ry step a writer takes,
He’s closely question’d as to time and place,
He ne’er can end his work with easy grace.
To those, from whom just credence I receive,
Their tales I promise fully to believe.

AT length, when our advent’rers round had play’d,
And danc’d with ev’ry widow, wife, and maid,
The full blown lily and the tender rose,
Astolphus said, though clearly I suppose,
We can as many hearts securely link,

As e'er we like, yet better now, I think,
To stop a while in some delightful spot,
And that before satiety we've got;
For true it is, with love as with our meat;
If we, variety of dishes eat,
The doctors tell us inj'ry will ensue,
And too much raking none can well pursue.
Let us some pleasing fair-one then engage,
To serve us both:—enough she'll prove I'll wage.

JOCONDE at once replied, with all my heart,
And I a lady know who'll take the part;
She's beautiful; possesses store of wit;
And is the wife of one above a cit.

WITH such to meddle would be indiscreet,
Replied the king, more charms we often meet,
Beneath a chambermaid or laundress' dress,
Than any rich coquette can well possess.
Besides, with those, less form is oft requir'd,
While dames of quality must be admir'd;
Their whims complied with, though suspicions rise;
And ev'ry hour produces fresh surprise,
But this sweet charmer of inferior birth
A treasure proves; a source of bliss on earth.
No trouble she to carry here nor there;
No balls she visits, and requires no care;
The conquest easy, we may talk or not;
The only difficulty we have got,
Is how to find one, we may faithful view;
So let us choose a girl, to love quite new.

SINCE these, replied the YOUTH, your thoughts appear,
What think you of our landlord's daughter here?
That she's a perfect virgin I've no doubt,
Nor can we find a chaster round about;
Her very doll more innocent won't prove,
Than this sweet nymph design'd with us to move.

THE scheme our prince's approbation met;
The very girl, said he, I wish'd to get;
This night be our attack; and if her heart
Surrenders when our wishes we impart,
But one perplexity will then remain;
'Tis who her virgin favours shall obtain?
The honour 's all a whim, and I, as king,
At once assuredly should claim this thing:
The rest 'tis very easy to arrange;
As matters suit we presently can change.

IF ceremony 'twere, Joconde replied,
All cavil then we quickly could decide;
Precedence would no doubt with you remain:
But this is quite another case 'tis plain;
And equity demands that we agree,
By lot to settle which the man shall be.

THE noble youths no arguments would spare,
And each contended for the spoiler's care;
Howe'er Joconde obtained the lucky hit,
And first embrac'd this fancied dainty bit.

THE girl who was the noble rival's aim,

That ev'ning to the room for something came;
Our heroes gave her instantly a chair,
And lavished praises on her face and hair;
A diamond ring soon sparkled in her eyes;
Its pleasing pow'rs at sight obtain'd the prize.

THE bargain made, she, in the dead of night,
When silence reign'd and all was void of light,
With careful steps their anxious wish obey'd,
And 'tween them both, she presently was laid;
'Twas Paradise they thought, where all is nice,
And our young spark believ'd he broke the ice.

THE folly I forgive him;—'tis in vain
On this to reason—idle to complain;
The WISE have oft been dup'd it is confest,
And Solomon it seems among the rest.
But gay Joconde felt nothing of the kind,
A secret pleasure glow'd within his mind;
He thought Astolphus wond'rous bliss had missed,
And that himself alone the fair had kiss'd;
A clod howe'er, who liv'd within the place,
Had, prior to the Roman, her embrace.

THE soft amour extended through the night,
The girl was pleas'd, and all proceeded right;
The foll'wing night, the next, 'twas still the same;
Young Clod at length her coldness 'gan to blame;
And as he felt suspicious of the act,
He watch'd her steps and verified the fact:
A quarrel instantly between them rose;

Howe'er the fair, his anger to compose,
And favour not to lose, on honour vow'd,
That when the sparks were gone, and time allow'd,
She would oblige his craving, fierce desire;—
To which the village lad replied with ire:—
Pray what care I for any tavern guest,
Of either sex; to you I now protest,
If I be not indulg'd this very night,
I'll publish your amours in mere despite.

HOW can we manage it, replied the belle,
I'm quite distressed—indeed the truth to tell,
I've promis'd them this night to come again,
And if I fail, no doubt can then remain,
But I shall lose the ring, their pledg'd reward,
Which would, you know for me, be very hard.

TO you I wish the ring, replied young Clod,
But do they sleep in bed, or only nod?
Tell me, pray; oh, said she, they sleep most sound;
But then between them plac'd shall I be found,
And while the one amidst Love's frolicks sports,
The other quiet lies, or Morpheus courts.
On hearing this the rustick lad proposed,
To visit her when others' eyes were closed.
Oh! never risk it, quickly she replied;
'Twere folly to attempt it by their side.
He answer'd, never fear, but only leave
The door ajar, and me they'll not perceive.

THE door she left exactly as he said;

The spark arriv'd, and then approach'd the bed,
('Twas near the foot,) then 'tween the sheets he slid,
But God knows how he lay, or what he did.
Astolphus and Joconde ne'er smelt a rat,
Nor ever dreamt of what their girl was at,
At length when each had turn'd and op'd his eyes,
Continual movement fill'd him with surprise.
The monarch softly said:—why how is this?
My friend has eaten something, for in bliss,
He revels on, and truly much I fear,
His health will show, it may be bought too dear.

THIS very sentiment Joconde bethought;
But Clod a breathing moment having caught,
Resum'd his fun, and that so oft would seek:
He gratified his wishes for a week;
Then watching carefully, he found once more;
Our noble heroes had begun to snore,
On which he slyly took himself away,
The road he came, and ere 'twas break of day;
The girl soon follow'd, since she justly fear'd,
Still more fatigues:—so off she quickly steer'd,

AT length when both the nobles were awake;
Astolphus said, my friend you rest should take,
'Twere better till to-morrow keep in bed,
Since sleep, with such fatigues, of course has fled:
You talk at random, cried the Roman youth;
More rest I fancy you require in truth;
You've led a pretty life throughout the night;
I? said the king; why I was weary quite,

So long I waited; you no respite gave,
But wholly seem'd our little nymph t' enslave;
At length to try if I from rage could keep,
I turn'd my back once more, and went to sleep.
If you had willingly the belle resign'd,
I was, my friend, to take a turn inclin'd;
That had sufficed for me, since I, like you,
Perpetual motion never can pursue.

YOUR raillery, the Roman youth replied,
Quite disconcerted, pray now lay aside,
And talk of something else; you've fully shown,
That I'm your vassal, and since you are grown
So fond that you to keep the girl desire,
E'en wholly to yourself, why I'll retire;
Do with her what you please, and we shall see,
How long this furor will with you agree.

IT may, replied the king, for ever last,
If ev'ry night like this, I'm doom'd to fast.

SIRE, said Joconde, no longer let us thus,
In terms of playful raillery discuss;
Since such your pleasure, send me from your view;
On this the youthful monarch angry grew,
And many words between the friends arose;
The presence of the nymph Astolphus chose;
To her they said, between us judge, sweet fair,
And every thing was stated then with care.

THE girl with blushing cheeks before them kneel'd,

And the mysterious tale at once reveal'd.
Our heroes laugh'd; the treach'ry vile excus'd;
And gave the ring, which much delight diffus'd;
Together with a handsome sum of gold,
Which soon a husband in her train enroll'd,
Who, for a maid, the pretty fair-one took;
And then our heroes wand'ring pranks forsook,
With laurels cover'd, which in future times,
Will make them famous through the Western climes;
More glorious since, they only cost, we find,
Those sweet ATTENTIONS pleasing to the MIND.

So many conquests proud of having made,
And over full the BOOK of—those who'd play'd;
Said gay Astolphus we will now, my friend,
Return the shortest road and poaching end;
If false our mates, yet we'll console ourselves,
That many others have inconstant elves.
Perhaps, in things a change will be one day,
And only tender flames LOVE'S torch display;
But now it seems some evil star presides,
And Hymen's flock the devil surely rides.
Besides, vile fiends the universe pervade,
Whose constant aim is mortals to degrade,
And cheat us to our noses if they can,
(Hell's imps in human shape, disgrace to man!)
Perhaps these wretches have bewitch'd our wives,
And made us fancy errors in their lives.
Then let us like good citizens, our days
In future pass amidst domestick ways;
Our absence may indeed restore their hearts,

For jealousy oft virtuous truths imparts.

IN this Astolphus certainly believ'd;
The friends return'd, and kindly were receiv'd;
A little scolding first assail'd the ear;
But blissful kisses banish'd ev'ry fear.
To balls and banquets ALL themselves resigned;
Of dwarf or valet nothing more we find;
Each with his wife contentedly remained:—
'Tis thus alone true happiness is gained.

The Cudgelled and Contented Cuckold

SOME time ago from Rome, in smart array,
A younger brother homeward bent his way,
Not much improved, as frequently the case
With those who travel to that famous place.
Upon the road oft finding, where he stayed,
Delightful wines, and handsome belle or maid,
With careless ease he loitered up and down.—
One day there passed him in a country town,
Attended by a page, a lady fair,
Whose charming form and all-engaging air,
At once his bosom fired with fond desire;
And nearer still, her beauties to admire.
He most gallantly saw her safely home;
Attentions charm the sex where'er we roam.

OUR thoughtless rambler pleasures always sought:
From Rome this spark had num'rous pardons brought;
But,—as to virtues (this too oft we find),
He'd left them,—with his HOLINESS behind!

THE lady was, by ev'ry one, confessed,
Of beauty, youth, and elegance possessed;
She wanted naught to form her bliss below,

But one whose love would ever fondly flow.

INDEED so fickle proved this giddy youth,
That nothing long would please his heart or tooth;
Howe'er he earnestly inquired her name,
And ev'ry other circumstance the same.
She's lady, they replied, to great 'squire Good,
Who's almost bald from age 'tis understood;
But as he's rich, and high in rank appears,
Why that's a recompense you know for years.

THESE facts our young gallant no sooner gained,
But ardent hopes at once he entertained;
To wily plots his mind he quickly bent,
And to a neighb'ring town his servants sent;
Then, at the house where dwelled our noble 'squire,
His humble services proposed for hire.

PRETENDING ev'ry sort of work he knew,
He soon a fav'rite with old Square-toes grew,
Who (first advising with his charming mate),
Chief falc'ner made him o'er his fine estate.

THE new domestick much the lady pleased;
He watched and eagerly the moment seized,
His ardent passion boldly to declare,
In which he showed a novice had no share.

'TWAS managed well, for nothing but the chase,
Could Square-toes tempt to quit her fond embrace,
And then our falc'ner must his steps attend:—

The very time he wished at home to spend.
The lady similar emotions showed;
For opportunity their bosoms glowed;
And who will feel in argument so bold,
When this I say, the contrary to hold?
At length with pity Cupid saw the case,
And kindly lent his aid to their embrace.

ONE night the lady said, with eager eyes,
My dear, among our servants, which d'ye prize,
For moral conduct most and upright heart?
To this her spouse replied, the faithful part
Is with the falc'ner found, I must decide:
To him my life I'd readily confide.

THEN you are wrong, said she,—most truly so,
For he's a good-for-nothing wretch I know;
You'll scarcely credit it, but t'other day,
He had the barefaced impudence to say,
He loved me much, and then his passion pressed:
I'd nearly fallen, I was so distressed.
To tear his eyes out, I designed at first,
And e'en to choke this wretch, of knaves the worst;
By prudence solely was I then restrained,
For fear the world should think his point was gained.

THE better then to prove his dark intent,
I feigned an inclination to consent,
And in the garden, promised as to-night,
I'd near the pear-tree meet this roguish wight.
Said I, my husband never moves from hence;

No jealous fancy, but to show the sense
He entertains of my pure, virtuous life,
And fond affection for a loving wife.
Thus circumstanced, your wishes see are vain,
Unless when he's asleep a march I gain,
And softly stealing from his torpid side,
With trembling steps I, to my lover, glide.
So things remain, my dear; an odd affair:—
On this Square-toes 'gan to curse and swear;
But his fond rib most earnestly besought,
His rage to stifle, as she clearly thought,
He might in person, if he'd take the pain,
Secure the rascal and redress obtain
You know, said she, the tree is near the door,
Upon the left and bears of fruit great store;
But if I may my sentiments express,
In cap and petticoats you'd best to dress;
His insolence is great, and you'll be right,
To give your strokes with double force to night;
Well work his back; flat lay him on the ground:—
A rascal! honourable ladies round,
No doubt he many times has served the same;
'Tis such impostors characters defame.
To rouse his wrath the story quite sufficed;
The spouse resolved to do as she advised.
Howe'er to dupe him was an easy lot;
The hour arrived, his dress he soon had got,
Away he ran with anxious fond delight.
In hopes the wily spark to trap that night.
But no one there our easy fool could see,
And while he waited near the fav'rite tree,

Half dead with cold, the falc'ner slyly stole,
To her who had so well contrived the whole;
Time, place, and disposition, all combined
The loving pair to mutual joys resigned.
When our expert gallant had with the dame,
An hour or more indulged his ardent flame,
Though forced at length to quit the loving lass,
'Twas not without the favourite parting glass;
He then the garden sought, where long the 'squire,
Upon the knave had wished to vent his ire.

NO sooner he the silly husband spied,
But feigning 'twas the wily wife he eyed,
At once he cried,—ah, vilest of the sex!
Are these thy tricks, so good a man to vex?
Oh shame upon thee! thus to treat his love,
As pure as snow, descending from above.
I could not think thou hadst so base a heart,
But clear it is, thou need'st a friendly part,
And that I'll act: I asked this rendezvous
With full intent to see if thou wert true;
And, God be praised, without a loose design,
To plunge in luxuries pronounced divine.
Protect me Heav'n! poor sinner that I'm here!
To guard thy honour I will persevere.
My worthy master could I thus disgrace?
Thou wanton baggage with unblushing face,
Thee on the spot I'll instantly chastise,
And then thy husband of the fact advise.

THE fierce harangue o'er Square-toes pleasure spread,

Who, mutt'ring 'tween his teeth, with fervour said:
O gracious Lord! to thee my thanks are due—
To have a wife so chaste—a man so true!
But presently he felt upon his back
The falc'ner's cudgel vigorously thwack,
Who soundly basted him as on he ran,
To gain the house, with terror, pale and wan.

THE squire had wished his trusty man, no doubt,
Had not, at cudgelling, been quite so stout;
But since he showed himself so true a friend,
And with his actions could such prudence blend,
The master fully pardoned what he knew,
And quickly to his wife in bed he flew,
When he related every thing that passed
Were we, cried he, a hundred years to last,
My lovely dear, we ne'er on earth could find
A man so faithful, and so well inclined.
I'd have him take within our town a wife,
And you and I'll regard him during life.
In that, replied the lady, we agree,
And heartily thereto I pledged will be.

The Husband-Confessor

WHEN Francis (named the first) o'er Frenchmen reign'd,
In Italy young Arthur laurels gained,
And oft such daring valour showed in fight,
With ev'ry honour he was made a knight;
The monarch placed the spur upon his heel,
That all around his proper worth might feel.
Then household deities at home he sought,
Where—not at prayers his beauteous dame he caught:
He'd left her, truly, quite dissolv'd in tears;
But now the belle had bid adieu to fears;
And oft was dancing joyously around,
With all the company that could be found.

GALLANTS in crowds Sir Arthur soon perceived;
At sight of these the knight was sorely grieved;
And, turning in his mind how best to act;
Cried he, Can this be truly held a fact,
That I've been worthy while I'd fame in view,
Of cuckoldom at home, and knighthood too?
It ought to be but half:—the truth let's know;
From constancy the purest blessings flow.
Then like a father-confessor he dressed,
And took his seat where priests their flock confessed.
His lady absolution sought that day,

And on her knees before him 'gan to pray;
The minor sins were told with downcast eyes,
And then for hearing those of larger size,
The husband-confessor prepared his ears:—
Said she, Good father, ('mid a flood of tears),
My bed receives, (the fault I fear's not slight,)
A gentleman, a parson, and a knight.
Still more had followed, but, by rage o'ercome,
Sir Arthur cut the thread, and she was mum;
Though, doubtless, had the fair been let proceed,
Quite long her Litany had been decreed.

THE husband, in a rage, exclaimed, thou jade,
A parson, say'st thou? t'whom dost think thou'st made
This curst confession?—To my spouse, cried she,
I saw you enter here, and came with glee,
Supposing you'd a trick to raise surprise;
Howe'er 'tis strange that one so very wise,
The riddle should not fully comprehend:—
A KNIGHT, the king created you, my friend;
A GENTLEMAN, your rank was long ago;
A PARSON, you have made yourself you know.
Goon heav'ns! exclaimed the knight, 'tis very clear,
And I a blockhead surely must appear.

THE COBBLER

WE'RE told, that once a cobbler, BLASE by name;
A wife had got, whose charms so high in fame;
But as it happened, that their cash was spent,
The honest couple to a neighbour went,
A corn-factor by trade, not overwise

To whom they stated facts without disguise;
And begged, with falt'ring voice denoting care,
That he, of wheat, would half a measure spare,
Upon their note, which readily he gave,
And all advantages desired to wave.

THE time for payment came; the money used;
The cash our factor would not be refused;
Of writs he talked, attorneys, and distress;
The reason:—heav'n can tell, and you may guess;
In short, 'twas clear our gay gallant desired,
To cheer the wife, whose beauty all admired.

SAID he, what anxiously I wish to get,
You've plenty stored, and never wanted yet;
You surely know my meaning?—Yes, she cried;
I'll turn it in my mind, and we'll decide
How best to act. Away she quickly flew,
And Blase informed, what Ninny had in view.
Zounds! said the cobbler, we must see, my dear,
To hook this little sum:—the way is clear;
No risk I'm confident; for prithee run
And tell him I've a journey just begun;
That he may hither come and have his will;
But 'ere he touch thy lips, demand the bill;
He'll not refuse the boon I'm very sure;
Meantime, myself I'll hide and all secure.
The note obtained, cough loudly, strong, and clear;
Twice let it be, that I may plainly hear;
Then forth I'll sally from my lurking place,
And, spite of folly's frowns, prevent disgrace.

THE plot succeeded as the pair desired;
The cobbler laughed, and ALL his scheme admired:

A PURSE-PROUD cit thereon observed and swore;
'Twere better to have coughed when all was o'er;
Then you, all three, would have enjoyed your wish,
And been in future all as mute as fish.

OH! sir, replied the cobbler's wife at ease,
Do you suppose that use can hope to please,
And like your ladies full of sense appear?
(For two were seated with his wedded dear;)
Perhaps my lady 'd act as you describe,
But ev'ry one such prudence don't imbibe.

The Peasant and his Angry Lord

ONCE on a time, as hist'ry's page relates,
A lord, possessed of many large estates,
Was angry with a poor and humble clod,
Who tilled his grounds and feared his very nod.
Th'offence (as often happens) was but small,
But on him, vowed the peer, his rage should fall—
Said he, a halter, rascal, you deserve;
You'll never from the gallows-turnpike swerve:
Or, soon or late you swinging will be found
Who, born for hanging, ever yet was drowned?
Howe'er you'll smile to hear my lenient voice;
Observe, three punishments await your choice;
Take which you will.—The first is, you shall eat,
Of strongest garlick, thirty heads complete;
No drink you'll have between, nor sleep, nor rest;
You know a breach of promise I detest.
Or, on your shoulders further I propose,
To give you, with a cudgel, thirty blows.
Or, if more pleasing, that you truly pay,
The sum of thirty pounds without delay.

THE peasant 'gan to turn things in his mind:—
Said he, to take the heads I'm not inclined;
No drink, you say, between; that makes it worse;

To eat the garlick thus, would prove a curse.
Nor can I suffer on my tender back,
That, with a cudgel, thirty blows you thwack.
Still harder thirty pounds to pay appeared;
Uncertain how to act, he hanging feared.
The noble peer he begged, upon his knees,
His penitence to hear, and sentence ease.
But mercy dwelled not with the angry lord
Is this, cried he, the answer?—bring a cord.
The peasant, trembling lest his life was sought;
The garlick chose, which presently was brought.

UPON a dish my lord the number told;
Clod no way liked the garlick to behold.
With piteous mien the garlick head he took,
Then on it num'rous ways was led to look,
And grumbling much, began to spit and eat,
just like a cat with mustard on her meat,
To touch it with his tongue he durst not do;
He knew not how to act or what pursue.
The peer, delighted at the man's distress,
The garlick made him bite, and chew, and press,
Then gulp it down as if delicious fare;
The first he passed; the second made him swear;
The third he found was every whit as sad,
He wished the devil had it, 'twas so bad.
In short, when at the twelfth our wight arrived,
He thought his mouth and throat of skin deprived.
Said he, some drink I earnestly intreat;
What, Greg'ry, cried my lord, dost feel a heat;
In thy repasts dost love to wet thy jaws?

Well! well! I won't object; thou know'st my laws;
Much good may't do thee; here, some wine, some wine!
Yet recollect, to drink, since you design,
That afterward, my friend, you'll have to choose
The thirty blows, or thirty pounds to lose.
But, cried the peasant, I sincerely pray,
Your lordship's goodness, that the garlick may
Be taken in the account, for as to pelf,
Where can an humble lab'rer, like myself,
Expect the sum of thirty pounds to seize?
Then, said the peer, be cudgelled if you please;
Take thirty thwacks; for naught the garlick goes.
To moisten well his throat, and ease his woes,
The peasant drank a copious draught of wine,
And then to bear the cudgel would resign.

A SINGLE blow he patiently endured;
The second, howsoe'er, his patience cured;
The third was more severe, and each was worse;
The punishment he now began to curse;
Two lusty wights, with cudgels thrashed his back
And regularly gave him thwack and thwack;
He cried, he roared, for grace he begged his lord,
Who marked each blow, and would no ease accord;
But carefully observed, from time to time,
That lenity he always thought sublime;
His gravity preserved; considered too
The blows received and what continued due.

AT length, when Greg'ry twenty strokes had got,
He piteously exclaimed:—if more's my lot

I never shall survive! Oh! pray forgive,
If you desire, my lord, that I should live.
Then down with thirty pounds, replied the peer,
Since you the blows so much pretend to fear;
I'm sorry for you; but if all the gold
Be not prepared, your godfather, I'm told,
Can lend a part; yet, since so far you've been,
To flinch the rest you surely won't be seen.

THE wretched peasant to his lordship flew,
And trembling cried—'tis up! the number view!
A scrutiny was made, which nothing gained;
No choice but pay the money now remained;
This grieved him much, and o'er the fellow's face;
The dewy drops were seen to flow apace.
All useless proved:—the full demand he sent,
With which the peer expressed himself content.
Unlucky he whoe'er his lord offends!
To golden ore, howe'er, the proud man bends:

'TWAS vain that Gregory a pardon prayed;
For trivial faults the peasant dearly paid;
His throat enflamed—his tender back well beat—
His money gone—and all to make complete,
Without the least deduction for the pain,
The blows and garlick gave the trembling swain.

The Muleteer

THE Lombard princes oft pervade my mind;
The present tale Boccace relates you'll find;
Agiluf was the noble monarch's name;
Teudelingua he married, beauteous dame,
The last king's widow, who had left no heir,
And whose dominions proved our prince's share.

NO Beauty round compare could with the queen;
And ev'ry blessing on the throne was seen,
When Cupid, in a playful moment, came,
And o'er Agiluf's stable placed his flame;
There left it carelessly to burn at will,
Which soon began a muleteer to fill,
With LOVE'S all-powerful, all-consuming fire,
That naught controls, and youthful breasts desire.

THE muleteer was pleasing to the sight:
Gallant, good-humoured, airy, and polite,
And ev'ry way his humble birth belied;
A handsome person, nor was sense denied;
He showed it well, for when the youth beheld,
With eyes of love, the queen, who all excelled,
And ev'ry effort anxiously had made,
To stop the flames that would his heart invade;

When vain it proved, he took a prudent part:—

WHO can, like Cupid, manage wily art?
Whate'er stupidity we may discern,
His pupils more within a day can learn,
Than MASTERS knowledge in the schools can gain,
Though they in study should ten years remain;
The lowest clown he presently inspires,
With ev'ry tendency that love requires;
Of this our present tale's a proof direct,
And none that feel—its truths will e'er suspect:

THE am'rous muleteer his thoughts employed;
Consid'ring how his wish might be enjoyed.
Without success to certainty were brought,
Life seemed to him not worth a slender thought;
To hazard ev'ry thing; to live or die!
Possession have!—or in the grave to lie!

THE Lombard custom was, that when the king,
Who slept not with his queen, (a common thing
In other countries too), desired to greet
His royal consort, and in bed to meet,
A night-gown solely o'er his back he threw,
And then proceeded to the interview,
Knocked softly at the door, on which a fair,
Who waited on the queen with anxious care,
Allowed the prince to enter; took his light,
(Which only glimmered in the midst of night,)
Then put it out, and quickly left the room:—
A little lantern to dispel the gloom,

With waxen taper that emitted rays—
In diff'rent countries various are their ways!

OUR wily, prying, crafty muleteer,
Knew well these forms were current through the year:
He, like the king, at night himself equipped,
And to the queen's superb apartment slipped.
His face concealed the fellow tried to keep;
The waiting dame was more than half asleep;
The lover got access:—soon all was clear;
The prince's coming he had but to fear,
And, as the latter had, throughout the day,
The chase attended an extensive way,
'Twas more than probable he'd not be led,
(Since such fatigue he'd had,) to quit his bed.

PERFUMED, quite neat, and lively as a bird,
Our spark (safe entered) uttered not a word.
'Twas often customary with the king,
When state affairs, or other weighty thing,
Displeasure gave, to take of love his fill,
Yet let his tongue the while continue still.
A singularity we needs must own,
With this the wife was long familiar grown.

OUR am'rous wight more joys than one received,
If our narrator of the tale's believed;
(In bed a muleteer is worth three kings,
And value oft is found in humble things.)
The queen began to think her husband's rage
Had proved a stimulus such wars to wage,

And made him wond'rous stout in pleasure's sport,
Though all the while his thoughts were-'bout the court.

WITH perfect justice Heav'n its gifts bestows;
But equal talents all should not compose.
The prince's virtues doubtless were designed,
To take command, and govern o'er mankind.
The lawyer, points of difficulty views,
Decides with judgment, and the truth pursues.
In Cupid's scenes the muleteer succeeds:—
Each has his part:—none universal meeds.

WITH pleasures feasted, our gallant retired,
Before the morn fresh blushes had acquired.
But scarcely had he left the tender scene,
'Ere king Agiluf came to see his queen,
Who much surprise expressed, and to him said:
My dear, I know your love, but from this bed,
You'll recollect how recently you went,
And having wonders done, should be content.
For heav'n's sake, consider more your health;
'Tis dearer far to me than Croesus' wealth.

WITHIN the royal breast suspicions rose,
But nothing then the monarch would disclose.
He instantly withdrew without a word;
His sentiments to speak had been absurd,
And to the stable flew, since he believed
The circumstances, which his bosom grieved,
Whate'er mysterious doubts might then appear,
Proceeded from some am'rous muleteer.

WHEN round the dorture he began to creep,
The troop appeared as if dissolved in sleep,
And so they truly were, save our gallant,
Whose terrors made him tremble, sigh, and pant:
No light the king had got; it still was dark;
Agiluf groped about to find the spark,
Persuaded that the culprit might be known,
By rapid beating of the pulse alone.
The thought was good; to feel the prince began,
And at the second venture, found his man,
Who, whether from the pleasures he'd enjoyed,
Or fear, or dread discov'ry to avoid,
Experienced (spite of ev'ry wily art,)
At once quick beating of the pulse and heart.
In doubt how this adventure yet might end,
He thought to seem asleep would him befriend.

MEANWHILE the king, though not without much pains,
Obtained the scissors used for horses' manes.
With these, he said, I'll mark the fond gallant,
That I may know again the one I want.

THE monarch from the muleteer with care,
In front, snipt off a bulky lock of hair.
This having done, he suddenly withdrew;
But carelessly away the trophy threw;
Of which the sly gallant advantage took,
And thus the prince's subtle project shook;
For instantly began our artful spark,
His fellow servants like himself to mark.

WHEN day arrived the monarch was surprised,
To see each muleteer alike disguised;
No hair in front of either now was seen;
Why, how is this? said he: What can it mean?
Fifteen or more, if I believe my sight,
My wife has satisfied this very night.
Well! well! he'll now escape if mum he prove;
But there again I trust he ne'er shall move.

The Servant Girl Justified

BOCCACE alone is not my only source;
T'another shop I now shall have recourse;
Though, certainly, this famed Italian wit
Has many stories for my purpose fit.
But since of diff'rent dishes we should taste;
Upon an ancient work my hands I've placed;
Where full a hundred narratives are told,
And various characters we may behold;
From life, Navarre's fair queen the fact relates;
My story int'rest in her page creates;
Beyond dispute from her we always find,
Simplicity with striking art combin'd.
Yet, whether 'tis the queen who writes, or not;
I shall, as usual, here and there allot
Whate'er additions requisite appear;
Without such license I'd not persevere,
But quit, at once, narrations of the sort;
Some may be long, though others are too short.

LET us proceed, howe'er (our plan explained:)
A pretty servant-girl a man retain'd.
She pleas'd his eye, and presently he thought,
With ease she might to am'rous sports be brought;
He prov'd not wrong; the wench was blithe and gay,

A buxom lass, most able ev'ry way.

AT dawn, one summer's morn, the spark was led
To rise, and leave his wife asleep in bed;
He sought at once the garden, where he found
The servant-girl collecting flow'rs around,
To make a nosegay for his better half,
Whose birth-day 'twas:—he soon began to laugh,
And while the ranging of the flow'rs he prais'd,
The servant's neckerchief he slyly rais'd.
Who, suddenly, on feeling of the hand,
Resistance feign'd, and seem'd to make a stand;
But since these liberties were nothing new,
They other fun and frolicks would pursue;
The nosegay at the fond gallant was thrown;
The flow'rs he kiss'd, and now more ardent grown
They romp'd and rattl'd, play'd and skipt around;
At length the fair one fell upon the ground;
Our am'rous spark advantage took of this,
And nothing with the couple seem'd amiss.

UNLUCKILY, a neighbour's prying eyes
Beheld their playful pranks with great surprise,
She, from her window, could the scene o'erlook;
When this the fond gallant observ'd, he shook;
Said he, by heav'ns! our frolicking is seen,
By that old haggard, envious, prying quean;
But do not heed it; instantly he chose
To run and wake his wife, who quickly rose;—
So much the dame he fondl'd and caress'd,
The garden walk she took at his request,

To have a nosegay, where he play'd anew
Pranks just the same as those of recent view,
Which highly gratified our lady fair,
Who felt dispos'd, and would at eve repair,
To her good neighbour, whom she bursting found,
With what she'd seen that morn upon the ground.

THE usual greetings o'er, our envious dame,
With scowling brow exclaim'd,—my dear, your fame,
I love too much not fully to detail,
What I have witnessed, and with truth bewail;
Will you continue, in your house to keep
A girl, whose conduct almost makes me weep?
Anon I'd kick her from your house, I say;
The strumpet should not stay another day.
The wife replied, you surely are deceiv'd;
An honest, virtuous creature she's believ'd.
Well, I can easily, my friend, suppose,
Rejoin'd the neighbour, whence this favour flows;
But look about, and be convinc'd, this morn
From my own window (true as you are born,)
Within the garden I your husband spi'd
And presently the servant girl I ey'd;
At one another various flow'rs they threw,
And then the minx a little graver grew.
I understand you, cried the list'ning fair;
You are deceiv'd:—myself alone was there.

NEIGHBOUR
But patience, if you please: attend I pray
You've no conception what I meant to say:

The playful fair was actively employ'd,
In plucking am'rous flow'rs—they kiss'd and toy'd.

WIFE
'Twas clearly I, howe'er, for her you took.

NEIGHBOUR
The flow'rs for bosoms quickly they forsook;
Large handfuls frequently they seem'd to grasp,
And ev'ry beauty in its turn to clasp.

WIFE
But still, why think you, friend, it was not I?
Has not your spouse with you a right to try
What freaks he likes?

NEIGHBOUR
But then, upon the ground
This girl was thrown, and never cried nor frown'd;
You laugh.—

WIFE
Indeed I do, 'twas myself.

NEIGHBOUR
A flannel petticoat display'd the elf.

WIFE
'Twas mine:

NEIGHBOUR
Be patient:—and inform me, pray,
If this were worn by you or her to-day?
There lies the point, for, if you'll me believe,
Your husband did—the most you can conceive.

WIFE
How hard of credence!—'twas myself I vow.

NEIGHBOUR
Oh! that's conclusive; I'll be silent now;
Though truly I am led to think, my eyes
Are pretty sharp, and much I feel surprise
At what you say; in fact, I would have sworn,
I saw them thus at romps this very morn;
Excuse the hint, and do not turn her off.

WIFE
Why, turn her off?—the very thought I scoff;
She serves me well.

NEIGHBOUR
And so it seems is taught;
By all means keep her then, since thus she's thought.

The Three Gossips' Wager

AS o'er their wine one day, three gossips sat,
Discoursing various pranks in pleasant chat,
Each had a loving friend, and two of these
Most clearly managed matters at their ease.

SAID one, a princely husband I have got.
A better in the world there's surely not;
With him I can adjust as humour fits,
No need to rise at early dawn, like cits,
To prove to him that two and three make four,
Or ask his leave to ope or shut the door.

UPON my word, replied another fair,
If he were mine, I openly declare,
To judge from what so pleasantly you say,
I'd make a present of him new-year's day.
For pleasure never gives me full delight,
Unless a little pain the bliss invite.
No doubt your husband moves as he is led;
Thank heav'n a different mortal claims my bed;
To take him in, great nicety we need;
But howsoe'er, at times I can succeed;
The satisfaction doubly then is felt:—
In fond emotion bosoms freely melt.

With neither of you, husband or gallant,
Would I exchange, though these so much you vaunt.

ON this, the third with candour interfer'd;
She thought that oft the god of love appear'd,
Good husbands playfully to fret and vex,
Sometimes to rally couples: then perplex;
But warmer as the conversation grew,
She, anxious that each disputant might view
Herself victorious, (or believe it so,)
Exclaim'd, if either of you wish to show
Who's in the right, with argument have done,
And let us practise some new scheme of fun,
To dupe our husbands; she who don't succeed
Shall pay a forfeit; all replied, "Agreed."
But then, continued she, we ought to take
An oath, that we will full discov'ry make,
To one another of the various facts,
Without disguising even trifling acts.
And then, good upright Macae shall decide;
Thus things arrang'd, the ladies homeward plied.

SHE, 'mong the three, who felt the most constraint
Ador'd a youth, contemporaries paint,
Well made and handsome, but with beardless chin,
Which led the pair a project to begin;
For yet no opportunity they'd found,
T' enjoy their wishes, save by stealth around;
Most ardently she sought to be at ease,
And 'twas agreed the lucky thought to seize
That like a chambermaid he should be dress'd,

And then proceed to execute the jest,
Attend upon the wily, wedded pair,
And offer services with modest air
And downcast eyes; the husband on her leer'd,
And in her favour prepossess'd appear'd,
In hopes one day, to find those pleasing charms
Resign'd in secret to his longing arms.
Such pretty cheeks and sparkling eyes he thought,
Had ne'er till then his roving fancy caught;
The girl was hir'd, but seemingly with pain,
Since PRUDENCE ultimately might complain,
That (maid and master both so very young)
'Twould not be wonderful if things went wrong.

AT first the husband inattention show'd,
And scarcely on the maid a look bestow'd;
But presently he chang'd his conduct quite,
And presents gave, with promises not slight;
At length the servant feign'd to lend an ear,
And anxious seem'd obliging to appear.

THE trap our cunning lovers having laid,
One eve this message brought the smiling maid;
My lady, sir, is ill, and rest requires,
To sleep alone to-night she much desires.
To grant the master's wish the girl was led,
And they together hurried off to bed.

THE husband 'tween the sheets himself had plac'd;
The nymph was in her petticoat, unlac'd;
When suddenly appear'd the wily wife,

And promis'd harmony was turn'd to strife.
Are these your freaks, cried she with mark'd surprise;
Your usual dish it seems then don't suffice;
You want, indeed, to have some nicer fare?
A little sooner, by the saints I swear,
You'd me a pretty trick, 'tis clear, have shown,
And doubtless, then, tit bits to keep been prone.
This, howsoe'er, to get you're not design'd,
So elsewhere you may try what you can find.
And as to you, miss Prettyface, you jade,
Good heav'ns! to think a paltry servant maid
Should rival me? I'll beat you black and blue!
The bread I eat, indeed, must be for you?
But I know better, and indeed am clear,
Not one around will fancy I appear
So void of charms, so faded, wither'd, lost,
That I should out of doors at once be tost;
But I will manage matters:—I design
This girl no other bed shall have than mine;
Then who so bold to touch her there will dare?
Come, Miss, let's to my room at once repair;
Away—your things to-morrow you can seek;
If scandal 'twould spread around, I'd wreak
My vengeance instantly, and turn you out;
But I am lenient, and desire no rout;
Perhaps your ruin may be sav'd by care;
So night and day your company I'll share;
No more my bosom then will feel dismay,
For I shall see that you no frolicks play.

ON this the trembling girl, o'ercome with fears;

Held down her head and seem'd to hide her tears;
Pick'd up her clothes and quickly stole away,
As if afraid her mistress more might say;
And hop'd to act the maid while Sol gave light,
But play at ease the fond gallant at night;
At once she fill'd two places in the house,
And thought in both the husband she should chouse,
Who bless'd his stars that he'd escap'd so well,
And sneak'd alone to rest within his cell,
While our gay, am'rous pair advantage took,
To play at will, and ev'ry solace hook,
Convinc'd most thoroughly, once lovers kiss'd,
That OPPORTUNITY should n'er be miss'd.
Here ends the trick our wily gossip play'd;
But now let's see the plot another laid.

THE second dame, whose husband was so meek,
That only from her lips the truth he'd seek,
When seated with him 'neath a pear tree's shade,
Contriv'd at ease and her arrangement made.
The story I shall presently relate;
The butler, strong, well dress'd, and full of prate:
Who often made the other servants trot,
Stood near when madam hit upon her plot,
To whom she said, I wish the fruit to taste;
On which the man prepar'd with ev'ry haste,
To climb the tree, and off the produce shook;
But while above, the fellow gave a look
Upon the ground below, and feign'd he saw
The spouse and wife—do more than kiss and paw:
The servant rubb'd his eyes, as if in doubt,

And cried: why truly, sir, if you're so stout,
That you must revel 'mid your lady's charms,
Pray elsewhere take her to your longing arms,
Where you at ease may frolick hours or days,
Without my witnessing your loving ways;
Indeed, I'm quite surprised at what I spy
In publick, 'neath a tree such pranks to try!
And, if you don't a servant's presence heed,
With decency howe'er you should proceed.
What, still go on? for shame, I say, for shame!
Pray wait till by and by; you're much to blame;
Besides, the nights are long enough you'll find;
Heav'n genial joys for privacy design'd;
And why this place, when you've nice chambers got?
What, cried the lady, says this noisy sot?
He surely dreams; Where can he learn these tales?
Come down; let's see what 'tis the fellow ails.
Down William came. How? said the master, how?
Are we at play?

WILLIAM
Not now, sir, no, not now.

HUSBAND
Why, when then, friend?

WILLIAM
While I was in the tree,
Alive, sir, flay me, if I did not see
You on the verdant lawn my lady lay,
And kiss, and toy, and other frolicks play.

WIFE
'Twere surely better if thou held'st thy tongue,
Or thou'lt a beating get before 'tis long.

HUSBAND
No, no, my dear, he's mad, and I design
The fellow in a madhouse to confine.

WILLIAM
Is't folly, pray, to see what we behold?

WIFE
What hast thou seen?

WILLIAM
What I've already told:—
My master and yourself at Cupid's game,
Or else the tree 's enchanted I proclaim.

WIFE
ENCHANTED! nonsense; such a sight to see!

HUSBAND
To know the truth myself, I'll climb the tree,
Then you the fact will quickly from me learn;
We may believe what we ourselves discern.

SOON as the master they above descried,
And that below our pair he sharply eyed,
The butler took the lady in his arms,
And grew at once familiar with her charms;

At sight of this the husband gave a yell:
Made haste to reach the ground, and nearly fell;
Such liberties he wish'd at once to stop,
Since what he'd seen had nearly made him drop.
How! how!—cried he:—what, e'en before my sight?
What can you mean? said she without affright.

HUSBAND
DAR'ST thou to ask again?

WIFE
AND why not, pray?

HUSBAND
FINE, pretty doings!—Presently you'll say;
That what I've seen 'tis folly to believe.

WIFE
Too much is this:—such accusations grieve.

HUSBAND
Thou did'st most clearly suffer his embrace.

WIFE
I? WHY, you dream!

HUSBAND
This seems a curious case.
MY reason's flown'! or have I lost my eyes?

WIFE

CAN you suppose my character I prize
So very little, that these pranks I'd play
Before your face, when I might ev'ry day
Find minutes to divert myself at will,
And (if lik'd such frolicks) take my fill?

HUSBAND
I KNOW not what to think nor what to do;
P'rhaps this same tree can tricks at will pursue;
Let's see again; aloft he went once more,
And William acted as he'd done before;
But now the husband saw the playful squeeze;
Without emotion, and returned at ease.
To find the cause, said he, no longer try,
The tree's enchanted, we may well rely.

SINCE, that's the fact, replied the cunning jade;
To burn it, quickly William seek fort aid;
The tree accurst no longer shall remain;
Her will the servant wish'd not to restrain,
But soon some workmen brought, who felled the tree;
And wondered what the fault our fair could see.
Down hew it, cried the lady, that's your task;
More concerns you not; folly 'tis to ask.

OUR second gossip thus obtained success;
But now the third: we'll see if she had less:
To female friends she often visits paid,
And various pastimes there had daily play'd;
A leering lover who was weary grown,
Desired ONE night she'd meet him quite alone.

TWO, if you will, replied the smiling fair;
A trifle 'tis you ask, and I'll repair
Where'er you wish, and we'll recline at ease;
My husband I can manage, if I please,
While thus engag'd.—The parties soon agreed;
But still the lady for her wits had need,
Since her dear man from home but rarely went,
No pardons sought at Rome, but was content
With what he nearer got, while his sweet wife
More fondness mark'd for gratifying life,
And ever anxious, warmest zeal to show,
Was always wishing distant scenes to know;
As pilgrim oft she'd trod a foreign road,
But now desir'd those ancient ways t'explode;
A plan more rare and difficult she sought,
And round her toe our wily dame bethought,
To tie a pack-thread, fasten'd to the door,
Which open'd to the street: then feign'd to snore
Beside her husband, Harry Berlinguier,
(So, usually, they nam'd her wedded dear.)

HOWE'ER, so cunningly with him she dealt,
That Harry turn'd, and soon the pack-thread felt,
Which rais'd distrust, and led him to suspect
Some bad design the thread was meant t'effect.

A LITTLE time, as if asleep, he lay
Considering how to act, or what to say;
Then rose, (his spouse believing not awake,)
And softly treading, lest the room should shake;
The pack-thread follow'd to the outer door,

And thence concluded (what he might deplore,)
That his dear partner from her faith would stray,
And some gallant that night design'd to play
The lover's part and draw the secret clue,
When she would rise, and with him freaks pursue,
While he (good husband!) quietly in bed
Might sleep, not dreaming that his wife had fled.

FOR otherwise, what use such pains to take?
A visit cuckoldom, perhaps, might make;
An honour that he'd willingly decline;
On which he studied how to countermine;
And like a sentinel mov'd to and fro',
To watch if any one would thither go
To pull the string, that he could see with ease,
And then he'd instantly the culprit seize.

THE reader will perceive, we may suppose,
Besides the entrance which the husband chose,
On t'other side a door, where our gallant
Could enter readily, as he might want,
And there the spark a chambermaid let in:—
Oft servants prone are found a bribe to win.

WHILE Berlinguier thus watch'd around and round;
The friends with one another pleasures found;
But heav'n alone knows how nor what they were:—
No fact transpir'd save all was free from care;
So well the servant kept the careful watch,
That not a chance was given the pair to catch:
THE spark at dawn the lady left alone,

And ere the husband came the bird was flown;
Then Harry, weary, took his place again,
Complaining, that he'd felt such racking pain,
And dreading, lest alarms her breast should seize,
Within another room he'd sought for ease.

TWO days had pass'd, when madam thought once more,
To set the thread, as she had done before;
He left the bed, pretending he was sick,
Resumed his post; again the lover came,
And, with my lady, play'd the former game.

THE scheme so well succeeded, that the pair
Thrice wish'd to try the wily pack-thread snare;
The husband with the cholic mov'd away,
His place the bold gallant resum'd till day.

AT length their ardour 'gan, it seems, to cool,
And Harry, they no longer tried to fool;
'Twas time to seek the myst'ry of the plot,
Since, to three acts, the comedy was got.

AT midnight, when the spark had left the bed;
A servant, by his orders, drew the thread;
On whom the husband, without fear, laid hold,
And with him enter'd like a soldier bold,
Not then supposing he'd a valet seiz'd;
Well tim'd it prov'd, howe'er;—the lady pleas'd
Her voice to raise, on hearing what was said,
And through the house confusion quickly spread.
THE valet now before them bent the knee,

And openly declar'd, he came to see
The chambermaid, whom he was wont to greet,
And by the thread to rouse when time to meet:

ARE these your knavish tricks, replied the dame,
With eyes upon her maid that darted flame;
When I by chance observ'd about your toe,
A thread one night, I then resolv'd to know
Your scheme in full, and round my own I tied
A clue, on which I thoroughly relied,
To catch this gay gallant, that you pretend
Your husband will become, I apprehend.

Be that as 'twill, to-night from hence you go.
My dear, said Berlinguier, I'd fain say no;
Let things remain until to-morrow, pray
And then my lady presently gave way.
A fortune Harry on the girl bestow'd;
The like our valet to his master ow'd;
To church the happy couple smiling went:—
They'd known each other long, and were content.

THUS ended then, the third and last amour;
The trio hasten'd Macae to implore,
To say which gain'd the bet, who soon replied:—
I find it, friends, not easy to decide.

THE case hangs up, and there will long remain;
'Tis often thus when justice we'd obtain:

The Old Man's Calendar

OFT have I seen in wedlock with surprise,
That most forgot from which true bliss would rise
When marriage for a daughter is designed,
The parents solely riches seem to mind;
All other boons are left to heav'n above,
And sweet SIXTEEN must SIXTY learn to love!
Yet still in other things they nicer seem,
Their chariot-horses and their oxen-team
Are truly matched;—in height exact are these,
While those each shade alike must have to please;
Without the choice 'twere wonderful to find,
Or coach or wagon travel to their mind.
The marriage journey full of cares appears,
When couples match in neither souls nor years!
An instance of the kind I'll now detail:
The feeling bosom will such lots bewail!

QUINZICA, (Richard), as the story goes,
Indulged his wife at balls, and feasts, and shows,
Expecting other duties she'd forget,
In which howe'er he disappointment met.
A judge in Pisa, Richard was, it seems,
In law most learned: wily in his schemes;
But silver beard and locks too clearly told,

He ought to have a wife of diff'rent mould;
Though he had taken one of noble birth,
Quite young, most beautiful, and formed for mirth,
Bartholomea Galandi her name;
The lady's parents were of rank and fame;
Our JUDGE herein had little wisdom shown,
And sneering friends around were often known
To say, his children ne'er could fathers lack:
At giving counsel some have got a knack,
Who, were they but at home to turn their eyes,
Might find, perhaps, they're not so over-wise.

QUINZICA, then perceiving that his pow'rs
Fell short of what a bird like his devours,
T'excuse himself and satisfy his dear,
Pretended that, no day within the year,
To Hymen, as a saint, was e'er assigned,
In calendar, or book of any kind,
When full ATTENTION to the god was paid:—
To aged sires a nice convenient aid;
But this the sex by no means fancy right;
Few days to PLEASURE could his heart invite
At times, the week entire he'd have a fast;
At others, say the day 'mong saints was classed,
Though no one ever heard its holy name;—
FAST ev'ry Friday—Saturday the same,
Since Sunday followed, consecrated day;
Then Monday came:—still he'd abstain from play;
Each morning find excuse, but solemn feasts
Were days most sacred held by all the priests;
On abstinence, then, Richard lectures read,

And long before the time, was always led
By sense of right, from dainties to refrain:
A period afterward would also gain;
The like observed before and after Lent;
And ev'ry feast had got the same extent;
These times were gracious for our aged man;
And never pass them was his constant plan.

OF patron saints he always had a list;
Th' evangelists, apostles, none he miss'd;
And that his scruples might have constant food;
Some days malign, he said, were understood;
Then foggy weather;—dog-days' fervent heat:
To seek excuses he was most complete,
And ne'er asham'd but manag'd things so well,
Four times a year, by special grace, they tell,
Our sage regal'd his youthful blooming wife,
A little with the sweets of marriage life.

WITH this exception he was truly kind,
Fine dresses, jewels, all to please her mind;
But these are bawbles which alone controul
Those belles, like dolls, mere bodies void of soul.
Bartholomea was of diff'rent clay;
Her only pleasure (as our hist'ries say),
To go in summer to the neighb'ring coast,
Where her good spouse a charming house could boast,
In which they took their lodging once a week;
At times they pleasure on the waves would seek,
As fishing with the lady would agree,
And she was wond'rous partial to the sea,

Though far to sail they always would refuse.
One day it happened better to amuse,
Our couple diff'rent fishing vessels took,
And skimm'd the wave to try who most could hook,
Of fish and pleasure; and they laid a bet,
The greatest number which of them should get.
On board they had a man or two at most.
And each the best adventure hop'd to boast.

A CERTAIN pirate soon observ'd the ship,
In which this charming lady made the trip,
And presently attack'd and seiz'd the same;
But Richard's bark to shore in safety came;
So near the land, or else he would not brave,
To any great extent, the stormy wave,
Or that the robber thought if both he took,
He could not decently for favours look,
And he preferr'd those joys the FAIR bestow,
To all the riches which to mortals flow.

ALTHOUGH a pirate, he had always shown
Much honour in his acts, as well was known;
But Cupid's frolicks were his heart's delight:
None truly brave can ever beauty slight;
A sailor's always bold and kind and free,
Good lib'ral fellows, such they'll ever be;
'Mong saints indeed 'twere vain their names to seek!
The man was good howe'er of whom we speak;
His usual name was Pagamin Montegue;
For hours the lady's screams were heard a league,
While he each minute anxiously would seize,

To cheer her spirits and her heart to please;
T'attain his wish he ev'ry art combined;
At length the lovely captive all resigned.
'Twas Cupid conquer'd, Cupid with his dart;
A thousand times more pirate in his art,
Than Pagamin; on bleeding hearts he preys,
But little quarter gives, nor grace displays:
To pay her ransom she'd enough of gold;
For this her spouse was truly never cold;
No fast nor festival therein appear'd,
And her captivity he greatly fear'd.

THIS calendar o'erspread with rubrick days;
She soon forgot and learn'd the pirate's ways;
The matrimonial zone aside was thrown,
And only mentioned where the fact was known:

OUR lawyer would his fingers sooner burn;
Than have his wife but virtuous home return;
By means of gold he entertain'd no doubt,
Her restoration might be brought about.
A passport from the pirate he obtain'd,
Then waited on him and his wish explain'd;
To pay he offer'd what soe'er he'd ask;
His terms accept, though hard perhaps the task;

THE robber answer'd, if my name around,
Be not for honourable acts renown'd,
'Tis quite unjust:—your partner I'll restore
In health, without a ransom:—would you more?
A friendship so respect'd, heav'n forefend!

Should ever, by my conduct, have an end.
The fair, whom you so ardently admire,
Shall to your arms return as you desire,
Such pleasure to a friend I would not sell;
Convince me that she's your's, and all is well;
For if another I to you should give,
(And many that I've taken with me live,)
I surely should incur a heavy blame;
I lately captur'd one, a charming dame,
With auburn locks, a little fat, tall, young;
If she declare she does to you belong,
When you she's seen, I will the belle concede;
You'll take her instantly; I'll not impede.

THE sage replied, your conduct's truly wise;
Such wond'rous kindness fills me with surprise;
But since 'tis said that every trade must live,
The sum just mention:—I'll the ransom give;
No compliment I wish, my purse behold
You know the money presently is told;
Consider me a stranger now I pray;
With you I'd equal probity display,
And so will act, I swear, as you shall see;
There 's not a doubt the fair will go with me;
My word for this I would not have you take:—
You'll see how happy 'twill the lady make
To find me here; to my embrace she'll fly;
My only fears—that she of joy will die.
To them the charmer now was instant brought,
Who eyed her husband as beneath a thought;
Received him coldly, just as if he'd been

A stranger from Peru, she ne'er had seen.

LOOK, said Quinzica, she's ashamed 'tis plain
So many lookers on her love restrain;
But be assured, if we were left alone,
Around my neck her arms would soon be thrown.

IF this, replied the pirate, you believe,
Attend her toilet:—naught can then deceive.
Away they went, and closely shut the door;
When Richard said, thou darling of my store,
How can'st thou thus behave? my pretty dove,
'Tis thy Quinzica, come to seek his love,
In all the same, except about his wife;
Dost in this face a change observe my life?
'Tis grieving for thy loss that makes me ill;
Did ever I in aught deny thy will?
In dress or play could any thee exceed?
And had'st thou not whatever thou might'st need?
To please thee, oft I made myself a slave;
Such thou art now; but thee again I crave.
Then what dost think about thy honour, dear?—
Said she, with ire, I neither know nor fear;
Is this a time to guard it, do you say?
What pain was shown by any one, I pray;
When I was forc'd to wed a man like you,
Old, impotent, and hateful to the view,
While I was young and blooming as the morn,
Deserving truly, something less forlorn,
And seemingly intended to possess
What Hymen best in store has got to bless;

For I was thought by all the world around,
Most worthy ev'ry bliss in wedlock found.

YET things took quite another turn with me
In tune my husband never proved to be,
Except a feast or two throughout the year;
From Pagamin I met a diff'rent cheer;
Another lesson presently he taught;
The life's sweet pleasures more the pirate brought,
In two short days, than e'er I had from you
In those four years that only you I knew.

PRAY leave me husband:—let me have my will
Insist not on my living with you still;
No calendars with Pagamin are seen—
Far better treated with the man I've been.
My other friends and you much worse deserved:
The spouse, for taking me when quite unnerved,
And they, for giving preference base to gold,
To those pure joys—far better thought than told.
But Pagamin in ev'ry way can please;
And though no code he owns, yet all is ease;
Himself will tell you what has passed this morn,
His actions would a sov'reign prince adorn.
Such information may excite surprise,
But now the truth, 'twere useless to disguise,
Nothing will gain belief, we've no one near
To witness our discourse:—adieu, my dear,
To all your festivals—I'm flesh and blood:—
Gems, dresses, ornaments, do little good;
You know full well, betwixt the head and heel,

Though little's said, yet much we often feel.
On this she stopt, and Richard dropt his chin,
Rejoiced to 'scape from such unwelcome din.

BARTHOLOMEA, pleased with what had passed;
No disposition showed to hold him fast;
The downcast husband felt such poignant grief,
With ills where age can scarcely hope relief,
That soon he left this busy stage of life,
And Pagamin the widow took to wife.
The deed was just, for neither of the two
E'er felt what oft in Richard rose to view;
From feeling proof arose their mutual choice;
And 'tween them ne'er was heard the jarring voice.

BEHOLD a lesson for the aged man;
Who thinks, when old, to act as he began;
But, if the sage a yielding dotard seems,
His work is done by those the wife esteems;
Complaints are never heard; no thrilling fears;
And ev'ry one around at ease appears.

The Avaricious Wife and Tricking Gallant

WHO knows the world will never feel surprise,
When men are duped by artful women's eyes;
Though death his weapon freely will unfold;
Love's pranks, we find, are ever ruled by gold.
To vain coquettes I doubtless here allude;
But spite of arts with which they're oft endued;
I hope to show (our honour to maintain,)
We can, among a hundred of the train,
Catch one at least, and play some cunning trick:—
For instance, take blithe Gulphar's wily nick,
Who gained (old soldier-like) his ardent aim,
And gratis got an avaricious dame.

LOOK well at this, ye heroes of the sword,
Howe'er with wily freaks your heads be stored,
Beyond a doubt, at court I now could find,
A host of lovers of the Gulphar kind.

To Gasperin's so often went our wight,
The wife at length became his sole delight,
Whose youth and beauty were by all confessed;
But, 'midst these charms, such av'rice she possessed,
The warmest love was checked—a thing not rare,

In modern times at least, among the FAIR.
'Tis true, as I've already said, with such
Sighs naught avail, and promises not much;
Without a purse, who wishes should express,
Would vainly hope to gain a soft caress.
The god of love no other charm employs,
Then cards, and dress, and pleasure's cheering joys;
From whose gay shops more cuckolds we behold,
Than heroes sallied from Troy's horse of old.

BUT to our lady's humour let's adhere;
Sighs passed for naught: they entered not her ear;
'Twas speaking only would the charmer please,
The reader, without doubt, my meaning sees;
Gay Gulphar plainly spoke, and named a sum
A hundred pounds, she listened:—was o'ercome.

OUR wight the cash by Gasperin was lent;
And then the husband to the country went,
Without suspecting that his loving mate,
Designed with horns to ornament his pate.

THE money artful Gulphar gave the dame,
While friends were round who could observe the same;
Here, said the spark, a hundred pounds receive,
'Tis for your spouse:—the cash with you I leave.
The lady fancied what the swain had said,
Was policy, and to concealment led.

NEXT morn our belle regaled the arch gallant,
Fulfilled his promise:—and his eager want.

Day after day he followed up the game;
For cash he took, and int'rest on the same;
Good payers get, we always may conclude,
Full measure served, whatever is pursued.

WHEN Gasperin returned, our crafty wight,
Before the wife addressed her spouse at sight;
Said he the cash I've to your lady paid,
Not having (as I feared) required its aid;
To save mistakes, pray cross it in your book;
The lady, thunderstruck, with terror shook;
Allowed the payment; 'twas a case too clear;
In truth for character she 'gan to fear.
But most howe'er she grudged the surplus joy,
Bestowed on such a vile, deceitful boy.

THE loss was doubtless great in ev'ry view
Around the town the wicked Gulphar flew;
In all the streets, at every house to tell,
How nicely he had trick'd the greedy belle.

TO blame him useless 'twere you must allow;
The French such frolicks readily avow.

The Jealous Husband

A CERTAIN husband who, from jealous fear,
With one eye slept while t'other watched his dear,
Deprived his wife of every social joy,
(Friends oft the jealous character annoy,)
And made a fine collection in a book,
Of tricks with which the sex their wishes hook.
Strange fool! as if their wiles, to speak the truth,
Were not a hydra, both in age and youth.

HIS wife howe'er engaged his constant cares;
He counted e'en the number of her hairs;
And kept a hag who followed every hour,
Where'er she went, each motion to devour;
Duenna like, true semblance of a shade,
That never quits, yet moves as if afraid.

THIS arch collection, like a prayer-book bound;
Was in the blockhead's pocket always found,
The form religious of the work, he thought,
Would prove a charm 'gainst vice whenever sought!

ONE holy day, it happened that our dame,
As from the neighb'ring church she homeward came;
And passed a house, some wight, concealed from view;

A basket full of filth upon her threw.

WITH anxious care apologies were made;
The lady, frightened by the frolick played,
Quite unsuspicious to the mansion went;
Her aged friend for other clothes she sent,
Who hurried home, and ent'ring out of breath;
Informed old hunks—what pained him more than death

ZOUNDS! cried the latter, vainly I may look
To find a case like this within my book;
A dupe I'm made, and nothing can be worse:—
Hell seize the work—'tis thoroughly a curse!

NOT wrong he proved, for, truly to confess;
This throwing dirt upon the lady's dress
Was done to get the hag, with Argus' eyes
Removed a certain distance from the prize.
The gay gallant, who watched the lucky hour,
Felt doubly blessed to have her in his power.

HOW vain our schemes to guard the wily sex!
Oft plots we find, that ev'ry sense perplex.
Go, jealous husbands, books of cases burn;
Caresses lavish, and you'll find return.

The Gascon Punished

A GASCON (being heard one day to swear,
That he'd possess'd a certain lovely fair,)
Was played a wily trick, and nicely served;
'Twas clear, from truth he shamefully had swerved:
But those who scandal propagate below,
Are prophets thought, and ev'ry action know;
While good, if spoken, scarcely is believed,
And must be viewed, or not for truth received.

THE dame, indeed, the Gascon only jeered,
And e'er denied herself when he appeared;
But when she met the wight, who sought to shine;
And called her angel, beauteous and divine,
She fled and hastened to a female friend,
Where she could laugh, and at her ease unbend.

NEAR Phillis, (our fair fugitive) there dwelled
One Eurilas, his nearest neighbour held;
His wife was Cloris; 'twas with her our dove
Took shelter from the Gascon's forward love,
Whose name was Dorilas; and Damon young,
(The Gascon's friend) on whom gay Cloris hung.

SWEET Phillis, by her manner, you might see,

From sly amours and dark intrigues was free;
The value to possess her no one knew,
Though all admired the lovely belle at view.
Just twenty years she counted at the time,
And now a widow was, though in her prime,
(Her spouse, an aged dotard, worth a plum:—
Of those whose loss to mourn no tears e'er come.)

OUR seraph fair, such loveliness possessed,
In num'rous ways a Gascon could have blessed;
Above, below, appeared angelic charms;
'Twas Paradise, 'twas Heav'n, within her arms!

THE Gascon was—a Gascon;—would you more?
Who knows a Gascon knows at least a score.
I need not say what solemn vows he made;
Alike with Normans Gascons are portrayed;
Their oaths, indeed, won't pass for Gospel truth;
But we believe that Dorilas (the youth)
Loved Phillis to his soul, our lady fair,
Yet he would fain be thought successful there.

ONE day, said Phillis, with unusual glee,
Pretending with the Gascon to be free:—
A favour do me:—nothing very great;
Assist to dupe one jealous of his mate;
You'll find it very easy to be done,
And doubtless 'twill produce a deal of fun.
'Tis our request (the plot you'll say is deep,)
That you this night with Cloris's husband sleep
Some disagreement with her gay gallant

Requires, that she a night at least should grant,
To settle diff'rences; now we desire,
That you'll to bed with Eurilas retire,
There's not a doubt he'll think his Cloris near;
He never touches her:—so nothing fear;
For whether jealousy, or other pains,
He constantly from intercourse abstains,
Snores through the night, and, if a cap he sees,
Believes his wife in bed, and feels at ease.
We'll properly equip you as a belle,
And I will certainly reward you well.

TO gain but Phillis's smiles, the Gascon said,
He'd with the very devil go to bed.

THE night arrived, our wight the chamber traced;
The lights extinguished; Eurilas, too, placed;
The Gascon 'gan to tremble in a trice,
And soon with terror grew as cold as ice;
Durst neither spit nor cough; still less encroach;
And seemed to shrink, least t'other should approach;
Crept near the edge; would scarcely room afford,
And could have passed the scabbard of a sword.

OFT in the night his bed-fellow turned round;
At length a finger on his nose he found,
Which Dorilas exceedingly distressed;
But more inquietude was in his breast,
For fear the husband amorous should grow,
From which incalculable ills might flow.

OUR Gascon ev'ry minute knew alarm;
'Twas now a leg stretched out, and then an arm;
He even thought he felt the husband's beard;
But presently arrived what more he feared.

A BELL, conveniently, was near the bed,
Which Eurilas to ring was often led;
At this the Gascon swooned, so great his fear,
And swore, for ever he'd renounce his dear.
But no one coming, Eurilas, once more,
Resumed his place, and 'gan again to snore.

AT length, before the sun his head had reared;
The door was opened, and a torch appeared.
Misfortune then he fancied full in sight;
More pleased he'd been to rise without a light,
And clearly thought 'twas over with him now;
The flame approached;—the drops ran o'er his brow;
With terror he for pardon humbly prayed:—
You have it, cried a fair: be not dismayed;
'Twas Phillis spoke, who Eurilas's place
Had filled, throughout the night, with wily grace,
And now to Damon and his Cloris flew,
With ridicule the Gascon to pursue;
Recounted all the terrors and affright,
Which Dorilas had felt throughout the night.
To mortify still more the silly swain,
And fill his soul with ev'ry poignant pain,
She gave a glimpse of beauties to his view,
And from his presence instantly withdrew.

The Princess Betrothed to the King of Garba

WHAT various ways in which a thing is told
Some truth abuse, while others fiction hold;
In stories we invention may admit;
But diff'rent 'tis with what historick writ;
Posterity demands that truth should then
Inspire relation, and direct the pen.

ALACIEL'S story's of another kind,
And I've a little altered it, you'll find;
Faults some may see, and others disbelieve;
'Tis all the same:—'twill never make me grieve;
Alaciel's mem'ry, it is very clear,
Can scarcely by it lose; there's naught to fear.
Two facts important I have kept in view,
In which the author fully I pursue;
The one—no less than eight the belle possessed,
Before a husband's sight her eyes had blessed;
The other is, the prince she was to wed
Ne'er seemed to heed this trespass on his bed,
But thought, perhaps, the beauty she had got
Would prove to any one a happy lot.

HOWE'ER this fair, amid adventures dire,

More sufferings shared than malice could desire;
Though eight times, doubtless, she exchanged her knight
No proof, that she her spouse was led to slight;
'Twas gratitude, compassion, or good will;
The dread of worse;—she'd truly had her fill;
Excuses just, to vindicate her fame,
Who, spite of troubles, fanned the monarch's flame:
Of eight the relict, still a maid received;—
Apparently, the prince her pure believed;
For, though at times we may be duped in this,
Yet, after such a number—strange to miss!
And I submit to those who've passed the scene,
If they, to my opinion, do not lean.

THE king of Alexandria, Zarus named,
A daughter had, who all his fondness claimed,
A star divine Alaciel shone around,
The charms of beauty's queen were in her found;
With soul celestial, gracious, good, and kind,
And all-accomplished, all-complying mind.

THE rumour of her worth spread far and wide,
The king of Garba asked her for his bride,
And Mamolin (the sov'reign of the spot,)
To other princes had a pref'rence got.

THE fair, howe'er, already felt the smart
Of Cupid's arrow, and had lost her heart;
But 'twas not known: princesses love conceal,
And scarcely dare its whispers fond reveal;
Within their bosoms poignant pain remains,

Though flesh and blood, like lasses of the plains.

THE noble Hispal, one of zarus' court,
A handsome youth, as histories report,
Alaciel pleased; a mutual flame arose,
Though this they durst not venture to disclose
Or, if expressed, 'twas solely by the eyes:—
Soul-speaking language, nothing can disguise!

AFFIANCED thus, the princess, with a sigh,
Prepared to part, and fully to comply.
The father trusted her to Hispal's care,
Without the least suspicion of the snare;
They soon embarked and ploughed the briny main;
With anxious hopes in time the port to gain.

WHEN they, from Egypt's coast had sailed a week;
To gain the wind they saw a pirate seek,
Which having done, he t'wards them bore in haste,
To take the ship in which our fair was placed.

THE battle quickly raged; alike they erred;
The pirates slaughter loved, and blood preferred,
And, long accustomed to the stormy tide,
Were most expert, and on their skill relied.
In numbers, too, superior they were found;
But Hisipal's valour greatly shone around,
And kept the combat undecided long;
At length Grifonio, wond'rous large and strong;
With twenty sturdy, pirates got on board,
And many soon lay gasping by the sword.

Where'er he trod, grim death and horrour reigned;
At length, the round the noble Hispal gained.
His nervous arm laid many wretches low
Rage marked his eyes, whene'er he dealt a blow:

BUT, while the youth was thus engaged in fight,
Grifonio ran to gain a sweeter sight;
The princess was on board full well he knew;
No time he lost, but to her chamber flew;
And, since his pleasures seemed to be her doom;
He bore her like a sparrow from the room:
But not content with such a charming fair,
He took her diamonds, ornaments for hair,
And those dear pledges ladies oft receive,
When they a lover's ardent flame believe.
Indeed, I've heard it hinted as a truth,
(And very probable for such a youth,)
That Hispal, while on board, his flame revealed;
And what chagrin she felt was then concealed,
The passage thinking an improper time,
To shew a marked displeasure at his crime.

THE pirate-chief who carried off his prey,
Had short-lived joy, for, wishing to convey
His charming captive from the ship with speed;
One vessel chanced a little to recede,
Although securely fastened by the crew,
With grappling hooks, as usually they do,
When quite intent to pass, young Hispal made
A blow, that dead at once the ruffian laid;
His head and shoulders, severed from the trunk;

Fell in the sea, and to the bottom sunk,
Abjuring Mahomet, and all the tribe
Of idle prophets, Catholics proscribe;
Erect the rest upon the legs remained;
The very posture as before retained;
This curious sight no doubt a laugh had raised,—
But in the moment, she, so lately praised,
With dread Grifonio, fell beyond their view;
To save her, straight the gallant Hispal flew.
The ships, for want of pilots at the helm,
At random drifted over Neptune's realm.

GRIM death the pirate forced to quit his slave;
Buoyed up by clothes, she floated on the wave,
'Till Hispal succour lent, who saw 'twas vain
To try with her the vessel to regain.
He could, with greater ease, the fair convey
To certain rocks, and thither bent his way;
Those rocks to sailors oft destruction proved,
But now the couple saved, who thither moved:
'Tis even said the jewels were not lost,
But sweet Alaciel, howsoever tost,
Preserved the caskets, which with strings were tied;
And seizing these, the treasure drew aside.

OUR swimmer on his back the princess bore;
The rock attained; but hardships were not o'er;
Misfortunes dire the noble pair pursued
And famine, worst of ills, around was viewed.
No ship was near; the light soon passed away;
The night the same; again appeared the day;

No vessel hove in sight; no food to eat;
Our couple's wretchedness seemed now complete;
Hope left them both, and, mutual passion moved,
Their situation more tormenting proved.

LONG time in silence they each other eyed
At length, to speak the lovely charmer tried
Said she, 'tis useless, Hispal, to bewail:
Tears, with the cruel Parcae, naught avail;
Each other to console be now our aim;
Grim death his course will follow still the same.
To mitigate the smart let's try anew;
In such a place as this few joys accrue.

CONSOLE each other, say you? Hispal cried;
What can console when forced one's love to hide?
Besides, fair princess, ev'ry way 'tis clear,
Improper 'twere for you to love while here;
I equally could death or famine brave;
But you I tremble for, and wish to save.

THESE words so pained the fair, that gushing tears
Bedewed Alaciel's cheeks, her looks spoke fears;
The ardent flame which she'd so long concealed;
Burst forth in sighs, and all its warmth revealed;
While such emotion Hispal's eyes expressed,
That more than words his anxious wish confessed.
These tender scenes were followed by a kiss,
The prelude sweet of soft enchanting bliss;
But whether taken, or by choice bestowed,
Alike 'twas clear, their heaving bosoms glowed.

THOSE vows now o'er, said Hispal with a sigh,
In this adventure, if we're doomed to die,
Indiff'rent surely 'tis, the prey to be
Of birds of air, or fishes of the sea;
My reason tells me ev'ry grave's the same,
Return we must, at last, from whence we came,
Here ling'ring death alone we can expect;
To brave the waves 'tis better to elect;
I yet have strength, and 'tis not far to land;
The wind sets fair: let's try to gain the strand;
From rock to rock we'll go: I many view,
Where I can rest; to THIS we'll bid adieu.

TO move, Alaciel readily agreed;
Again our couple ventured to proceed;
The casket safe in tow; the weather hot;
From rock to rock with care our swimmer got;
The princess, anxious on his back to keep:—
New mode of traversing the wat'ry deep.

WITH Heav'n's assistance, and the rocks for rest,
The youth, by hunger and fatigue oppressed,
Uneasiness of mind, weighed down with care,
Not for himself, but safety of the fair,
A fast of two long tedious days now o'er,
The casket and the belle he brought on shore:

I THINK you cry—how wond'rously exact,
To bring the casket into ev'ry act!
Is that a circumstance of weight I pray?
It truly seems so, and without delay,

You'll see if I be wrong; no airy flight,
Or jeer, or raillery, have I in sight.
Had I embarked our couple in a ship
Without or cash or jewels for the trip,
Distress had followed, you must be aware;
'Tis past our pow'r to live on love or air;
In vain AFFECTION ev'ry effort tries
Inexorable hunger ALL defies.

THE casket, with the diamonds proved a source,
To which 'twas requisite to have recourse;
Some Hispal sold, and others put in pawn,
And purchased, near the coast, a house and lawn;
With woods, extensive park, and pleasure ground;
And many bow'rs and shady walks around,
Where charming hours they passed, and this 'twas plain,
Without the casket they could n'er obtain.

BENEATH the wood there was a secret grot,
Where lovers, when they pleased, concealment got,
A quiet, gloomy, solitary place,
Designed by nature for the billing race.

ONE day, as through the grove a walk they sought,
The god of love our couple thither brought;
His wishes, Hispal, as they went along,
Explained im part by words direct and strong;
The rest his sighs expressed, (they spoke the soul;)—
The princess, trembling, listened to the whole.

SAID he, we now are in a place retired,

Unknown to man, (such spots how oft desired!)
Let's take advantage of the present hour:
No joys, but those of LOVE, are in our pow'r;
All others see withdrawn! and no one knows
We even live; perhaps both friends and foes
Believe us in the belly of a whale;
Allow me, lovely princess, to prevail;
Bestow your kindness, or, without delay,
Those charms to Mamolin let me convey.
Yet, why go thither?—happy you could make
The man, whose constancy no perils shake,
What would you more?—his passion's ardent grown;
And surely you've enough resistance shown.

SUCH tender elocution Hispal used,
That e'en to marble, 'Twould have warmth infused;
While fair Alaciel, on the bark of trees,
With bodkin wrote, apparently at ease.
But Cupid drew her thoughts to higher things,
Than merely graving what from fancy springs.
Her lover and the place, at once assured,
That such a secret would be well secured;
A tempting bait, which made her, with regret,
Resist the witching charm that her beset.

UNLUCKILY, 'twas then the month of May,
When youthful hearts are often led astray,
And soft desire can scarcely be concealed,
But presses through the pores to be revealed.
How many do we see, by slow degrees,
And, step by step, accord their ALL to please,

Who, at the onset, never dreamed to grant
The smallest favour to their fond gallant.
The god of love so archly acts his part,
And, in unguarded moments, melts the heart,
That many belles have tumbled in the snare,
Who, how it happened, scarcely could declare.

WHEN they had reached the pleasing secret spot;
Young Hispal wished to go within the grot;
Though nearly overcome, she this declined;
But then his services arose to mind;
Her life from Ocean's waves, her honour too,
To him she owed; what could he have in view?
A something, which already has been shown,
Was saved through Hispal's nervous arm alone:
Said he, far better bless a real friend,
Than have each treasure rifled in the end,
By some successful ruffian; think it o'er;
You little dream for whom you guard the store.

THE princess felt the truth of this remark,
And half surrendered to the loving spark;
A show'r obliged the pair, without delay,
To seek a shed:—the place I need not say;
The rest within the grotto lies concealed:—
The scenes of Cupid ne'er should be revealed.
Alaciel blame, or not—I've many known,
With less excuses, who've like favours shown.

ALONE the cavern witnessed not their bliss;
In love, a point once gained, naught feels amiss,

If trees could speak that grew within the dell,
What joys they viewed—what stories they might tell!
The park, the lawn, the pleasure grounds, and bow'rs,
The belts of roses, and the beds of flow'rs,
All, all could whisper something of the kind;
At length, both longed their friends again to find,
Quite cloyed with love, they sighed to be at court;
Thus spoke the fair her wishes to support.

LOVED youth, to ME you must be ever dear;
To doubt it would ungen'rous now appear;
But tell me, pray, what's love without desire,
Devoid of fear, and nothing to acquire?
Flame unconfined is soon exhausted found,
But, thwarted in its course 'twill long abound;
I fear this spot, which we so highly prize,
Will soon appear a desert in our eyes,
And prove at last our grave; relieve my woe;
At once to Alexandria, Hispal go;
Alive pronounced, you presently will see,
What worthy people think of you and me;
Conceal our residence, declare you came,
My journey to prepare, (your certain aim,)
And see that I've a num'rous escort sent,
To guard me from a similar event.
By it, believe me, you shall nothing lose;
And this is what I willingly would choose;
For, be I single, or in Hymen's band,
I'd have you follow me by sea and land,
And be assured, should favour I withdraw,
That I've observed in you some glaring flaw.

WERE her intentions fully as expressed,
Or contrary to what her lips confessed,
No matter which her view, ‘twas very plain,
If she would Hispal’s services retain,
‘Twere right the youth with promises to feed,
While his assistance she so much must need:
As soon as he was ready to depart
She pressed him fondly to her glowing heart,
And charged him with a letter to the king;
This Hispal hastened to the prince to bring;
Each sail he crowded:—plied with ev’ry oar;
A wind quite fair soon brought him to shore;
To court he went, where all with eager eyes,
Demanded if he lived, amid surprise,
And where he left the princess; what her state?
These questions answered, Hispal, quite elate,
Procured the escort, which, without delay,
Though leaving him behind, was sent away:
No dark mistrust retained the noble youth;
But Zarus wished it: such appeared the truth.

BY one of early years the troop was led,
A handsome lad, and elegantly bred.
He landed with his party near the park.
And these in two divided ere ‘twas dark.

ONE half he left a guard upon the shore,
And with the other hastened to the door,
Where dwelled the belle, who daily fairer grew:
Our chief was smitten instantly at view;
And, fearing opportunity again,

Like this, perhaps, he never might obtain,
Avowed at once his passion to the fair;
At which she frowned, and told him, with an air;
To recollect his duty, and her rank:—
With equals only, he should be so frank.

ON these occasions, prudent 'tis to show
Your disappointment by a face of woe;
Seem ev'ry way the picture of despair:—
This countenance our knight appeared to wear;
To starve himself he vowed was his design;
To use the poniard he should ne'er incline,
For then no time for penitence would rest.—
The princess of his folly made a jest.
He fasted one whole day; she-tried in vain
To make him from the enterprise refrain.

AT length, the second day she 'gan to feel,
And strong emotion scarcely could conceal.
What! let a person die her charms could save!
'Twas cruel, thus to treat a youth so brave.
Through pity, she at last, to please the chief,
Consented to bestow on him relief;
For, favours, when conferred with sullen air,
But little gratify she was aware.

WHen satisfied the smart gallant appeared,
And anxiously to putting off adhered,
Pretending that the wind and tide would fail;
The galleys sometimes were unfit to sail,
Repairs required; then further heard the news,

That certain pirates had unpleasant views;
To fall upon the escort they'd contrived:
At length, a pirate suddenly arrived,
Surprized the party left upon the shore,
Destroyed the whole; then sought the house for more,
And scaled the walls while darkness spread around.
The pirate was Grifonio's second found,
Who, in a trice, the noble mansion took,
And joy gave place to grief in ev'ry look.

THE Alexandrian swore and cursed his lot;
The pirate soon the lady's story got,
And, taking her aside, his share required
Such impudence Alaciel's patience tired,
Who, ev'ry thing refused with haughty air;
Of this, howe'er, the robber was aware;
In Venus' court no novice was he thought;
To gain the princess anxiously he sought;
Said he, you'd better take me as a friend;
I'm more than pirate, and you'll comprehend,
As you've obliged one dying swain to fast,
You fast in turn, or you'll give way at last;
'Tis justice this demands: we sons of sea
Know how to deal with those of each degree;
Remember you will nothing have to eat,
Till your surrender fully is complete.

NO haggling, princess pray, my word receive;
What could be done, her terror to relieve?
Above all law is might:—'twill take its course;
Entire submission is the last resource.

OFT what we would not, we're obliged to do,
When fate our steps with rigour will pursue.
No folly greater than to heighten pain,
When we are sensible relief is vain.
What she, through pity, to another gave,
Might well be granted when herself 'twould save.

AT length she yielded to this suitor rude:—
No grief so great, but what may be subdued.
'Twould in the pirate doubtless have been wise,
The belle to move, and thus prevent surprise;
But who, from folly in amours is free?
The god of love and wisdom ne'er agree.

WHILE our gay pirate thought himself at ease,
The wind quite fair to sail when he might please,
Dame Fortune, sleepy only while we wake,
And slily watching when repose we take,
Contrived a trick the cunning knave to play,
And this was put in force ere break of day.

A LORD, the owner of a neighb'ring seat,
Unmarried;—fond of what was nice and neat,
Without attachment, and devoid of care,
Save something new to meet among the FAIR;
Grew tired of those he long around had viewed,
Now constantly, in thought, our belle pursued.
He'd money, friends, and credit all his days,
And could two thousand men at pleasure raise:
One charming morn, together these he brought;
Said he, brave fellows, can it well be thought,

That we allow a pirate, (dire disgrace!)
To plunder as he likes before our face,
And make a slave of one whose form 's divine?
Let's to the castle, such is my design,
And from the ruffian liberate the fair;
This evening ev'ry one will here repair,
Well armed, and then in silence we'll proceed,
(By night 'tis nothing will impede,)
And ere Aurora peeps, perform the task;
The only booty that I mean to ask
Is this fair dame; but not a slave to make,
I anxiously desire to let her take
Whate'er is her's:—restore her honour too;
All other things I freely leave to you;
Men, horses, baggage, in a word, the whole
Of what the knavish rascals now control.
Another thing, howe'er:—I wish to hang
The pirate instantly, before his gang.

THIS speech so well succeeded to inspire,
That scarcely could the men retain their ire.

THE evening came, the party soon arrived;
They ate not much, but drink their rage revived.
By such expensive treats we've armies known,
In Germany and Flanders overthrown;
And our commander was of this aware
'Twas prudent, surely, no expense to spare.

THEY carried ladders for the escalade,
And each was furnished with a tempered blade;

No other thing embarrassing they'd got;
No drums; but all was silent as the grot.

THEY reached the house when nearly break of day,
The time old Morpheus' slumbers often weigh;
The gang, with few exceptions, (then asleep),
Were sent, their vigils with grim death to keep.

THE chief hung up:—the princess soon appeared;
Her spirits presently our champion cheered;
The pirate scarcely had her bosom moved:—
No tears at least a marked affection proved;
But, by her prayers she pardon sought to gain,
For some who were not in the conflict slain;
Consoled the dying, and lamented those,
Who, by the sword, had closed their book of woes:
Then left the place without the least regret,
Where such adventures and alarms she'd met.
'Tis said, indeed, she presently forgot
The two gallants who last became her lot;
And I can easily the fact believe:
Removed from sight, but few for lovers grieve.

SHE, by her neighbour, was received, we're told,
'Mid costly furniture and burnished gold;
We may suppose what splendour shone around,
When all-attracting he would fain be found;
The best of wines; each dish considered rare:—
The gods themselves received not better fare:
Till then, Alaciel ne'er had tasted wine;
Her faith forbade a liquor so divine;

And, unacquainted with the potent juice,
She much indulged at table in its use.
If lately LOVE disquieted her brain,
New poison now pervaded ev'ry vein;
Both fraught with danger to the beauteous FAIR,
Whose charms should guarded be with ev'ry care.

THE princess by the maids in bed was placed;
Then thither went the host with anxious haste,
What sought he? you will ask:—mere torpid charms:—
I wish the like were clasped within my arms.
Give me as much, said one the other week,
And see if I'd a neighbour's kindness seek.
Through Morpheus' sleepy pow'r, and Bacchus' wine:
Our host, at length, completed his design.

ALACIEL, when at morn, she oped her eyes,
Was quite o'ercome with terror and surprise,
No tears would flow, and fear restrained her voice;
Unable to resist, she'd got no choice.

A NIGHT thus passed, the wily lover said,
Must surely give a license to your bed.
The princess thought the same; but our gallant,
Soon cloyed, for other conquests 'gan to pant.

THE host one evening from the mansion went;
A friend he left himself to represent,
And with the charming fair supply his place,
Which, in the dark he thought, with easy grace,
Might be effected, if he held his tongue,

And properly behaved the whole night long.
To this the other willingly agreed;
(What friend would be refused, if thus in need?)
And this new-comer had complete success
He scarcely could his ecstacy express.

THE dame exclaimed:—pray how could he pretend;
To treat me so, and leave me to a friend?
The other thought the host was much to blame;
But since 'tis o'er, said he, be now your aim,
To punish his contempt of beauteous charms;
With favours load me—take me to your arms;
Caress with fond embrace; bestow delight;
And seem to love me, though in mere despite.

SHE followed his advice: avenged the wrong;
And naught omitted, pleasures to prolong.
If he obtained his wishes from the fair,
The host about it scarcely seemed to care.

THE sixth adventure of our charming belle,
Some writers one way, some another tell;
Whence many think that favour I have shown,
And for her, one gallant the less would own.
Mere scandal this; from truth I would nor swerve,
To please the fair: more credence I deserve;
Her husband only eight precursors had;
The fact was such;—I none suppress nor add.

THE host returned and found his friend content;
To pardon him Alaciel gave consent;

And 'tween them things would equally divide
Of royal bosoms clemency's the pride.

WHILE thus the princess passed from hand to hand
She oft amused her fancy 'mong a band
Of charming belles that on her would attend,
And one of these she made an humble friend.
The fav'rite in the house a lover had,
A smart, engaging, handsome, clever lad,
Well born, but much to violence inclined
A wooer that could scarcely be confined
To gentle means, but oft his suit began,
Where others end, who follow Cupid's plan.

IT one day happened, that this forward spark;
The girl we speak of, met within the park,
And to a summer-house the fav'rite drew;
The course they took the princess chanced to view
As wand'ring near; but neither swain nor fair,
Suspicion had, that any one was there;
And this gallant most confidently thought,
The girl by force, might to his terms be brought!
His wretched temper, obstacle to love,
And ev'ry bliss bestowed by heav'n above,
Had oft his hopes of favours lately marred;
And fear, with those designs, had also jarred:
The girl, howe'er, would likely have been kind,
If opportunities had pleased her mind.

THE lover, now convinced that he was feared;
In dark designs upon her persevered.

No sooner had she entered, than our man
Locked instantly the door, but vain his plan;
To open it the princess had a key;
The girl her fault perceived, and tried to flee;
He held her fast; the charmer loudly called;
The princess came—or vainly she had squalled.

QUITE disappointed: overcome with ire,
He wholly lost respect amid desire,
And swore by all the gods, that, ere they went,
The one or other should to him consent;
Their hands he'd firmly tie to have his way;
For help (the place so far) 'twere vain to pray;
To take a lot was all that he'd allow;
Come, draw, he said; to Fortune you must bow;
No haggling I request—comply; be still:
Resolved I am with one to have my will.

WHAT has the princess done? the girl replied,
That you, to make her suffer, thus decide
Yes, said the spark, if on her fall the lot,
Then you'll, at least for present, be forgot.

NO, cried Alaciel, ne'er I'll have it said,
To sacrifice I saw a maiden led;
I'll suffer rather all that you expect,
If you will spare my friend as I direct.
'Twas all in vain, the lots were drawn at last,
And on the princess was the burthen cast;
The other was permitted to retire,
And each was sworn that nothing should transpire:

But our gallant would sooner have been hung,
Than have upon such secrets held his tongue;
'Tis clear, no longer silent he remained,
Than one to listen to his tale he'd gained.

THIS change of favourites the princess grieved;
That Cupid trifled with her she perceived;
With much regret she saw her blooming charms,
The Helen of too many Paris' arms.

ONE day it happened, as our beauteous belle
Was sleeping in a wood beside a dell,
By chance there passed, quite near, a wand'ring knight,
Like those the ladies followed with delight,
When they on palfreys rode in days of old,
And purity were always thought to hold.

THIS knight, who copied those of famed romance,
Sir Roger, and the rest, in complisance,
No sooner saw the princess thus asleep,
Than instantly he wished a kiss to reap.
While thinking, whether from the neck or lip,
'Twere best the tempting balm of bliss to sip,
He suddenly began to recollect
The laws of chivalry he should respect.
Although the thought retained, his fervent prayer
To Cupid was, that while the nymph was there,
Her fascinating charms he might enjoy;
Sure love's soft senses were ne'er designed to cloy!

THE princess woke, and great surprise expressed;

Oh! charming fair, said he, be not distressed;
No savage of the woods nor giant 's nigh,
A wand'ring knight alone you now descry,
Delighted thus to meet a beauteous belle
Such charms divine, what angel can excel!

THIS compliment was followed by his sighs,
And frank confession, both from tongue and eyes;
Our lover far in little time could go;
At length, he offered on her to bestow,
His hand and heart, and ev'ry thing beside,
Which custom sanctions when we seek a bride.

WITH courtesy his offer was received,
And she related what her bosom grieved;
Detailed her hist'ry, but with care concealed
The six gallants, as wrong to be revealed.
The knight, in what he wished, indulgence got;
And, while the princess much deplored her lot,
The youth proposed Alaciel he should bring,
To Mamolin, or Alexandria's king.

TO Mamolin? replied the princess fair,
No, no—I now indeed would fain repair,
(Could I my wishes have), to Zarus' court,
My native country:—thither give support.

IF Cupid grant me life, rejoined the knight,
You there shall go, and I'll assist your flight;
To have redress, upon yourself depends,
As well as to requite the best of friends;

But should I perish in the bold design,
Submit you must, as wills the pow'rs divine.
I'll freely say, howe'er, that I regard,
My services enough to claim reward.

ALACIEL readily to this agreed;
And favours fondly promised to concede;
T'ensure, indeed, his guarding her throughout,
They were to be conferred upon the route,
From time to time as onward they should go,
Not all at once, but daily some to flow.

THINGS thus arranged, the fair behind the knight
Got up at once, and with him took to flight.
Our cavalier his servants sought to find,
That, when he crossed the wood, he left behind;
With these a nephew and his tutor rode;
The belle a palfrey took, as more the mode,
But, by her walked attentively the spark,
A tale he'd now relate; at times remark
The passing scene; then press his ardent flame;
And thus amused our royal, beauteous dame.

THE treaty was most faithfully observed;
No calculation wrong; from naught they swerved.
At length they reached the sea; on ship-board got;
A quick and pleasing passage was their lot;
Delightfully serene, which joy increased;
To land they came (from perils thought released;)
At Joppa they debarked; two days remained:
And when refreshed, the proper road they gained;

Their escort was the lover's train alone;
On Asia's shores to plunder bands are prone;
By these were met our spark and lovely fair;
New dangers they, alas! were forced to share.

TO cede, at first, their numbers forced the train;
But rallied by our knight they were again;
A desp'rate push he made; repulsed their force;
And by his valour stopt, at length, their course;
In which attack a mortal wound he got,
But was not left for dead upon the spot.

BEFORE his death he full instructions gave,
To grant the belle whatever she might crave;
He ordered too, his nephew should convey,
Alaciel to her home without delay,
Bequeathing him whatever he possessed,
And—what the princess owed among the rest.

AT length, from dread alarms and tears released,
The pair fulfilled the will of our deceased;
Discharged each favour was, of which the last
Was cancelled just as they the frontiers passed.

THE nephew here his precious charge resigned,
For fear the king should be displeased to find,
His daughter guarded by a youthful swain:—
The tutor only with her could remain.

NO words of mine, no language can express
The monarch's joy his child to re-possess;

And, since the difficulty I perceive,
I'll imitate old Sol's retreat at eve,
Who falls with such rapidity of view,
He seems to plunge, dame Thetis to pursue.

THE tutor liked his own details to hear,
And entertaining made his tales appear:
The num'rous perils that the fair had fled,
Who laughed aside, no doubt, at what he said.

I SHOULD observe, the aged tutor cried,
The princess, while for liberty she sighed,
And quite alone remained (by Hispal left,)
That she might be of idleness bereft,
Resolved most fervently a god to serve,
From whom she scarcely since would ever swerve,
A god much worshipped 'mong the people there,
With num'rous temples which his honours share,
Denominated cabinets and bow'rs,
In which, from high respect to heav'nly pow'rs,
They represent the image of a bird,
A pleasing sight, though (what appears absurd)
'Tis bare of plumage, save about the wings;
To this each youthful bosom incense brings,
While other gods, as I've been often told,
They scarcely notice, till they're growing old.

DID you but know the virtuous steps she trod,
While thus devoted to the little god,
You'd thank a hundred times the pow'rs above,
That gave you such a child to bless your love.

But many other customs there abound:—
The FAIR with perfect liberty are found:
Can go and come, whene'er the humour fits;
No eunuch (shadow like) that never quits;
But watches ev'ry movement:—always feared;
No men, but who've upon the chin a beard:
Your daughter from the first, their manners took:
So easy is her ev'ry act and look,
And truly to her honour I may say,
She's all-accommodating ev'ry way.

THE king delighted seemed at what he heard;
But since her journey could not be deferred,
The princess, with a num'rous escort, tried
Again o'er seas t'wards Garba's shores to glide,
And, there arrived, was cordially received
By Mamolin, who loved, she soon believed,
To fond excess; and, all her suite to aid,
A handsome gift to ev'ry one was made.

THE king with noble feasts the court regaled,
At which Alaciel pleasantly detailed
just what she liked, or true or false, 'twas clear;
The prince and courtiers were disposed to hear.

AT night the queen retired to soft repose,
From whence next morn with honour she arose;
The king was found much pleasure to express;
Alaciel asked no more, you well may guess.

BY this we learn, that husbands who aver

Their wond'rous penetration often err;
And while they fancy things so very plain,
They've been preceded by a fav'rite swain.
The safest rule 's to be upon your guard;
Fear ev'ry guile; yet hope the full reward.

SWEET, charming FAIR, your characters revere;
The Mamolin's a bird not common here.
With us Love's fascination is so soon
Succeeded by the licensed honey moon,
There's scarcely opportunity to fool,
Though oft the husband proves an easy tool.

YOUR friendships may be very chaste and pure,
But strangely Cupid's lessons will allure.
Defeat his wiles; resist his tempting charms
E'en from suspicion suffer not alarms.
Don't laugh at my advice; 'twere like the boys,
Who better might amuse themselves with toys.

IF any one, howe'er unable seem,
To make resistance 'gainst the flame supreme
Turn ALL to jest; though right to keep the crown
Yet lost, 'there wrong, yourself to hang or drown.

The Magick Cup

THE worst of ills, with jealousy compared,
Are trifling torments ev'ry where declared.

IMAGINE, to yourself a silly fool,
To dark suspicion grown an easy tool;
No soft repose he finds, by night or day;
But rings his ear, he's wretched ev'ry way!
Continually he dreams his forehead sprouts;
The truth of reveries he never doubts.
But this I would not fully guaranty,
For he who dreams, 'tis said, asleep should be;
And those who've caught, from time to time, a peep,
Pretend to say—the jealous never sleep.

A MAN who has suspicions soon will rouse;
But buz a fly around his precious spouse,
At once he fancies cuckoldom is brought,
And nothing can eradicate the thought;
In spite of reason he must have a place,
And numbered be, among the horned race;
A cuckold to himself he freely owns,
Though otherwise perhaps in flesh and bones.

GOOD folks, of cuckoldom, pray what's the harm,

To give, from time to time, such dire alarm?
What injury 's received, and what 's the wrong,
At which so many sneer and loll their tongue?
While unacquainted with the fact, 'tis naught;
If known:—e'en then 'tis scarcely worth a thought.
You think, however, 'tis a serious grief;
Then try to doubt it, which may bring relief,
And don't resemble him who took a sup,
From out the celebrated magick cup.
Be warned by others' ills; the tale I'll tell;
Perhaps your irksomeness it may dispel.

BUT first, by reason let me prove, I pray,
That evil such as this, and which you say,
Oft weighs you down with soul-corroding care;
Is only in the mind:—mere spright of air:
Your hat upon your head for instance place,
Less gently rather than's your usual case;
Pray, don't it presently at ease remain?
And from it do you aught amiss retain?
Not e'en a spot; there's nothing half so clear;
The features, too, they as before appear?
No difference assuredly you see?
Then how can cuckoldom an evil be?
Such my conclusion, spite of fools or brutes,
With whose ideas reason never suits.

YES, yes, but honour has, you know, a claim:
Who e'er denied it?—never 'twas my aim.
But what of honour?—nothing else is heard;
At Rome a different conduct is preferred;

The cuckold there, who takes the thing to heart,
Is thought a fool, and acts a blockhead's part;
While he, who laughs, is always well received
And honest fellow through the town believed.
Were this misfortune viewed with proper eyes,
Such ills from cuckoldom would ne'er arise.

THAT advantageous 'tis, we now will prove:
Folks laugh; your wife a pliant glove shall move;
But, if you've twenty favourites around,
A single syllable will ne'er resound.
Whene'er you speak, each word has double force;
At table, you've precedency of course,
And oft will get the very nicest parts;
Well pleased who serves you!—all the household smarts
No means neglect your favour to obtain;
You've full command; resistance would be vain.
Whence this conclusion must directly spring:
To be a cuckold is a useful thing.

AT cards, should adverse fortune you pursue;
To take revenge is ever thought your due;
And your opponent often will revoke,
That you for better luck may have a cloak:
If you've a friend o'er head and ears in debt:
At once, to help him numbers you can get.
You fancy these your rind regales and cheers
She's better for it; more beautiful appears;
The Spartan king, in Helen found new charms,
When he'd recovered her from Paris' arms.

YOUR wife the same; to make her, in your eye,
More beautiful 's the aim you may rely;
For, if unkind, she would a hag be thought,
Incapable soft love scenes to be taught.
These reasons make me to my thesis cling,—
To be a cuckold is a useful thing.

IF much too long this introduction seem,
The obvious cause is clearly in the theme,
And should not certainly be hurried o'er,
But now for something from th' historick store.

A CERTAIN man, no matter for his name,
His country, rank, nor residence nor fame,
Through fear of accidents had firmly sworn,
The marriage chain should ne'er by him be worn;
No tie but friendship, from the sex he'd crave:
If wrong or right, the question we will wave.
Be this as 't will, since Hymen could not find
Our wight to bear the wedded knot inclined,
The god of love, to manage for him tried,
And what he wished, from time to time supplied;
A lively fair he got, who charms displayed,
And made him father to a little maid;
Then died, and left the spark dissolved in tears:
Not such as flow for wives, (as oft appears)
When mourning 's nothing more than change of dress:
His anguish spoke the soul in great distress.

THE daughter grew in years, improved in mien,
And soon the woman in her air was seen;

Time rolls apace, and once she's ridded of her bib,
Then alters daily, and her tongue gets glib,
Each year still taller, till she's found at length;
A perfect belle in look, in age, in strength.
His forward child, the father justly feared,
Would cheat the priest of fees so much revered;
The lawyer too, and god of marriage-joys;
Sad fault, that future prospects oft destroys:
To trust her virtue was not quite so sure;
He chose a convent, to be more secure,
Where this young charmer learned to pray and sew;
No wicked books, unfit for girls to know,
Corruption's page the senses to beguile
Dan Cupid never writes in convent style:

OF nothing would she talk but holy-writ;
On which she could herself so well acquit,
That oft the gravest teachers were confused;
To praise her beauty, scarcely was excused;
No flatt'ry pleasure gave, and she'd reply:
Good sister stay!—consider, we must die;
Each feature perishes:—'tis naught but clay;
And soon will worms upon our bodies prey:
Superior needle-work our fair could do;
The spindle turn at ease:—embroider too;
Minerva's skill, or Clotho's, could impart;
In tapestry she'd gained Arachne's art;
And other talents, too, the daughter showed;
Her sense, wealth, beauty, soon were spread abroad:
But most her wealth a marked attention drew;
The belle had been immured with prudent view,

To keep her safely till a spouse was found,
Who with sufficient riches should abound.
From convents, heiresses are often led
Directly to the altar to be wed.

SOME time the father had the girl declared
His lawful child, who all his fondness shared.
As soon as she was free from convent walls,
Her taste at once was changed from books to balls;
Around Calista (such was named our fair)
A host of lovers showed attentive care;
Cits, courtiers, officers, the beau, the sage,
Adventurers of ev'ry rank and age.

FROM these Calista presently made choice,
Of one for whom her father gave his voice;
A handsome lad, and thought good humoured too
Few otherwise appear when first they woo.
Her fortune ample was; the dow'r the same;
The belle an only child; the like her flame.
But better still, our couple's chief delight,
Was mutual love and pleasure to excite.

TWO years in paradise thus passed the pair,
When bliss was changed to Hell's worst cank'ring care;
A fit of jealousy the husband grieved,
And, strange to tell, he all at once believed,
A lover with success his wife addressed,
When, but for him, the suit had ne'er been pressed;
For though the spark, the charming fair to gain,
Would ev'ry wily method try, 'twas plain,

Yet had the husband never terrors shown,
The lover, in despair, had quickly flown.

WHAT should a husband do whose wife is sought,
With anxious fondness by another? Naught.
'Tis this that leads me ever to advise,
To sleep at ease whichever side he lies.
In case she lends the spark a willing ear,
'Twill not be better if you interfere:
She'll seek more opportunities you'll find;
But if to pay attention she's inclined,
You'll raise the inclination in her brain,
And then the danger will begin again.

WHERE'ER suspicion dwells you may be sure,
To cuckoldom 'twill prove a place secure.
But Damon (such the husband's name), 'tis clear,
Thought otherwise, as we shall make appear.
He merits pity, and should be excused,
Since he, by bad advice, was much abused;
When had he trusted to himself to guide,
He'd acted wisely,'—hear and you'll decide.

THE Enchantress Neria flourished in those days;
E'en Circe, she excelled in Satan's ways;
The storms she made obedient to her will,
And regulated with superior skill;
In chains the destinies she kept around;
The gentle zephyrs were her sages found;
The winds, her lacqueys, flew with rapid course;
Alert, but obstinate, with pow'rful force.

WITH all her art th' enchantress could not find,
A charm to guard her 'gainst the urchin blind;
Though she'd the pow'r to stop the star of day,
She burned to gain a being formed of clay.
If merely a salute her wish had been,
She might have had it, easily was seen;
But bliss unbounded clearly was her view,
And this with anxious ardour she'd pursue.
Though charms she had, still Damon would remain,
To her who had his heart a faithful swain:
In vain she sought the genial soft caress:
To Neria naught but friendship he'd express.
Like Damon, husbands nowhere now are found,
And I'm not certain, such were e'er on ground.
I rather fancy, hist'ry is not here,
What we would wish, since truth it don't revere,
I nothing in the hippogriff perceive,
Or lance enchanted, but we may believe;
Yet this I must confess has raised surprise,
Howe'er, to pass it will perhaps suffice;
I've many passed the same,—in ancient days;
Men different were from us: had other ways;
Unlike the present manners, we'll suppose;
Or history would other facts disclose.

THE am'rous Neria to obtain her end,
Made use of philters, and would e'en descend;
To ev'ry wily look and secret art,
That could to him she loved her flame impart.
Our swain his marriage vow to this opposed;
At which th' enchantress much surprise disclosed.

You doubtless fancy, she exclaimed one day,
That your fidelity must worth display;
But I should like to know if equal care,
Calista takes to act upon the square.
Suppose your wife had got a smart gallant,
Would you refuse as much a fair to grant?
And if Calista, careless of your fame,
Should carry to extremes a guilty flame,
Would you but half way go? I truly thought,
By sturdy hymen thus you'd not be caught.
Domestick joys should be to cits confined;
For none but such were scenes like those designed.

BUT as to you:—decline Love's choice pursuit!
No anxious wish to taste forbidden fruit?
Though such you banish from your thoughts I see,
A friend thereto I fain would have you be.
Come make the trial: you'll Calista find,
Quite new again when to her arms resigned.
But let me tell you, though your wife be chaste,
Erastus to your mansion oft is traced.

AND do you think, cried Damon with an air,
Erastus visits as a lover there?
Too much he seems, my friend, to act a part,
That proves the villain both in head and heart.

SAID Neria, mortified at this reply,
Though he's a friend on whom you may rely,
Calista beauty has; much worth the man,
With smart address to execute his plan;

And when we meet accomplishments so rare;
Few women but will tumble in the snare.

THIS conversation was by Damon felt,
A wife, brisk, young, and formed 'mid joys to melt;
A man well versed in Cupid's wily way;
No courtier bolder of the present day;
Well made and handsome, with attractive mind;
Wo what might happen was the husband blind?
Whoever trusts implicitly to friends,
Too oft will find, on shadows he depends.
Pray where's the devotee, who could withstand,
The tempting glimpse of charms that all command;
Which first invite by halves: then bolder grow,
Till fascination spreads, and bosoms glow?
Our Damon fancied this already done,
Or, at the best, might be too soon begun:
On these foundations gloomy views arose,
Chimeras dire, destructive of repose.

TH'enchantress presently a hint received,
That those suspicions much the husband grieved;
And better to succeed and make him fret,
She told him of a thing, 'mong witches met,
'Twas metamorphose-water (such the name)
With this could Damon take Erastus' frame;
His gait, his look, his carriage, air and voice
Thus changed, he easily could mark her choice,
Each step observe:—enough, he asked no more,
Erastus' shape the husband quickly bore;
His easy manner, and appearance caught:

With captivating smiles his wife he sought.
And thus addressed the fair with ev'ry grace:—
How blithe that look! enchanting is your face;
Your beauty's always great, I needs must say,
But never more delightful than to-day.

CALISTA saw the flatt'ring lover's scheme;
And turned to ridicule the wily theme.
His manner Damon changed, from gay to grave:
Now sighs, then tears; but nothing could enslave;
The lady, virtue firmly would maintain;
At length, the husband, seeing all was vain,
Proposed a bribe, and offered such a sum,
Her anger dropt: the belle was overcome.
The price was very large, it might excuse,
Though she at first was prompted to refuse;
At last, howe'er her chastity gave way:
To gold's allurements few will offer nay!
The cash, resistance had so fully laid,
Surrender would at any time be made.
The precious ore has universal charms,
Enchains the will, or sets the world in arms!

THOUGH elegant your form, and smart your dress,
Your air, your language, ev'ry warmth express
Yet, if a banker, or a financier,
With handsome presents happen to appear,
At once is blessed the wealthy paramour,
While you a year may languish at the door.

THIS heart, inflexible, it seems, gave ground,

To money's pow'rful, all-subduing sound;
The rock now disappeared—and, in its stead,
A lamb was found, quite easy to be led,
Who, as a proof, resistance she would wave,
A kiss, by way of earnest freely gave.
No further would the husband push the dame,
Nor be himself a witness of his shame,
But straight resumed his form, and to his wife,
Cried, O Calista! once my soul and life
Calista, whom I fondly cherished long;
Calista, whose affection was so strong;
Is gold more dear than hearts in union twined?
To wash thy guilt, thy blood should be assigned.
But still I love thee, spite of evil thought;
My death will pay the ills thou'st on me brought.

THE metamorphosis our dame surprised;
To give relief her tears but just sufficed;
She scarcely spoke; the husband, days remained,
Reflecting on the circumstance that pained.
Himself a cuckold could he ever make,
By mere design a liberty to take?
But, horned or not? the question seemed to be,
When Neria told him, if from doubts not free,
Drink from the cup:—with so much art 'tis made,
That, whose'er of cuckoldom 's afraid,
Let him but put it to his eager lips
If he's a cuckold, out the liquor slips;
He naught can swallow; and the whole is thrown
About his face or clothes, as oft 's been shown.
But should, from out his brow, no horns yet pop—

He drinks the whole, nor spills a single drop.

THE doubt to solve, our husband took a sup,
From this famed, formidably, magick cup;
Nor did he any of the liquor waste:—
Well, I am safe, said he, my wife is chaste,
Though on myself it wholly could depend;
But from it what have I to apprehend?
Make room, good folks, who leafless branches wear;
If you desire those honours I should share.
Thus Damon spoke, and to his precious wife
A curious sermon preached, it seems, on life.

IF cuckoldom, my friends, such torments give;
'Tis better far 'mong savages to live!

LEST worse should happen, Damon settled spies,
Who, o'er his lady watched with Argus' eyes.
She turned coquette; restraints the FAIR awake,
And only prompt more liberties to take.
The silly husband secrets tried to know,
And rather seemed to seek the wily foe,
Which fear has often rendered fatal round,
When otherwise the ill had ne'er been found.

FOUR times an hour his lips to sip he placed;
And clearly, for a week was not disgraced.
Howe'er, no further went his ease of mind;
Oh, fatal science! fatally designed!
With fury Damon threw the cup away,
And, in his rage, himself inclined to slay.

HIS wife he straight shut up within a tower,
Where, morn and night, he showed a husband's pow'r,
Reproach bestowed: while she bewailed her lot,
'Twere better far, if he'd concealed the blot;
For now, from mouth to mouth, and ear to ear,
It echoed, and re-echoed far and near.

MEANWHILE Calista led a wretched life;
No gold nor jewels Damon left his wife,
Which made the jailer faithful, since 'twere vain
To hope, unbribed, this Cerberus to gain.

AT length, the wife a lucky moment sought,
When Damon seemed by soft caresses caught.
Said she, I've guilty been, I freely own;
But though my crime is great, I'm not alone;
Alas! how few escape from like mishap;
'Mong Hymen's band so common is the trap;
And though at you the immaculate may smile,
What use to fret and all the sex revile?

WELL I'll console myself, and pardon you,
Cried Damon, when sufficient I can view,
Of ornamented foreheads, just like mine,
To form among themselves a royal line;
'Tis only to employ the magick cup,
From which I learned your secrets by a sup.

HIS plan to execute, the husband went,
And ev'ry passenger was thither sent,
Where Damon entertained, with sumptuous fare;

And, at the end, proposed the magick snare:
Said he, my wife played truant to my bed;
Wish you to know if your's be e'er misled?
'Tis right how things go on at home to trace,
And if upon the cup your lips you place,
In case your wife be chaste, there'll naught go wrong;
But, if to Vulcan's troop you should belong,
And prove an antlered brother, you will spill
The liquor ev'ry way, in spite of skill.

TO all the men, that Damon could collect,
The cup he offered, and they tried th' effect;
But few escaped, at which they laughed or cried,
As feelings led, or cuckoldom they spied,
Whose surly countenance the wags believed,
In many houses near, might be perceived.

ALREADY Damon had sufficient found,
To form a regiment and march around;
At times they threatened governors to hang,
Unless they would surrender to their gang;
But few they wanted to complete the force,
And soon a royal army made of course.
From day to day their numbers would augment,
Without the beat of drum, to great extent;
Their rank was always fixed by length of horn:
Foot soldiers those, whose branches short were borne;
Dragoons, lieutenants, captains, some became,
And even colonels, those of greater fame.
The portion spilled by each from out the vase
Was taken for the length, and fixed the place.

A wight, who in an instant spilled the whole,
Was made a gen'ral: not commander sole,
For many followed of the same degree,
And 'twas determined they should equals be.

THE rank and file now nearly found complete,
And full enough an enemy to beat,
Young Reynold, nephew of famed Charlemain,
By chance came by: the spark they tried to gain,
And, after treating him with sumptuous cheer,
At length the magick cup mas made appear;
But no way Reynold could be led to drink:
My wife, cried he, I truly faithful think,
And that's enough; the cup can nothing more;
Should I, who sleep with two eyes, sleep with four?
I feel at ease, thank heav'n, and have no dread,
Then why to seek new cares should I be led?
Perhaps, if I the cup should hold awry,
The liquor out might on a sudden fly;
I'm sometimes awkward, and in case the cup
Should fancy me another, who would sup,
The error, doubtless, might unpleasant be:
To any thing but this I will agree,
To give you pleasure, Damon, so adieu;
Then Reynold from the antlered corps withdrew.

SAID Damon, gentlemen, 'tis pretty clear,
So wise as Reynold, none of us appear;
But let's console ourselves;—'tis very plain,
The same are others:—to repine were vain.

AT length, such numbers on their rolls they bore;
Calista liberty obtained once more,
As promised formerly, and then her charms
Again were taken to her spouse's arms.

LET Reynold's conduct, husbands, be your line;
Who Damon's follows surely will repine.
Perhaps the first should have been made the chief;
Though, doubtless, that is matter of belief.
No mortal can from danger feel secure;
To be exempt from spilling, who is sure?
Nor Roland, Reynold, nor famed Charlemain,
But what had acted wrong to risk the stain.

The Falcon

I RECOLLECT, that lately much I blamed,
The sort of lover, avaricious named;
And if in opposites we reason see,
The liberal in paradise should be.
The rule is just and, with the warmest zeal,
To prove the fact I to the CHURCH appeal.

IN Florence once there dwelled a gentle youth,
Who loved a certain beauteous belle with truth;
O'er all his actions she had full controul;—
To please he would have sold his very soul.
If she amusements wished, he'd lavish gold,
Convinced in love or war you should be bold;
The cash ne'er spare:—invincible its pow'rs,
O'erturning walls or doors where'er it show'rs.
The precious ore can every thing o'ercome;
'Twill silence barking curs: make servants dumb;
And these can render eloquent at will:—
Excel e'en Tully in persuasive skill;
In short he'd leave no quarter unsubdued,
Unless therein the fair he could include.

SHE stood th' attack howe'er, and Frederick failed;
His force was vain whenever he assailed;

Without the least return his wealth he spent:
Lands, houses, manors of immense extent,
Were ev'ry now and then to auction brought;
To gratify his love was all he thought.

THE rank of 'squire till lately he had claimed;
Now scarcely was he even mister named;
Of wealth by Cupid's stratagems bereft,
A single farm was all the man had left;
Friends very few, and such as God alone,
Could tell if friendship they might not disown;
The best were led their pity to express;
'Twas all he got: it could not well be less;
To lend without security was wrong,
And former favours they'd forgotten long;
With all that Frederick could or say or do,
His liberal conduct soon was lost to view.

WITH Clytia he no longer was received,
Than while he was a man of wealth believed;
Balls, concerts, op'ras, tournaments, and plays,
Expensive dresses, all engaging ways,
Were used to captivate this lady fair,
While scarcely one around but in despair,
Wife, widow, maid, his fond affection sought;
To gain him, ev'ry wily art was brought;
But all in vain:—by passion overpow'red,
The belle, whose conduct others would have soured,
To him appeared a goddess full of charms,
Superior e'en to Helen, in his arms;
From whence we may conclude, the beauteous dame

Was always deaf to Fred'rick's ardent flame.

ENAMOURED of the belle, his lands he sold;
The family estates were turned to gold;
And many who the purchases had made,
With pelf accumulated by their trade,
Assumed the airs of men of noble birth:—
Fair subjects oft for ridicule and mirth!

RICH Clytia was, and her good spouse, 'tis said,
Had lands which far and wide around were spread;
No cash nor presents she would ever take,
Yet suffered Frederick splendid treats to make,
Without designing recompense to grant,
Or being more than merely complaisant.

ALREADY, if my mem'ry do not fail,
I've said, the youth's estates were put to sale,
To pay for feasts the fair to entertain,
And what he'd left was only one domain,
A petty farm to which he now retired;
Ashamed to show where once so much admired,
And wretched too, a prey to lorn despair,
Unable to obtain by splendid care,
A beauty he'd pursued six years and more,
And should for ever fervently adore.
His want of merit was the cause he thought,
That she could never to his wish be brought,
While from him not a syllable was heard,
Against the lovely belle his soul preferred.

'MID poverty oft Fred'rick sighed and wept;
A toothless hag—his only servant kept;
His kitchen cold; (where commonly he dwelled;)
A pretty decent horse his stable held;
A falcon too; and round about the grange,
Our quondam 'squire repeatedly would range,
Where oft, to melancholy, he was led,
To sacrifice the game which near him fed;
By Clytia's cruelty the gun was seized,
And feathered victims black chagrin appeased.

'TWAS thus the lover whiled his hours away;
His heart-felt torments nothing could allay;
Blessed if with fortune love he'd also lost,
Which constantly his earthly comforts crossed;
But this lorn passion preyed upon his mind:—
Where'er he rode, BLACK CARE would mount behind.

DEATH took at length the husband of the fair;
An only son appointed was his heir,
A sickly child, whose life, 'twas pretty plain,
Could scarcely last till spring returned again,
Which made the husband, by his will, decree,
His wife the infant's successor should be,
In case the babe at early years should die,
Who soon grew worse and raised the widow's sigh.

TOO much affection parents ne'er can show:—
A mother's feelings none but mothers know.

FAIR Clytia round her child with anxious care,

Watched day and night, and no expense would spare;
Inquired if this or that would please his taste;
What he desired should be procured with haste;
But nothing would he have that she proposed;
An ardent wish howe'er the boy disclosed,
For Fred'rick's Falcon, and most anxious grew:—
Tear followed tear, and nothing else would do.
When once a child has got a whim in brain,
No peace, no rest, till he the boon obtain.

WE should observe our belle, near Fred'rick's cot,
A handsome house and many lands had got;
'Twas there the lovely babe had lately heard,
Most wondrous stories of the bird averred;
No partridge e'er escaped its rapid wing:—
On every morn down numbers it would bring;
No money for it would its owner take;
Much grieved was Clytia such request to make.
The man, for her, of wealth had been bereft;
How ask the only treasure he had left?
And him if she were led to importune,
Could she expect that he'd accord the boon?
Alas! ungratefully she oft repaid,
His liberal treats, his concerts, serenade,
And haughtily behaved from first to last:
How be so bold, (reflecting on the past,)
To see the man that she so ill had used?
And ask a favour?—could she be excused?
But then her child!—perhaps his life 'twould save;
Naught would he take; the falcon she must crave.

THAT her sweet babe might be induced to eat,
So meant the bird of Fred'rick to intreat;
Her boy was heard continually to cry,
Unless he had the falcon, he should die.

THESE reasons strongly with the mother weighed;
Her visit to the 'squire was not delayed;
With fond affection for her darling heir,
One morn, alone she sought the lorn repair.

TO Fred'rick's eye an angel she appeared;
But shame he felt, that she, his soul revered,
Should find him poor:—no servants to attend,
Nor means to give a dinner to a friend.
The poverty in which he now was viewed,
Distressed his mind and all his griefs renewed.
Why come? said he; what led you thus to trace,
An humble slave of your celestial face?
A villager, a wretched being here;
Too great the honour doubtless must appear;
'Twas somewhere else you surely meant to go?
The lady in a moment answered no.
Cried he, I've neither cook nor kettle left;
Then how can I receive you, thus bereft?
But you have bread, said Clytia:—that will do;—
The lover quickly to the poultry flew,
In search of eggs; some bacon too he found;
But nothing else, except the hawk renowned,
Which caught his eye, and instantly was seized,
Slain, plucked, and made a fricassee that pleased.

MEANWHILE the house-keeper for linen sought;
Knives, forks, plates, spoons, cups, glass and chairs she brought;
The fricassee was served, the dame partook,
And on the dish with pleasure seemed to look.

THE dinner o'er, the widow then resolved,
To ask the boon which in her mind resolved.
She thus begun:—good sir, you'll think me mad,
To come and to your breast fresh trouble add;
I've much to ask, and you will feel surprise,
That one, for whom your love could ne'er suffice,
Should now request your celebrated bird;
Can I expect the grant?—the thought 's absurd
But pardon pray a mother's anxious fear;
'Tis for my child:—his life to me is dear.
The falcon solely can the infant save;
Yet since to you I nothing ever gave,
For all your kindness oft on me bestowed;
Your fortune wasted:—e'en your nice abode,
Alas! disposed of, large supplies to raise,
To entertain and please in various ways:
I cannot hope this falcon to obtain;
For sure I am the expectation's vane;
No, rather perish child and mother too;
Than such uneasiness should you pursue:
Allow howe'er this parent, I beseech,
Who loves her offspring 'yond the pow'r of speech,
Or language to express, her only boy,
Sole hope, sole comfort, all her earthly joy,
True mother like, to seek her child's relief,

And in your breast deposit now her grief.
Affection's pow'r none better know than you,—
How few to love were ever half so true!
From such a bosom I may pardon crave
Soft pity's ever with the good and brave!

ALAS! the wretched lover straight replied,
The bird was all I could for you provide;
'Twas served for dinner.—Dead?—exclaimed the dame,
While trembling terror overspread her frame.
No jest, said he, and from the soul I wish,
My heart, instead of that, had been the dish;
But doomed alas! am I by fate, 'tis clear,
To find no grace with her my soul holds dear:
I'd nothing left; and when I saw the bird,
To kill it instantly the thought occurred;
Those naught we grudge nor spare to entertain,
Who o'er our feeling bosoms sov'reign reign:
All I can do is speedily to get,
Another falcon: easily they're met;
And by to-morrow I'll the bird procure.
No, Fred'rick, she replied, I now conjure
You'll think no more about it; what you've done
Is all that fondness could have shown a son;
And whether fate has doomed the child to die,
Or with my prayers the pow'rs above comply;
For you my gratitude will never end—
Pray let us hope to see you as a friend.

THEN Clytia took her leave, and gave her hand;
A proof his love no more she would withstand.

He kissed and bathed her fingers with his tears;
The second day grim death confirmed their fears:

THE mourning lasted long and mother's grief;
But days and months at length bestowed relief;
No wretchedness so great, we may depend,
But what, to time's all-conqu'ring sithe will bend:

TWO famed physicians managed with such care;
That they recovered her from wild despair,
And tears gave place to cheerfulness and joy:—
The one was TIME the other Venus' Boy.
Her hand fair Clytia on the youth bestowed,
As much from love as what to him she owed.

LET not this instance howsoe'r mislead;
'Twere wrong with hope our fond desires to feed,
And waste our substance thus:—not all the FAIR,
Possess of gratitude a decent share.
With this exception they appear divine;
In lovely WOMAN angel-charms combine;
The whole indeed I do not here include;
Alas; too many act the jilt and prude.
When kind, they're ev'ry blessing found below:
When otherwise a curse we often know.

The Little Dog

THE key, which opes the chest of hoarded gold.
Unlocks the heart that favours would withhold.
To this the god of love has oft recourse,
When arrows fail to reach the secret source,
And I'll maintain he's right, for, 'mong mankind,
Nice presents ev'ry where we pleasing find;
Kings, princes, potentates, receive the same,
And when a lady thinks she's not to blame,
To do what custom tolerates around;
When Venus' acts are only Themis' found,
I'll nothing 'gainst her say; more faults than one,
Besides the present, have their course begun.

A MANTUAN judge espoused a beauteous fair:
Her name was Argia:—Anselm was her care,
An aged dotard, trembling with alarms,
While she was young, and blessed with seraph charms.
But, not content with such a pleasing prize,
His jealousy appeared without disguise,
Which greater admiration round her drew,
Who doubtless merited, in ev'ry view,
Attention from the first in rank or place
So elegant her form, so fine her face.

'TWOULD endless prove, and nothing would avail,
Each lover's pain minutely to detail:
Their arts and wiles; enough 'twill be no doubt,
To say the lady's heart was found so stout,
She let them sigh their precious hours away,
And scarcely seemed emotion to betray.

WHILE at the judge's, Cupid was employed,
Some weighty things the Mantuan state annoyed,
Of such importance, that the rulers meant,
An embassy should to the Pope be sent.
As Anselm was a judge of high degree,
No one so well embassador could be.

'TWAS with reluctance he agreed to go,
And be at Rome their mighty Plenipo';
The business would be long, and he must dwell
Six months or more abroad, he could not tell.
Though great the honour, he should leave his dove,
Which would be painful to connubial love.
Long embassies and journeys far from home
Oft cuckoldom around induce to roam.

THE husband, full of fears about his wife;
Exclaimed—my ever—darling, precious life,
I must away; adieu, be faithful pray,
To one whose heart from you can never stray
But swear to me, my duck, (for, truth to tell,
I've reason to be jealous of my belle,)
Now swear these sparks, whose ardour I perceive,
Have sighed without success, and I'll believe.

But still your honour better to secure,
From slander's tongue, and virtue to ensure,
I'd have you to our country-house repair;
The city quit:—these sly gallants beware;
Their presents too, accurst invention found,
With danger fraught, and ever much renowned;
For always in the world, where lovers move,
These gifts the parent of assentment prove.
'Gainst those declare at once; nor lend an ear
To flattery, their cunning sister-peer.
If they approach, shut straight both ears and eyes;
For nothing you shall want that wealth supplies;
My store you may command; the key behold,
Where I've deposited my notes and gold.
Receive my rents; expend whate'er you please;
I'll look for no accounts; live quite at ease;
I shall be satisfied with what you do,
If naught therein to raise a blush I view;
You've full permission to amuse your mind;
Your love, howe'er, for me alone's designed;
That, recollect, must be for my return,
For which our bosoms will with ardour burn.

THE good man's bounty seemingly was sweet;
All pleasures, one excepted, she might greet;
But that, alas! by bosoms unpossessed,
No happiness arises from the rest:
His lady promised ev'ry thing required:—
Deaf, blind, and cruel,—whosoe'er admired;
And not a present would her hand receive
At his return, he fully might believe,

She would be found the same as when he went,
Without gallant, or aught to discontent.

HER husband gone, she presently retired
Where Anselm had so earnestly desired;
The lovers came, but they were soon dismissed,
And told, from visits they must all desist;
Their assiduities were irksome grown,
And she was weary of their lovesick tone.
Save one, they all were odious to the fair;
A handsome youth, with smart engaging air;
But whose attentions to the belle were vain;
In spite of arts, his aim he could not gain;
His name was Atis, known to love and arms,
Who grudged no pains, could he possess her charms.
Each wile he tried, and if he'd kept to sighs,
No doubt the source is one that never dries;
But often diff'rent with expense 'tis found;
His wealth was wasted rapidly around
He wretched grew; at length for debt he fled,
And sought a desert to conceal his head.
As on the road he moved, a clown he met,
Who with his stick an adder tried to get,
From out a thicket, where it hissing lay,
And hoped to drive the countryman away:
Our knight his object asked; the clown replied,
To slay the reptile anxiously I tried;
Wherever met, an adder I would kill:
The race should be extinct if I'd my will.

WHY would'st thou, friend, said Atis, these destroy?

God meant that all should freely life enjoy.
The youthful knight for reptiles had, we find,
Less dread than what prevails with human kind;
He bore them in his arms:—they marked his birth;
From noble Cadmus sprung, who, when on earth,
At last, to serpent was in age transformed;
The adder's bush the clown no longer stormed;
No more the spotted reptile sought to stay,
But seized the time, and quickly crept away.

AT length our lover to a wood retired;
To live concealed was what the youth desired;
Lorn silence reigned, except from birds that sang,
And dells that oft with sweetest echo rang.
There HAPPINESS and frightful MIS'RY lay,
Quite undistinguished: classed with beasts of prey;
That growling prowled in search of food around:
There Atis consolation never found.
LOVE thither followed, and, however viewed,
'Twas vain to hope his passion to elude;
Retirement fed the tender, ardent flame,
And irksome ev'ry minute soon became.
Let us return, cried he, since such our fate:
'Tis better, Atis, bear her frowns and hate,
Than of her beauteous features lose the view;
Ye nightingales and streams, ye woods adieu!
When far from her I neither see nor hear:
'Tis she alone my senses still revere;
A slave I am, who fled her dire disdain;
Yet seek once more to wear the cruel chain.

AS near some noble walls our knight arrived,
Which fairy-hands to raise had once contrived,
His eyes beheld, at peep of early morn,
When bright Aurora's beams the earth adorn,
A beauteous nymph in royal robes attired,
Of noble mien, and formed to be admired,
Who t'ward him drew, with pleasing, gracious air,
While he was wrapped in thought, a prey to care.

SAID she, I'd have you, Atis, happy be;
'Tis in my pow'r, and this I hope to see;
A fairy greet me, Manto is my name:—
Your friend, and one you've served unknown:—the same
My fame you've heard, no doubt; from me proceeds
The Mantuan town, renowned for ancient deeds;
In days of yore I these foundations laid,
Which in duration, equal I have made,
To those of Memphis, where the Nile's proud course
Majestically flows from hidden source.
The cruel Parcae are to us unknown;
We wond'rous magick pow'rs have often shown;
But wretched, spite of this, appears our lot
Death never comes, though various ills we've got,
For we to human maladies are prone,
And suffer greatly oft, I freely own.

ONCE, in each week to serpents we are changed;
Do you remember how you here arranged,
To save an adder from a clown's attack?
'Twas I, the furious rustick wished to hack,
When you assisted me to get away;

For recompense, my friend, without delay,
I'll you procure the kindness of the fair,
Who makes you love and drives you to despair:
We'll go and see her:—be assured from me,
Before two days are passed, as I foresee,
You'll gain, by presents, Argia and the rest,
Who round her watch, and are the suitor's pest.
Grudge no expense, be gen'rous, and be bold,
Your handfuls scatter, lavish be of gold.
Assured you shall not want the precious ore;
For I command the whole of Plutus' store,
Preserved, to please me, in the shades below;
This charmer soon our magick pow'r shall know.

THE better to approach the cruel belle,
And to your suit her prompt consent compel,
Myself transformed you'll presently perceive;
And, as a little dog, I'll much achieve,
Around and round I'll gambol o'er the lawn,
And ev'ry way attempt to please and fawn,
While you, a pilgrim, shall the bag-pipe play;
Come, bring me to the dame without delay.

NO sooner said, the lover quickly changed,
Together with the fairy, as arranged;
A pilgrim he, like Orpheus, piped and sang;
While Manto, as a dog, skipt, jumped, and sprang.

THEY thus proceeded to the beauteous dame;
Soon valets, maids, and others round them came;
The dog and pilgrim gave extreme delight

And all were quite diverted at the sight.

THE lady heard the noise, and sent her maid,
To learn the reason why they romped and played:
She soon returned and told the lovely belle,
A spaniel danced, and even spoke so well,
it ev'ry thing could fully understand,
And showed obedience to the least command.
'Twere better come herself and take a view:
The things were wond'rous that the dog could do.

THE dame at any price the dog would buy,
In case the master should the boon deny.
To give the dog our pilgrim was desired;
But though he would not grant the thing required;
He whispered to the maid the price he'd take,
And some proposals was induced to make.
Said he, 'tis true, the creature 's not for sale;
Nor would I give it: prayers will ne'er prevail;
Whate'er I chance to want from day to day,
It furnishes without the least delay.
To have my wish, three words alone I use,
Its paw I squeeze, and whatsoe'er I choose,
Of gold, or jewels, fall upon the ground;
Search all the world, there's nothing like it found.
Your lady's rich, and money does not want;
Howe'er, my little dog to her I'll grant
If she'll a night permit me in her bed,
The treasure shall at once to her be led.

THE maid at this proposal felt surprise;

Her mistress truly! less might well suffice;
A paltry knave! cried she, it makes me laugh;
What! take within her bed a pilgrim's staff!
Were such a circumstance abroad to get,
My lady would with ridicule be met;
The dog and master, probably, were last
Beneath a hedge, or on a dunghill cast;
A house like this they'll never see agen;—
But then the master is the pride of men,
And that in love is ev'ry thing we find
Much wealth and beauty please all womankind!

HIS features and his mien the knight had changed;
Each air and look for conquest were arranged.
The maid exclaimed: when such a lover sues,
How can a woman any thing refuse?
Besides the pilgrim has a dog, ‘tis plain,
Not all the wealth of China could obtain.
Yet to possess my lady for a night,
Would to the master be supreme delight:

I SHOULD have mentioned, that our cunning spark;
The dog would whisper (feigning some remark,)
On which ten ducats tumbled at his feet;
These Atis gave the maid, (O deed discreet;)
Then fell a diamond: this our wily wight
Took up, and smiling at the precious sight,
Said he, what now I hold I beg you'll bear,
To her you serve, so worthy of your care;
Present my compliments, and to her say,
I'm her devoted servant from to-day.

THU female quickly to her mistress went;
Our charming little dog to represent:
The various pow'rs displayed, and wonders done;
Yet scarcely had she on the knight begun,
And mentioned what he wished her to unfold,
But Argia could her rage no longer hold;
A fellow! to presume, cried she, to speak
Of me with freedom!—I am not so weak,
To listen to such infamy, not I
A pilgrim too!—no, you may well rely,
E'en were he Atis, it would be the same,
To whom I now my cruel conduct blame:
Such things he never would to me propose;
Not e'en a monarch would the like disclose;
I'm 'bove temptation, presents would not do:—
Not Plutus' stores, if offered to my view;
A paltry pilgrim to presume indeed,
To think that I would such a blackguard heed,
Ambassadress my rank! and to admit
A fellow, only for the gallows fit!

THIS pilgrim, cried the maid, has got the means
Not only belles to get, but even queens;
Or beauteous goddesses he could obtain:—
He's worth a thousand Atis's 'tis plain.
Bur, said the wife, my husband made me vow.
What? cried the maid, you'd not bedeck his brow!
A pretty promise truly:—can you think,
You less from this, than from the first, should shrink?
Who'll know the fact, or publish it around?
Consider well, how many might be found,

Who, were they marked with spot upon the nose,
When things had taken place that we suppose,
Would not their heads so very lofty place,
I'm well assured, but feel their own disgrace.
For such a thing, are we the worse a hair?
No, no, good lady, who presumes to swear,
He can discern the lips which have been pressed,
By those that never have the fact confessed,
Must be possessed of penetrating eyes,
Which pierce the sable veil of dark disguise.
This favour, whether you accord or not,
'Twill not a whit be less nor more a blot.
For whom, I pray, LOVE'S treasures would you hoard?
For one, who never will a treat afford,
Or what is much the same, has not the pow'r?
All he may want you'll give him in an hour,
At his return; he's very weak and old,
And, doubtless, ev'ry way is icy cold!

THE cunning girl such rhetorick displayed,
That all she said, her mistress, having weighed,
Began to doubt alone, and not deny
The spaniel's art, and pilgrim's piercing eye:
To her the master and his dog were led,
To satisfy her mind while still in bed;
For bright Aurora, from the wat'ry deep,
Not more reluctantly arose from sleep.

OUR spark approached the dame with easy air,
Which seemed the man of fashion to declare;
His compliments were made with ev'ry grace,

That minds most difficult could wish to trace.

THE fair was charmed, and with him quite content;
You do not look, said she, like one who meant
Saint James of Compostella soon to see,
Though, doubtless, oft to saints you bend the knee.

TO entertain the smiling beauteous dame,
The dog, by various tricks, confirmed his flame,
To please the maid and mistress he'd in view:
Too much for these of course he could not do;
Though, for the husband, he would never move,
The little fav'rite sought again to prove
His wond'rous worth, and scattered o'er the ground,
With sudden shake, among the servants round,
Nice pearls, which they on strings arranged with care;
And these the pilgrim offered to the fair:
Gallantly fastened them around her arms,
Admired their whiteness and extolled her charms:
So well he managed, 'twas at length agreed,
In what his heart desired he should succeed;
The dog was bought: the belle bestowed a kiss,
As earnest of the promised future bliss.

THE night arrived, when Atis fondly pressed,
Within his arms, the lady thus caressed;
Himself he suddenly became again,
On which she scarcely could her joy contain:—
Th' ambassador she more respect should show,
Than favours on a pilgrim to bestow.

THE fair and spark so much admired the night;
That others followed equal in delight;
Each felt the same, for where's the perfect shade;
That can conceal when joys like these pervade?
Expression strongly marks the youthful face,
And all that are not blind the truth can trace.
Some months had passed, when Anselm was dismissed;
Of gifts and pardons, long appeared his list;
A load of honours from the Pope he got:—
The CHURCH will these most lib'rally allot.

FROM his vicegerent quickly he received
A good account, and friends his fears relieved;
The servants never dropt a single word
Of what had passed, but all to please concurred.

THE judge, both maid and servants, questioned much;
But not a hint he got, their care was such.
Yet, as it often happens 'mong the FAIR,
The devil entered on a sudden there;
Such quarrels 'tween the maid and mistress rose,
The former vowed she would the tale disclose.
Revenge induced her ev'ry thing to tell,
Though she were implicated with the belle.

SO great the husband's rage, no words can speak:
His fury somewhere he of course would wreak;
But, since to paint it clearly would be vain—
You'll by the sequel judge his poignant pain.

A SERVANT Anselm ordered to convey

His wife a note, who was, without delay,
To come to town her honoured spouse to see;
Extremely ill (for such he feigned to be.)
As yet the lady in the country stayed;
Her husband to and fro' his visits paid.

SAID he, remember, when upon the road,
Conducting Argia from her lone abode,
You must contrive her men to get away,
And with her none but you presume to stay.—
A jade! she horns has planted on my brow:
Her death shall be the consequence I vow.

WITH force a poinard in her bosom thrust;
Watch well th' occasion:—die, I say, she must,
The deed performed, escape; here's for you aid;
The money take:—pursuit you can evade;
As I request, proceed; then trust to me:—
You naught shall want wherever you may be.

TO seek fair Argia instantly he went;
She, by her dog, was warned of his intent.
How these can warn? if asked, I shall reply,
They grumble, bark, complain, or fawn, or sigh;
Pull petticoat or gown, and snarl at all,
Who happen in their way just then to fall;
But few so dull as not to comprehend;
Howe'er, this fav'rite whispered to his friend,
The dangers that awaited her around;
But go, said he, protection you have found;
Confide in me:—I'll ev'ry ill prevent,

For which the rascal hither has been sent.
As on they moved, a wood was in the way,
Where robbers often waited for their prey;
The villain whom the husband had employed,
Sent forward those whose company annoyed,
And would prevent his execrable plan;
The last of horrid crimes.—disgrace to man!
No sooner had the wretch his orders told,
But Argia vanished—none could her behold;
The beauteous belle was quickly lost to view:
A cloud, the fairy Manto o'er her threw.

THIS circumstance astonished much the wretch,
Who ran to give our doating spouse a sketch
Of what had passed so strange upon the way;
Old Anselm thither went without delay,
When, marvellous to think! with great surprise,
He saw a palace of extensive size,
Erected where, an hour or two before,
A hovel was not seen, nor e'en a door.

THE husband stood aghast!—admired the place,
Not built for man, e'en gods 'twould not disgrace.
The rooms were gilt; the decorations fine;
The gardens and the pleasure-grounds divine;
Such rich magnificence was never seen;
Superb the whole, a charming blessed demesne.
The entrance ev'ry way was open found;
But not a person could be viewed around,
Except a negro, hideous to behold,
Who much resembled AEsop, famed of old.

OUR judge the negro for a porter took,
Who was the house to clean and overlook;
And taking him for such, the black addressed,
With full belief the title was the best,
And that he greatly honoured him, 'twas plain
(Of ev'ry colour men are proud and vain:)
Said he, my friend, what god this palace owns?
Too much it seems for those of earthly thrones;
No king, of consequence enough could be;
The palace, cried the black, belongs to me.

THE judge was instantly upon his knees,
The negro's pardon asked, and sought to please;
I trust, said he, my lord, you'll overlook
The fault I made: my ignorance mistook.
The universe has not so nice a spot;
The world so beautiful a palace got!

DOST wish me, said the black, the house to give,
For thee and thine therein at ease to live?
On one condition thou shalt have the place
For thee I seriously intend the grace,
If thou 'lt on me a day or two attend,
As page of honour:—dost thou comprehend?
The custom know'st thou—better I'll expound;
A cup-bearer with Jupiter is found,
Thou'st heard no doubt.

ANSELM
What, Ganymede?

NEGRO
The same;
And I'm that Jupiter of mighty fame;
The chief supreme who rules above the skies;
Be thou the lad with fascinating eyes,
Though not so handsome, nor in truth so young.

ANSELM
You jest, my lord; to youth I don't belong;
'Tis very clear;—my judge's dress—my age!

NEGRO
I jest? thou dream'st.

ANSELM
My lord?

NEGRO
You won't engage?
Just as you will:—'tis all the same you'll find.

ANSELM
My lord! . . . The learned judge himself resigned,
The black's mysterious wishes to obey;—
Alas! curst presents, how they always weigh!

A PAGE the magistrate was quickly seen,
In dress, in look, in age, in air, in mien;
His hat became a cap; his beard alone
Remained unchanged; the rest had wholly flown.

THUS metamorphosed to a pretty boy,
The judge proceeded in the black's employ.
Within a corner hidden, Argia lay,
And heard what Anselm had been led to say.
The Moor howe'er was Manto, most renowned,
Transformed, as oft the fairy we have found;
She built the charming palace by her art,—
Now youthful features would to age impart.

AT length, as Anselm through a passage came,
He suddenly beheld his beauteous dame.
What! learned Anselm do I see, said she,
In this disguise?—It surely cannot be;
My eyes deceive me:—Anselm, grave and wise;
Give such a lesson? I am all surprise.

'TIS doubtless he: oh, oh! our bald-pate sire;
Ambassador and judge, we must admire,
To see your honour thus in masquerade:—
At your age, truly, suffer to be made
A—modesty denies my tongue its powr's
What!—you condemn to death for freaks like ours?
You, whom I've found * * * you understand—for shame
Your crimes are such as all must blush to name.
Though I may have a negro for gallant,
And erred when Atis for me seemed to pant,
His merit and the black's superior rank,
Must lessen, if not quite excuse my prank.
Howe'er, old boy, you presently shall see,
If any belle solicited should be,
To grant indulgencies, with presents sweet,

She will not straight capitulation beat;
At least, if they be such as I have viewed:—
Moor, change to dog; immediately ensued
The metamorphose that the fair required,
The black'moor was again a dog admired.
Dance, fav'rite; instantly he skipped and played;
And to the judge his pretty paw conveyed.
Spaniel, scatter gold; presently there fell
Large sums of money, as the sound could tell.
Such strong temptation who can e'er evade?
The dog a present to your wife was made.
Then show me, if you can, upon the earth,
A queen, a princess, of the highest birth,
Who would not virtue presently concede,
If such excuses for it she could plead;
Particularly if the giver proved
A handsome lad that elegantly moved.

I, TRULY, for the spaniel was exchanged;
What you'd too much of, freely I arranged,
To grant away, this jewel to obtain
My value 's nothing great, you think, 'tis plain;
And, surely, you'd have thought me very wrong,
When such a prize I met, to haggle long.
'Twas he this palace raised; but I have done;
Remember, since you've yet a course to run,
Take care again how you command my death;
In spite of your designs I draw my breath.
Though none but Atis with me had success,
I now desire, he may Lucretia bless,
And wish her to surrender up her charms,

(Just like myself) to his extended arms.
If you approve, our peace at once is made:
If not—while I've this dog I'm not afraid,
But you defy: I dread not swords nor bowl;
The little dog can warn me of the whole;
The jealous he confounds; be that no more;
Such folly hence determine to give o'er.
If you, to put restraints on women choose,
You'll sooner far their fond affections lose.

THE whole our judge conceded;—could he less?
The secret of his recent change of dress
Was promised to be kept: and that unknown,
E'en cuckoldom again might there have flown.

OUR couple mutual compensation made,
Then bade adieu to hill, and dale, and glade.

SOME critick asks the handsome palace' fate;
I answer:—that, my friend, I shan't relate;
It disappeared, no matter how nor when.
Why put such questions?—strict is not my pen.
The little dog, pray what of that became?
To serve the lover was his constant aim.

AND how was that?—You're troublesome my friend:
The dog perhaps would more assistance lend;
On new intrigues his master might be bent;
With single conquest who was e'er content?

THE fav'rite spaniel oft was missing found;

But when the little rogue had gone his round,
He'd then return, as if from work relieved,
To her who first his services received.
His fondness into fervent friendship grew;
As such gay Atis visited anew;
He often came, but Argia was sincere,
And firmly to her vow would now adhere:
Old Anselm too, had sworn, by heav'n above;
No more to be suspicious of his love;
And, if he ever page became again,
To suffer punishment's severest pain.

The Eel Pie

HOWEVER exquisite we BEAUTY find,
It satiates sense, and palls upon the mind:
Brown bread as well as white must be for me;
My motto ever is—VARIETY.

THAT brisk brunette, with languid, sleepy eye,
Delights my fancy; Can you tell me why?
The reason 's plain enough:—she 's something new.
The other mistress, long within my view,
Though lily fair, with seraph features blessed,
No more emotion raises in my breast;
Her heart assents, while mine reluctant proves;
Whence this diversity that in us moves?
From hence it rises, to be plain and free,
My motto ever is—VARIETY.

THE same in other words, I've often said;
'Tis right, at times, disguise with care to spread.
The maxim's good, and with it I agree:
My motto ever is—VARIETY.

A CERTAIN spouse the same devise had got,
Whose wife by all was thought a handsome lot.
His love, howe'er, was over very soon;

It lasted only through the honeymoon;
Possession had his passion quite destroyed;
In Hymen's bands too oft the lover 's cloyed.

ONE, 'mong his valets, had a pretty wife;
The master was himself quite full of life,
And soon the charmer to his wishes drew,
With which the husband discontented grew,
And having caught them in the very fact,
He rang his mate the changes for the act;
Sad names he called her, howsoever just,
A silly blockhead! thus to raise a dust,
For what, in ev'ry town 's so common found;
May we worse fortune never meet around!

HE made the paramour a grave harangue
Don't others give, said he, the poignant pang;
But ev'ry one allow to keep his own,
As God and reason oft to man have shown,
And recommended fully to observe;
You from it surely have not cause to swerve;
You cannot plead that you for beauty pine
You've one at home who far surpasses mine;
No longer give yourself such trouble, pray:
You, to my help-mate, too much honour pay;
Such marked attentions she can ne'er require
Let each of us, alone his own admire.
To others' WELLs you never ought to go,
While your's with sweets is found to overflow;
I willingly appeal to connoisseurs;
If heav'n had blessed me with such bliss as your's,

That when I please, your lady I could take,
I would not for a queen such charms forsake.
But since we can't prevent what now is known,
I wish, good sir, contented with your own,
(And 'tis, I hope, without offence I speak,)
You'll favours from my wife no longer seek.

THE master, neither no nor yes replied,
But orders gave, his man they should provide;
For dinner ev'ry day, what pleased his taste,
A pie of eels, which near him should be placed.

HIS appetite at first was wond'rous great;
Again, the second time, as much he ate;
But when the third appeared, he felt disgust,
And not another morsel down could thrust.
The valet fain would try a diff'rent dish;
'Twas not allowed;—you've got, said they, your wish;
'Tis pie alone; you like it best you know,
And no objection you must dare to show.

I'M surfeited, cried he, 'tis far too much:
Pie ev'ry day! and nothing else to touch!
Not e'en a roasted eel, or stewed, or fried!
Dry bread I'd rather you'd for me provide.
Of your's allow me some at any rate,
Pies, (devil take them!) thoroughly I hate;
They'll follow me to Paradise I fear,
Or further yet;—Heav'n keep me from such cheer!

THEIR noisy mirth the master thither drew,

Who much desired the frolick to pursue;
My friend, said he, I greatly feel surprise,
That you so soon are weary grown of pies;
Have I not heard you frequently declare,
Eel-pie 's of all, the most delicious fare?
Quite fickle, certainly, must be your taste;
Can any thing in me so strange be traced?
When I exchange a food which you admire;
You blame and say, I never ought to tire;
You do the very same; in truth, my friend,
No mark of folly 'tis, you may depend,
In lord or squire, or citizen or clown,
To change the bread that's white for bit of brown:
With more experience, you'll with me agree,—
My motto ever is—VARIETY.

WHEN thus the master had himself expressed,
The valet presently was less distressed;
Some arguments, howe'er, at first he used;
For, after all—are fully we excused,
When we our pleasure solely have in view;
Without regarding what's to others due?
I relish change; well, take it; but 'tis best,
To gain the belles with love of gold possessed;
And that appears to me the proper plan;
In truth, our lover very soon began
To practise this advice;—his voice and way
Could angel-sweetness instantly convey.

HIS words were always gilt; (impressive tongue!)
To gilded words will sure success belong.

In soft amours they're ev'ry thing 'tis plain
The maxim 's certain, and our aim will gain;
My meaning doubtless easily is seen;
A hundred times repeated this has been
Th' impression should be made so very deep,
That I thereon can never silence keep;
And this the constant burden of my song—
To gilded words will sure success belong.

THEY easily persuade the beauteous dame;
Her dog, her maid, duenna, all the same;
The husband sometimes too, and him we've shown
'Twas necessary here to gain alone;
By golden eloquence his soul was lulled;
Although from ancient orators not culled:
Their books retained have nothing of the kind;
Our jealous spouse indulgent grew we find.
He followed e'en, 'tis said, the other's plan—
And, thence his dishes to exchange began.

THE master and his fav'rite's freaks around;
Continually the table-talk were found;
He always thought the newest face the best:
Where'er he could, each beauty he caressed;
The wife, the widow, daughter, servant-maid,
The nymph of field or town:—with all he played;
And, while he breathed, the same would always be;
His motto ever was—VARIETY.

The Magnificent

SOME wit, handsome form and gen'rous mind;
A triple engine prove in love we find;
By these the strongest fortresses are gained
E'en rocks 'gainst such can never be sustained.
If you've some talents, with a pleasing face,
Your purse-strings open free, and you've the place.
At times, no doubt, without these things, success
Attends the gay gallant, we must confess;
But then, good sense should o'er his actions rule;
At all events, he must not be a fool.
The stingy, women ever will detest;
Words puppies want;—the lib'ral are the best.

A Florentine, MAGNIFICENT by name,
Was what we've just described, in fact and fame;
The title was bestowed upon the knight,
For noble deeds performed by him in fight.
The honour ev'ry way he well deserved;
His upright conduct (whence he never swerved,)
Expensive equipage, and presents made,
Proclaimed him all around what we've pourtrayed.

WITH handsome person and a pleasing mien,
Gallant, a polished air, and soul serene;

A certain fair of noble birth he sought,
Whose conquest, doubtless, brilliant would be thought;
Which in our lover doubly raised desire;
Renown and pleasure lent his bosom fire.

THE jealous husband of the beauteous fair
Was Aldobrandin, whose suspicious care
Resembled more, what frequently is shown
For fav'rites mistresses, than wives alone.
He watched her every step with all his eyes;
A hundred thousand scarcely would suffice;
Indeed, quite useless Cupid these can make;
And Argus oft is subject to mistake:
Repeatedly they're duped, although our wight,
(Who fancied he in ev'ry thing was right,)
Himself so perfectly secure believed,
By gay gallants he ne'er could be deceived.

TO suitors, howsoe'er, he was not blind;
To covet presents, greatly he inclined.
The lover yet had no occasion found,
To drop a word to charms so much renowned;
He thought his passion was not even seen;
And if it had, would things have better been?
What would have followed? what had been the end?
The reader needs no hint to comprehend.

BUT to return to our forlorn gallant,
Whose bosom for the lady's 'gan to pant;
He, to his doctor, not a word had said;
Now here, now there, he tried to pop his head.

But neither door nor window could he find,
Where he might glimpse the object of his mind,
Or even hear her voice, or sound her name;
No fortress had he ever found the same;
Yet still to conquer he was quite resolved,
And oft the manner in his mind revolved.
This plan at length he thought would best succeed,
To execute it doubtless he had need
Of ev'ry wily art he could devise,
Surrounded as he was by eagle-eyes.

I THINK the reader I've already told,
Our husband loved rich presents to behold;
Though none he made, yet all he would receive;
Whate'er was offered he would never leave.

MAGNIFICENT a handsome horse had got,
It ambled well, or cantered, or would trot;
He greatly valued it, and for its pace,
'Twas called the Pad; it stept with wond'rous grace:
By Aldobrandin it was highly praised;
Enough was this: the knight's fond hopes were raised;
Who offered to exchange, but t'other thought,
He in a barter might perhaps be caught.
'Tis not, said he, that I the horse refuse;
But I, in trucking, never fail to lose.

ON this, Magnificent, who saw his aim;
Replied, well, well, a better scheme we'll frame;
No changing we'll allow, but you'll permit,
That for the horse, I with your lady sit,

You present all the while, 'tis what I want;
I'm curious, I confess, and fort it pant.
Besides, your friends assuredly should know
What mind, what sentiments may from her flow.
Just fifteen minutes, I no more desire:
What! cried the other, you my wife require?
No, no, pray keep your horse, that won't be right.
But you'll be present, said the courteous knight.
And what of that? rejoined the wily spouse.
Why, cried Magnificent, then naught should rouse
Your fears or cares, for how can ill arise,
While watched by you, possessed of eagle-eyes?

THE husband 'gan to turn it in his mind;
Thought he, if present, what can be designed?
The plan is such as dissipates my fears;
The offer advantageous too appears;
He's surely mad; I can't conceive his aim;
But, to secure myself and wife from shame;
Without his knowledge, I'll forbid the fair
Her lips to open, and for this prepare.

COME, cried old Aldobrandin, I'll consent:
But, said the other, recollect 'tis meant,
So distant from us, all the while you stay,
That not a word you hear of what I say.
Agreed, rejoined the husband:—let's begin;
Away he flew, and brought the lady in.

WHEN our gallant the charming belle perceived;
Elysium seemed around, he half believed.

The salutations o'er, they went and sat
Together in a corner, where their chat
Could not be heard, if they to talk inclined;
Our brisk gallant no long harangues designed,
But to the point advanced without delay;
Cried he, I've neither time nor place to say
What I could wish, and useless 'twere to seek
Expressions that but indirectly speak
The sentiments which animate the soul;
In terms direct, 'tis better state the whole.

THUS circumstanced, fair lady, let me, pray;
To you at once, my adoration pay;
No words my admiration can express;
Your charms enslave my senses, I confess;
Can you suppose to answer would be wrong?
Too much good sense to you should now belong;
Had I the leisure, I'd in form disclose
The tender flame with which my bosom glows;
Each horrid torment; but by Fate denied
Blessed opportunities, let me not hide,
While moments offer, what pervades my heart,
And openly avow the burning smart
Few minutes I have got to travel o'er
What gen'rally requires six months or more.
Cold is that lover who will not pursue,
With ev'ry ardour, beauty, when in view.
But why this silence?—not a word you say!
You surely will not send me thus away!
That heav'n, an angel made you, none deny;
But still, to what is asked you should reply.

Your husband this contrived I plainly see,
Who fancies that replies were not to be,
Since in our bargain they were never named;
For shuffling conduct he was ever famed;
But I'll come round him, spite of all his art;
I can reply for you, and from the heart,
Since I can read your wishes in your eyes;
'Tis thus to say—Good, sir, I would advise
That you regard me, not as marble cold;
Your various tournaments and actions bold,
Your serenades, and gen'ral conduct prove,
What tender sentiments your bosom move.

YOUR fond affection constantly I praised,
And quickly felt a flame within me raised;
Yet what avails?—Oh, that I'll soon disclose;
Since we agree, allow me to propose,
Our mutual wishes we enjoy to-night;
And turn to ridicule that jealous Wight;
In short, reward him for his wily fear,
In watching us so very closely here.
Your garden will be quite the thing, I guess;
Go thither, pray, and never fear success;
Depend upon it, soon his country seat
Your spouse will visit:—then the hunks we'll cheat.
When plunged in sleep the grave duennas lie,
Arise, furred gown put on, and quickly fly;
With careful steps you'll to the garden haste;
I've got a ladder ready to be placed
Against the wall which joins your neighbour's square:
I've his permission thither to repair;

'Tis better than the street:—fear naught my dove.—
Ah! dear Magnificent, my fondest love;
As you desire, I'll readily proceed;
My heart is your's: we fully are agreed.
'T's you who speaks, and, would that in my arms
Permission I had got to clasp your charms!

MAGNIFICENT (for her he now replied,)
This flame you'll soon no reason have to hide
Through dread or fear of my old jealous fool,
Who wisely fancies he can woman rule.

THE lover, feigning rare, the lady left,
And grumbling much, as if of hope bereft,
Addressed the husband thus: you're vastly kind;
As well with no-one converse I might find;
If horses you so easily procure,
You Fortune's frowns may very well endure.
Mine neighs, at least, but this fair image seems,
Mere pretty fish; I've satisfied my schemes;
What now of precious minutes may remain,
If any one desire my chance to gain,
A bargain he shall have:—most cheap the prize;
The husband laughed till tears bedewed his eyes.
Said he, these youths have always in their head
Some wond'rous fancies; follies round them spread.
Friend, from pursuit you much too soon retire:
With time we oft obtain our fond desire.
But I shall always keep a watchful eye;
Some knowing tricks methinks I yet can spy;
Howe'er, the horse must now be clearly mine,

And you'll the pad of course to me resign;
To you no more expense; and from to-day,
Be not displeased to see me on it, pray;
At ease I'll ride my country house to view;—
That very night he to the mansion flew,
And our good folks immediately repaired,
Where gay Magnificent no pains had spared
To get access; what passed we won't detail;
Soft scenes, you'll doubtless guess, should there prevail.

THE dame was lively, beautiful, and young;
The lover handsome, finely formed, and strong;
Alike enchanted with each other's charms,
Three meetings were contrived without alarms;
A fair so captivating to possess,
What mortal could be satisfied with less?
In golden dreams the sage duennas slept;
A female sentinel to watch was kept.

A SUMMER-HOUSE was at the garden end,
Which to the pair much ease was found to lend;
Old Aldobrandin, when he built the same,
Ne'er fancied LOVE, would in it freak and game.
In cuckoldom he took his full degrees;
The horse he daily mounted at his ease,
And so delighted with his bargain seemed,
Three days, to prove it, requisite he deemed.
The country house received him ev'ry night;
At home he never dreamed but all was right.

WHAT numbers round, whom Fortune favours less;

Have got a wife, but not a horse possess;
And, what yet still more wond'rous may appear,
Know ev'ry thing that passes with their dear.

The Ephesian Matron[*]

IF there's a tale more common than the rest,
The one I mean to give is such confessed.
Why choose it then? you ask; at whose desire?
Hast not enough already tuned thy lyre?
What favour can thy MATRON now expect,
Since novelty thou clearly dost neglect?
Besides, thou'lt doubtless raise the critick's rage.
See if it looks more modern in my page.

AT Ephesus, in former times, once shone,
A fair, whose charms would dignify a throne;
And, if to publick rumour credit 's due,
Celestial bliss her husband with her knew.
Naught else was talked of but her beauteous face,
And chastity that adds the highest grace;
From ev'ry quarter numbers flocked to see
This belle, regarded as from errors free.
The honour of her sex, and country too;
As such, old mothers held her up to view,
And wished their offspring's wives like her to act:
The sons desired the very same in fact;
From her, beyond a doubt, our PRUDES descend,
An ancient, celebrated house, depend.

---

[*] See Chapters 111 and 112 from The Satyricon by Petronius Arbiter.

THE spouse adored his beauteous charming wife:
But soon, alas! he lost his precious life;
'Twere useless on particulars to dwell:
His testament, indeed, provided well
For her he loved on earth to fond excess,
Which, 'yond a doubt, would have relieved distress;
Could gold a cherished husband's loss repair,
That filled her soul with black corroding care.

A WIDOW, howsoever, oft appears
Distracted 'mid incessant floods of tears,
Who thoroughly her int'rest recollects,
And, spite of sobs, her property inspects.

OUR Matron's cries were loudly heard around,
And feeling bosoms shuddered at the sound;
Though, we, on these occasions, truly know,
The plaint is always greater than the woe.
Some ostentation ever is with grief
Those who weep most the soonest gain relief.

EACH friend endeavoured to console the fair;
Of sorrow, she'd already had her share:
'Twas wrong herself so fully to resign;—
Such pious preachings only more incline
The soul to anguish 'mid distractions dire:
Extremes in ev'ry thing will soonest tire.

AT length, resolved to shun the glorious light,
Since her dear spouse no longer had the sight,
O'erwhelmed with grief she sought Death's dreary cell,

Her love to follow, and with him to dwell.

A SLAVE, through pity, with the widow went;
To live or die with her she was content;
To die, howe'er, she never could intend:
No doubt she only thought about her friend,
The mistress whom she never wished to quit,
Since from her birth with her she used to sit.
They loved each other with a friendship true:
From early years it daily stronger grew;
Look through the universe you'll scarcely find,
So great a likeness, both in heart and mind.
The slave, more clever than the lady fair,
At first her mistress left to wild despair;
She then essayed to soothe each torment dire;
But reason 's fruitless, with a soul on fire.
No consolation would the belle receive,
For one no more, she constantly would grieve,
And sought to follow him to regions blessed:—
The sword had shortest proved, if not the best.

BUT still the lady anxious was to view,
Again those precious relicks, and pursue,
E'en in the tomb what yet her soul held dear
No aliment she took her mind to cheer;
The gate of famine was the one she chose,
By which to leave this nether world of woes.

A DAY she passed; another day the same;
Her only sustenance, sobs, sighs, and flame
Still unappeased; she murmur'd 'gainst her fate;

But nothing could her direful woes abate.

ANOTHER corpse a residence had got,
A trifling distance from the gloomy spot;
But very diff'rent, since, by way of tomb,
Enchained on gibbet was the latter's doom;
To frighten robbers was the form designed,
And show the punishment that rogues should find.

A SOLDIER, as a sentinel was set,
To guard the gallows, who good payment met;
'Twas ruled, howe'er, if robbers, parents, friends,
The body carried off, to make amends,
The sentinel at once should take its place
Severity too great for such a case;
But publick safety fully to maintain,
'Twas right the sentry pardon should not gain.

WHILE moving round his post, he saw at night
Shine, cross the tomb, a strange, unusual light,
Which thither drew him, curious to unfold
What, through the chinks, his eyesight could behold.

OUR wight soon heard the lady's cries distressed,
On which he entered, and with ardour pressed,
The cause of such excessive grief to know,
And if 'twas in his pow'r to ease her woe.

DISSOLVED in tears, and quite o'ercome with care;
She scarcely noticed that a man was there.
The corpse, howe'er, too plainly told her pain,

And fully seemed the myst'ry to explain.
We've sworn, exclaimed the slave, what's 'yond belief,
That here we'll die of famine and of grief.

THOUGH eloquence was not the soldier's art,
He both convinced 'twas wrong with life to part:
The dame was great attention led to pay,
To what the son of Mars inclined to say,
Which seemed to soften her severe distress:
With time each poignant smart is rendered less.

IF, said the soldier, you have made a vow,
That you, some food to take will not allow;
Yet, looking on while I my supper eat,
Will not prolong your lives, nor oaths defeat.

HIS open manner much was formed to please;
The lady and her maid grew more at ease,
Which made the gen'rous sentinel conclude,
To bring his meat they would not fancy rude.

THIS done, the slave no longer was inclined
To follow Death, as soon she changed her mind.
Said she, good madam, pleasing thoughts I've got;
Don't you believe that, if you live or not,
'Tis to your husband ev'ry whit the same?
Had you gone first, would he have had the name
Of following to the grave as you design?
No, no, he'd to another course incline.
Long years of comfort we may clearly crave;
At twenty years it's surely wrong to brave

Both death and famine in a gloomy tomb
There's time enough to think of such a doom.
At best, too soon we die; do let us wait;
Here's nothing now at least to haste our fate.
In truth, I wish to see a good old age:
To bury charms like your's, would that be sage?
Of what advantage, I should wish to know,
To carry beauty to the shades below?
Those heavenly features make my bosom sigh,
To think from earthly praise they mean to fly.

THIS flatt'ry roused the beauteous widowed fair;
The god of soft persuasion soon was there,
And from his quiver in a moment drew
Two arrows keen, which from his bow-string flew;
With one he pierced the soldier to the heart,
The lady slightly felt the other dart.
Her youth and beauty, spite of tears, appeared,
And men of taste such charms had long revered;
A mind of tender feeling might, through life.
Have loved her—even though she were a wife.

THE sentinel was smitten with her charms;
Grief, pity, sighs, belong to Cupid's arms;
When bosoms heave and eyes are drowned in tears,
Then beauty oft with conq'ring grace appears.

BEHOLD our widow list'ning to his praise,
Incipient fuel Cupid's flame to raise;
Behold her, even glad to view the wight,
Whose well tim'd flatt'ry filled her with delight

AT length, to eat he on the fair prevailed,
And pleased her better than the dead bewailed.
So well he managed, that she changed her plan,
And, by degrees, to love him fondly 'gan.
The son of Mars a darling husband grew,
While yet her former dear was full in view.

MEANTIME the corpse, that long in chains had swung,
By thieves was carried off from where it hung.
The noise was heard, and thither ran our wight;
But vain his efforts:—they were out of sight;
Confused, distressed, he sought again the tomb,
To tell his grief and settle, 'mid the gloom,
How best to act, and where his head to hide,
Since hang he must, the laws would now decide.

THE slave replied, your gibbet-thief, you say,
Some lurking rogues this night have borne away:
The law, it seems, will ne'er accord you grace
The corpse that's here, let's set in t'other's place:
The passers-by the change will never tell
The lady gave consent, and all was well.

O FICKLE females, ever you're the same;
A woman's a woman, both in mind and name
Some fair we find, and some unlike the dove,
But CONSTANCY'S the highest charm of love.

YE prudes, for ever doubt of full success;
Don't boast at all: too much you may profess,
How good soever your design may be,

Not less is ours, you easily may see;
The MATRON'S tale is not beyond belief:
To entertain, our object is in chief.

THE widow's only errors were her cries;
And mad design her life to sacrifice;
For, merely setting husband-dead in place
of one of this patibulary race,
Was surely not a fault so very grave:
Her lover's life was what she sought to save.

A LIVING drum-boy, truly be it said,
Is better far, than any monarch dead.

Belphegor

(addressed to Miss de Chammelay)

YOUR name with ev'ry pleasure here I place,
The last effusions of my muse to grace.
O charming Phillis! may the same extend
Through time's dark night: our praise together blend;
To this we surely may pretend to aim
Your acting and my rhymes attention claim.
Long, long in mem'ry's page your fame shall live;
You, who such ecstacy so often give;
O'er minds, o'er hearts triumphantly you reign:
In Berenice, in Phaedra, and Chimene,
Your tears and plaintive accents all engage:
Beyond compare in proud Camilla's rage;
Your voice and manner auditors delight;
Who strong emotions can so well excite?
No fine eulogium from my pen expect:
With you each air and grace appear correct
My first of Phillis's you ought to be;
My sole affection had been placed on thee;
Long since, had I presumed the truth to tell;
But he who loves would fain be loved as well.

NO hope of gaining such a charming fair,
Too soon, perhaps, I ceded to despair;

Your friend, was all I ventured to be thought,
Though in your net I more than half was caught.
Most willingly your lover I'd have been;
But time it is our story should be seen.

ONE, day, old Satan, sov'reign dread of hell;
Reviewed his subjects, as our hist'ries tell;
The diff'rent ranks, confounded as they stood,
Kings, nobles, females, and plebeian blood,
Such grief expressed, and made such horrid cries,
As almost stunned, and filled him with surprise.
The monarch, as he passed, desired to know
The cause that sent each shade to realms below.
Some said—my HUSBAND; others WIFE replied;
The same was echoed loud from ev'ry side.

HIS majesty on this was heard to say:
If truth these shadows to my ears convey,
With ease our glory we may now augment:
I'm fully bent to try th' experiment.
With this design we must some demon send,
Who wily art with prudence well can blend;
And, not content with watching Hymen's flock,
Must add his own experience to the stock.

THE sable senate instantly approved
The proposition that the monarch moved;
Belphegor was to execute the work;
The proper talent in him seemed to lurk:
All ears and eyes, a prying knave in grain
In short, the very thing they wished to gain.

THAT he might all expense and cost defray,
They gave him num'rous bills without delay,
And credit too, in ev'ry place of note,
With various things that might their plan promote.
He was, besides, the human lot to fill,
Of pleasure and of pain:—of good and ill;
In fact, whate'er for mortals was designed,
With his legation was to be combined.
He might by industry and wily art,
His own afflictions dissipate in part;
But die he could not, nor his country see,
Till he ten years complete on earth should be.

BEHOLD him trav'lling o'er th' extensive space;
Between the realms of darkness and our race.
To pass it, scarcely he a moment took;
On Florence instantly he cast a look;—
Delighted with the beauty of the spot,
He there resolved to fix his earthly lot,
Regarding it as proper for his wiles,
A city famed for wanton freaks and guiles.
Belphegor soon a noble mansion hired,
And furnished it with ev'ry thing desired;
As signor Roderick he designed to pass;
His equipage was large of ev'ry class;
Expense anticipating day by day,
What, in ten years, he had to throw away.

HIS noble entertainments raised surprise;
Magnificence alone would not suffice;
Delightful pleasures he dispensed around,

And flattery abundantly was found,
An art in which a demon should excel:
No devil surely e'er was liked so well.
His heart was soon the object of the FAIR;
To please Belphegor was their constant care.

WHO lib'rally with presents smoothes the road,
Will meet no obstacles to LOVE'S abode.
In ev'ry situation they are sweet,
I've often said, and now the same repeat:
The primum mobile of human kind,
Are gold and silver, through the world we find.

OUR envoy kept two books, in which he wrote
The names of all the married pairs of note;
But that assigned to couples satisfied,
He scarcely for it could a name provide,
Which made the demon almost blush to see,
How few, alas! in wedlock's chains agree;
While presently the other, which contained
Th' unhappy—not a leaf in blank remained.

NO other choice Belphegor now had got,
Than—try himself the hymeneal knot.
In Florence he beheld a certain fair,
With charming face and smart engaging air;
Of noble birth, but puffed with empty pride;
Some marks of virtue, though not much beside.
For Roderick was asked this lofty dame;

The father said Honesta[*] (such her name)
Had many eligible offers found;
But, 'mong the num'rous band that hovered round,
Perhaps his daughter, Rod'rick's suit might take,
Though he should wish for time the choice to make.
This approbation met, and Rod'rick 'gan
To use his arts and execute his plan.

THE entertainments, balls, and serenades,
Plays, concerts, presents, feasts, and masquerades,
Much lessened what the demon with him brought;
He nothing grudged:—whate'er was wished he bought.
The dame believed high honour she bestowed,
When she attention to his offer showed;
And, after prayers, entreaties, and the rest,
To be his wife she full assent expressed.

BUT first a pettifogger to him came,
Of whom (aside) Belphegor made a game;
What! said the demon, is a lady gained
just like a house?—these scoundrels have obtained
Such pow'r and sway, without them nothing's done;
But hell will get them when their course is run.
He reasoned properly; when faith's no more,
True honesty is forced to leave the door;
When men with confidence no longer view
Their fellow-mortals,—happiness adieu!
The very means we use t' escape the snare,
Oft deeper plunge us in the gulph of care;

---

[*] By this character La Fontaine is supposed to have meant his own wife.

Avoid attorneys, if you comfort crave
Who knows a PETTIFOGGER, knows a KNAVE;
Their contracts, filled with IFS and FORS, appear
The gate through which STRIFE found admittance here.
In vain we hope again the earth 'twill leave
Still STRIFE remains, and we ourselves deceive:
In spite of solemn forms and laws we see,
That LOVE and HYMEN often disagree.
The heart alone can tranquilize the mind;
In mutual passion ev'ry bliss we find.

HOW diff'rent things in other states appear!
With friends—'tis who can be the most sincere;
With lovers—all is sweetness, balm of life;
While all is IRKSOMENESS with man and wife.
We daily see from DUTY springs disgust,
And PLEASURE likes true LIBERTY to trust.

ARE happy marriages for ever flown?
On full consideration I will own,
That when each other's follies couples bear;
They then deserve the name of HAPPY PAIR.

ENOUGH of this:—no sooner had our wight
The belle possessed, and passed the month's delight;
But he perceived what marriage must be here,
With such a demon in our nether sphere.
For ever jars and discords rang around;
Of follies, ev'ry class our couple found;
Honesta often times such noise would make,
Her screams and cries the neighbours kept awake,

Who, running thither, by the wife were told:—
Some paltry tradesman's daughter, coarse and bold,
He should have had:—not one of rank like me;
To treat me thus, what villain he must be!
A wife so virtuous, could he e'er deserve!
My scruples are too great, or I should swerve;
Indeed, without dispute, 'twould serve him right:—
We are not sure she nothing did in spite;
These prudes can make us credit what they please:
Few ponder long when they can dupe with ease.

THIS wife and husband, as our hist'ries say,
Each moment squabbled through the passing day;
Their disagreements often would arise
About a petticoat, cards, tables, pies,
Gowns, chairs, dice, summer-houses, in a word,
Things most ridiculous and quite absurd.

WELL might this spouse regret his Hell profound,
When he considered what he'd met on ground.
To make our demon's wretchedness complete,
Honesta's relatives, from ev'ry street,
He seemed to marry, since he daily fed
The father, mother, sister (fit to wed,)
And little brother, whom he sent to school;
While MISS he portioned to a wealthy fool.

HIS utter ruin, howsoe'er, arose
From his attorney-steward that he chose.
What's that? you ask—a wily sneaking knave,
Who, while his master spends, contrives to save;

Till, in the end, grown rich, the lands he buys,
Which his good lord is forced to sacrifice.

IF, in the course of time, the master take
The place of steward, and his fortune make,
'Twould only to their proper rank restore,
Those who become just what they were before.

POOR Rod'rick now no other hope had got,
Than what the chance of traffick might allot;
Illusion vain, or doubtful at the best:—
Though some grow rich, yet all are not so blessed.
'Twas said our husband never would succeed;
And truly, such it seemed to be decreed.
His agents (similar to those we see
In modern days) were with his treasure free;
His ships were wrecked; his commerce came to naught;
Deceived by knaves, of whom he well had thought;
Obliged to borrow money, which to pay,
He was unable at th' appointed day,
He fled, and with a farmer shelter took,
Where he might hope the bailiffs would not look.

HE told to Matthew, (such the farmer's name,)
His situation, character, and fame:
By duns assailed, and harassed by a wife,
Who proved the very torment of his life,
He knew no place of safety to obtain,
Like ent'ring other bodies, where 'twas plain,
He might escape the catchpole's prowling eye,
Honesta's wrath, and all her rage defy.

From these he promised he would thrice retire;
Whenever Matthew should the same desire:
Thrice, but no more, t'oblige this worthy man,
Who shelter gave when from the fiends he ran.
THE AMBASSADOR commenced his form to change:—
From human frame to frame he 'gan to range;
But what became his own fantastick state,
Our books are silent, nor the facts relate.

AN only daughter was the first he seized,
Whose charms corporeal much our demon pleased;
But Matthew, for a handsome sum of gold,
Obliged him, at a word, to quit his hold.
This passed at Naples—next to Rome he came,
Where, with another fair, he did the same;
But still the farmer banished him again,
So well he could the devil's will restrain;
Another weighty purse to him was paid
Thrice Matthew drove him out from belle and maid.

THE king of Naples had a daughter fair,
Admired, adored:—her parents' darling care;
In wedlock oft by many princes sought;
Within her form, the wily demon thought
He might be sheltered from Honesta's rage;
And none to drive him thence would dare engage.

NAUGHT else was talked of, in or out of town,
But devils driven by the cunning clown;
Large sums were offered, if, by any art,
He'd make the demon from the fair depart.

AFFLICTED much was Matthew, now to lose
The gold thus tendered, but he could not choose,
For since Belphegor had obliged him thrice,
He durst not hope the demon to entice;
Poor man was he, a sinner, who, by chance,
(He knew not how, it surely was romance,)
Had some few devils, truly, driven out:
Most worthy of contempt without a doubt.
But all in vain:—the man they took by force;
Proceed he must, or hanged he'd be of course.

THE demon was before our farmer placed;
The sight was by the prince in person graced;
The wond'rous contest numbers ran to see,
And all the world spectators fain would be.

IF vanquished by the devil:—he must swing;
If vanquisher:—'twould thousands to him bring:
The gallows was, no doubt, a horrid view;
Yet, at the purse, his glances often flew;
The evil spirit laughed within his sleeve,
To see the farmer tremble, fret, and grieve.
He pleaded that the wight he'd thrice obeyed;
The demon was by Matthew often prayed;
But all in vain,—the more he terror showed,
The more Belphegor ridicule bestowed.

AT length the clown was driven to declare,
The fiend he was unable to ensnare;
Away they Matthew to the gallows led;
But as he went, it entered in his head,

And, in a sort of whisper he averred
(As was in fact the case) a drum he heard.

THE demon, with surprise, to Matthew cried;
What noise is that? Honesta, he replied,
Who you demands, and every where pursues,
The spouse who treats her with such vile abuse.

THESE words were thunder to Belphegor's ears,
Who instantly took flight, so great his fears;
To hell's abyss he fled without delay,
To tell adventures through the realms of day.
Sire, said the demon, it is clearly true,
Damnation does the marriage knot pursue.
Your highness often hither sees arrive,
Not squads, but regiments, who, when alive,
By Hymen were indissolubly tied:—
In person I the fact have fully tried.
Th' institution, perhaps, most just could be:
Past ages far more happiness might see;
But ev'ry thing, with time, corruption shows;
No jewel in your crown more lustre throws.

BELPHEGOR'S tale by Satan was believed;
Reward he got: the term, which-sorely grieved,
Was now reduced; indeed, what had he done,
That should prevent it?—If away he'd run,
Who would not do the same who weds a shrew?
Sure worse below the devil never knew!
A brawling woman's tongue, what saint can bear?
E'en Job, Honesta would have taught despair.

WHAT is the inference? you ask:—I'll tell;—
Live single, if you know you are well;
But if old Hymen o'er your senses reign,
Beware Honestas, or you'll rue the chain.

The Little Bell

HOW weak is man! how changeable his mind!
His promises are naught, too oft we find;
I vowed (I hope in tolerable verse,)
Again no idle story to rehearse.
And whence this promise?—Not two days ago;
I'm quite confounded; better I should know:
A rhymer hear then, who himself can boast,
Quite steady for—a minute at the most.
The pow'rs above could PRUDENCE ne'er design;
For those who fondly court the SISTERS NINE.
Some means to please they've got, you will confess;
But none with certainty the charm possess.
If, howsoever, I were doomed to find
Such lines as fully would content the mind:
Though I should fail in matter, still in art;
I might contrive some pleasure to impart.

LET'S see what we are able to obtain:—
A bachelor resided in Touraine.
A sprightly youth, who oft the maids beset,
And liked to prattle to the girls he met,
With sparkling eyes, white teeth, and easy air,
Plain russet petticoat and flowing hair,
Beside a rivulet, while Io round,

With little bell that gave a tinkling sound,
On herbs her palate gratified at will,
And gazed and played, and fondly took her fill.

AMONG the rustic nymphs our spark perceived
A charming girl, for whom his bosom heaved;
Too young, however, to feel the poignant smart,
By Cupid oft inflicted on the heart.
I will not say thirteen's an age unfit
The contrary most fully I admit;
The LAW supposes (such its prudent fears)
Maturity at still more early years;
But this apparently refers to towns,
While LOVE was born for groves, and lawns, and downs.

THE youth exerted ev'ry art to please;
But all in vain: he only seemed to teaze:
Whate'er he said, however nicely graced,
Ill-humour, inexperience, or distaste,
Induced the belle, unlearned in Cupid's book;
To treat his passion with a froward look.

BELIEVING ev'ry artifice in love
Was tolerated by the pow'rs above,
One eve he turned a heifer from the rest;
Conducted by the girl his thoughts possessed;
The others left, not counted by the fair,
(Youth seldom shows the necessary care,)
With easy, loit'ring steps the cottage sought,
Where ev'ry night they usually were brought.

HER mother, more experienced than the maid,
Observed, that from the cattle one had strayed;
The girl was scolded much, and sent to find
The heifer indiscreetly left behind.
Fair Isabella gave a vent to tears;
Invoked sweet echo to disperse her fears:
Solicited with fervent, piercing cry,
To tell her where lorn Io she might spy,
Whose little bell the spark deprived of sound;
When he withdrew her from the herd around.

THE lover now the tinkling metal shook;
The path that t'wards it led the charmer took.
The well known note was pleasing to her ear;
Without suspecting treachery was near,
She followed to a wood, both deep and large,
In hopes at least she might regain her charge.

GUESS her surprise, good reader, when she heard,
A lover's voice, who would not be deterred.
Said he, fair maid whene'er the heart's on fire,
'Tis all permitted that can quench desire.
On this, with piercing cries she rent the air;
But no one came:—she sunk to dire despair.

YE beauteous dames avoid the Sylvan shade;
Dread dangers solitary woods pervade.

The Glutton

A STURGEON, once, a glutton famed was led
To have for supper—all, except the head.
With wond'rous glee he feasted on the fish;
And quickly swallowed down the royal dish.
O'ercharged, howe'er, his stomach soon gave way;
And doctors were required without delay.

THE danger imminent, his friends desired
He'd settle ev'ry thing affairs required.
Said he, in that respect I'm quite prepared;
And, since my time so little is declared,
With diligence, I earnestly request,
The sturgeon's head you'll get me nicely dressed.

The Two Friends

AXIOCHUS, a handsome youth of old,
And Alcibiades, (both gay and bold,)
So well agreed, they kept a beauteous belle,
With whom by turns they equally would dwell.

IT happened, one of them so nicely played,
The fav'rite lass produced a little maid,
Which both extolled, and each his own believed,
Though doubtless one or t'other was deceived.

BUT when to riper years the bantling grew,
And sought her mother's foot-steps to pursue,
Each friend desired to be her chosen swain,
And neither would a parent's name retain.

SAID one, why brother, she's your very shade;
The features are the same-:-your looks pervade.
Oh no, the other cried, it cannot be
Her chin, mouth, nose, and eyes, with your's agree;
But that as 'twill, let me her favours win,
And for the pleasure I will risk the sin.

The Country Justice

TWO lawyers to their cause so well adhered,
A country justice quite confused appeared,
By them the facts were rendered so obscure
With which the truth remained he was not sure.
At length, completely tired, two straws he sought
Of diff'rent lengths, and to the parties brought.
These in his hand he held:—the plaintiff drew
(So fate decreed) the shortest of the two.
On this the other homeward took his way,
To boast how nicely he had gained the day.

THE bench complained: the magistrate replied
Don't blame I pray—'tis nothing new I've tried;
Courts often judge at hazard in the law,
Without deciding by the longest straw.

Alice Sick

SICK, Alice grown, and fearing dire event,
Some friend advised a servant should be sent
Her confessor to bring and ease her mind;—
Yes, she replied, to see him I'm inclined;
Let father Andrew instantly be sought:—
By him salvation usually I'm taught.

A MESSENGER was told, without delay,
To take, with rapid steps, the convent way;
He rang the bell—a monk enquired his name,
And asked for what, or whom, the fellow came.
I father Andrew want, the wight replied,
Who's oft to Alice confessor and guide:
With Andrew, cried the other, would you speak?
If that's the case, he's far enough to seek;
Poor man! he's left us for the regions blessed,
And has in Paradise ten years confessed.

The Kiss Returned

AS WILLIAM walking with his wife was seen,
A man of rank admired her lovely mien.
Who gave you such a charming fair? he cried,
May I presume to kiss your beauteous bride?
With all my heart, replied the humble swain,
You're welcome, sir:—I beg you'll not refrain;
She's at your service: take the boon, I pray;
You'll not such offers meet with ev'ry day.

THE gentleman proceeded as desired;
To get a kiss, alone he had aspired;
So fervently howe'er he pressed her lip,
That Petronella blushed at ev'ry sip.

SEVEN days had scarcely run, when to his arms,
The other took a wife with seraph charms;
And William was allowed to have a kiss,
That filled his soul with soft ecstatick bliss.
Cried he, I wish, (and truly I am grieved)
That when the gentleman a kiss received,
From her I love, he'd gone to greater height,
And with my Petronella passed the night.

Sister Jane

WHEN Sister Jane, who had produced a child,
In prayer and penance all her hours beguiled
Her sister-nuns around the lattice pressed;
On which the abbess thus her flock addressed:
Live like our sister Jane, and bid adieu
To worldly cares:—have better things in view.

YES, they replied, we sage like her shall be,
When we with love have equally been free.

An Imitation of Anacreon

PAINTER in Paphos and Cythera famed
Depict, I pray, the absent Iris' face.
Thou hast not seen the lovely nymph I've named;
The better for thy peace.—Then will I trace
For thy instruction her transcendent grace.
Begin with lily white and blushing rose,
Take then the Loves and Graces... But what good
Words, idle words? for Beauty's Goddess could
By Iris be replaced, nor one suppose
The secret fraud—their grace so equal shows.
Thou at Cythera couldst, at Paphos too,
Of the same Iris Venus form anew.

Another Imitation of Anacreon

PRONE, on my couch I calmly slept
Against my wont. A little child
Awoke me as he gently crept
And beat my door. A tempest wild
Was raging-dark and cold the night.
"Have pity on my naked plight,"
He begged, "and ope thy door."—"Thy name?"
I asked admitting him.—"The same
"Anon I'll tell, but first must dry
"My weary limbs, then let me try
"My mois'ened bow."—Despite my fear
The hearth I lit, then drew me near
My guest, and chafed his fingers cold.
"Why fear?" I thought. "Let me be bold
"No Polyphemus he; what harm
"In such a child?—Then I'll be calm!"
The playful boy drew out a dart,
Shook his fair locks, and to my heart
His shaft he launch'd.—"Love is my name,"
He thankless cried, "I hither came
"To tame thee. In thine ardent pain
"Of Cupid think and young Climene."—
"Ah! now I know thee, little scamp,
"Ungrateful, cruel boy! Decamp!"

Cupid a saucy caper cut,
Skipped through the door, and as it shut,
"My bow," he taunting cried, "is sound,
"Thy heart, poor comrade, feels the wound."

Tales
and
Trifles
of
Jean de la Fontaine

Volume II

The Author's Preface to his Second Book of These Tales

These are the last works of this style that will come from the pen of the Author, and consequently this is the last opportunity he has of vindicating the boldness and privilege which he has assumed. We make no mention of villainous rhymes, of lines that run into the next, of two vowels without elision, nor, in general, of such kinds of carelessness as he would not allow himself in another style of poetry, but which are part and parcel, so to say, of this style. Too anxious a care in avoiding such would force a tale-writer into a labyrinth of shifts, into narratives as dull as they are grand, into straits that are utterly useless, and would make him disregard the pleasure of the heart in order to labour for the gratification of the ear. We must leave studied narrative for lofty subjects, and not compose an epic poem of the Adventures of Renaud d'Ast. Suppose the Author, who has put these tales into rhyme, had brought to bear on them all the care and preciseness required of him; not only would this care be observed, especially as it is unnecessary, but it would also transgress the precept lain down by Ouintilian, still the Author would not have attained the main object, which is to interest the reader, to charm him, to rivet his attention in spite of himself,—in a word, to please him. As everybody knows, the secret of pleasing the reader is not always based on regulation, nor even on symmetry; there is need of smartness and tastefulness, if we would strike home. How many of those perfect types of beauty do we see which never strike home, and of which nobody feels enamoured! We do not wish to rob Modern Authors of the praise that is due to them. Nicely turned lines, fine language, accuracy, elegance of rhyme are accomplishments in a poet. However that may be, let us consider of our own epigrams wherein all these qualities are combined, perhaps we shall find in them far less point, nay, I would venture to add, far less charm than in those of Marot or Saint-Gelais, although almost all the works of the latter poets are full of the same faults as are attributed to us. We will be told that these were not faults in their day, whereas they are very great faults in ours. To this we answer by a similar kind of argument, by saying, as we have already said, that these would undoubtedly be faults in another style of poetry, but not in this. The late M. de Voiture is a proof in point. We need only read the works in which he brings to life again the character of Marot. For our Author does not lay claim to praise for himself, nor to rounds of applause from the public for having put a few tales into rhyme. Without doubt he has entered on quite a new path, and has pursued it to the utmost of his power, choosing now one road, now another, and always treading with surer step when he has followed the manner of our old poets "quorum in hae re imitari negligentiam exoptat potius quam istorum diligentiam."

But while saying that we wished to waive this question, we have unconsciously involved ourselves in its discussion. Perhaps this has not been without advantage; for there is nothing that resembles faults more than these licenses. Let us now consider the liberty which the Author has assumed in cutting into the property of others as well as his own, without making exception even to the best known stories, none of which he scruples to tamper with. He curtails, enlarges, and alters incidents and details, at times the main issue and the sequel; in short, the story is no longer the same; it is, in point of fact, quite a new tale; its original author would find it no small difficulty to recognise in it his own work. "Non sic decet contaminari fabulas," Critics will say. Why should they not? They twitted Terence in just the same way; but Terence sneered at them, and claimed a right to treat the matter as he did. He has mingled his own ideas with the subjects he drew from Menander, just as Sophocles and Euripides mingled theirs with the subjects they drew from former writers, sparing neither history nor romance, where "decorum" and the rules of the Drama were at issue. Shall this privilege cease with respect to fictitious stories? Must we in future have more scrupulous or religious regard, if we may be allowed the expression, for falsehood than the Ancients had for truth? What people call a good tale never passes from hand to hand without receiving some fresh touch of embellishment. How comes it then, we may be asked, that in many passages the Author curtails instead of enlarging on the original? On that point we are agreed: the Author does so in order to avoid lengthiness and ambiguity,—two faults which are inadmissible in such matters, especially the latter. For if lucidity is to be commended in all literary works, we may say that it is especially necessary in narratives, where one thing is, as a rule, the sequel and the result of another; where the less important sometimes lays the basis of the more important; so that, once the thread becomes broken, the reader cannot gather it up again. Besides, as narratives in verse are very awkward, the author must clog himself with details as little as possible; by means of this you relieve not only yourself, but also the reader, for whom an author should not fail to prepare pleasure unalloyed. Whenever the Author has altered a few particulars and even a few catastrophes, he has been forced to do so by the cause of that catastrophe and the urgency of giving it a happy termination. He has fancied that in tales of this kind everyone ought to be satisfied with the end: it pleases the reader at any rate, if the author has not given the characters too distasteful a rendering. But he must not go so far as that, if possible, nor make the reader laugh and cry in the same tale. This medley shocks Horace above all things; his wish is not that our works should border on the grotesque, and that we should draw a picture half woman half fish. These are the general motives the Author has had in view. We might still quote special motives and vindicate each point; but we must needs leave something to the capacity and leniency of our readers. They will be satisfied, then, with the motives we have mentioned. We would have stated them more clearly and have set more by them, had the general compass of a Preface so allowed.

Friar Philip's Geese

IF these gay tales give pleasure to the FAIR,
The honour's great conferred, I'm well aware;
Yet, why suppose the sex my pages shun?
Enough, if they condemn where follies run;
Laugh in their sleeve at tricks they disapprove,
And, false or true, a muscle never move.
A playful jest can scarcely give offence:
Who knows too much, oft shows a want of sense.
From flatt'ry oft more dire effects arise,
Enflame the heart and take it by surprise;
Ye beauteous belles, beware each sighing swain,
Discard his vows:—my book with care retain;
Your safety then I'll guarantee at ease.—
But why dismiss?—their wishes are to please:
And, truly, no necessity appears
For solitude:—consider well your years.
I HAVE, and feel convinced they do you wrong,
Who think no virtue can to such belong;
White crows and phoenixes do not abound;
But lucky lovers still are sometimes found;
And though, as these famed birds, not quite so rare,
The numbers are not great that favours share;
I own my works a diff'rent sense express,
But these are tales:—mere tales in easy dress.

TO beauty's wiles, in ev'ry class, I've bowed;
Fawned, flattered, sighed, e'en constancy have vowed
What gained? you ask—but little I admit;
Howe'er we aim, too oft we fail to hit.
My latter days I'll now devote with care,
To guard the sex from ev'ry latent snare.
Tales I'll detail, and these relate at ease:
Narrations clear and neat will always please;
Like me, to this attention criticks pay;
Then sleep, on either side, from night till day.
If awkward, vulgar phrase intervene,
Or rhymes imperfect o'er the page be seen,
Condemn at will; but stratagems and art,
Pass, shut your eyes, who'd heed the idle part?
Some mothers, husbands, may perhaps be led,
To pull my locks for stories white or red;
So matters stand: a fine affair, no doubt,
And what I've failed to do—my book makes out.

THE FAIR my pages safely may pursue,
And this apology they'll not refuse.
What recompense can I presume to make?
A tale I'll give, where female charms partake,
And prove resistless whatsoe'er assail:
Blessed BEAUTY, NATURE ever should prevail.

HAD Fate decreed our YOUTH, at early morn,
To view the angel features you adorn,
The captivating pow'rs AURORA bless,
Or airy SPRING bedecked in beauteous dress,
And all the azure canopy on high

Had vanished like a dream, once you were nigh.
And when his eyes at length your charms beheld,
His glowing breast with softest passion swelled;
Superior lustre beamed at ev'ry view;
No pleasures pleased: his soul was fixed on you.
Crowns, jewels, palaces, appeared as naught.
'Twas solely beauteous woman now he sought.

A WOOD, from earliest years, his home had been,
And birds the only company he'd seen,
Whose notes harmonious often lulled his care,
Beguiled his hours, and saved him from despair;
Delightful sounds! from nightingale and dove
Unknown their tongue, yet indicant of love.

THIS savage, solitary, rustick school,
The father chose his infancy to rule.
The mother's recent death induced the sire,
To place the son where only beasts retire;
And long the forest habitants alone
Were all his youthful sight had ever known.

TWO reasons, good or bad, the father led
To fly the world:—all intercourse to dread
Since fate had torn his lovely spouse from hence;
Misanthropy and fear o'ercame each sense;
Of the world grown tired, he hated all around:—
Too oft in solitude is sorrow found.
His partner's death produced distaste of life,
And made him fear to seek another wife.
A hermit's gloomy, mossy cell he took,

And wished his child might thither solely look.

AMONG the poor his little wealth he threw,
And with his infant son alone withdrew;
The forest's dreary wilds concealed his cell;
There Philip (such his name) resolved to dwell.

BY holy motives led, and not chagrin,
The hermit never spoke of what he'd seen;
But, from the youth's discernment, strove to hide,
Whate'er regarded love, and much beside,
The softer sex, with all their magick charms,
That fill the feeling bosom with alarms.
As years advanced, the boy with care he taught;
What suited best his age before him brought;
At five he showed him animals and flow'rs,
The birds of air, the beasts, their sev'ral pow'rs;
And now and then of hell he gave a hint,
Old Satan's wrath, and what might awe imprint,
How formed, and doomed to infamy below;
In childhood FEAR 's the lesson first we know!

THE years had passed away, when Philip tried,
In matters more profound his son to guide;
He spoke of Paradise and Heav'n above;
But not a word of woman,—nor of LOVE.
Fifteen arrived, the sire with anxious care,
Of NATURE'S works declaimed,—but not the FAIR:
An age, when those, for solitude designed,
Should be to scenes of seriousness confined,
Nor joys of youth, nor soft ideas praised

The flame soon spreads when Cupid's torch is raised.

AT length, when twenty summers time had run,
The father to the city brought his son;
With years weighed down, the hermit scarcely knew
His daily course of duty to pursue;
And when Death's venomed shaft should on him fall;
On whom could then his boy for succour call?
How life support, unknowing and unknown?
Wolves, foxes, bears, ne'er charity have shown;
And all the sire could give his darling care,
A staff and wallet, he was well aware
Fine patrimony, truly, for a child!
To which his mind was no way reconciled.
Bread few, 'twas clear, the hermit would deny,
And rich he might have been you may rely;
When he drew near, the children quickly cried
Here's father Philip—haste, the alms provide;
And many pious men his friends were found,
But not one female devotee around:
None would he hear; the FAIR he always fled
Their smiles and wiles the friar kept in dread.

OUR hermit, when he thought his darling youth;
Well fixed in duty and religious truth,
Conveyed him 'mong his pious friends, to learn
How food to beg, and other ways discern.
In tears he viewed his son the forest quit,
And fain would have him for the world unfit.

THE city's palaces and lofty spires,

Our rustick's bosom filled with new desires.
The prince's residence great splendour showed,
And lively pleasure on the youth bestowed.
What's here? said he; The court, his friends replied:—
What there?—The mansions where the great reside:—
And these?—Fine statues, noble works of art:
All gave delight and gratitude his heart.
But when the beauteous FAIR first caught his view,
To ev'ry other sight he bade adieu;
The palace, court, or mansions he admired,
No longer proved the objects he desired;
Another cause of admiration rose,
His breast pervaded, and disturbed repose.
What's this, he cried, so elegantly neat?
O tell me, father; make my joy complete!

WHAT gave the son such exquisite delight,
The parent filled with agonizing fright.
To answer, howsoe'er he'd no excuse,
So told the youth—a bird they call a goose.

O BEAUTEOUS bird, exclaimed th' enraptured boy,
Sing, sound thy voice, 'twill fill my soul with joy;
To thee I'd anxiously be better known;
O father, let me have one for my own!
A thousand times I fondly ask the boon;
Let's take it to the woods: 'tis not too soon;
Young as it is, I'll feed it morn and night,
And always make it my supreme delight.

Richard Minutolo

IN ev'ry age, at Naples, we are told,
Intrigue and gallantry reign uncontrolled;
With beauteous objects in abundance blessed.
No country round so many has possessed;
Such fascinating charms the FAIR disclose,
That irresistibly soft passion flows.

'MONG these a belle, enchanting to behold,
Was loved by one, of birth and store of gold;
Minutolo (and Richard) was his name,
In Cupid's train a youth of brilliant fame:
'Tween Rome and Paris none was more gallant,
And num'rous hearts were for him known to pant.

CATELLA (thus was called our lady fair,)
So long, howe'er, resisted Richard's snare,
That prayers, and vows, and promises were vain;
A favour Minutolo could not gain.
At length, our hero weary, coldness showed,
And dropt attendance, since no kindness flowed;
Pretended to be cured:—another sought,
And feigned her charms his tender heart had caught:
Catella laughed, but jealousy was nigh;
'Twas for her friend that now He heaved the sigh.

THESE dames together met, and Richard too,
The gay gallant a glowing picture drew,
Of certain husbands, lovers, prudes, and wives;
Who led in secret most lascivious lives.
Though none he named, Catella was amazed;
His hints suspicions of her husband raised;
And such her agitation and affright,
That, anxious to procure more certain light,
In haste she took Minutolo aside,
And begged the names he would not from her hide,
With all particulars, from first to last:—
Her ardent wish to know whate'er had passed.

SO long your reign, said Richard, o'er my mind,
Deny I could not, howsoe'er inclined;
With Mrs. Simon often is your spouse;
Her character no doubt your spleen will rouse;
I've no design, observe to give offence,
But, when I see your int'rest in suspense,
I cannot silent keep; though, were I still
A slave, devoted wholly to your will,
As late I moved, I would not drop a word
Mistrust of lovers may not be absurd;
Besides, you'd fancy other motives led
To tell you of your husband what was said;
But heav'n be praised, of you I nothing want;
My object's plain—no more the fond gallant.

I'VE lately certain information had,
Your spouse (I scarcely thought the man so bad,)
Has with the lady an appointment made;

At Jack's nice bagnio he will meet the jade.

NOW clearly Jack's not rich, and there's no doubt;
A hundred ducats give, and—ALL will out;
Let him but have a handsome sum in view,
And any thing you wish, be sure he'll do;
You then can manage ev'ry way so well,
That, at the place assigned to meet his belle,
You'll take this truant husband by surprise;—
Permit me in this nice affair to advise.

THE lady has agreed, you will remark,
That in a room where ev'ry part is dark,
(Perhaps to 'scape the keeper's prying sight,
Or shame directs exclusion of the light,)
She will receive your gay inconstant spouse;
Now, take her place; the case deceit allows;
Make Jack your friend; nor haggle at the price;
A hundred ducats give, is my advice;
He'll place you in the room where darkness reigns;
Think not too fast, nor suffer heavy chains;
Do what you wish, and utter not a word;
To speak, assuredly would be absurd;
'Twould spoil the whole; destroy the project quite;
Attend, and see if all things be not right.

THE project pleased Catella to the soul;
Her wrath, no longer able to controul,
She Richard stopt; enough, enough, she cried;
I fully understand:—leave me to guide;
I'll play the fellow and his wanton lass

A pretty trick-shall all their art surpass,
Unless the string gives way and spoils my scheme;
What, take me for a nincompoop?—they dream.

THIS said, she sought excuse to get away,
And went in quest of Jack without delay.
The keeper, howsoe'er, a hint had got;
Minutolo had schooled him for the plot;
Oft cash does wonders, and, if such the case
In France or Britain, when conferred a grace,
The bribe is taken, and the truth abused,
In Italy it will not be refused;
There this sole quiver Cupid useful finds,—

A PURSE well stored—all binds, gunlocks, or blinds:
Jack took the pelf from Richard and the dame;
Had Satan offered—'twould have been the same.
In short, Minutolo had full success,
All came about, and marked the spark's address.

THE lady had at first some warm dispute
To many questions Jack was even mute;
But when he saw the golden charms unmasked,
Far more he promised than Catella asked.

THE time of rendezvous arrived, our spark
To Jack's repaired, and found the room quite dark;
So well arranged, no crevice could he find,
Through which the light might hurt what he designed.

NOT long he waited, ere our jealous dame,

Who longed to find her faithless husband, came,
Most thoroughly prepared his ears to greet.
Jack brought the couple presently to meet.
The lady found, howe'er, not what she sought:
No guilty spouse, nor Mrs. Simon caught;
But wily Richard, who, without alarms,
In silence took Catella in his arms.
What further passed between the easy pair,
Think what you will, I mean not to declare;
The lover certainly received delight
The lady showed no terror nor affright;
On neither side a syllable was dropt
With care Minutolo his laughter stopt;
Though difficult, our spark succeeded well;
No words of mine can Richard's pleasure tell.
His fav'rite beauteous belle he now possessed,
And triumphed where so oft he'd been repressed,
Yet fondly hoped her pardon he should get,
Since they together had so gaily met.

AT length, the fair could no longer contain:
Vile wretch, she cried, I've borne too much 'tis plain;
I'm not the fav'rite whom thou had'st in view:
To tear thy eyes out justly were thy due,
'Tis this, indeed, that makes thee silent keep,
Each morn feign sickness, and pretend to sleep,
Thyself reserving doubtless for amours:—
Speak, villain! say, of charms have I less stores?
Or what has Mrs. Simon more than I?
A wanton wench, in tricks so wondrous sly!
Where my love less? though truly now I hate;

Would that I'd seen thee hung, thou wretch ingrate!

MINUTOLO, while thus Catella spoke,
Caressed her much, but silence never broke;
A kiss e'en tried to gain, without success;
She struggled, and refused to acquiesce;
Begone! said she, nor treat me like a child;
Stand off!—away!—thy taction is defiled;
My tears express an injured woman's grief;
No more thy wife I'll be, but seek relief;
Return my fortune—go:—thy mistress seek;
To be so constant:—How was I so weak?
It surely would be nothing more than right,
Were Richard I to see this very night,
Who adoration constantly has paid:—
You much deserve to be a cuckold made;
I'm half inclined, I vow, to do the worst.
At this our arch gallant with laughter burst.
What impudence!—You mock me too? she cried
Let's see, with blushes if his face be dyed?
When from his arms she sprang, a window sought;
The shutters ope'd, and then a view she caught;
Minutolo, her lover! * * * what surprise!
Pale, faint, she instant grew, and closed her eyes:
Who would have thought, said she, thou wert so base?
I'm lost! * * * for ever sunk in dire disgrace!

WHO'LL, know it? Richard earnestly replied;
In Jack's concealment we may both confide;
Excuse the trick I've played and ne'er repine;
Address, force, treachery, in love combine;

All are permitted when intrigue 's the word;
To hold the contrary were quite absurd.
Till stratagem was used I naught could gain,
But looks and darts from eyes, for all my pain.
I've paid myself;—Would you have done it?—No;
'Tis all as might be wished;—come, smiles bestow;
I'm satisfied, the fault was not with you.
In this, to make you wretched, naught I view;
Why sigh and groan?—What numbers could I name,
Who would be happy to be served the same.

HIS reas'ning yet could not the belle appease;
She wept, and sought by tears her mind to ease;
Affliction highly added to her charms;
Minutolo still gave her new alarms;
He took her hand, which she at once withdrew:
Away, she cried; no longer me pursue;
Be satisfied; you surely don't desire
That I assistance from the house require,
Or rouse the neighbours with my plaintive cries
I'll ev'ry thing declare without disguise.

SUCH folly don't commit, replied the spark;
Your wisest plan is nothing to remark:
The world at present is become so vile,
If you the truth divulge, they'll only smile;
Not one a word of treachery would believe,
But think you came—and money to receive:
Suppose, besides, it reached your husband's ears;
Th' effect has reason to excite your fears;
'Twould give displeasure and occasion strife:

Would you in duels wish to risk his life?
Whatever makes you with him disagree,
At all events, I'm full as bad as he.

THESE reasons with Catella greatly weighed
Since things, continued he, are thus displayed;
And cannot be repaired, console your mind;
A perfect being never was designed.
If, howsoe'er you will * * * but say no more;
Such thoughts for ever banish, I implore.
'Mid all my perseverance, zeal, and art,
I nothing got but frowns that pierced the heart:
'Twill now on you depend if pleasure prove
This day imperfect, ere from hence we move.
What more remains to do? the worst is past;
'Tis step the first that costs, however classed.

SO well Minutolo preferred his suit,
The lady with him more would not dispute,
With downcast eyes she listened to his prayer,
And looked disposed to tranquilize his care;
From easy freedom soon he 'gan to soar;
A smile received:—a kiss bestowed and more:
At length, the lady passed resistance by,
And all conceded, e'en without a sigh.

OUR hero felt a thousand times more blessed
Than when he first the beauteous fair caressed;
For when a flame reciprocal is raised,
The bliss redoubles, and by all is praised.

THUS Richard pleasantly employed his time,
Contented lived, concentring joys sublime.
A sample, now, we have given of his pow'rs,
And who would wish for more delightful hours?
O grant, kind heav'n! that I the like may meet,
And ever prove so wary and discreet.

The Monks of Catalonia

TO you, my friends, allow me to detail,
The feats of monks in Catalonia's vale,
Where oft the holy fathers pow'rs displayed,
And showed such charity to wife and maid,
That o'er their minds sweet fascination reigned,
And made them think, they Paradise had gained.

SUCH characters oft preciously advise,
And youthful easy female minds surprise,
The beauteous FAIR encircle with their net,
And, of the feeling heart, possession get:
Work in the holy vineyard, you may guess,
And, as our tale will show, with full success.

IN times of old, when learning 'mong the FAIR,
Enough to read the testament, was rare,
(Times howsoe'er thought difficult to quote,)
A swarm of monks of gormandizing note,
Arrived and fixed themselves within a town,
For young and beauteous belles of great renown,
While, of gallants, there seemed but very few,
Though num'rous aged husbands you might view.

A NOBLE chapel soon the fathers raised,
To which the females ran and highly praised,
Surveyed it o'er and confidently thought,
'Twas there, of course, salvation should be sought.
And when their faith had thoroughly been proved,
To gain their point the monks the veil removed.—
Good father Andrew scorned to use finesse,
And in discourse the sex would thus address.

IF any thing prevent your sov'reign bliss,
And Paradise incautiously you miss,
Most certainly the evil will arise,
From keeping for your husbands large supplies,
Of what a surplus you have clearly got,
And more than requisite to them allot,
Without bestowing on your trusty friends,
The saving that to no one blessings lends.

PERHAPS you'll tell me, marriage boons we shun;
'Tis true, and Heav'n be praised enough is done,
Without those duties to require our share
You know from direful sin we guard the FAIR.
Ingratitude 's declared the height of crimes,
And God pronounced it such in early times;
For this eternally was Satan curst;
Howe'er you err, be careful of the worst.
Return to Heav'n your thanks for bounteous care,
And then to us a tithe of surplus spare,
Which costs you nothing worth a moment's thought;
And marks the zeal with which our faith is taught,
A claim legitimate our order opes,

Bestowed, for holy offices, by popes,
No charitable gift, but lawful right:
Priests well supported are a glorious sight.
Four times a year, exactly to a day,
Each wife this tithe should personally pay
Our holy saint requires that you submit:
'Tis founded on decrees of holy writ.
All Nature carefully the law reveres,
That gratitude and fealty endears.

NOW marriage works we rank as an estate,
And tithe is due for that at any rate.
We'll take it patiently, whate'er the toil:
Nor be o'er nice about the justful spoil.
Our order have not, you must surely know,
By many comforts, what we wish below.

'TIS right, however, that I now suggest,
Whatever passes must not be expressed;
But naught to husbands, parents, friends, reveal;
From ev'ry one the mysterious conceal.
Three words th' apostle taught: be these your care;
FAITH, CHARITY, and PRUDENCE learn to share.

THE holy father, by his fine discourse,
Delivered with the most impressive force,
Gave wonderous satisfaction and surprise,
And passed with all for Solomon the wise;
Few slept while Andrew preached, and ev'ry wife,
His precepts guarded as she would her life;
And these not solely treasured in the mind,

But showed to practise them the heart inclined,
Each hastened tithe to bring without delay,
And quarrelled who should be the first to pay;
Loud murmurs rang, and many city dames,
Were forced to keep till morn the friar's claims,
And HOLY CHURCH, not knowing what to do,
Such numbers seemed to be in paying cue,
At length was forced, without restraint, to say,
The Lord commands that, till a future day,
You give us time to breathe:—so large the lot,
To serve for present we enough have got;
Too much the whole at once, but by degrees,
Your tithe we'll take and all contrive to please.
With us arrange the hour you would be here,
And some to-day:—to-morrow more we'll cheer;
The whole in order, and you'll clearly see,
That SOFTLY with FAIRLY best agree.

THE sex inclined to follow this advice;
About receipts however they were not nice;
The entertainment greatly was admired,
And pure devotion all their bosoms fired,
A glass of cordial some apart received;
Good cheer was given, may be well believed;
Ten youthful dames brisk friar Fripart took,
Gay, airy, and engaging ev'ry look,
Who paid with pleasure all the monk could wish;
Some had fifteen:—some twelve to taste their dish;
Good friar Rock had twenty for his share,
And gave such satisfaction to the FAIR,
That some, to show they never grudged the price,

And proved their punctuality,—paid twice.

So much indeed, that satiated with ways,
That six long months engaged their nights and days:
They gladly credit would have given now,
But found the ladies would not this allow,
Believing it most positively wrong,
To keep whate'er might to the church belong.
No tithe arrears were any where around,
So zealous were the dames in duty found,
They often in advance paid holy dues,
How pure the monks!—how just the ladies views!
The friars used despatch alone with those,
That for their fascinating charms they chose,
And sent the sempiternals to bestow,
The tribute they had brought on those below,
For in the refuse tithes that were their lot,
The laicks oft pleasant pickings got.
In short 'twas difficult to say,
What charity was shown from day to day.

IT happened that one night a married dame,
Desirous to convey the monks their claim,
And walking with her spouse just by the spot,
Where dwelled the arch contrivers of the plot,
Good Heavens! said she, I well remember now,
I've business with a friar here, I vow;
'Twill presently be done if you'll but wait;
Religious duties we must ne'er abate.
What duties? cried the husband with surprise;
You're surely mad:—'tis midnight I surmise;

Confess yourself to-morrow if required;
The holy fathers are to bed retired.
That makes no difference, the lady cried.—
I think it does, the husband straight replied,
And thither I'll not let you go to-night:—
What heinous sins so terribly affright,
That in such haste the mind you wish to ease?
To-morrow morn repair whene'er you please:

YOU do me wrong, rejoined the charming fair;
I neither want confession nor a prayer,
But anxiously desire what is due to pay;
For if incautiously I should delay,
Long time 'would be ere I the monk should see,
With other matters he'll so busy be.
But what can you the holy fathers owe?
To which the lady said:—what don't you know?
A tithe, my dear, the friars always claim.—
What tithe? cried he; it surely has a name.
Not know! astonishingly, replied the wife.—
To which the husband answered:—On my life,
That women friars pay is very strange;
Will you particulars with me arrange?
How cunningly, said she, you seem to act;
Why clearly you're acquainted with the fact?
'Tis Hymeneal works:—What works? cried he—
Lord! said the dame, assuredly you see,
Why I had paid an hour ago or more
And you've prevented me when at the door;
I'm sure, of those who owe, I'm not the worst,
For I, in paying, always was the first.

THE husband quite astonished now appeared;
At once a hundred diff'rent ills he feared;
But questioning his wife howe'er, he found,
That many other dames who lived around,
Like her; in paying tithes, the monks obeyed,
Which consolation to his breast conveyed.
Poor innocent! she nothing wished to hide;
Said she, not one but tithe they make provide;
Good friar Aubrey takes your sister's dues;
To father Fabry Mrs. B's accrues;
The mayoress friar William likes to greet,
A monk more handsome scarcely you will meet;
And I to friar Gerard always go;
I wished this night to pay him all I owe.

ALAS! when tongues unbridled drop disguise,
What direful ills, what discords oft arise!
The cunning husband having thus obtained,
Particulars of what the fathers gained,
At first designed in secret to disclose,
Those scenes of fraud and matrimonial woes:
The mayor and citizens should know, he thought;
What dues were paid: what tithes the friars sought;
But since 'twas rather difficult to place,
Full credence, at the first, in such a case,
He judged it best to make the fellow speak,
To whom his wife had shown herself so weak.

FOR father Gerard in the morn he sent,
Who, unsuspecting, to the husband went,
When, in the presence of the injured wife,

He drew his sword and swore he'd take his life,
Unless the mystery he would disclose,
Which he reluctantly through terror chose.
Then having bound the friar hand and foot,
And in another room his lady put,
He sallied forth his hapless lot to tell,
And to the mayor exposed the wily spell;
The corporation next; then up and down,
The secret he divulged throughout the town.

A CRY for vengeance presently was heard;
The whole at once to slaughter, some preferred
While others would the place with fire surround,
And burn the house with those within it found.
Some wished to drown them, bound within their dress;
With various other projects you may guess;
But all agreed that death should be their lot,
And those for burning had most voices got.

WITHOUT delay they to the convent flew;
But when the holy mansion came in view,
Respect, the place of execution changed;
A citizen his barn for this arranged;
The crafty crew together were confined,
And in the blaze their wretched lives resigned,
While round the husbands danced at sound of drum,
And burnt whatever to their hands had come;
Naught 'scaped their fury, monks of all degrees,
Robes, mantles, capuchins, and mock decrees:
All perished properly within the flames;
But nothing more I find about the dames;

And friar Gerard, in another place,
Had met apart his merited disgrace.

The Cradle

NEAR Rome, of yore, close to the Florence road,
Was seen a humble innkeeper's abode;
Small sums were charged; few guests the night would stay;
And these could seldom much afford to pay.
A pleasing active partner had the host
Her age not much 'bove thirty at the most;
Two children she her loving husband bore;
The boy was one year old: the daughter more;
Just fifteen summers o'er her form had smiled;
In person charming, and in temper mild.

IT happened that Pinucio, young and gay,
A youth of family, oft passed the way,
Admired the girl, and thought she might be gained,
Attentions showed, and like return obtained;
The mistress was not deaf, nor lover mute;
Pinucio seemed the lady's taste to suit,
Of pleasing person and engaging air;
And 'mong the equals of our youthful fair,
As yet, not one a pref'rence had received;
Nor had she e'er in golden dreams believed;
But, spite of tender years, her mind was high,
And village lads she would not let come nigh.

COLUTTA, (such her name,) though much admired;
And many in the place her hand desired,
Rejected some, and others would not take,
And this most clearly for Pinucio's sake.
Long conversations she could rarely get,
And various obstacles the lovers met;
No interviews where they might be at ease,
But ev'ry thing conspired to fret and teaze.
O parents, husbands! be advised by me;
Constraint with wives or children won't agree;
'Tis then the god of love exerts his art,
To find admittance to the throbbing heart.

PINUCIO and a friend, one stormy night,
The landlord's reached and would in haste alight;
They asked for beds, but were too late they found:
You know, sir, cried the host, we don't abound;
And now the very garrets we have let:
You'd better elsewhere try your wish to get,
And spite of weather, further on pursue
At best, our lodging is unfit for you.

HAVE you no truckle bed? the lover cried;
No corner left?—we fain would here abide:
Why, truly, said the host, we always keep
Two beds within the chamber where we sleep;
My wife and I, of course, take one of these;
Together lie in t'other if you please.
The spark replied, this we will gladly do;
Come, supper get; that o'er, the friends withdrew:
Pinucio, by Coletta's sage advice,

In looking o'er the room was very nice;
With eagle-eyes particulars he traced,
Then 'tween the clothes himself and friend he placed.
A camp-bed for the girl was on the floor;
The landlord's, 'gainst the wall and next the door;
Another opposite the last was set,
And this, to guests, at certain times was let;
And 'tween the two, but near the parents' best,
A cradle for the child to rest its head,
From which a pleasant accident arrived,
That our gallant's young friend of rest deprived.

WHEN midnight came, and this gay spark supposed
The host and hostess' eyes in sleep were closed,
Convinced the time appointed was at hand,
To put in execution what was planned,
He to the camp-bed silently repaired,
And found the belle by Morpheus not insnared;
Coletta taught a play that mortals find
Fatigues the body more than plagues the mind:
A truce succeeded, but 'twas quickly o'er:
Those rest not long who pilfer Cupid's store.

AGAIN, when to the room the hostess came,
And found the cradle rested not the same,
Good heav'ns! cried she, it joins my husband's head:
And, but for that, I truly had been led
To lay myself unthinkingly beside
The strangers whom with lodging we provide;
But, God be praised, this cradle shows the place
Where my good husband's pillow I must trace.

This said, she with the friend was quickly laid,
Without suspecting what mistake she'd made.

BETWEEN the lovers all was blithe and gay,
When suddenly the friend, though far from day,
Was forced to rise ('twas plain a pressing case,)
And move the infant's cradle from its place,
To ope the door, and lest he noise might make,
Or any way by chance the child should wake,
He set it carefully beside his bed,
And (softly treading) to the garden sped.

ON his return he passed the cradle by;
To place it as before he would not try,
But went to sleep; when presently a sound,
From something that had tumbled, rang around,
Awoke his wife, who ran below,
That what had happened she might clearly know.
No fool in such adventures was our Wight:
The opportunity he would not slight,
But played the husband well: no, no, I'm wrong;
He played it ill:—too oft, too much, too long;
For whosoe'er would wish to do it well,
Should softly go:—the gentle most excel.

IN truth, the wife was quite surprised to find
Her spouse so much to frolicking inclined;
Said she, what ails the man, he's grown so gay?
A lad of twenty's not more fond of play.
Well! let's enjoy the moments while we can;
God's will be done, since life is but a span!

THE words were scarcely said, when our gallant
Renewed his fun, and nothing seemed to want;
Indeed, the hostess still her charms possessed,
And, on occasion, well might be caressed.

MEANWHILE Coletta, dreading a surprise,
Prevailed upon her paramour to rise;
'Twas nearly break of day when he withdrew,
But, groping to his place the way anew,
Pinucio, by the cradle too, was led
To miss his friend's and take the landlord's bed.
No sooner in than with an under voice,
(Intriguers oft too eagerly rejoice,)
Said he, my friend, I wish I could relate
The pleasure I've received; my bliss is great;
To you, I'm sorry, Fortune proves so cold;
Like happiness I'd fain in you behold;
Coletta is a morsel for a king;
Inestimable girl!—to me she'll cling.
I've many seen, but such a charming fair,
There's not another like her any where.

WITH softest skin, delightful form and mien;
Her ev'ry act resembles BEAUTY's queen;
In short, before we'd ended with our fun,
Six posts (without a fiction) we had run.
The host was struck with what the spark averred,
And muttered something indistinctly heard.

THE hostess whispered HIM she thought her spouse:—
Again, my dear, such sparks let's never house;

Pray don't you hear how they together chat?—
Just then the husband raised himself and sat;
Is this your plan? said he with mighty rage;
Was it for THIS you would my house engage?
You understand me, but I'll seek redress;
Think you so very cheap to have success?
What, would you ruin families at will,
And with our daughters take at ease your fill?
Away, I say! my house this moment quit;
And as for You, abominable chit,
I'll have your life: this hour you breathe your last;
Such creatures only can with beasts be classed.

PINUCIO heard the lecture with dismay,
At once was mute, and grew as cold as clay;
A moment's silence through the room prevailed;
Coletta trembled, and her lot bewailed.
The hostess now, on ev'ry side perceived
Her peril great, and for the error grieved.
The friend, howe'er, the cradle called to mind,
Which caused the many ills we've seen combined,
And instantly he cried:—Pinucio! strange
You thus allow yourself about to range;
Did I not tell you when the wine you took,
'Twould make many sad misfortunes hook?
Whene'er you freely drink, 'tis known fall well,
Your sleep's disturbed, you walk, and nonsense tell.
Come, come to bed: the morning soon will peep;
Pinucio took the hint, pretended sleep,
And carried on so artfully the wile,
The husband no suspicion had of guile.

The stratagem our hostess likewise tried,
And to her daughter's bed in silence hied,
Where she conceived her fortress was so strong,
She presently began to use her tongue,
And cried aloud:—Impossible the fact;
Such things he could not with Coletta act;
I've with her been in bed throughout the night,
And she, no more than I, has swerved from right;
'Twere mighty pretty, truly, here to come;
At this the host a little while was dumb;
But in a lower tone at length replied
I nought with your account I'm satisfied.

THE party rose; the titter circled round;
And each sufficient reason for it found;
The whole was secret, and whoe'er had gained,
With care upon the subject mute remained.

St. Julian's Prayer

TO charms and philters, secret spells and prayers,
How many round attribute all their cares!
In these howe'er I never can believe,
And laugh at follies that so much deceive.
Yet with the beauteous FAIR, 'tis very true,
These WORDS, as SACRED VIRTUES, oft they view;
The spell and philter wonders work in love
Hearts melt with charms supposed from pow'rs above!

MY aim is now to have recourse to these,
And give a story that I trust will please,
In which Saint Julian's prayer, to Reynold D'Ast,
Produced a benefit, good fortune classed.
Had he neglected to repeat the charm,
Believed so thoroughly to guard from harm,
He would have found his cash accounts not right,
And passed assuredly a wretched night.

ONE day, to William's castle as he moved.
Three men, whose looks he very much approved,
And thought such honest fellows he had round,
Their like could nowhere be discovered round;
Without suspecting any thing was wrong,
The three, with complaisance and fluent tongue,

Saluted him in humble servile style,
And asked, (the minutes better to beguile,)
If they might bear him company the way;
The honour would be great, and no delay;
Besides, in travelling 'tis safer found,
And far more pleasant, when the party's round;
So many robbers through the province range,
(Continued they) 'tis wonderfully strange,
The prince should not these villains more restrain;
But there:—bad MEN will somewhere still remain.

TO their proposal Reynold soon agreed,
And they resolved together to proceed.
When 'bout a league the travellers had moved,
Discussing freely, as they all approved,
The conversation turned on spells and prayer,
Their pow'r o'er worms of earth, or birds of air;
To charm the wolf, or guard from thunder's roar,
And many wonderful achievements more;
Besides the cures a prayer would oft produce;
To man and beast it proves of sov'reign use,
Far greater than from doctors e'er you'll view,
Who, with their Latin, make so much ado.

IN turn, the three pretended knowledge great,
And mystick facts affected to relate,
While Reynold silently attention paid
To all the words the honest fellows said:—
Possess you not, said one, some secret prayer
To bring you aid, when dangers round you stare?
To this our Reynold seriously replied,

Myself, on secret spells, I do not pride;
But still some WORDS I have that I repeat,
Each morn I travel, that I may not meet
A horrid lodging where I stop at night;
'Tis called SAINT JULIAN'S PRAYER that I recite,
And truly I have found, that when I fail
To say this prayer, I've reason to bewail.
But rarely I neglect so good a thing,
That ills averts, and may such blessings bring.
And have you clearly said it, sir, to day?
Cried one of those he met upon his way.
Yes, Reynold answered. Well, replied the Wight;
I'll wage, I'm better lodged than you to-night.

'TWAS very cold, and darkness 'gan to peep;
The place was distant yet, where they might sleep.
Perhaps, said Reynold, 'tis your usual care,
In travelling, to say, like me, this prayer.
Not so, the other cried, to you I vow,
Invoking saints is not my practice now;
But should I lose, thenceforth I'll them address.—
Said Reynold, readily I acquiesce;
My life I'd venture, should you to an inn,
For, in the town, I've neither friend nor kin,
And, if you like, we'll this exception make.
The other answered: Well, the bet I'll take;
Your horse and coat against my purse you wage,
And, sure of gaining, readily engage.
Our Wight might then have thoroughly perceived,
His horse was lost—no chance to be relieved.

BESIDE a wood, as on the party moved,
The one, who betting had so much approved,
Now changed his tone, and in a surly way,
Exclaimed:—Alight—you'll find it time to pray;
Let me apprize you, distant is the place,
And much you'll need Saint Julian's special grace.
Come off, I tell you:—instantly they took
His purse, horse, clothes, and all their hands could hook
E'en seized his boots, and said with subtle sneer,
Your feet, by walking, won't the worse appear;
Then sought a diff'rent road by rapid flight,
And, presently the knaves were out of sight;
While Reynold still with stockings, drawers, and shirt,
But wet to skin, and covered o'er with dirt:
(The wind north-east in front—as cold as clay;)
In doleful dumps proceeded on his way,
And justly feared, that spite of faith and prayer,
He now should meet, at night, with wretched fare.

HOWEVER, some pleasing hopes he still had yet,
That, from his cloak-bag, he some clothes might get;
For, we should note, a servant he had brought,
Who in the neighbourhood a farrier sought.
To set a shoe upon his horse, and then
Should join his master on the road agen;
But that, as we shall find, was not the case,
And Reynold's dire misfortune thence we trace.
In fact, the fellow, worthless we'll suppose,
Had viewed from far what accidents arose,
Then turned aside, his safety to secure,
And left his master dangers to endure;

So steadily be kept upon the trot,
To Castle-William, ere 'twas night, he got,
And took the inn which had the most renown;
For fare and furniture within the town,
There waited Reynold's coming at his ease,
With fire and cheer that could not fail to please.
His master, up to neck in dirt and wet,
Had num'rous difficulties o'er to get;
And when the snow, in flakes obscured the air,
With piercing cold and winds, he felt despair;
Such ills he bore, that hanging might be thought
A bed of roses rather to be sought.
CHANCE so arranges ev'ry thing around
ALL good, or ALL that's bad is solely found;
When favours flow the numbers are so great,
That ev'ry wish upon us seems to wait;
But, if disposed, misfortunes to bestow;
No ills forgot: each poignant pang we know.
In proof, attend my friends, this very night,
The sad adventures that befell our wight,
Who, Castle-William did not reach till late,
When they, an hour or more, had shut the gate.

AT length our traveller approached the wall,
And, somehow to the foot contrived to crawl;
A roofed projection fortune led him near,
That joined a house, and 'gan his heart to cheer.
Delighted with the change he now had got,
He placed himself upon the sheltered spot;
A lucky hit but seldom comes alone;
Some straw, by chance, was near the mansion thrown,

Which Reynold 'neath the jutting penthouse placed
There, God be praised, cried he, a bed I've traced.

MEANWHILE, the storm from ev'ry quarter pressed;
Our traveller was soon to death distressed;
With cold benumbed; by fell despair o'erspread;
He trembled, groaned:—teeth chattered in his head;
So loud his plaints, at length they reached the ear
Of one who dwelled within the mansion near:
A servant girl; her mistress brisk and gay:
A youthful widow, charming as the day;
The governor she privately received:
A noble marquis, who her cares relieved.
Oft interrupted when he sought the fair,
And wished at ease her company to share;
Desirous too of passing quite unknown,
A private door he presently was shown,
That opened to the fields, and gave access:
Through this he visited with such address,
That none within the town his commerce viewed,
Nor e'en a servant's eye his course pursued.
Surprise I feel, since pleasures of the mind,
Apparently were not for lords designed;
More pleased they seem when made the talk around
And soft amours divulged, delights are found.

IT happened that the night our Job arrived,
And, stretched on straw, misfortune just survived,
The lady thought her fond gallant to see,
And ev'ry moment hoped with him to be.
The supper ready, and the room prepared,

Each rarity was served: no trouble spared;
Baths, perfumes, wines, most exquisite, in place,
And ev'ry thing around displaying grace,
With Cupid's whole artillery in view,
Not his, who would with sighs alone pursue,
But that kind god who always favour shows,
The source of happiness, whence pleasure flows.

MEANWHILE, however, while thus the lady sought.
By ev'ry charm to please, a note was brought;
A page conveyed it, by the marquis sent,
To say his coming business would prevent.
The disappointment doubtless was severe,
But consolation certainly was near;
It proved to Reynold wonderfully kind,
For scarcely had our traveller resigned,
And groaned aloud, but, tender as her dame,
In haste the confidential servant came,
And to the widow said:—I hear below
Some poor unfortunate o'ercome with woe;
'Tis piercing cold, and he perhaps will die
Some place, pray grant, where he to-night may lie.

MOST readily, replied the courteous fair,
We never use the garret:—lodge him there;
Some straw upon a couch will make a bed,
On which the wand'rer may repose his head;
Shut well the door, but first provide some meat,
And then permit him thither to retreat.

WITHOUT this timely help 'twas clear our wight

Had ne'er survived the horrors of the night;
The door was ope'd, and Reynold blessed the hand
That gave relief, and stopt life's ebbing sand.
His tale he told; got spirits, strength, and ease;
In person tall, well made, and formed to please,
He looked not like a novice in amour,
Though young, and seeking shelter at a door.
His want of dress and miserable state
Raised shame indeed, and showed distress was great.
Though LOVE be seen in Nature's pure array,
No dirt appears, however you survey.

THIS servant girl now hastened to the fair,
And ev'ry circumstance detailed with care.
See, said the lady, if within the press
There be not clothes to furnish him a dress;
My husband, now no more, must some have left;
Yes, said the girl, you're not of them bereft,
I recollect his wardrobe did abound;
And presently a handsome suit she found.

MEANWHILE the lady having learned the name
Of Reynold D'Ast, his quality and fame,
(Himself it seems particulars detailed,
While all around his suff'rings keen bewailed,)
Her orders gave, the bath for her prepared
Should now receive the man her care had spared.
Unasked, the stranger this attention got,
And well perfumed ere clothes they would allot.
When dressed, he waited on the widow fair,
And paid his compliments with graceful air.

THE supper (for the marquis first designed)
At length was served with taste the most refined.
Our trav'ller glad, an appetite displayed;
The lady carefully her guest surveyed,
And anxious seemed to gratify his wish,
By helping what appeared his favourite dish.
Already, perhaps, she felt a Cupid's dart,
And in her throbbing bosom knew the smart;
Or sympathy, or pity for his woes,
Might touch the spring whence softest passion flows.
On ev'ry side assailed the youthful dame
Herself surrendered unto Cupid's flame.
Should I give way, said she, who'll tell the tale?
No risk is run if secrecy prevail.
The marquis merits to be played the trick;
He no excuse can have, unless he's sick.
One sin against another I may weigh,
And man for man will equally repay.

SO inexperienced Reynold was not found,
But that he saw how things were going round,
And, that Saint Julian's Prayer would yet succeed,
To give him all the lodging he might need.

THE supper o'er, our couple left alone,
What fairer field could truly have been shown?
The belle now wore a smart becoming dress,
Designed, in ev'ry view, to prepossess.
'Twas NEGLIGENCE, so requisite to please
And fascinate, with airy, careless ease,
According to the taste which I pursue,

That made her charms so exquisite to view.
No gaudy tinsel: all was flowing light;
Though not superb, yet pleasing to the sight;
A neckerchief, where much should be concealed,
Was made so narrow,—beauties half revealed;
Beneath is shade—what words can ne'er express;
And Reynold saw enough the rest to guess.
No more I say; the belle indeed was fair,
Possessed of youth and all engaging air;
Tall, nicely formed; each grace, that hearts could win;
Not much of fat, nor yet appeared too thin.
Emotion, at the view, who would not feel?
To soft delight what bosom proves of steel?
No marble bust, philosopher, nor stone,
But similar sensation would have shown.

THE silence first was broken by the dame;
Who spoke so freely, Reynold bolder came.
He knew not well, howe'er, discourse to find;
To help him out the widow was inclined;
Said she, you much remind me of a friend,
Whose ev'ry wish I sought with mine to blend
My husband (rest his soul!) had just those eyes,
That look, air, mouth:—the very height and size:
You greatly honour me, the spark replied:
Your charms howe'er might well have been his pride;
I ne'er beheld such soft engaging mien:
On earth, like beauty never yet was seen.
But, in extremes to be, appears my lot;
Just now I felt quite chilled:—at present hot;
Pray tell me which is best? The fair looked down,

And humbly seemed to wave the proffered crown,
That she might still more flattery receive
Address not small, if we'll our eyes believe.
The swain now praised each charm within his view,
And whatsoe'er his wishes could pursue;
Where hope was strong, and expectation high,
She would not long be cruel and deny.
To give the praise, your due, the lover cried,
And note the beauties that my heart divide,
'Twould take an age, and I've a single night,
Which surely might be passed with more delight.
The widow smiled; enough it seems was said;
And Reynold shortened—what to nothing led.
In war or love, time equally is dear;
More happy than our spark none could appear;
No point but what he gained; the smiling dame
Resistance only showed to raise the flame;
Nor more nor less; each belle like art has got,
And practises at will, or maid or not.

BUT truly, it was never my intent
To count each favour she to Reynold lent;
Particulars exact of ev'ry kiss,
And all the preludes incident to bliss;
Both, doubtless, knew more ways than one to please;
And sought, with anxious care, love's charms to seize.
On recollection of the wretched state
In which our traveller had moved of late,
Some favour was bestowed:—there, cried the dame,
Is something to repay the road you came;
This for the cold; that fear; there thieves disgraced;

So, one by one, the whole was soon effaced.
In this way to be paid for ills we meet,
Who'd not be satisfied with boons so sweet?
And we conclude, that Reynold on the spot,
Love's am'rous recompense of pleasures got.
Now easy conversation was renewed;
Then mutual kisses; ev'ry sweet pursued.
'Twas time for bed; howe'er, the widow fair
Determined that her own the spark should share;
'Twas prudent, doubtless; like a lady wise;
Gallantly done: one room would well suffice.

WHAT further passed betwixt the pair that night;
I cannot say, though we'll believe 'twas right;
Between the clothes when laid, and unrestrained,
Most clearly, Reynold all his wishes gained.
There he was recompensed for ev'ry grief;
The lady too, received so much relief,
That she desired his company again,
But still these visits secrets should remain;
'Twas requisite the governor to see;
Howe'er the dame delighted seemed to be,
And not content with what she had bestowed,
A purse well stored with gold to Reynold showed:
He took no more, indeed, than what would pay
The bare expenses on his homeward way;
Then sought the street that to the tavern led,
Where still his lazy servant was in bed;
The fellow mauled; then changed throughout his dress;
Since to the cloak-bag now he had access.
His fortune to complete, that day they took

The very wretches that he wished to hook.
He to the judge repaired with ev'ry haste;
In such a case you never time should waste;
For, once the things are into court received,
'Tis like the lion's den: naught e'er 's retrieved;
Their hands are closed, not 'gainst what may be brought
But to secure what from their grasp is sought.
Who seeks redress by law, facts oft have shown,
May bless his stars if he but keep his own.

THE trial o'er, a gallows treble-faced,
Was, for their swinging, in the market placed,
ONE of the three harangued the mob around,
(His speech was for the others also found)
Then, 'bout their necks the halters being tied,
Repentant and confessed the culprits died.

WHO, after this, will doubt the pow'r of prayers?
These silly knaves had banished all their cares;
And when at ease they thought to skip and prance,
Were seized and quickly taught another dance.
On t'other hand, where dire distress prevailed,
And death, in various ways, our spark assailed,
A beauty suddenly his senses charmed,
Who might a prelate's bosom have alarmed.
So truly fortunate, indeed, his lot,
Again his money, baggage, horse he got;
And, thank Saint Julian, howsoever tossed,
He passed a blissful night that nothing cost.

The Countryman who Sought his Calf

A COUNTRYMAN, one day, his calf had lost,
And, seeking it, a neighbouring forest crossed;
The tallest tree that in the district grew,
He climbed to get a more extensive view.
Just then a lady with her lover came;
The place was pleasing, both to spark and dame;
Their mutual wishes, looks and eyes expressed,
And on the grass the lady was caressed.
At sights of charms, enchanting to the eyes,
The gay gallant exclaimed, with fond surprise:—
Ye gods, what striking beauties now I see!
No objects named; but spoke with anxious glee.
The clod, who, on the tree had mounted high,
And heard at ease the conversation nigh,
Now cried:—Good man! who see with such delight;
Pray tell me if my calf be in your sight?

Hans Carvel's Ring

HANS CARVEL took, when weak and late in life;
A girl, with youth and beauteous charms to wife;
And with her, num'rous troubles, cares and fears;
For, scarcely one without the rest appears.
Bab (such her name, and daughter of a knight)
Was airy, buxom: formed for am'rous fight.
Hans, holding jeers and cuckoldom in dread,
Would have his precious rib with caution tread,
And nothing but the Bible e'er peruse;
All other books he daily would abuse;
Blamed secret visits; frowned at loose attire;
And censured ev'ry thing gallants admire.
The dame, howe'er, was deaf to all he said;
No preaching pleased but what to pleasure led,
Which made the aged husband hold his tongue.
And wish for death, since all round went wrong.
Some easy moments he perhaps might get;
A full detail in hist'ry's page is met.
One night, when company he'd had to dine,
And pretty well was fill'd with gen'rous wine,
Hans dreamed, as near his wife he snoring lay,
The devil came his compliments to pay,
And having on his finger put a ring,
Said he, friend Hans, I know thou feel'st a sting;

Thy trouble 's great: I pity much thy case;
Let but this ring, howe'er, thy finger grace,
And while 'tis there I'll answer with my head,
THAT ne'er shall happen which is now thy dread:
Hans, quite delighted, forced his finger through;
You drunken beast, cried Bab, what would you do?
To love's devoirs quite lost, you take no care,
And now have thrust your finger God knows where!

The Hermit

WHEN Venus and Hypocrisy combine,
Oft pranks are played that show a deep design;
Men are but men, and friars full as weak:
I'm not by Envy moved these truths to speak.
Have you a sister, daughter, pretty wife?
Beware the monks as you would guard your life;
If in their snares a simple belle be caught:
The trap succeeds: to ruin she is brought.
To show that monks are knaves in Virtue's mask;
Pray read my tale:—no other proof I ask.

A HERMIT, full of youth, was thought around,
A saint, and worthy of the legend found.
The holy man a knotted cincture wore;
But, 'neath his garb:—heart-rotten to the core.
A chaplet from his twisted girdle hung,
Of size extreme, and regularly strung,
On t'other side was worn a little bell;
The hypocrite in ALL, he acted well;
And if a female near his cell appeared,
He'd keep within as if the sex he feared,
With downcast eyes and looks of woe complete,
You'd ne'er suppose that butter he could eat.

NOT far from where the hermit's cell was placed,
Within a village dwelled a widow chaste;
Her residence was at the further end
And all her store—a daughter as a friend,
Who candour, youth, and charms supreme possessed;
And still a virgin lived, howe'er distressed.
Though if the real truth perhaps we name,
'Twas more simplicity than virtuous aim;
Not much of industry, but honest heart;
No wealth, nor lovers, who might hope impart.
In Adam's days, when all with clothes were born,
She doubtless might like finery have worn;
A house was furnished then without expense;
For sheets or mattresses you'd no pretence;
Not e'en a bed was necessary thought
No blankets, pillowbiers, nor quilts were bought.
Those times are o'er; then Hymen came alone;
But now a lawyer in his train is shown.

OUR anchorite, in begging through the place;
This girl beheld,—but not with eyes of grace.
Said he, she'll do, and, if thou manag'st right,
Lucius, at times, with her to pass the night.
No time he lost, his wishes to secure:
The means, we may suppose, not over pure.

QUITE near the open fields they lived, I've said;
An humble, boarded cottage o'er their head.
One charming night—no, I mistake 'tis plain,
Our hermit, favoured much by wind and rain,
Pierced in the boarding, where by time 'twas worn;

A hole through which he introduced a horn;
And loudly bawled:—attend to what I say,
Ye women, my commands at once obey.
This voice spread terror through the little cot;
Both hid their heads and trembled for their lot;
But still our monk his horn would sound aloud
Awake! cried he; your favour God has vowed;
My faithful servant, Lucius, haste to seek;
At early dawn go find this hermit meek
To no one say a word: 'tis Heav'n ordains;
Fear nothing, Lucius ever blessed remains;
I'll show the way myself: your daughter place,
Good widow, with this holy man of grace;
And from their intercourse a pope shall spring,
Who back to virtue christendom will bring.

HE spoke to them so very loud and clear,
They heard, though 'neath the clothes half dead with fear.
Some time howe'er the females lay in dread;
At length the daughter ventured out her head,
And, pulling hastily her parent's arm,
Said she, dear mother, (not suspecting harm)
Good Heav'ns! must I obey and thither go?
What would the holy man on me bestow?
I know not what to say nor how to act;
Now cousin Anne would with him be exact,
And better recollect his sage advice:—
Fool! said the mother, never be so nice;
Go, nothing fear, and do whate'er's desired;
Much understanding will not be required;
The first or second time thou'lt get thy cue,

And cousin Anne will less know what to do.
Indeed? the girl replied; well, let's away,
And we'll return to bed without delay.
But softly, cried the mother with a smile;
Not quite so fast, for Satan may beguile;
And if 'twere so, hast taken proper care?
I think he spoke like one who would ensnare.
To be precipitate, in such a case,
Perhaps might lead at once to dire disgrace.
If thou wert terrified and did'st not hear,
Myself I'm sure was quite o'ercome with fear.
No, no, rejoined the daughter, I am right:
I clearly heard, dear mother, spite of fright.
Well then, replied the widow, let us pray,
That we by Satan be not led astray.

AT length they both arose when morning came,
And through the day the converse was the same.
At night howe'er the horn was heard once more,
And terrified the females as before.
Thou unbelieving woman, cried the voice,
For certain purposes of God the choice;
No more delay, but to the hermit fly,
Or 'tis decreed that thou shalt quickly die.
Now, mother, said the girl, I told you well;
Come, let us hasten to the hermit's cell;
So much I dread your death, I'll nothing shun;
And if 'tis requisite, I'll even run.
Away then, cried the mother, let us go;
Some pains to dress, the daughter would bestow,
Without reflecting what might be her fare:—

To PLEASE is ev'ry blooming lass's care.

OUR monk was on the watch you may suppose;
A hole he made that would a glimpse disclose;
By which, when near his cell the females drew,
They might, with whip in hand the hermit view,
Who, like a culprit punished for his crimes,
Received the lash, and that so many times,
It sounded like the discipline of schools,
And made more noise than flogging fifty fools.

WHEN first our pilgrims knocked, he would not hear;
And, for the moment, whipping would appear;
The holy lash severely he applied,
Which, through the hole, with pain our females spied;
At length the door he ope'd, but from his eyes
No satisfaction beamed: he showed surprise.
With trembling knees and blushes o'er the face,
The widow now explained the mystick case.
Six steps behind, the beauteous daughter stood,
And waited the decree she thought so good.
The hypocrite howe'er the hermit played,
And sent these humble pilgrims back dismayed.
Said he, the evil spirit much I dread;
No female to my cell should e'er be led;
Excuse me then: such acts would sorrow bring;
From me the HOLY FATHER ne'er spring.
What ne'er from you? the widow straight replied:
And why should not the blessing, pray, be tried?
No other answer howsoe'er she got;
So back they trudged once more to gain their cot.

Ah! mother, said the girl, 'tis my belief,
Our many heavy sins have caused thus grief.

WHEN night arrived and they in sleep were lost,
Again the hermit's horn the woodwork crossed;
Return, return, cried he with horrid tone;
To-morrow you'll have due attention shown;
I've changed the hermit's cold fastidious mind,
And when you come, he'll act as I've designed.

THE couple left their bed at break of day,
And to the cell repaired without delay
Our tale to shorten, Lucius kind appeared
To rigid rules no longer he adhered.
The mother with him let her girl remain,
And hastened to her humble roof again.
The belle complying looked:—he took her arm,
And soon familiar grew with ev'ry charm.

O HYPOCRITES! how oft your wily art
Deceives the world and causes poignant smart.

AT matins they so very often met,
Some awkward indications caused regret.
The fair at length her apron-string perceived
Grew daily shorter, which her bosom grieved;
But nothing to the hermit she'd unfold,
Nor e'en those feelings to her mother told;
She dreaded lest she should be sent away,
And be deprived at once of Cupid's play.
You'll tell me whence so much discernment came?

From this same play:—the tree of art by name.
For sev'n long months the nymph her visits paid;
Her inexperience doubtless wanted aid.

BUT when the mother saw her daughter's case,
She made her thank the monk, and leave the place.
The hermit blessed the Lord for what was done;
A pleasant course his humble slave had run.
He told the mother and her daughter fair,
The child, by God's permission, gifts would share.
Howe'er, be careful, said the wily wight,
That with your infant ev'ry thing goes right;
To you, from thence, great happiness will spring:
You'll reign the parent of what's more than king;
Your relatives to noble rank will rise:
Some will be princes; others lords comprise;
Your nephews cardinals; your cousins too
Will dukes become, if they the truth pursue;
And places, castles, palaces, there'll be,
For you and them of every high degree;
You'll nothing want: eternal is the source,
Like waters flowing in the river's course.
This long prediction o'er: with features grave,
His benediction to them both he gave.

WHEN home returned, the girl, each day and night,
Amused her mind with prospects of delight;
By fancy's aid she saw the future pope,
And all prepared to greet her fondest hope;
But what arrived the whole at once o'erthrew
Hats, dukedoms, castles, vanished from the view:

The promised elevation of the NAME
Dissolved to air:-a little female came!

The Convent Gardener of Lamporechio

WHEN Cupid with his dart, would hearts assail,
The rampart most secure is not the VEIL;
A husband better will the FAIR protect,
Than walls or lattices, I much suspect.
Those parents, who in nunneries have got
Their daughters (whether willingly or not),
Most clearly in a glaring error prove,
To fancy God will round their actions move;
'Tis an abuse of what we hold divine;
The Devil with them surely must combine.
Besides, 'twere folly to suppose that vice
Ne'er entered convent walls, and nuns were ice.
A very diff'rent sentiment I hold:
Girls, who in publick move, however bold,
Have greater terrors lest they get a stain;
For, honour lost, they never fame regain.
Few enemies their modesty attack;
The others have but one their minds to rack.
TEMPTATION, daughter of the drowsy dame,
That hates to move, and IDLENESS we name,
Is ever practising each wily art,
To spread her snares around the throbbing heart;
And fond DESIRE, the child of lorn CONSTRAINT,

Is anxious to the soul soft scenes to paint.
If I've a worthy daughter made a nun,
Is that a reason she's a saint?—Mere fun!
Avaunt such folly!—three in four you'll find,
Of those who wear the veil—have changed their mind;
Their fingers bite, and often do much worse:
Those convent vows, full soon, become a curse;
Such things at least have sometimes reached my ear
(For doubtless I must speak from others here);
Of his Boccace a merry tale has told,
Which into rhyme I've put, as you'll behold.

WITHIN a nunnery, in days of yore,
A good old man supplied the garden-store;
The nuns, in general, were smart and gay,
And kept their tongues in motion through the day.
Religious duties they regarded less,
Than for the parlour* to be nice in dress
Arranging ev'ry article to please,
That each might captivate and charm at ease;
The changes constantly they rang around,
And made the convent-walls with din resound.
Eight sisters and an abbess held the place,
And strange to say—there DISCORD you might trace.
All nine had youth, and many beauty too:
Young friars round the place were oft in view,
Who reckoned ev'ry step they took so well,
That always in the proper road they fell.

---

* The parlour in a convent is the room where the nuns are permitted to speak to their friends through a lattice.

Th' aged gard'ner, of whom ere now we spoke,
Was oft bewildered, they would so provoke;
Capricious, whimsical, from day to day,
Each would command and try to have her way;
And as they ne'er agreed among themselves,
He suffered more than if with fifty elves;
When one was pleased, another soon complained:
At length to quit the nuns he was constrained.
He left them, poor and wretched as he came;
No cross, pile, money:—e'en his coat the same.

A YOUTH of Lamporechio, gay and bold,
One day this gard'ner met as I am told;
And after conversation 'bout the place,
Said, he should like nun's service to embrace,
And that he wished sincerely to be hired:
He'd gratis do whatever was required.
'Twas clear indeed his object was not pelf;
He thought however he might reward himself;
And as the sisters were not over wise,
A nun he now and then might make his prize;
Proceed from one to more with like address,
Till with the whole he'd had complete success.
Said Nuto (such we find the gard'ner's name),
Believe me, friend, you will be much to blame;
Some other service seek, I recommend;
These convent-dames will ne'er their whimseys end.
I'd rather live without or soup or bread,
Than work for them, however nicely fed.

STRANGE creatures are these nuns, upon my word;

Their ways ridiculous and e'en absurd;
Who, with the sisterhood, has never been,
Has clearly yet, not perfect torment seen,
Such service, prithee, never try to gain;
To do what they require I know is vain;
One will have soft, and t'other asks for hard:
Thou'lt be a fool such ninnies to regard;
No work thou'lt do, whatever be the want:
THIS cabbages,—THAT carrots tells thee plant:
Said t'other, fain I'd bring it to the test;
I'm but a simpleton, it is confessed;
Yet still a month in place, and thou wilt see;
How well I with the convent-dames agree.
The reason is, my life is in its prime,
While thou art sunk in years and worn by time,
I'm proper for their work, and only ask,
To be admitted to the drudging task.
Well, said the former, if resolved to try,
To their factotum instantly apply;
Come; let's away. Lead on, the other cried;
I've got a thought, which I'll to you confide:—
I'll seem an idiot, and quite dumb appear.—
In that, said Nuto, only persevere,
And then perhaps the confessor thou'lt find,
With their factotum carelessly inclined;
No fears nor dark suspicions of a mute:
Thou'lt ev'ry way, my friend, their wishes suit.

THE place, as was expected, soon he got;
And half the grounds to trench, at once his lot:
He acted well the nincompoop and fool,

Yet still was steady to the garden tool;
The nuns continually would flock around,
And much amusement in his anticks found.

ONE day, as sleeping lay our sprightly wight,
Or feigning sleep, no matter which is right,
(Boccace pretends the latter was the fact)
Two nuns (perhaps not two the most exact,)
Observing him extended on the sward,
While summer's heat from air so much debarred;
That few would venture from the convent-roof,
Lest, 'gainst the sun, their cheeks should not be proof:
Said one, approaching him, let's take this fool,
And place him in the garden-house to cool.
The lad was handsome, with engaging mien:
The nun admired the features she had seen,
And Cupid raised a wish to be at ease,
Where she, without restraint, herself might please.
What would you, cried the other, with him do?
You'll see, rejoined the first, if we pursue;
Just what might be expected from the place;
Christ! said the second (with a cross of grace),
You would not surely do what is forbid?
Suppose increase? it never could be hid;
Besides, should we be seen, 'twill be the cause,
Of dire disgrace to break such sacred laws.

WE shall not be observed, the first replied;
These ills thy fancy forms: haste, let's decide,
And seize the moment while 'tis in our reach,
Without regard to what old dotards teach,

Or what may happen at a future hour;
Here's no one near: 'tis fully in our pow'r;
The time and place so thoroughly agree,
'Twill be impossible our freaks to see;
But 'twill be right that one should watch with care;
While t'other with the lad seeks joys to share,
And irksome gloom endeavours to dispel:
He's dumb, you know, and tales can never tell.
The other answered, since 'tis your desire,
I'll acquiesce and do what you require;
You'll take him first: I see it is your aim;
And since it will oblige, I'll wave my claim;
Go, pleasure seek, and satisfy each wish:
You're always anxious for a fav'rite dish;
'Tis only to oblige that I comply.
That, said the other, clearly I descry;
I'm well persuaded, thou art always kind;
But still I think thou would'st not be inclined;
In such a scene to take the leading part,
Thy bashfulness would counteract thy heart.

SOME time the squeamish sister watched the spot;
At length the other, who'd her wishes got,
The station took; the lab'rer tried to please
The second as the first, but less at ease;
So many favours fell not to her share,
And only treble comfort proved her fare.

THE garden-path, and summer-house as well,
Were well remembered by each wanton belle;
No need of guides; and soon our spark contrived;

With sister Agnes also to be hived
A press-house at the convent end he chose,
in which he showed her how soft pleasure flows;
Nor Claudia nor Angelica would miss
The dormitory that, and cellar this;
In short the garret and the vaulted cave
Knew fully how the sisters could behave;
Not one but what he first or last regaled
E'en with the rigid abbess he prevailed,
To take a dance, and as the dame required
Her treble share of what was most admired,
The other nuns were oft obliged to fast,
While with the convent-head his time was passed.

TO no restoratives our Wight would run;
Though these do little, where much work is done:
So oft the lad was pressed for cheering play,
That with the abbess, when engaged one day,
He said, where'er I go, 'tis common talk,
With only sev'n an able bird should walk,
Yet constantly I've got no less than nine:—
The abbess cried,—A miracle divine!
Here nuns, pray haste, and quickly come around;
We've fasted with success:—his tongue is found.
The eight encircled him with great surprise;
No longer dumb.—they viewed with eager eyes:
A consultation instantly was had,
When 'twas agreed to honour well the lad,
And try to make him secrecy observe;
But if dismissed, from silence he might swerve.
The active youth, well fed, well paid, thus blessed,

Did all he could,—and others did the rest.
He for the nuns procured a little lot,
That afterward two little friars got,
And in the sequel fathers soon became;
The sisters mothers too, in spite of shame;
But never name more justly was applied:
In vain their mysteries they strove to hide.

The Mandrake

FLORENTINE we now design to show;—
A greater blockhead ne'er appeared below;
It seems a prudent woman he had wed,
With beauty that might grace a monarch's bed;
Young, brisk, good-humoured, with engaging mien;
None in the town, or round, the like was seen:
Her praises every voice inclined to sing,
And judged her worthy of a mighty king;
At least a better husband she deserved:
An arrant fool he looked, and quite unnerved.
This Nicia Calfucci (for such his name)
Was fully bent to have a father's fame,
And thought his country honour he could do,
Could he contrive his lineage to pursue.
No holy saint in Paradise was blessed,
But what this husband fervently addressed;
From day to day, so oft he teazed for grace,
They scarcely knew his off'rings where to place.
No matron, quack, nor conjurer around,
But what he tried their qualities profound;
Yet all in vain: in spite of charm or book,
No father he, whatever pains he took.

TO Florence then returned a youth from France;

Where he had studied,—more than complaisance:
Well trained as any from that polished court;
To Fortune's favours anxious to resort;
Gallant and seeking ev'ry FAIR to please;
Each house, road, alley, soon he knew at ease;
The husbands, good or bad, their whims and years,
With ev'ry thing that moved their hopes or fears;
What sort of fuel best their females charmed;
What spies were kept by those who felt alarmed;
The if's, for's, to's, and ev'ry artful wile,
That might in love a confidant beguile,
Or nurse, or father-confessor, or dog;
When passion prompts, few obstacles can clog.

THE snares were spread, each stratagem was laid;
And every thing arranged to furnish aid,
When our gay spark determined to invest
Old Nicia with the cuckold's branching crest.
The plan no doubt was well conceived and bold;
The lady to her friends appeared not cold;
Within her husband's house she seemed polite;
But ne'er familiarly was seen invite,
No further could a lover dare proceed;
Not one had hope the belle his flame would heed.

OUR youth, Calimachus, no sooner came,
But he howe'er appeared to please the dame;
His camp he pitched and entered on the siege
Of fair Lucretia, faithful to her liege,
Who presently the haughty tigress played,
And sent him, like the rest, away dismayed.

HE, scarcely knew what saint he could invoke;
When Nicia's folly served him for a cloak;
However strange, no stratagem nor snare,
But what the fool would willingly prepare
With all his heart, and nothing fancy wrong;
That might to others possibly belong.
The lover and himself, as learned men,
Had conversations ev'ry now and then;
For Nicia was a doctor in the law:
Degree, to him, not worth a single straw;
Far better had he common prudence traced;
And not his confidence so badly placed.

ONE day he to Calimachus complained,
Of want of heirs, and wished they could be gained:
Where lay the fault? He was a gay gallant;
Lucretia young with features to enchant.
When I at Paris was, replied our wight,
There passed a clever man, a curious sight,
His company with anxious care I sought,
And was at length a hundred secrets taught;
'Mong others how, at will, to get an heir:—
A certain thing, he often would declare;
The great Mogul had tried it on his queen,
just two years since, the heir might then be seen;
And many other princesses of fame,
Had added by it to their husband's name.
'Twas very true; I've seen it fully proved:
The remedy all obstacles removed;
'Tis from the root of certain tree expressed;
A juice most potent ev'ry where confessed,

And Mandrake called, which taken by a wife;
More pow’r evinces o’er organick life,
Than from conventual grace was e’er derived,
Though in the cloister youthful friars hived.

TEN months from hence I’ll you a father make;
No longer time than that I ask to take;
This period o’er, the child to church we’ll bring,—
If true, said Nicia, what a glorious thing!
You’ll do me services I can’t express.—
Don’t doubt it, cried the spark of smart address:
Must I the fact so oft to you repeat?
I’ve seen it with my eyes; ‘tis most complete;
You mean to jest, assuredly my friend;
Would you by doubts the great Mogul offend?
So handsomely this traveller he paid,
No sign of discontent he e’er betrayed.

‘TIS excellent, the Florentine replied;
Lucretia must be pleased to have it tried;
What satisfaction! in her arms to view
An infant that my lineage will renew.
Now, worthy friend, you god-father shall stand;
This very day pray take the thing in hand.

NOT quite so fast, rejoined our smart gallant,
First know the plan, before consent you grant;
There is an ill attends the whole affair;
But what below, alas! is free from care;
This juice, possessing virtues so divine,
Has also pow’rs that prove the most malign:

Whoe'er receives the patient's first embrace;
Too fatally the dire effects will trace;
Death oft succeeds the momentary joy;
We scarcely good can find without alloy.

YOUR servant; sir, said Nicia with surprise;
No more of this: the name will me suffice;
Lucretia we will let remain at ease:
What you propose can never truly please;
If I must die by getting of a son,
'Tis better far the benefit to shun;
Go find some other for your wondrous art;
In fact I'm not inclined with life to part.

HOW strange your conduct, cried the sprightly youth:
Extremes you seek, and overleap the truth;
Just now the fond desire to have a boy
Chased ev'ry care and filled your heart with joy;
At present quite the contrary appears
A moment changed your fondest hopes to fears;
Come, hear the rest; no longer waste your breath:
Kind Nature all can cure, excepting death.
What's necessary pray, that things succeed?
Some youthful clod for once should take the lead,
And clear the way of ev'ry venom round
Then you with safety may commence to sound;
No time you'll lose, but instantly begin
And you'll most certainly your object win.
This step is necessary to the end;
Some lad of little worth I recommend;
But not ill made, nor savagely robust,

To give your lady terror nor disgust.
We know that, used to Nicia's soft caress,
Lucretia would disrelish rude address;
Indeed 'tis possible in such event,
Her tender heart would never give consent;
This led me to propose a man that's young;
Besides, the more he proves for action strong,
The less of venom will behind remain,
And I'll engage that ev'ry drop he'll drain.

AT first the husband disapproved the plan,
The infamy, and danger which they ran
Perhaps the magistrate might have him sought,
And he, of murder, guilty might be thought;
The sudden death would mightily perplex;
A fellow's creature's loss would sorely vex;
Lucretia, who'd withstood each tempter's charms,
Was now to be disgraced in rustick arms!

CALIMACHUS, with eagerness replied;
I would a man of consequence provide,
Or one, at all events, whose anxious aim
Would be, aloud the myst'ry, to proclaim!
But fear and folly would contain the clown,
Or money at the worst would stop renown,
Your better half apparently resigned;
The clod without intention of the kind;
In short whate'er arrived, 'tis clear your case
Could not with Cuckoldom be well in place.
Besides 'tis no way certain but our blade,
By strength of nerves the poison may evade;

And that's a double reason for the choice,
Since with more certainty we shall rejoice:
The venom may evaporate in fume,
And Mandrake pleasing pow'rs at once assume;
For when I spoke of death, I did not mean,
That nothing from it would the person screen;
To-morrow we the rustick lad must name;
To-night the potion given your charming dame;
I've some already with me, all prepared;
Let nothing of your project be declared:
You should not seem to know what we've designed;
Ligurio you'll permit this clod to find;
You can most thoroughly in him confide:
Discretion, secrecy, with him reside.
One thing, however, nearly I'd forgot;
A bandage for the eyes we should allot;
And when well bound he nothing e'er can trace
Of whom, or what, the lady, or the place.

THE whole arrangement Nicia much approved;
But now 'twas time the lady should be moved.
At first she thought it jest, then angry grew,
And vowed the plan she never would pursue;
Her life she'd rather forfeit than her name:
Once known, for ever lost would be her fame
Besides the heinous sin and vile offence,
God knew she rather would with all dispense;
Mere complaisance had led her to comply;
Would she admit a wretch with blearing eye,
To incommode, and banish tranquil ease?
Who could conceive her formed a clod to please?

Can I, said she, the paths of honour quit,
And in my bed a loathsome brute permit?
Or e'er regard the plan but with disdain?
No, by saint John, I ever will maintain,
Nor beau, nor clown, nor king, nor lord, nor 'squire,
Save Nicia, with me freely shall retire.

THE fair Lucretia seemed so firmly bent,
To father Timothy at length they went,
Who preached the lady such a fine discourse,
She ceded more through penitence than force.

MOREOVER she was promised that the lad
Should be nor clownish, nor in person bad;
Nor such as any way might give disgust,
But one to whom she perfectly might trust.

THE wondrous draught was taken by the fair;
Next day our Wight prepared his wily snare:
Himself bepowdered like a miller's man,
With beard and whiskers to complete his plan;
A better metamorphose ne'er was seen;
Ligurio, who had in the secret been,
So thoroughly disguised the lover thought,
At midnight him to Nicia freely brought,
With bandage o'er the eyes and hair disdained,
Not once the husband of deceit complained.

BESIDE the dame in silence slid our spark;
In silence she attended in the dark,
Perfumed and nicely ev'ry way bedecked;

For what? you ask, or whom did she expect;
Were all these pains a miller to receive?—
Too much they cannot take, the sex believe;
And whether kings or millers be their aim,
The wish to please is ever found the same.
'Tis double honour in a woman thought,
When by her charms a torpid heart is caught;
She, who in icy bosoms flame can raise,
Deserving doubtless is of treble praise.

THE spark disguised, his place no sooner took,
But awkwardness he presently forsook;
No more the miller, but the smart gallant:
The lady found him kind and complaisant;
Such moments we'll suppose were well employed;
Though trembling fears not perfectly destroyed.

SHE, to herself, remarked, 'tis very strange,
This lad's demeanour should so quickly change;
He's quite another character, 'tis clear;
What pity that his end should be so near;
Alas! he merits not so hard a fate;
I feel regret the lot should him await;
And while soft pleasure seems his heart's delight;
His soul is doomed from hence to take its flight.

THE husband who so fully gave consent,
Was led his partner's suff'rings to lament
The spirit of a queen in truth she showed,
When cuckoldom was on her spouse bestowed;
In decoration, forced to acquiesce,

She would not condescend to join caress.

LUCRETIA howsoe'er the lad approved;
His winning manners much her favour moved.

WHEN he the subtle venom had subdued,
He took her hand, and having fondly sued,
Said he, your pardon lady now I ask;
Be not displeased when I remove the mask;
Your rage restrain; a trick on you's been played;
Calimachus am I; be not dismayed;
Approve my sacrifice; the secret's known;
Your rigour would be useless now if shown;
Should I be doomed howe'er to breathe my last,
I die content, rememb'ring what has passed;
You have the means my life at will to take;
More havock with me soft delight could make,
Than any poison that the draught possessed;
Mere folly, imposition, all the rest.

TILL then Lucretia had resistance made;
To seem submissive she was still afraid;
The lover was not hated by the belle,
But bashfulness she could not well dispel,
Which, joined to simple manners mixed with fear,
Ungrateful made her, spite of self, appear.

IN silence wrapt, and scarcely drawing breath,
By passion moved, and yet ashamed to death,
Not knowing how to act, so great her grief,
From tears, her throbbing bosom sought relief.

Look, could she e'er her lover in the face?
Will he not think me covered with disgrace?
Said she, within herself;—what else believe?
My wits were lost to let him thus deceive.
O'ercome by sorrow, then she turned her head,
And tried to hide herself within the bed,
At furthest end, but vain alas her aim,
The lover thither in a moment came:
Her only ground, remaining unsubdued,
Surrendered when the vanquisher pursued,
Who every thing submitted to his will,
And tears no more her eyes were found to fill;
Shame took to flight, and scruples spread the wing;
How happy those whom duping GAIN can bring!

TOO soon Aurora for our spark appeared;
Too soon for her so thoroughly revered;
Said he, the poison, that can life devour,
Requires repeated acts to crush its pow'r.
The foll'wing days our youthful am'rous pair
Found opportunities for pleasing fare.
The husband scarcely could himself contain,
So anxiously he wished his aim to gain.

THE lover from the belle at length arose,
And hastened to his house to seek repose;
But scarcely had he placed himself in bed,
When our good husband's footsteps thither led;
He, to the spark, related with delight,
How mandrake-juice succeeded in the night.
Said he, at first beside the bed I crept,

And listened if the miller near her kept,
Or whether he to converse was inclined,
And ev'ry way to act as was designed.
I then my wife was anxious to address,
And whispered that she should the youth caress;
Nor dread too much the spoiling of her charms:
Indeed 'twas all embarrassing alarms.
Don't think, said I, that either can deceive;
I ev'ry thing shall hear, you may believe;
Know, Nicia is a man, who well may say,
He's trusted without measure ev'ry day.

PRAY recollect my very life 's at stake,
And do not many difficulties make.
Convince thereby how much your spouse you love;
'Twill pleasure doubtless give the pow'rs above.
But should the blockhead any how prove shy
Send instantly to me; I shall be nigh;
I'm going now to rest; by no means fail;
We'll soon contrive and ev'ry way prevail.
But there was no necessity for this;
'Tis pretty clear that nothing went amiss.
In fact the rustick liked the business well,
And seemed unwilling to resign the belle,
I pity him, and much lament his lot;
But—he must die and soon will be forgot:
A fig for those who used to crack their jest;
In nine months' time a child will be the test.

The Rhemese

NO city I to Rheims would e'er prefer:
Of France the pride and honour I aver;
The Holy Ampoule* and delicious wine,
Which ev'ry one regards as most divine,
We'll set apart, and other objects take:
The beauties round a paradise might make!
I mean not tow'rs nor churches, gates, nor streets;
But charming belles with soft enchanting sweets:
Such oft among the fair Rhemese we view:
Kings might be proud those graces to pursue.

ONE 'mong these belles had to the altar led,
A painter, much esteemed, and who had bread.
What more was requisite!—he lived at ease,
And by his occupation sought to please.
A happy woman all believed his wife;
The husband's talents pleased her to the life:
For gallantry howe'er he was renowned,
And many am'rous dames, who dwelled around,
Would seek the artist with a double aim:
So all our chronicles record his fame.

---

* The Saint Ampoule, or Holy Ampulla, a vial said to have descended from heaven, in which was oil for anointing the kings of France at the coronation, and formerly kept at Rheims.

But since much penetration 's not my boast,
I just believe—what's requisite at most.

WHENE'ER the painter had in hand a fair,
He'd jest his wife, and laugh with easy air;
But Hymen's rights proceeding as they ought,
With jealous fears her breast was never fraught.
She might indeed repay his tricks in kind,
And gratify, in soft amours, her mind,
Except that she less confidence had shown,
And was not led to him the truth to own.

AMONG the men attracted by her smiles,
Two neighbours, much delighted with her wiles;
Were often tempted, by her sprightly wit,
To listen to her chat, and with her sit;
For she had far the most engaging mien,
Of any charmer that around was seen.
Superior understanding she possessed;
Though fond of laughter, frolick, fun, and jest.
She to her husband presently disclosed
The love these cit-gallants to her proposed;
Both known for arrant blockheads through the town,
And ever boasting of their own renown.
To him she gave their various speeches, tones,
Each silly air: their tears, and sighs, and groans;
They'd read, or rather heard, we may believe,
That, when in love, with sighs fond bosoms heave.
Their utmost to succeed these coxcombs tried,
And seemed convinced they should not be denied;
A common cause they would the business hold,

And what one knew the other must be told.
Whichever first a favour might obtain,
Should tell his happiness to t'other swain.

YE FAIR 'tis thus they oft your kindness treat:
The pleasure that he wished alone is sweet.
LOVE, is no more; of t'other, laid in earth,
We've here no traces scarcely from the birth.
You serve for sport and prey, to giddy youth,
Devoid of talents, principles, and truth.
'Tis right they should suppose, still two are found;
Who take their course continually round.
The first that in your pleasure grounds appears;
I'd have you, on his wings, to use the shears.

OUR lady then, her lovers to deceive,
One day observed—you shall, my friends, this eve;
Drink wine with me:—my husband will away,
And, what's delightful, till to-morrow stay;
We shall ourselves be able to amuse,
And laugh, and sing, and talk as we may choose.
'Tis excellent, cried they: things well you frame;
And at the promised hour, the heroes came.

WHEN introduced, and all supposing clear,
A sudden knocking turned their joy to fear;
The door was barred; she to the window flew;
I think, said she, that's to the master due;
And should it prove to be as I suspect:—
'Tis he, I vow:—fly, hide, he'll you detect;
Some accident, suspicion, or design,

Has brought him back to sleep, I now divine:

OUR two gallants, when dangers round them pressed,
A closet entered, mightily distressed;
To get away 'twere folly to have tried;
The husband came, the roast he quickly spied;
With pigeons too, in diff'rent fashions cooked;
Why, hey! said he, as round about he looked:
What guests have you that supper you prepare?
The wife replied: two neighbours taste our fare:
Sweet Alice, and good Simonetta, mean
To-night, at table with us to be seen;
I'm quite rejoiced to think that you are here:
The company will more complete appear;
These dames will, by your presence, nothing lose;
I'll run and hasten them: 'twill you amuse;
The whole is ready; I'll at once away,
And beg, in coming, they'll no more delay.

THE ladies named were wives of our gallants,
So fond of contraband, and smuggled grants,
Who, vexed to be confined, still praised the dame,
For skewing such address to 'scape from blame.
She soon returned, and with her brought the FAIR,
Who, gaily singing, entered free from care.
The painter them received with bow and kiss;
To praise their beauty he was not remiss;
Their dress was charming; all he much admired;
Their presence frolick, fun, and jest inspired,
Which no way pleased the husbands in the cage,
Who saw the freaks with marks of bursting rage:

The door half open gave a view complete,
How freely he their wives was led to treat.

THINGS thus commenced, the supper next was served;
From playful tricks the painter never swerved,
But placed himself at table 'twist the two,
And jest and frolicking would still pursue.
To women, wine, and fun, said he, I drink;
Put round the toast; none from it e'er must shrink;
The order was obeyed; the glass oft filled
The party soon had all the liquor swilled:

THE wife just then, it seems, no servant kept;
More wine to get, she to the cellar stept.
But dreading ghosts, she Simonetta prayed;
To light her down, she was so much afraid.

THE painter was alone with Alice left,
A country belle, of beauty not bereft:
Slight, nicely made, with rather pretty face,
She thought herself possessed of ev'ry grace,
And, in a country town, she well might get
The appellation of a gay coquette.

THE wily spark, perceiving no one near;
Soon ran from compliment to sweet and dear;
Her lips assailed;—the tucker drew aside,
And stole a kiss that hurt her husband's pride,
Who all beheld; but spouses, that are sage,
No trifles heed, nor peccadillos page;
Though, doubtless, when such meetings are possessed,

The simple kiss gives room to dread the rest;
For when the devil whispers in the ear
Of one that sleeps, he wakes at once to fear.

THE husband, howsoe'er, at length perceived
Still more concessions, which his bosom grieved;
While on the neck a hand appeared to please,
The other wandered equally at ease;
Be not offended, love! was often said;
To frantick rage the sight her sposo led,
Who, beating in his hat, was on the move
To sally forth, his wrath to let them prove,
To thrash his wife, and force her spark to feel
his nervous arm could quickly make him reel.

BE not so silly, whispered t'other Wight;
To stir up noise could ne'er be reckoned right;
Be quiet now: consider where we are;
Keep close, or else you'll all our pleasures mar;
Remember, written 'tis, By others do
The same as you would like they should by you;
'Tis proper in this place we should remain
Till all is hushed in sleep: then freedom gain;
That's my opinion how we ought to act
Are you not half a cuckold now, in fact?
Fair Alice has consented:-that's enough;
The rest is mere compliance, nonsense, stuff!

THE husband seemed the reasons to approve;
Some slight attempts the lady made to move;
No time for more. What then? you ask:—Why, then—

The lady put her cap to rights agen;
No mark appeared suspicion to awake,
Except her cheek a scarlet hue might take.
Mere trifle that; from talking it might spring;
And other causes, doubtless, we could bring.

ONE of the belles, howe'er, who went for wine,
Smiled, on returning, at the blushing sign:
The painter's wife; but soon they filled each glass,
And briskly round the bottle seemed to pass;
They drank the host, the hostess, and the FAIR,
Who, 'mong the three, should first her wishes share.

AT length, a second time the bottle failed;
The hostess' fear of ghosts again prevailed,
And mistress Alice now for escort went,
Though much she wished the other to have sent;
With Simonetta she was forced to change,
And leave the painter at his ease to range.

THIS dame at first appeared to be severe
Would leave the room, and feigned to be sincere;
But when the painter seized her by the gown,
She prudence showed, and feared he'd pull her down;
Her clothes might tear, which led her to remain:
On this the husband scarcely could contain;
He seemed resolved his hiding place to leave;
But instantly the other pulled his sleeve;
Be easy friend, said he, it is but right,
That equal favours we should have to-night,
And cuckoldom should take you to his care,

That we alike in ev'ry thing may fare.

ARE we not brothers in adventure, pray?
And such our solemn promises, to-day.
Since one the painter clearly has disgraced,
The other equally should be embraced.
In spite of ev'ry thing you now advance,
Your wife as well as mine shall have a dance;
A hand I'll lend, if wanting it be found;
Say what you will, I'll see she has her round.
She had it then:—our painter tried to please;
The lady equally appeared at ease;
Full time the others gave, and when they came,
More wine was not required by spark nor dame;
'Twas late, and for the day enough he'd done;
Good night was said: their course the belles had run;
The painter, satisfied, retired to rest;
The gay gallants, who lay so long distressed,
The wily hostess from the closet drew,
Abashed, disconsolate, and cuckolds too;
Still worse to think, with all their care and pain;
That neither of them could his wish obtain,
Or e'en return the dame what she procured
Their wives, whom she so cleverly allured.

HERE ends our tale; the business is complete;
In soft amours success alone is sweet.

The Amorous Courtesan

DAN CUPID, though the god of soft amour,
In ev'ry age works miracles a store;
Can Catos change to male coquets at ease;
And fools make oracles whene'er he please;
Turn wolves to sheep, and ev'ry thing so well,
That naught remains the former shape to tell:
Remember, Hercules, with wond'rous pow'r,
And Polyphemus, who would men devour:
The one upon a rock himself would fling,
And to the winds his am'rous ditties sing;
To cut his beard a nymph could him inspire;
And, in the water, he'd his face admire.
His club the other to a spindle changed,
To please the belle with whom he often ranged.

A HUNDRED instances the fact attest,
But sage Boccace has one, it is confessed,
Which seems to me, howe'er we search around,
To be a sample, rarely to be found.
'Tis Chimon that I mean, a savage youth,
Well formed in person, but the rest uncouth,
A-bear in mind, but Cupid much can do,
LOVE licked the cub, and decent soon he grew.
A fine gallant at length the lad appeared;

From whence the change?—Fine eyes his bosom cheered
The piercing rays no sooner reached his sight,
But all the savage took at once to flight;
He felt the tender flame; polite became;
You'll find howe'er, our tale is not the same.

I MEAN to state how once an easy fair,
Who oft amused the youth devoid of care,
A tender flame within her heart retained,
Though haughty, singular, and unrestrained.
Not easy 'twas her favours to procure;
Rome was the place where dwelled this belle impure;
The mitre and the cross with her were naught;
Though at her feet, she'd give them not a thought;
And those who were not of the highest class,
No moments were allowed with her to pass.
A member of the conclave, first in rank,
To be her slave, she'd scarcely deign to thank;
Unless a cardinal's gay nephew came,
And then, perhaps, she'd listen to his flame;
The pope himself, had he perceived her charms,
Would not have been too good to grace her arms.
Her pride appeared in clothes as well as air,
And on her sparkled gold and jewels rare;
In all the elegance of dress arrayed,
Embroidery and lace, her taste displayed.

THE god of soft amour beheld her aim;
And sought at once her haughty soul to tame;
A Roman gentleman, of finest form,
Soon in her bosom raised a furious storm;

Camillus was the name this youth had got;
The nymph's was Constance, that LOVE'S arrow shot:
Though he was mild, good humoured, and serene,
No sooner Constance had his person seen,
And in her breast received the urchin's dart,
Than throbs, and trembling fears o'erwhelmed her heart.
The flame she durst declare no other way,
Than by those sighs, which feelings oft betray.
Till then, nor shame nor aught could her retain;
Now all was changed:—her bashfulness was plain.
As none, howe'er, could think the subtle flame
Would lie concealed with such a haughty dame,
Camillus nothing of the kind supposed.
Though she incessantly by looks disclosed,
That something unrevealed disturbed the soul,
And o'er her mind had absolute control.
Whatever presents Constance might receive,
Still pensive sighs her breast appeared to heave:
Her tints of beauty too, began to fail,
And o'er the rose, the lily to prevail.

ONE night Camillus had a party met,
Of youthful beaux and belles, a charming set,
And, 'mong the rest, fair Constance was a guest;
The evening passed in jollity and jest;
For few to holy converse seemed inclined,
And none for Methodists appeared designed:
Not one, but Constance, deaf to wit was found,
And, on her, raillery went briskly round.

THE supper o'er the company withdrew,

But Constance suddenly was lost to view;
Beside a certain bed she took her seat,
Where no one ever dreamed she would retreat,
And all supposed, that ill, or spirits weak,
She home had run, or something wished to seek.

THE company retired, Camillus said,
He meant to write before he went to bed,
And told his valet he might go to rest
A lucky circumstance, it is confessed.
Thus left alone, and as the belle desired;
Who, from her soul, the spark so much admired;
Yet knew not how the subject to disclose,
Or, in what way her wishes to propose;
At length, with trembling accents, she revealed;
The flame she longer could not keep concealed.

EXCEEDINGLY surprised Camillus seemed,
And scarcely could believe but what he dreamed;
Why, hey! said he, good lady, is it thus,
With favoured friends, you doubtful points discuss?
He made her sit, and then his seat regained
Who would have thought, cried he, you here remained;
Now who this hiding place to you could tell?
'Twas LOVE, fond LOVE! replied the beauteous belle;
And straight a blush her lovely cheek suffused,
So rare with those to Cyprian revels used;
For Venus's vot'ries, to pranks resigned,
Another way, to get a colour, find.

CAMILLUS, truly, some suspicions had,

That he was loved, though neither fool nor mad;
Nor such a novice in the Paphian scene,
But what he could at once some notions glean:
More certain tokens, howsoe'er, to get,
And set the lady's feelings on the fret,
By trying if the gloom that o'er her reigned
Was only sly pretence, he coldness feigned.

SHE often sighed as if her heart would break;
At length love's piercing anguish made her speak:
What you will say, cried she, I cannot guess,
To see me thus a fervent flame confess.
The very thought my face with crimson dyes;
My way of life no shield for this supplies;
The moment pure affection 's in the soul,
No longer wanton freaks the mind control.

MY conduct to excuse, what can I say?
O could my former life be done away,
And in your recollection naught remain,
But what might virtuous constancy maintain
At all event, my frankness overlook,
Too well I see, the fatal path I took
Has such displeasure to your breast conveyed,
My zeal will rather hurt than give me aid;
But hurt or not, I'll idolize you still:
Beat, drive away, contemn me as you will;
Or worse, if you the torment can contrive
I'm your's alone, Camillus, while alive.

TO this harangue the wary youth replied

In truth, fair lady, I could ne'er decide,
To criticise what others round may do.—
'Tis not the line I'd willingly pursue;
And I will freely say, that your discourse
Has much surprised me, though 'tis void of force.
To you it surely never can belong,
To say variety in love is wrong;
Besides, your sex, and decency, 'tis clear,
To ev'ry disadvantage you appear.
What use this eloquence, and what your aim?
Such charms alone as your's could me inflame;
Their pow'r is great, but fully I declare,
I do not like advances from the FAIR.

TO Constance this a thunder-clap appeared;
Howe'er, she in her purpose persevered.
Said she, this treatment doubtless I deserve;
But still, from truth my tongue can never swerve,
And if I may presume my thoughts to speak,
The plan which I've pursued your love to seek,
Had never proved injurious to my cause,
If still my beauty merited applause.
From what you've said, and what your looks express
To please your sight, no charms I now possess.
Whence comes this change?—to you I will refer;
Till now I was admired, you must aver;
And ev'ry one my person highly praised;
These precious gifts, that admiration raised,
Alas! are fled, and since I felt LOVE'S flame,
Experience whispers, I'm no more the same;
No longer have charms that please your eyes:

How happy I should feel if they'd suffice!

THE suppliant belle now hoped to be allowed
One half his bed to whom her sighs were vowed;
But terror closed her lips; she nothing said,
Though oft her eyes were to his pillow led.
To be confused the wily stripling feigned,
And like a statue for a time remained.

AT length he said:—I know not what to do;
Undressing, by myself, I can't pursue.
Shall I your valet call? rejoined the fair;
On no account, said he, with looks of care;
I would not have you in my chamber seen,
Nor thought that here, by night, a girl had been,
Your caution is enough, the belle replied:
Myself between the wall and bed I'll hide,
'Twill what you fear prevent, and ills avoid;
But bolt the door: you'll then be not annoyed;
Let no one come; for once I'll do my best,
And as your valet act till you're undressed;
To am'rous Constance this permission grant
The honour would her throbbing breast enchant.

THE youth to her proposal gave consent,
And Constance instantly to business went;
The means she used to take his clothes were such,
That scarcely once his person felt her touch;
She stopt not there, but even freely chose
To take from off his feet, both shoes and hose
What, say you:—With her hands did Constance this?

Pray tell me what you see therein amiss?
I wish sincerely I could do the same,
With one for whom I feel a tender flame.

BETWEEN the clothes in haste Camillus flew,
Without inviting Constance to pursue.
She thought at first he meant to try her love;
But raillery, this conduct was above.
His aim, howe'er more fully to unfold,
She presently observed:—'Tis very cold;
Where shall I sleep? said she:

CAMILLUS
Just where you please;

CONSTANCE
What, on this chair?

CAMILLUS
No, no, be more at ease;
Come into bed.

CONSTANCE
Unlace me then, I pray.

CAMILLUS
I cannot: I'm undressed, and cold as clay:
Unlace yourself.—

JUST then the belle perceived
A poinard, which anxiety relieved;

She drew it from the scabbard, cut her lace,
And many parts of dress designed for grace,
The works of months, embroidery and flow'r
Now perished in the sixtieth of an hour,
Without regret, or seeming to lament,
What more than life will of the sex content.

YE dames of Britain, Germany, or France,
Would you have done as much, through complaisance?
You would not, I'm convinced: the thing is clear;
But doubtless this, at Rome, must fine appear.

POOR Constance softly to the bed approached,
No longer now supposing she encroached,
And trusting that, no stratagem again
Would be contrived to give her bosom pain.
Camillus said: my sentiments I'll speak;
Dissimulation I will never seek;
She who can proffer what should be denied,
Shall never be admitted by my side;
But if the place your approbation meet,
I won't refuse your lying at my feet.

FAIR Constance such reproof could not withstand,
'Twas well the poinard was not in her hand;
Her bosom so severely felt the smart,
She would have plunged the dagger through her heart:
But Hope, sweet Hope! still fluttered to her view;
And young Camillus pretty well she knew;
Howe'er with such severity he spoke,
That e'en the mildest saint it would provoke;

Yet, in a swain so easy, gentle, kind,
'Twas strange so little lenity to find.

SHE placed herself, as order'd, cross the bed,
And at his feet at length reclined her head;
A kiss on them she ventured to impress,
But not too roughly, lest she should transgress:
We may conjecture if he were at ease;
What victory! to see her stoop to please;
A beauty so renowned for charms and pride,
'Twould take a week, to note each trait described;
No other fault than paleness he could trace,
Which gave her (causes known) still higher grace.

CAMILLUS stretched his legs, and on her breast
Familiarly allowed his feet to rest;
A cushion made of what so fair appeared,
That envy might from ivory be feared;
Then seemed as if to Morpheus he inclined,
And on the pillow sullenly resigned.
At last the sighs with which her bosom heaved,
Gave vent to floods of tears that much relieved;
This was the end:—Camillus silence broke,
And to tell the belle with pleasing accents spoke
I'm satisfied, said he, your love is pure;
Come hither charming girl and be secure.
She t'wards him moved; Camillus near her slid;
Could you, cried he, believe that what I did,
Was seriously the dictates of my soul,
To act the brute and ev'ry way control?
No, no, sweet fair, you know me not 'tis plain:

I truly wish your fondest love to gain;
Your heart I've probed, 'tis all that I desire;
Mid joys I swim; my bosom feels the fire.
Your rigour now in turn you may display;
It is but fair: be bountiful I pray;
Myself from hence your lover I declare;
No woman merits more my bed to share,
Whatever rank, or beauty, sense or life,
You equally deserve to be my wife;
Your husband I'll become; forget the past;
Unpleasant recollections should not last.
Yet there's one thing which much I wish to speak
The marriage must be secret that we seek;
There's no occasion reasons to disclose;
What I have said I trust will you dispose,
To act as I desire: you'll find it best:—
A wedding 's like amours while unconfessed;
One THEN both husband and gallant appears,
And ev'ry wily act the bosom cheers.
Till we, continued he, a priest can find,
Are you, to trust my promises inclined?
You safely may; he'll to his word adhere:
His heart is honest, and his tongue sincere.

TO this fair Constance answered not a word,
Which showed, with him, her sentiments concurred.
The spark, no novice in the dumb assent,
Received her silence fully as 'twas meant;
The rest involved in myst'ry deep remains;
Thus Constance was requitted for her pains.

YE Cyprian nymphs to profit turn my tale;
The god of LOVE, within his vot'ries pale,
Has many, if their sentiments were known,
That I'd prefer for Hymen's joys alone.
My wife, not always to the spindle true,
Will many things in life, not seem to view;
By Constance and her conduct you may see
How, with this theory, her acts agree;
She proved the truth of what I here advance,
And reaped the fruits produced by complaisance,
A horde of nuns I know who, ev'ry night,
Would such adventures wage with fond delight.

PERHAPS it will not be with ease believed,
That Constance from Camillus now received,
A proof of LOVE'S enchanting balmy sweet,
A proof perhaps you'll think her used to meet;
But ne'er till then she tasted pleasures pure;
Her former life no blisses could secure.
You ask the cause, and signs of doubt betray:
Who TRULY loves, the same will ever say.

Nicaise

TO serve the shop as 'prentice was the lot;
Of one who had the name of Nicaise got;
A lad quite ignorant beyond his trade,
And what arithmetick might lend him aid;
A perfect novice in the wily art,
That in amours is used to win the heart.
Good tradesmen formerly were late to learn
The tricks that soon in friars we discern;
They ne'er were known those lessons to begin,
Till more than down appeared upon the chin.
But now-a-days, in practice, 'tis confessed,
These shopkeepers are knowing as the best.

OUR lad of ancient date was less advanced;
At scenes of love his eyes had never glanced;
Be that as 'twill, he now was in the way,
And naught but want of wit produced delay:
A belle indeed had on him set her heart
His master's daughter felt LOVE'S poignant smart;
A girl of most engaging mind and mien,
And always steady in her conduct seen.
Sincerity of soul or humour free,
Or whether with her taste it might agree,
A fool 'twas clear presided o'er her soul,

And all her thoughts and actions felt control.
Some bold gallant would p'erhaps inform her plain,
She ever kept wild Folly in her train,
And nothing say to me who tales relate;
But oft on reason such proceedings wait.
If you a goddess love, advance she'll make;
Our belle the same advantages would take.
Her fortune, wit, and charm, attention drew,
And many sparks would anxiously pursue;
How happy he who should her heart obtain,
And Hymen prove he had not sighed in vain!
But she had promised, to the modest youth,
Who first was named, her confidence and truth;
The little god of pleasing soft desire
With full compliance with his whims require.

THE belle was pleased the 'prentice to prefer:
A handsome lad with truth we may aver,
Quite young, well made, with fascinating eye:
Such charms are ne'er despised we may rely,
But treasures thought, no FAIR will e'er neglect;
Whate'er her senses say, she'll these respect.
For one that LOVE lays hold of by the soul,
A thousand by the eyes receive control.

THIS sprightly girl with soft endearing ease,
Exerted ev'ry care the lad to please,
To his regards she never shy appeared;
Now pinched his arm, then smiled and often leered;
Her hand across his eyes would sometimes put;
At others try to step upon his foot.

To this he nothing offered in reply,
Though oft his throbbing bosom heaved a sigh.

SO many tender scenes, at length we find,
Produced the explanation LOVE designed;
The youthful couple, we may well believe,
Would from each other mutual vows receive;
They neither promises nor kisses spared,
Incalculable were the numbers shared;
If he had tried to keep exact account,
He soon had been bewildered with th' amount;
To such infinity it clearly ran,
Mistakes would rise if he pursued the plan;
A ceremony solely was required,
Which prudent girls have always much admired,
Yet this to wait gave pain and made her grieve;
From you, said she, the boon I would receive;
Or while I live the rapture never know,
That Hymen at his altar can bestow;
To you I promise, by the pow'rs divine,
My hand and heart I truly will resign.
Howe'er I'll freely say, should Hymen fail
To make me your's and wishes not prevail,
You must not fancy I'll become a nun,
Though much I hope to act as I've begun;
To marry you would please me to the soul;
But how can WE the ruling pow'rs control?
Too much I'm confident you love my fame,
To aim at what might bring me soon to shame:
In wedlock I've been asked by that and this;
My father thinks these offers not amiss;

But, Nicaise, I'll allow you still to hope,
That if with others I'm obliged to cope,
No matter whether counsellor or judge.
Since clearly ev'ry thing to such I grudge,
The marriage eve, or morn, or day, or hour,
To you I'll give—the first enchanting flow'r.

THE lad most gratefully his thanks returned;
His breast with ev'ry soft emotion burned.
Within a week, to this sweet charmer came,
A rich young squire, who soon declared his flame;
On which she said to Nicaise:—he will do;
This spark will easily let matters through;
And as the belle was confident of that,
She gave consent and listened to his chat.
Soon all was settled and arranged the day,
When marriage they no longer would delay,
You'll fully notice this:—I think I view
The thoughts which move around and you pursue;
'Twas doubtless clear, whatever bliss in store,
The lady was betrothed, and nothing more.

THOUGH all was fixed a week before the day,
Yet fearing accidents might things delay,
Or even break the treaty ere complete,
She would not our apprentice fully greet,
Till on the very morn she gave her hand,
Lest chance defeated what was nicely planned.

HOWE'ER the belle was to the altar led,
A virgin still, and doomed the squire to wed,

Who, quite impatient, consummation sought,
As soon as he the charmer back had brought;
But she solicited the day apart,
And this obtained, alone by prayers and art.
'Twas early morn, and 'stead of bed she dressed,
In ev'ry thing a queen had thought the best;
With diamonds, pearls, and various jewels rare;
Her husband riches had, she was aware,
Which raised her into rank that dress required,
And all her neighbours envied and admired.
Her lover, to secure the promised bliss,
An hour's indulgence gained to take a kiss.
A bow'r within a garden was the spot,
Which, for their private meeting, they had got.
A confidant had been employed around,
To watch if any one were lurking found.

THE lady was the first who thither came;
To get a nosegay was, she said, her aim;
And Nicaise presently her steps pursued,
Who, when the turf within the bow'r he viewed,
Exclaimed, oh la! how wet it is my dear!
Your handsome clothes will be spoiled I fear!
A carpet let me instantly provide?
Deuce take the clothes! the fair with anger cried;
Ne'er think of that: I'll say I had a fall;
Such accident a loss I would not call,
When Time so clearly on the wing appears,
'Tis right to banish scruples, cares, and fears;
Nor think of clothes nor dress, however fine,
But those to dirt or flames at once resign;

Far better this than precious time to waste,
Since frequently in minutes bliss we taste;
A quarter of an hour we now should prize,
The place no doubt will very well suffice;
With you it rests such moments to employ,
And mutually our bosoms fill with joy.
I scarcely ought to say what now I speak,
But anxiously your happiness I seek.

INDEED, the anxious, tender youth replied,
To save such costly clothes we should decide;
I'll run at once, and presently be here;
Two minutes will suffice I'm very clear.
AWAY the silly lad with ardour flew,
And left no time objections to renew.
His wondrous folly cured the charming dame;
Whose soul so much disdained her recent flame;
That instantly her heart resumed its place,
Which had too long been loaded with disgrace:
Go, prince of fools, she to herself exclaimed,
For ever, of thy conduct, be ashamed;
To lose thee surely I can ne'er regret,
Impossible a worse I could have met.
I've now considered, and 'tis very plain,
Thou merit'st not such favours to obtain;
From hence I swear, by ev'ry thing above;
My husband shall alone possess my love;
And least I might be tempted to betray,
To him I'll instantly the boon convey,
Which Nicaise might have easily received;
Thank Heav'n my breast from folly is relieved.

This said, by disappointment rendered sour,
The beauteous bride in anger left the bow'r.
Soon with the carpet simple Nicaise came,
And found that things no longer were the same.

THE lucky hour, ye suitors learn I pray,
Is not each time the clock strikes through the day,
In Cupid's alphabet I think I've read,
Old Time, by lovers, likes not to be led;
And since so closely he pursues his plan,
'Tis right to seize him, often as you can.
Delays are dangerous, in love or war,
And Nicaise is a proof they fortune mar.

QUITE out of breath with having quickly run;
Delighted too that he so soon had done,
The youth returned most anxious to employ,
The carpet for his mistress to enjoy,
But she alas! with rage upon her brow,
Had left the spot, he knew not why nor how;
And to her company returned in haste
The flame extinguished that her mind disgraced.
Perhaps she went the jewel to bestow,
Upon her spouse, whose breast with joy would glow:
What jewel pray?—The one that ev'ry maid
Pretends to have, whatever tricks she's played.
This I believe; but I'll no dangers run;
To burn my fingers I've not yet begun;
Yet I allow, howe'er, in such a case,
The girl, who fibs, therein no sin can trace.

OUR belle who, thanks to Nicaise, yet retained;
In spite of self, the flow'r he might have gained,
Was grumbling still, when he the lady met
Why, how is this, cried he, did you forget,
That for this carpet I had gone away?
When spread, how nicely on it we might play!
You'd soon to woman change the silly maid;
Come, let's return, and not the bliss evade;
No fear of dirt nor spoiling of your dress;
And then my love I fully will express.

NOT so, replied the disappointed dame,
We'll put it off:—perhaps 'twould hurt your frame
Your health I value, and I would advise,
To be at ease, take breath, and prudence prize;
Apprentice in a shop you now are bound
Next 'prentice go to some gallant around;
You'll not so soon his pleasing art require,
Nor to your tutorage can I now aspire.
Friend Nicaise take some neighb'ring servant maid,
You're quite a master in the shopping trade;
Stuffs you can sell, and ask the highest price;
And to advantage turn things in a trice.
But opportunity you can't discern;
To know its value,—prithee go and learn.

The Progress of Wit

DIVERTING in extreme there is a play,
Which oft resumes its fascinating sway;
Delights the sex, or ugly, fair, or sour;
By night or day:—'tis sweet at any hour.
The frolick, ev'ry where is known to fame;
Conjecture if you can, and tells its name.

THIS play's chief charm to husbands is unknown;
'Tis with the lover it excels alone;
No lookers-on, as umpires, are required;
No quarrels rise, though each appears inspired;
All seem delighted with the pleasing game:—
Conjecture if you can, and tell its name.

BE this as 'twill, and called whate'er it may;
No longer trifling with it I shall stay,
But now disclose a method to transmit
(As oft we find) to ninnies sense and wit.
Till Alice got instruction in this school,
She was regarded as a silly fool,
Her exercise appeared to spin and sew:—
Not hers indeed, the hands alone would go;
For sense or wit had in it no concern;
Whate'er the foolish girl had got to learn,

No part therein could ever take the mind;
Her doll, for thought, was just as well designed.
The mother would, a hundred times a day,
Abuse the stupid maid, and to her say
Go wretched lump and try some wit to gain.

THE girl, quite overcome with shame and pain;
Her neighbours asked to point her out the spot,
Where useful wit by purchase might be got.
The simple question laughter raised around;
At length they told her, that it might be found
With father Bonadventure, who'd a stock,
Which he at times disposed of to his flock.

AWAY in haste she to the cloister went,
To see the friar she was quite intent,
Though trembling lest she might disturb his ease;
And one of his high character displease.
The girl exclaimed, as on she moved,—Will he
Such presents willingly bestow on me,
Whose age, as yet, has scarcely reached fifteen?
With such can I be worthy to be seen?
Her innocence much added to her charms,
The gentle wily god of soft alarms
Had not a youthful maiden in his book,
That carried more temptation in her look.

MOST rev'rend sir, said she, by friends I'm told,
That in this convent wit is often sold,
Will you allow me some on trust to take?
My treasure won't afford that much I stake;

I can return if more I should require;
Howe'er, you'll take this pledge I much desire;
On which she tried to give the monk a ring,
That to her finger firmly seemed to cling.

BUT when the friar saw the girl's design,
He cried, good maid, the pledge we will decline,
And what is wished, provide for you the same;
'Tis merchandize, and whatsoe'er its fame,
To some 'tis freely giv'n:—to others taught
If not too dear, oft better when 'tis bought.
Come in and boldly follow where I lead;
None round can see: you've nothing here to heed;
They're all at prayers; the porter's at my will;
The very walls, of prudence have their fill.

SHE entered as the holy monk desired,
And they together to his cell retired.
The friar on the bed this maiden threw;
A kiss would take:—she from him rather drew;
And said.—To give one wit is this the way?
Yes, answered he, and round her 'gan to play:
Upon her bosom then he put his hand
What now, said she, am I to understand?
Is this the way?—Said he, 'tis so decreed;
Then patiently she let the monk proceed,
Who followed up, from point to point, his aim;
And wit, by easy steps, advancing came,
Till its progression with her was complete;
Then Alice laughed, success appeared so sweet.

A SECOND dose the friar soon bestowed,
And e'en a third, so fast his bounty flowed.
Well, said the monk, pray how d'ye find the play?
The girl replied: wit will not long delay;
'Twill soon arrive; but then I fear its flight:
I'm half afraid 'twill leave me ere 'tis night.
We'll see, rejoined the priest, that naught you lose;
But other secrets oftentimes we use.
Seek not those the smiling girl replied
With this most perfectly I'm satisfied;
Then be it so, said he, we'll recommence,
Nor longer keep the business in suspense,
But to the utmost length at once advance;
For this fair Alice showed much complaisance:
The secret by the friar was renewed;
Much pleasure in it Bonadventure viewed;
The belle a courtesy dropt, and then retired,
Reflecting on the wit she had acquired;
Reflecting, do you say?—To think inclined?
Yes, even more:—she sought excuse to find,
Not doubting that she should be forced to say,
Some cause for keeping her so long away.

TWO days had passed, when came a youthful friend;
Fair Nancy with her often would unbend;
Howe'er, so very thoughtful Alice seemed,
That Nancy (who was penetrating deemed)
Was well convinced whatever Alice sought,
So very absent she was not for naught.
In questioning she managed with such art,
That soon she learned—what Alice could impart

To listen she was thoroughly disposed,
While t'other ev'ry circumstance disclosed,
From first to last, each point and mystick hit,
And e'en the largeness of the friar's wit,
The repetitions, and the wondrous skill
With which he managed ev'ry thing at will.

BUT now, cried Alice, favour me I pray,
And tell at once, without reserve, the way
That you obtained such wit as you possess,
And all particulars to me confess.

IF I, said Nancy, must avow the truth,
Your brother Alan was the bounteous youth,
Who me obliged therewith, and freely taught,
What from the holy friar you'd have bought.
My brother Alan!—Alan! Alice cried;
He ne'er with any was himself supplied;
I'm all surprise; he's thought a heavy clot,
How could he give what he had never got?

FOOL! said the other, little thou can'st know;
For once, to me some information owe;
In such a case much skill is not required,
And Alan freely gave what I desired.
If me thou disbeliev'st, thy mother ask;
She thoroughly can undertake the task.

ON such a point we readily should say,
Long live the fools who wit so well display!

The Sick Abbess

EXAMPLE often proves of sov'reign use;
At other times it cherishes abuse;
'Tis not my purpose, howsoe'er, to tell
Which of the two I fancy to excel.
Some will conceive the Abbess acted right,
While others think her conduct very light
Be that as 'twill, her actions right or wrong,
I'll freely give a license to my tongue,
Or pen, at all events, and clearly show,
By what some nuns were led to undergo,
That flocks are equally of flesh and blood,
And, if one passes, hundreds stem the flood,
To follow up the course the first has run,
And imitate what t'other has begun.
When Agnes passed, another sister came,
And ev'ry nun desired to do the same;
At length the guardian of the flock appeared,
And likewise passed, though much at first she feared.
The tale is this, we purpose to relate;
And full particulars we now will state.

AN Abbess once a certain illness had,
Chlorosis named, which oft proves very bad,
Destroys the rose that decorates the cheek,

And renders females languid, pale, and weak.
Our lady's face was like a saint's in Lent:
Quite wan, though otherwise it marked content.
The faculty, consulted on her case,
And who the dire disorder's source would trace,
At length pronounced slow fever must succeed,
And death inevitably be decreed,
Unless;—but this unless is very strange
Unless indeed she some way could arrange;
To gratify her wish, which seemed to vex,
And converse be allowed with t'other sex:
Hippocrates, howe'er, more plainly speaks,
No circumlocutory phrase he seeks.

O JESUS! quite abashed the Abbess cried;
What is it?—fy!—a man would you provide?
Yes, they rejoined, 'tis clearly what you want,
And you will die without a brisk gallant;
One truly able will alone suffice;
And, if not such, take two we would advise.
This still was worse, though, if we rightly guess,
'Twas by her wished, durst she the truth confess.
But how the sisterhood would see her take
Such remedies and no objection make?
Shame often causes injury and pain;
And ills concealed bring others in their train.

SAID sister Agnes, Madam, take their word;
A remedy like this would be absurd,
If, like old death, it had a haggard look,
And you designed to get by hook or crook.

A hundred secrets you retain at ease;
Can one so greatly shock and you displease?—
You talk at random, Agnes, she replied;
Now, would you for the remedy decide,
Upon your word, if you were in my place?—
Yes, madam, said the nun, and think it grace;
Still more I'd do, if necessary thought;
Your health, by me, would ev'ry way be sought,
And, if required by you to suffer this,
Not one around would less appear remiss;
Sincere affection for you I have shown,
And my regard I'll ever proudly own.

A THOUSAND thanks the Abbess gave her friend;
The doctors said:—no use for them to send;
Throughout the convent sad distress appeared;
When Agnes, who to sage advice adhered,
And was not thought the weakest head around,
A kinder soul perhaps could not be found,
Said to the sisterhood,—What now retains
Our worthy Abbess, and her will enchains,
Is nothing but the shame of pow'rs divine,
Or else, to what's prescribed she would resign.
Through charity will no one take the lead,
And, by example, get her to proceed?

THE counsel was by ev'ry one approved,
And commendation through the circle moved.

IN this design not one, nor grave, nor old,
Nor young, nor prioress, at all seemed cold;

Notes flew around, and friends of worth and taste,
The black, the fair, the brown, appeared in haste;
The number was not small, our records say,
Not (what might be) appearance of delay,
But all most anxious seemed the road to show,
And what the Abbess feared, at once to know;
None more sincerely 'mong the nuns desired,
That shame should not prevent what was required.
Nor that the Abbess should, within her soul,
Retain what might injuriously control.

NO sooner one among the flock had made
The step, of which the Abbess was afraid,
But other sisters followed in the train:—
Not one behind consented to remain;
Each forward pressed, in dread to be the last;
At length, from prejudice the Abbess passed;
To such examples she at last gave way,
And, to a youth, no longer offered nay.

THE operation o'er, her lily face
Resumed the rose, and ev'ry other grace.
O remedy divine, prescription blessed!
Thy friendly aid to numbers stands confessed;
The friends of thousands, friend of nature too;
The friend of all, except where honour 's due.
This point of honour is another ill,
In which the faculty confess no skill.

WHAT ills in life! what mis'ries dire around,
While remedies so easy may be found!

The Truckers

THE change of food enjoyment is to man;
In this, t'include the woman is my plan.
I cannot guess why Rome will not allow
Exchange in wedlock, and its leave avow;
Not ev'ry time such wishes might arise,
But, once in life at least, 'twere not unwise;
Perhaps one day we may the boon obtain;
Amen, I say: my sentiments are plain;
The privilege in France may yet arrive
There trucking pleases, and exchanges thrive;
The people love variety, we find;
And such by heav'n was ere for them designed.

ONCE there dwelled, near Rouen, (sapient clime)
Two villagers, whose wives were in their prime,
And rather pleasing in their shape and mien,
For those in whom refinement 's scarcely seen.
Each looker-on conceives, LOVE needs not greet
Such humble wights, as he would prelates treat.

IT happened, howsoe'er, both weary grown,
Of halves that they so long had called their own;
One holyday, with them there chanced to drink
The village lawyer (bred in Satan's sink);

To him, said one of these, with jeering air,
Good mister Oudinet, a strange affair
Is in my head: you've doubtless often made
Variety of contracts; 'tis your trade:
Now, cannot you contrive, by one of these,
That men should barter wives, like goods, at ease?
Our pastor oft his benefice has changed;
Is trucking wives less easily arranged?
It cannot be, for well I recollect,
That Parson Gregory (whom none suspect)
Would always say, or much my mem'ry fails,
My flock 's my wife: love equally prevails;
He changed; let us, good neighbour do the same;
With all my heart, said t'other, that's my aim;
But well thou know'st that mine's the fairest face,
And, Mister Oudinet, since that's the case,
Should he not add, at least, his mule to boot?
My mule? rejoined the first, that will not suit;
In this world ev'ry thing has got its price:
Mine I will change for thine and that 's concise.
Wives are not viewed so near; naught will I add;
Why, neighbour Stephen, dost thou think me mad,
To give my mule to boot?—of mules the king;
Not e'en an ass I'd to the bargain bring;
Change wife for wife, the barter will be fair;
Then each will act with t'other on the square.

THE village lawyer now the friends addressed:
Said he, Antoinetta is confessed
To have superior charms to those of Jane;
But still, if I may venture to be plain,

Not always is the best what meets the eye,
For many beauties in concealment lie,
Which I prefer; and these are hid with care;
Deceptions, too, are practised by the FAIR;
Howe'er, we wish the whole to be disclosed,
Too much, 'tis said, they must not be exposed.

NOW, neighbours, let us fair arrangement make:
A pig in poke you'd neither give nor take;
Confront these halves in nature's birth-day suit;
To neither, then, will you deceit impute.
The project was most thoroughly approved;
Like inclination both the husbands moved.

ANTOINETTA, said the second spouse,
Has neither ill nor scratch her fears to rouse.
Jane, cried the first, is ev'ry way complete;
No freckles on the skin: as balm she's sweet:
Antoinetta is, her spouse replied,
Ambrosia ev'ry way: no fault to hide.

SAID t'other:—Don't so confident appear;
Thou know'st not Jane: her ways would marble cheer;
And there's a play:—thou understand'st no doubt?
To this rejoined the second village lout,
One diff'rence only have my wife and I:
Which plays the prettiest wiles is what we try;
Thou'lt very soon of these know how to think;
Here's to thee, neighbour; Mister Oud'net, drink;
Come, toast Antoinetta; likewise Jane;
The mule was granted, and the bargain plain:

Our village lawyer promised to prepare,
At once, the writings, which would all declare.
This Oudinet a good apostle proved
Well paid for parchment, or he never moved:
By whom was payment made?—by both the dames;
On neither husband showed he any claims.

THE village clowns some little time supposed
That all was secret: not a hint disclosed;
The parson of it, howsoe'er, obtained
Some intimation, and his off'rings gained.
I was not present, fully I admit;
But rarely clergymen their dues will quit.
The very clerk would not remit his fee:—
All those who serve the church in this agree.

THE permutation could not well be made,
But scandal would such practices upbraid;
In country villages each step is seen;
Thus, round the whisper went of what had been,
And placed at length the thorn where all was ease;
The pow'rs divine alone it could displease.
'Twas pleasant them together to behold;
The wives, in emulation, were not cold;
In easy talk they'd to each other say:
How pleasing to exchange from day to day!
What think you, neighbour, if, to try our luck,
For once we've something new, and valets truck?
This last, if made, the secret had respect;
The other had at first a good effect.

FOR one good month the whole proceeded well;
But, at the end, disgust dispersed the spell;
And neighbour Stephen, as we might suppose,
Began dissatisfaction to disclose;
Lamented much Antoinetta's stop;
No doubt he was a loser by the swop;
Yet neighbour Giles expressed extreme regret,
That t'other from him ought to boot should get:
Howe'er, he would retrucking not consent,
So much he otherwise appeared content.

IT happened on a day, as Stephen strayed
Within a wood, he saw, beneath a shade,
And near the stream, asleep, and quite alone,
Antoinetta, whom he wished his own.
He near her drew, and waked her with surprise;
The change ne'er struck her when she ope'd her eyes;
The gay gallant advantage quickly took,
And, what he wished, soon placed within his hook.
'Tis said, he found her better than at first;
Why so? you ask: was she then at the worst?
A curious question, truly, you've designed;
In Cupid's am'rous code of laws you'll find—
Bread got by stealth, and eat where none can spy,
Is better far than what you bake or buy;
For proof of this, ask those most learn'd in love
Truth we prefer, all other things above;
Yet Hymen, and the god of soft desire,
How much soe'er their union we admire,
Are not designed together bread to bake;
In proof, the sleeping scene for instance take.

Good cheer was there: each dish was served with taste;
The god of love, who often cooks in haste,
Most nicely seasoned things to relish well;
In this he's thought old Hymen to excel.

ANTOINETTA, to his clasp restored,
Our neighbour Stephen, who his wife adored,
Quite raw, howe'er, in this, exclaimed apart
Friend Giles has surely got some secret art,
For now my rib displays superior charms,
To what she had, before she left my arms.
Let's take her back, and play the Norman trick
Deny the whole, and by our priv'lege stick.

IMMEDIATELY he ev'ry effort tried,
To get the bargain fully set aside.
Giles, much distressed, exerted all his might,
To keep his prize, and prove his conduct right.
The cause was carried to the bishop's court;
Much noise it made, according to report.
At length the parliament would hear the claim,
And judge a case of such peculiar fame.

THE village lawyer, Oudinet, was brought;
From him, who drew the contract, truth was sought;
There rests the cause, for 'tis of recent date;
While undecided, more we cannot state.

HOW silly neighbour Stephen must appear!
He went against his int'rest now 'tis clear;
For, when superior pleasure he was shown,

The fascinating fair was not his own.
Good sense would whisper then, ‘twere full as well,
To let remain with Giles the beauteous belle;
Save now and then, within the leafy shade,
Where oft Antoinetta visits made,
And warbled to the shrubs and trees around;
There he might easily the nymph have found,
But, if with ease it could not be obtained,
Still greater pleasure he would then have gained.

GO preach me this to silly country louts;
These, howsoe’er, had managed well their bouts,
It must not be denied, and all was nice;
To do the like perhaps ‘twill some entice.
I much regret my lot was not the same,
Though doubtless many will my wishes blame.

The Case of Conscience

THOSE who in fables deal, bestow at ease
Both names and titles, freely as they please.
It costs them scarcely any thing, we find.
And each is nymph or shepherdess designed;
Some e'en are goddesses, that move below,
From whom celestial bliss of course must flow.

THIS Horace followed, with superior art:—
If, to the trav'ller's bed, with throbbing heart,
The chambermaid approached, 'twas Ilia found,
Or fair Egeria, or some nymph renowned.

GOD, in his goodness, made, one lovely day,
Apollo, who directs the lyrick lay,
And gave him pow'rs to call and name at will,
Like father Adam, with primordial skill.
Said he, go, names bestow that please the ear;
In ev'ry word let sweetest sound appear.
This ancient law then proves, by right divine,
WE oft are sponsors to the royal line.

WHEN pleasing tales and fables I endite,
I, who in humble verse presume to write,
May surely use this privilege of old,

And, to my fancy, appellations mould.
If I, instead of Anne, should Sylvia say,
And Master Thomas (when the case I weigh)
Should change to Adamas, the druid sage,
Must I a fine or punishment engage?
No, surely not:—at present I shall choose
Anne and the Parson for my tale to use.

WITHIN her village, Anne was thought the belle,
And ev'ry other charmer to excel.
As near a river once she chanced to stray,
She saw a youth in Nature's pure array,
Who bathed at ease within the gliding stream;
The girl was brisk, and worthy of esteem,
Her eyes were pleased; the object gave delight;
Not one defect could be produced in sight;
Already, by the shepherdess adored,
If with the belle to pleasing flights he'd soared,
The god of love had all they wished concealed
None better know what should not be revealed.
Anne nothing feared: the willows were her shade,
Which, like Venetian blinds, a cov'ring made;
Her eyes, howe'er, across had easy view,
And, o'er the youth, each beauty could pursue.

SHE back four paces drew, at first, through shame;
Then, led by LOVE, eight others forward came;
But scruples still arose that ardour foiled,
And nearly ev'ry thing had truly spoiled.
Anne had a conscience pure as holy fire;
But how could she abstain from soft desire?

If, in the bosom chance a flame should raise,
Is there a pow'r can then subdue the blaze?
At first these inclinations she withstood;
But doubting soon, how those of flesh and blood
Could sins commit by stepping in advance,
She took her seat upon the green expanse,
And there attentively the lad observed,
With eyes that scarcely from him ever swerved.

PERHAPS you've seen, from Nature, drawings made?
Some Eve, or Adam, artists then persuade,
In birth-attire to stand within their view,
While they with care and taste each trait pursue;
And, like our shepherdess, their stations take,
A perfect semblance ev'ry way to make.

ANNE in her mem'ry now his image placed;
Each line and feature thoroughly she traced,
And even now the fair would there remain,
If William (so was called this youthful swain)
Had not the water left; when she retired,
Though scarcely twenty steps from him admired,
Who, more alert than usual then appeared,
And, by the belle, in silence was revered.

WHEN such sensations once were in the breast,
Love there we may believe would hardly rest.

THE favours Anne reserved he thought his own,
Though expectations oft away have flown.
The more of this I think, the less I know;

Perhaps one half our bliss to chance we owe!

BE this as 'twill, the conscientious Anne
Would nothing venture to regale her man;
Howe'er, she stated what had raised her fear,
And ev'ry thing that made her persevere.

WHEN Easter came, new difficulties rose
Then, in confession, ALL she should disclose.
Anne, passing peccadillos in review,
This case aside, as an intruder threw;
But parson Thomas made her all relate;
And ev'ry circumstance most clearly state;
That he, by knowing fully each defect,
Might punishment accordingly direct,
In which no father-confessor should err,
Who absolution justly would confer.
The parson much his penitent abused;
Said he, with sensual views to be amused,
Is such a sin, 'tis scarcely worse to steal;
The sight is just the same as if you feel.

HOWE'ER, the punishment that he imposed
Was nothing great:—too slight to be disclosed;
Enough to say, that in the country round,
The father-confessors, who there abound,
As in our own, (perhaps in ev'ry part,)
Have devotees, who, when they ought to smart,
A tribute pay, according to their lot,
And thus indulgences are often got.

THIS tribute to discharge the current year,
Much troubled Anne, and filled her breast with fear,
When William, fishing, chanced a pike to hook,
And gave it to his dear at once to cook,
Who, quite delighted, hastened to the priest,
And begged his rev'rence on the fish to feast.
The parson with the present much was pleased;
A tap upon the shoulder care appeased;
And with a smile he to the bringer said
This fish, with trifles on the table spread,
Will all complete; 'twas holyday we find,
When other clergy with our rector dined.
Will you still more oblige, the parson cried,
And let the fish at home by you be fried?
Then bring it here:—my servant's very new,
And can't attempt to cook as well as you.
Anne hastened back; meanwhile the priests arrived,
Much noise, and rout of course, once these were hived;
Wines from the vault were brought without delay;
Each of the quality would something say.

THE dinner served; the dean at table placed;
Their conversation various points embraced;
To state the whole would clearly endless be;
In this no doubt the reader will agree.
They changed and changed, and healths went round and round;
No time for scandal while such cheer was found;
The first and second course away were cleared,
Dessert served up, yet still no pike appeared.
The dinner o'er without th' expected dish,

Or even a shadow of the promised fish.
When William learned the present Anne had made,
His wish, to have it cancelled, with her weighed.
The rector was surprised, you may suppose,
And, soon as from the table all arose,
He went to Anne, and called her fool and knave,
And, in his wrath, could scarcely secrets wave,
But nearly her reproached the bathing scene;
What, treat, said he, your priest like base and mean?

ANNE archly answered, with expression neat:—
The sight is just the same as if you eat!

The Devil of Pope-Fig Island

BY master Francis clearly 'tis expressed:
The folks of Papimania are blessed;
True sleep for them alone it seems was made
With US the copy only has been laid;
And by Saint John, if Heav'n my life will spare,
I'll see this place where sleeping 's free from care.
E'en better still I find, for naught they do:
'Tis that employment always I pursue.
Just add thereto a little honest love,
And I shall be as easy as a glove.

ON t'other hand an island may be seen,
Where all are hated, cursed, and full of spleen.
We know them by the thinness of their face
Long sleep is quite excluded from their race.

SHOULD you, good reader, any person meet,
With rosy, smiling looks, and cheeks replete,
The form not clumsy, you may safely say,
A Papimanian doubtless I survey.
But if, on t'other side, you chance to view,
A meagre figure, void of blooming hue,
With stupid, heavy eye, and gloomy mien
Conclude at once a Pope-figer, you've seen.

POPE-FIG 'S the name upon an isle bestowed,
Where once a fig the silly people showed,
As like the pope, and due devotion paid:—
By folly, blocks have often gods been made!
These islanders were punished for their crime;
Naught prospers, Francis tells us, in their clime;
To Lucifer was giv'n the hateful spot,
And there his country house he now has got.
His underlings appear throughout the isle,
Rude, wretched, poor, mean, sordid, base, and vile;
With tales, and horns, and claws, if we believe,
What many say who ought not to deceive.

ONE day it happened that a cunning clown
Was by an imp observed, without the town,
To turn the earth, which seemed to be accurst,
Since ev'ry trench was painful as the first.
This youthful devil was a titled lord;
In manners simple:—naught to be abhorred;
He might, so ignorant, be duped at ease;
As yet he'd scarcely ventured to displease:
Said he, I'd have thee know, I was not born,
Like clods to labour, dig nor sow the corn;
A devil thou in me beholdest here,
Of noble race: to toil I ne'er appear.

THOU know'st full well, these fields to us belong:
The islanders, it seems, had acted wrong;
And, for their crimes, the pope withdrew his cares;
Our subjects now you live, the law declares;

And therefore, fellow, I've undoubted right,
To take the produce of this field, at sight;
But I am kind, and clearly will decide
The year concluded, we'll the fruits divided.
What crop, pray tell me, dost thou mean to sow?
The clod replied, my lord, what best will grow
I think is Tousell; grain of hardy fame;
The imp rejoined, I never heard its name;
What is it. Tousell, say'st thou?—I agree,
If good return, 'twill be the same to me;
Work fellow, work; make haste, the ground prepare;
To dig and delve should be the rabble's care;
Don't think that I will ever lend a hand,
Or give the slightest aid to till the land;
I've told thee I'm a gentleman by birth,
Designed for ease: not doomed to turn the earth.
Howe'er I'll now the diff'rent parts allot,
And thus divide the produce of the plot:—
What shall above the heritage arise,
I'll leave to thee; 'twill very well suffice;
But what is in the soil shall be my share;
To this attend, see ev'ry thing is fair.

THIS beardless corn when ripe, with joy was reaped,
And then the stubble by the roots was heaped,
To satisfy the lordly devil's claim,
Who thought the seed and root were just the same,
And that the ear and stalk were useless parts,
Which nothing made if carried to the marts:
The labourer his produce housed with care;
The other to the market brought his ware,

Where ridicule and laughter he received;
'Twas nothing worth, which much his bosom grieved.

QUITE mortified, the devil quickly went;
To seek our clod, and mark his discontent:
The fellow had discreetly sold the corn,
In straw, unthrashed, and off the money borne,
Which he, with ev'ry wily care, concealed;
The imp was duped, and nothing was revealed.
Said he, thou rascal?—pretty tricks thou'st played;
It seems that cheating is thy daily trade;
But I'm a noble devil of the court,
Who tricking never knew, save by report.
What grain dost mean to sow th' ensuing year?
The labourer replied, I think it clear,
Instead of grain, 'twill better be to chop,
And take a carrot, or a turnip crop;
You then, my lord, will surely plenty find;
And radishes, if you are so inclined.

THESE carrots, radishes, and turnips too,
Said t'other, I am led to think will do;
My part shall be what 'bove the soil is found:
Thine, fellow, what remains within the ground;
No war with thee I'll have, unless constrained,
And thou hast never yet of me complained.
I now shall go and try to tempt a nun,
For I'm disposed to have a little fun.

THE time arrived again to house the store;
The labourer collected as before;

Leaves solely to his lordship were assigned,
Who sought for those a ready sale to find,
But through the market ridicule was heard,
And ev'ry one around his jest preferred:—
Pray, Mister Devil, where d'ye grow these greens?
How treasure up returns from your demesnes?

ENRAGED at what was said, he hurried back,
And, on the clown, proposed to make attack,
Who, full of joy, was laughing with his wife,
And tasting pleasantly the sweets of life.
By all the pow'rs of Hell, the demon cried,
He shall the forfeit pay, I now decide;
A pretty rascal truly, master Phil:
Here, pleasures you expect at will,
Well, well, proceed; gallant it while allowed;
For present I'll remit what I had vowed;
A charming lady I'm engaged to meet;
She's sometimes willing: then again discreet;
But soon as I, in cuckold's row, have placed
Her ninny husband, I'll return in haste,
And then so thoroughly I'll trim you o'er,
Such wily tricks you'll never practise more;
We'll see who best can use his claws and nails,
And from the fields obtain the richest sales.
Corn, carrots, radishes, or what you will:—
Crop as you like, and show your utmost skill
No stratagems howe'er with culture blend;
I'll take my portion from the better end;
Within a week, remember, I'll be here,
And recollect:—you've every thing to fear.

AMAZED at what the lordly devil said,
The clod could naught reply, so great his dread;
But at the gasconade Perretta smiled,
Who kept his house and weary hours beguiled,
A sprightly clever lass, with prying eye,
Who, when a shepherdess, could more descry,
Than sheep or lambs she watched upon the plain,
If other views or points she sought to gain.
Said she, weep not, I'll undertake at ease,
To gull this novice-devil as I please;
He's young and ignorant; has nothing seen;
Thee; from his rage, I thoroughly will skreen;
My little finger, if I like can show
More malice than his head and body know.

THE day arrived, our labourer, not brave,
Concealed himself, but not in vault nor cave;
He plunged within a vase extremely large,
Where holy-water always was in charge;
No demon would have thought to find him there,
So well the clod had chosen his repair;
In sacred stoles he muffled up his skin,
And, 'bove the water, only kept his chin;
There we will leave him, while the priests profound
Repeated Vade retro round and round.

PERRETTA at the house remained to greet
The lordly devil whom she hoped to cheat.
He soon appeared; when with dishevelled hair,
And flowing tears, as if o'erwhelmed with care,
She sallied forth, and bitterly complained,

How oft by Phil she had been scratched and caned;
Said she, the wretch has used me very ill;
Of cruelty he has obtained his fill;
For God's sake try, my lord, to get away:
Just now I heard the savage fellow say,
He'd with his claws your lordship tear and slash:
See, only see, my lord, he made this gash;
On which she showed:—what you will guess, no doubt,
And put the demon presently to rout,
Who crossed himself and trembled with affright:
He'd never seen nor heard of such a sight,
Where scratch from claws or nails had so appeared;
His fears prevailed, and off he quickly steered;
Perretta left, who, by her friends around,
Was complimented on her sense profound,
That could so well the demon's snares defeat;
The clergy too pronounced her plan discrete.

Feronde

IN Eastern climes, by means considered new;
The Mount's old-man, with terrors would pursue;
His large domains howe'er were not the cause,
Nor heaps of gold, that gave him such applause,
But manners strange his subjects to persuade;
In ev'ry wish, to serve him they were made.
Among his people boldest hearts he chose,
And to their view would Paradise disclose
Its blissful pleasures:—ev'ry soft delight,
Designed to gratify the sense and sight.
So plausible this prophet's tale appeared,
Each word he dropt was thoroughly revered.
Whence this delusion?—DRINK deranged the mind;
And, reason drowned, to madness they resigned.
Thus void of knowing clearly what they did,
They soon were brought to act as they were bid;
Conveyed to places, charming to the eye,
Enchanting gardens 'neath an azure sky,
With twining shrubs, meandring walks, and flow'rs,
And num'rous grottos, porticoes and bow'rs.
When they chanced to pass where all was gay,
From wine's inebriating pow'rful sway,
They wondered at the frolicking around,
And fancied they were got on fairy ground,

Which Mahomet pretended was assigned,
For those to his doctrine were inclined.
To tempt the men and girls to seek the scene,
And skip and play and dance upon the green,
To murm'ring streams, meandering along,
And lutes' soft notes and nightingales' sweet song:
No earthly pleasure but might there be viewed,
The best of wines and choicest fruits accrued,
To render sense bewildered at the sight,
And sink inebriated with delight.

THEN back they bore them motionless to sleep,
And wake with wishes further joys to reap.
From these enjoyments many fully thought,
To such enchanting scenes they should be brought,
In future times, eternal bliss to taste,
If death and danger valiantly they faced,
And tried the prophet Mahomet to please,
And ev'ry point to serve their prince would seize.

THE Mount's old man, by means like these, could say;
He'd men devoted to support his sway;
Upon the globe no empire more was feared,
Or king or potentate like him revered.
These circumstances I've minutely told,
To show, our tale was known in days of old.

FERONDE, a rich, but awkward, vulgar clown,
A ninny was believed throughout the town;
He had the charge of revenues not slight,
Which he collected for a friar white.

Of these I've known as good as any black,
When husbands some assistance seemed to lack,
And had so much to do, they monks might need;
Or other friends, their work at home to speed.
This friar for to-morrow never thought,
But squandered ev'ry thing as soon as brought;
No saint-apostle less of wealth retained;
Good cheer o'er ev'ry wish triumphant reigned,
Save now and then to have a little fun,
(Unknown to others) with a pretty nun.

FERONDE had got a spouse of pleasing sight,
Related nearly to our friar white,
Whose predecessor, uncle, sponsor kind,
Now gone to realms of night, had her consigned,
To be this silly blockhead's lawful wife,
Who thought her hand the honour of his life.
'Tis said that bastard-daughters oft retain
A disposition to the parent-train;
And this, the saying, truly ne'er bellied,
Nor was her spouse so weak but he descried,
Things clearer than was requisite believed,
And doubted much if he were not deceived.

THE wife would often to the prelate go,
Pretending business, proper he should know;
A thousand circumstances she could find;
'Twas then accounts: now sev'ral things combined;
In short no day nor hour within the week,
But something at the friar's she would seek.
The holy father then was always prone,

To send the servants off and be alone.
Howe'er the husband, doubting tricks were played;
Got troublesome; his wife would much upbraid
When she returned, and often beat her too;
In short,—he unaccommodating grew.

THE rural mind by nature jealous proves;
Suspicion shows of ev'ry thing that moves;
Unused to city ways, perverse appears,
And, undismayed, to principle adheres:

THE friar found his situation hard;
He loved his ease?—all trouble would discard;
As priests in gen'ral anxiously desire;
Their plan howe'er I never can admire,
And should not choose at once to take the town,
But by the escalade obtain the crown;
In LOVE I mean; to WAR I don't allude:
No silly bragging I would here intrude,
Nor be enrolled among the martial train:
'Tis Venus' court that I should like to gain.
Let t'other custom be the better way:
It matters not; no longer I'll delay,
But to my tale return, and fully state,
How our receiver, who misused his mate;
Was put in purgatory to be cured,
And, for a time, most thoroughly immured.

BY means of opiate powders, much renowned,
The friar plunged him in a sleep profound.
Thought dead; the fun'ral obsequies achieved,

He was surprised, and doubtless sorely grieved,
When he awoke and saw where he was placed,
With folks around, not much to suit his taste;
For in the coffin he at large was left,
And of the pow'r to move was not bereft,
But might arise and walk about the tomb,
Which opened to another vaulted room,
The gloomy, hollow mansion of the dead:
Fear quickly o'er his drooping spirits spread.
What's here? cried he: is't sleep, or is it death;
Some charm or spell perhaps withdraws their breath.
Our wight then asked their names and business there;
And why he was retained in such a snare?
In what had he offended God or man?—

SAID one, console thyself:—past moments scan;
When thou hast rested here a thousand years,
Thou'lt then ascend amid the Heav'nly spheres;
But first in holy purgatory learn,
To cleanse thyself from sins that we discern;
One day thy soul shall leave this loathsome place,
And, pure as ice, repair to realms of grace.
Then this consoling Angel gave a thwack,
And ten or dozen stripes laid on his back:—
'Tis thy unruly, jealous mind, said he,
Displeases God, and dooms thee here to be.

A MOURNFUL sigh the lorn receiver heaved,
His aching shoulders rubbed, and sobbed and grieved;
A thousand years, cried he, 'tis long indeed!
My very soul with horror seems to bleed.

WE should observe, this Angel was a wag,
A novice-friar and a convent fag;
Like him the others round had parts to act,
And were disguised in dresses quite exact.
Our penitent most humbly pardon sought;
Said he, if e'er to life again I'm brought,
No jealousy, suspicion's hateful bane,
Shall ever enter my distracted brain.
May I not have this grace, this wished for boon?
Some hopes they gave, but it could not be soon;
In short a year he lay upon the floor:
Just food for life received, and nothing more,
Each day on bread and water he was fed,
And o'er his back the cat-o'nine-tails spread:
Full twenty lashes were the number set,
Unless the friar should from Heav'n first get
Permission to remit at times a part,
For charity was glowing in his heart.

WE, must not doubt, he often offered prayers,
To ease the culprit's sufferings and cares.
The Angel likewise made a long discourse;
Said he, those vile suspicions were the source,
Of all thy sorrow, wretchedness, and pain:
Think'st thou such thoughts the clergy entertain?
A friar white!—too bad in ev'ry sense:
Ten strokes to one, if black, for such offence.
Repent, I say:—the other this desired,
Though scarcely he could tell what was required.

MEANWHILE the prelate with the fav'rite dame,

No time to lose, made ev'ry hour the same.
The husband, with a sigh, was heard to say:
I wonder what my wife's about to-day?
About?—whate'er it be 'tis doubtless right;
Our friar, to console her, takes delight;
Thy business too is managed as before,
And anxious care bestowed upon thy store.

HAS she as usual matters that demand
Attendance at the cloister to be scanned?—
No doubt was the reply, for having now
The whole affair upon her feeble brow,
Poor woman! be her wishes what they will,
She more assistance wants thy loss to fill.

DISCOURSE like this no pleasure gave the soul:
To call him so seems best upon the whole,
Since he'd not pow'r like others here to feed:—
Mere earthly shadow for a time decreed.

A MONTH was passed in fasting, pains, and prayer;
Some charity the friar made him share,
And now and then remission would direct;
The widow too he never would neglect,
But, all the consolation in his pow'r,
Bestowed upon her ev'ry leisure hour,
His tender cares unfruitful were not long;
Beyond his hopes the soil proved good and strong;
In short our Pater Abbas justly feared,
To make him father many signs appeared.

SINCE 'twere improper such a fact were known;
When proofs perhaps too clearly might be shown,
So many prayers were said and vigils kept,
At length the soul from purgatory crept,
So much reduced, and ev'ry way so thin
But little more he seemed than bones and skin.

A THING so strange filled numbers with surprise,
Who scarcely would believe their ears and eyes.
The friar passed for saint:—Feronde his fruit;
None durst presume to doubt nor to dispute;
A double miracle at once appeared
The dead's return: the lady's state revered.
With treble force Te Deum round was sung;
Sterility in marriage oft was rung,
And near the convent many offered prayers,
In hopes their fervent vows would gain them heirs.

THE humble spouse and wife we now shall leave
Let none, howe'er, suppose that we conceive,
Each husband merits, as our soul, the same,
To cure the jealous fears his breast inflame.

The Psalter

ONCE more permit me, nuns, and this the last;
I can't resist, whatever may have passed,
But must relate, what often I've been told;
Your tales of convent pranks are seldom cold;
They have a grace that no where else we find,
And, somehow, better seem to please designed.
Another then we'll have, which three will make:—
Three did I say?-'tis four, or I mistake;
Let's count them well:-The GARD'NER first, we'll name;
Then comes the ABBESS, whose declining frame
Required a youth, her malady to cure
A story thought, perhaps, not over pure;
And, as to SISTER JANE, who'd got a brat,
I cannot fancy we should alter that.
These are the whole, and four's a number round;
You'll probably remark, 'tis strange I've found
Such pleasure in detailing convent scenes:—
'Tis not my whim, but TASTE, that thither leans:
And, if you'd kept your breviary in view,
'Tis clear, you'd nothing had with this to do;
We know, howe'er, 'tis not your fondest care;
So, quickly to our hist'ry let's repair.

A CHARMING youth would frequent visits pay,

To nuns, whose convent near his dwelling lay;
And, 'mong the sisters, one his person saw,
Who, by her eyes, would fain attention draw;
Smiles she bestowed, and other complaisance,
But not a single step would he advance;
By old and young he greatly was admired;
Sighs burst around, but none his bosom fired.
Fair Isabella solely got his love,
A beauteous nun, and gentle as a dove,
Till then a novice in the flow'ry chain,
And envied doubly:—for her charms and swain.
Their soft amours were watched with eagle-eye:
No pleasure's free from care you may rely;
In life each comfort coupled is with ill,
And this to alter baffles all our skill.

THE sister nuns so vigilant had been,
One night when darkness overspread the scene;
And all was proper mysteries to hide,
Some words escaped her cell that doubts supplied,
And other matters too were heard around,
That in her breviary could not be found.
'Tis her gallant! said they: he's clearly caught;
Alarm pervaded; swarms were quickly brought;
Rage seemed to triumph; sentinels were placed;
The abbess too must know they were disgraced.
Away they hastened to convey surprise,
And, thund'ring at her door, cried, madam rise,
For sister Isabella, in her cell,
Has got a man, which surely can't be well.

YOU will observe, the dame was not at prayer,
Nor yet absorbed in sleep, devoid of care,
But with her then, this abbess had in bed
Good parson John, by kindness thither led,
A neighb'ring rector, confessor, and friend;
She rose in haste the sisters to attend,
And, seeking for her veil, with sense confused,
The parson's breeches took for what she used,
Which, in the dark, resembled what was worn
By nuns for veils, and called (perhaps in scorn),
Among themselves, their PSALTER, to express
Familiarly, a common, awkward dress.

WITH this new ornament, by way of veil,
She sallied forth and heard the woeful tale.
Then, irritated, she exclaimed with ire
To see this wretched creature I desire,
The devil's daughter, from her bold career,
Who'll bring our convent to disgrace, I fear;
But God forbid, I say, and with his leave,
We'll all restore:—rebuke she shall receive.
A chapter we will call:—the sisters came,
And stood around to hear their pious dame.

FAIR Isabella now the abbess sent,
Who straight obeyed, and to her tears gave vent,
Which overspread those lily cheeks and eyes,
A roguish youth so lately held his prize.
What! said the abbess: pretty scandal here,
When in the house of God such things appear;
Ashamed to death you ought to be, no doubt,

Who brought you thither?—such we always scout.

NOW Isabella, (—sister you must lose,
Henceforth, that name to you we cannot use;
The honour is too great,) in such a case,
Pray are you sensible of your disgrace,
And what's the punishment you'll undergo?
Before to-morrow, this you'll fully know;
Our institution chastisement decrees;
Come speak, I say, we'll hear you if you please.

POOR Isabella, with her sight on ground,
Confused, till then had scarcely looked around,
Now raised her eyes, and luckily perceived
The breeches, which her fears in part relieved,
And that the sisters, by surprise unnerved,
As oft's the case, had never once observed.
She courage took, and to the abbess said,
There's something from the Psalter, on your head,
That awkwardly hangs down; pray, madam, try
To put it right, or 'twill be in your eye.

'TWAS knee-strings, worn, at times, by priests and beaux,
For, more or less, all follow fashion's laws.
This veil, no doubt, had very much the air
Of those unmentionables parsons wear;
And this the nun, to frolicking inclined,
It seems had well impressed upon her mind.
What, cried the abbess, dares she still to sneer?
How great her insolence to laugh and jeer,
When sins so heavily upon her rest,

And ev'ry thing remains quite unconfessed.
Upon my word, she'd be a saint decreed;
My veil, young imp, your notice cannot need;
'Tis better think, you little hellish crow,
What pains your soul must undergo below.

THE mother abbess sermonized and fired,
And seemed as if her tongue would ne'er be tired.
Again the culprit said, your Psalter, pray,
Good madam, haste to set the proper way;
On which the sisters looked, both young and old
THOSE 'gan to laugh, while THESE were heard to scold.

OUR preacher, quite ashamed of what she'd done,
Now lost her voice, and noticed not the nun;
The murmur buzzed around, too well expressed,
What thoughts the holy sisterhood possessed.
At length the abbess said:—we've now not time
To take the chapter's votes upon her crime;
'Twould make it late; let each to bed return,
And, till to-morrow, we'll the case adjourn.
No chapter met, howe'er, when morrow came;
Another day arrived, and still the same;
The sages of the convent thought it best,
In fact, to let the mystick business rest.
Much noise, perhaps, would hurt religion's cause,
And, that considered, prudent 'twere to pause.
Base envy made them Isabella hate,
And dark suspicions to the abbess state.
In short, unable by their schemes to get
The morsel she'd so fortunately met,

Each nun exerted all her art to find,
What equally might satisfy the mind.
Old friends were willingly received again;
Her gallant our belle was suffered to retain;
The rector and the abbess had their will;
And, such their union, precepts to fulfill,
That if a nun had none to give her bliss,
To lend a friend was nothing thought amiss.

King Candaules and the Doctor of Laws

IN life oft ills from self-imprudence spring;
As proof, Candaules' story we will bring;
In folly's scenes the king was truly great:
His vassal, Gyges, had from him a bait,
The like in gallantry was rarely known,
And want of prudence never more was shown.

MY friend, said he, you frequently have seen
The beauteous face and features of the queen;
But these are naught, believe me, to the rest,
Which solely can be viewed when quite undressed.
Some day I'll let you gratify your eyes;
Without her knowledge I'll means devise;
But on condition:—you'll remember well
What you behold, to no one you will tell,
In ev'ry step most cautiously proceed,
And not your mind with silly wishes feed;
No sort of pleasure surely I could take,
To see vain passion you her lover make.
You must propose, this charming form to view,
As if mere marble, though to nature true;
And I'm convinced you'll readily declare,
Beyond nor art can reach, nor thought prepare;

Just now I left her in the bath at ease:
A judge you are, and shall the moment seize;
Come, witness my felicity supreme;
You know her beauties are my constant theme.

AWAY they went, and Gyges much admired;
Still more than that: in truth his breast was fired;
For when she moved astonishment was great,
And ev'ry grace upon her seemed to wait.
Emotion to suppress howe'er he tried,
Since he had promised what he felt to hide;
To hold his tongue he wished, but that might raise
Suspicions of designs and mystick ways.
Exaggeration was the better part,
And from the subject he would never start,
But fully praised each beauty in detail,
Without appearing any thing to veil.
Gods! Gyges cried, how truly, king, you're blessed;
The skin how fair—how charming all the rest!

THIS am'rous conversation by the queen
Was never heard, or she'd enraged have been;
In ancient days of ignorance, we find,
The sex, to show resentment, much inclined;
In diff'rent light at present this appears,
And fulsome praises ne'er offend their ears.

OUR arch observer struggled with his sighs
Those feelings much increased, so fair the prize:
The prince, in doubt, conducted him away;
But in his heart a hundred arrows lay;

Each magick charm directed pointed darts;
To flee were useless: LOVE such pain imparts,
That nothing can at times obstruct its course;
So quick the flight: so truly great the force.

WHILE near the king, much caution Gyges showed;
But soon the belle perceived his bosom glowed;
She learned the cause:—her spouse the tale disclosed,
And laughed and jeered, as he the facts exposed:
A silly blockhead! not to know a queen
Could raillery not bear on such a scene.
But had it pleased her wishes, still 'twere right
(Such honour's dictates) to discover spite;
And this she truly did, while in her mind,
To be revenged she fully was inclined.

FOR once, good reader, I should wish thee wife;
Or otherwise, thou never can'st in life,
Conceive the lengths a woman oft will go,
Whose breast is filled with wrath and secret woe.
A mortal was allowed these charms to view,
Which others' eyes could never dare pursue.
Such treasures were for gods, or rather kings
The privilege of both are beauteous things.

THESE thoughts induced the queen revenge to seek;
Rage moved her breast, and shame possessed her cheek.
E'en Cupid, we are told, assistance gave;
What from his aim effectually can save?
Fair in person was Gyges to behold;
Excuses for her easy 'twere to mould;

To show her charms, what baseness could excel?
And on th' exposer all her hatred fell.
Besides, he was a husband, which is worse
With these each sin receives a double curse.
What more shall I detail?—the facts are plain:
Detested was the king:—beloved the swain;
All was accomplished, and the monarch placed
Among the heroes who with horns are graced;
No doubt a dignity not much desired,
Though in repute, and easily acquired.

SUCH merit had the prince's folly got,
'In petto', Vulcan's brother was his lot;
The distance thence is little to the HAT:
The honour much the same of this or that.

SO far 'twas passing well, but, in the intrigue;
The cruel Parcae now appeared to league;
And soon the lovers, on possession bent,
To black Cocytus' shores the monarch sent;
Too much of certain potions forced to drink,
He quickly viewed the dreary, horrid brink;
While pleasing the objects Gyges' eyes beheld;
And in the palace presently he dwelled,
For, whether love or rage the widow fired,
Her throne and hand she gave, as was required.

T' EXTEND this tale was never my design;
Though known full well, I do not now repine;
The case so thoroughly my purpose served.
Ne'er from the narrative the object swerved;

And scarcely can I fancy, better light
The DOCTOR will afford to what I write.
The scenes that follow I from Rome have drawn;
Not Rome of old, ere manners had their dawn,
When customs were unpleasant and severe
The females, silly, and gallants in fear;
But Rome of modern days, delightful spot!
Where better tastes have into fashion got,
And pleasure solely occupies the mind
To rapture ev'ry bosom seems resigned.
A tempting journey truly it appears,
For youths from twenty on to thirty years.

NOT long ago, then, in the city dwelled,
A master, who in teaching law excelled;
In other matters he, howe'er, was thought
A man that jollity and laughter sought.
He criticised whatever passed around,
And oft, at others' cost, diversion found.

IT happened that our learned doctor had,
Among his many pupils (good and bad)
A Frenchman, less designed to study laws,
Than, in amours, perhaps, to gain applause.
One day, observing him with clouded mien,
My friend, said he, you surely have the spleen,
And, out of college, nothing seem to do;
No law books read:—some object I'd pursue;
A handsome Frenchman should his hours improve;
Seek soft intrigues, or as a lover move;
Talents you have, and gay coquettes are here

Not one, thank heav'n, but numbers oft appear.

THE student answered, I am new at Rome,
And, save the belles who sell their beauteous bloom,
I can't perceive, gallants much business find,
Each house, like monasteries, is designed,
With double doors, and bolts, and matrons sour,
And husbands Argus-eyed, who'd you devour.
Where can I go to follow up your plan,
And hope, in spots like these, a flame to fan?
'Twere not less difficult to reach the moon,
And with my teeth I'd bite it just as soon.

HA! HA! replied the doctor with delight,
The honour which you do us is not slight;
I pity men quite fresh and raw like you;
Our town, I see, you've hardly travelled through,
You fancy then, such wily snares are set,
'Tis difficult intrigues in Rome to get.
I'd have you know, we've creatures who devise,
To horn their husbands under Argus' eyes.
'Tis very common; only try around,
And soon you'll find, that sly amours abound.
Within the neighb'ring church go take your place,
And, to the dames who pass in search of grace,
Present your fingers dipt in water blessed:—
A sign for those who wish to be caressed.
In case the suppliant's air some lady please,
Who knows her trade, and how to act at ease,
She'll send a message, something to desire:
You'll soon be found, wherever you retire,

Though lodged so secretly, that God alone,
Till then, your place of residence had known.
An aged female will on you attend,
Who, used to this, will full assistance lend,
Arrange an interview with wily art;
No trouble take, you'll have an easy part;
No trouble did I say? why, that's too much;
Some things I would except, their pow'r is such;
And proper 'tis, my friend, that I should hint,
Attentions you at Rome should well imprint,
And be discrete; in France you favours boast:
Of ev'ry moment here you make the most;
The Romans to the greatest lengths proceed.

SO best, the spark replied, I like the deed;
And, though no Gascon, I may boldly say;
Superior prowess always I display.
Perhaps 'twas otherwise, for ev'ry wight;
In this, to play the Gascon, thinks it right.

TO all the doctor's words our youth adhered,
And presently within a church appeared,
Where daily came the choicest belles around,
And loves and graces in their train were found,
Or, if 'tis wished in modern phrase to speak,
Attention num'rous angels there would seek.
Beneath their veils were beauteous sparkling eyes;
The holy-water scarcely would suffice.

IN lucky spot the spark his station took,
And gave to each that passed a plaintive look;

To some he bowed; to others seemed to pray,
And holy water offered on their way.
One angel 'mong the rest the boon received,
With easy pleasing air, that much relieved;
On which the student to himself expressed,
A fond belief, with her he might be blessed.

WHEN home, an aged female to him came,
And soon a meeting place he heard her name.
To count particulars howe'er were vain
Their pranks were many, and their folly plain;
The belle was handsome; ev'ry bliss was sought,
And all their moments most delightful thought.

HE, to the doctor, ev'ry matter told
Discretion in a Frenchman would be cold;
'Tis out of nature, and bespeaks the cit;
Smells strong of shop, and would not fashion fit.

THE learned teacher satisfaction showed,
That such success from his instructions flowed,
Laughed heartily at husbands, silly wights,
Who had not wit to guard connubial rights,
And from their lamb the wily wolf to keep:
A shepherd will o'erlook a hundred sheep,
While foolish man's unable to protect,
E'en one where most he'd wish to be correct.
Howe'er, this care he thought was somewhat hard,
But not a thing impossible to guard;
And if he had not got a hundred eyes,
Thank heav'n, his wife, though cunning to devise,

He could defy:—her thoughts so well he knew,
That these intrigues she never would pursue.

YOU'LL, ne'er believe, good reader, without shame,
The doctor's wife was she our annals name;
And what's still worse, so many things he asked,
Her look, air, form, and secret charms unmasked,
That ev'ry answer fully seemed to say,
'Twas clearly she, who thus had gone astray.
One circumstance the lawyer led to doubt:
Some talents had the student pointed out,
Which she had never to her husband shown,
And this relief administered alone.
Thought he, those manners not to her belong,
But all the rest are indications strong,
And prove the case; yet she at home is dull;
While this appears to be a prattling trull,
And pleasing in her conversation too;
In other matters 'tis my wife we view,
Form, face, complexion, features, eyes, and hair,
The whole combined pronounces her the fair.

AT length, when to himself the sage had said
'Tis she; and then, 'tis not;—his senses led
To make him in the first opinion rest,
You well may guess what rage was in his breast.
A second meeting you have fixed? cried he;
Yes, said the Frenchman, that was made with glee;
We found the first so pleasing to our mind,
That to another both were well inclined,
And thoroughly resolved more fun to seek.

That's right, replied the doctor, have your freak;
The lady howsoe'er I now could name.
The scholar answered, that to me's the same;
I care not what she's called, Nor who she be:
'Tis quite enough that we so well agree.
By this time I'm convinced her loving spouse.
Possesses what an anchorite might rouse;
And if a failure any where be met,
At such a place to-morrow one may get,
What I shall hope, exactly at the hour,
To find resigned and fully in my pow'r:

IN bed I shall be instantly received,
And from anxiety be soon relieved.
The place of meeting is a room below,
Most nicely furnished, rich, but void of show.
At first I through a passage dark was led,
Where Sol's bright rays are ne'er allowed to spread;
But soon, by my conductress, I was brought,
'Mid LOVE'S delights, where all with charms was frought.

ON this you may suppose the doctor's pain;
But presently he thought a point to gain,
And take the student's place by wily art,
Where, acting in disguise the lover's part,
His rib he might entangle in a net,
And vassalage bestow she'd ne'er forget.
Our learned man was clearly in the wrong;
'Twere better far to sleep and hold his tongue;
Unless, with God's assistance, he could raise
A remedy that merited full praise.

Whenever wives have got a candidate,
To be admitted to the Cuckold's state,
If thence he get scot free 'tis luck indeed;
But once received, and ornaments decreed,
A blot the more will surely nothing add,
To one already in the garment clad.
The doctor otherwise however thought;
Yet still his reason no advantage brought;
Indeed he fancied, if he could forestall
The youth who now he might his master call;
The trick would to his wisdom credit do,
And show, superior wiles he could pursue.

AWAY the husband hastened to the place;
In full belief, that, hiding well his face,
And favoured by the darkness of the spot,
The silence marked, and myst'ry of the plot,
He, undiscovered, safely might be led,
Where such delicious fruits were ready spread.

MISFORTUNE, howsoe'er, would so direct
The aged female nothing to neglect,
Had with her got a lantern to conduct,
The light from which at will she could obstruct,
And, far more cunning than our learned sage,
Perceived at once with whom she had t'engage;
But, marking no surprise, she bade him wait,
While she, his coming, to her dame should state.
Said she, unless I tell her first you're here,
I dare not let you in her room appear.
Besides, you have not got the right attire;

Undressed, in truth, is what she would desire.
My lady, you must know, is gone to bed:—
Then, thrusting in a dressing room his head,
He there beheld the necessary fare,
Of night-cap, slippers, shirt, and combs for hair,
With perfumes too, in Rome the nicest known,
And fit for highest cardinals to own.
His clothes the learned doctor laid aside;
The aged female came his steps to guide;
Through passages she led him by the hand,
Where all was dark, and many turnings planned;
At once bewildered, and deprived of sight,
The lawyer tottered much for want of light.
At length she ope'd a door, and pushed the sage,
Where most unpleasantly he must engage,
Though doubtless ev'ry way his proper place:—
The school where he was used the LAWS to trace!
O'ercome with shame, confusion, and surprise,
He nearly fainted, vain 'twere to disguise.

THE circumstances ran throughout the town;
Each student then was waiting in his gown;
Enough, no doubt, his fortunes to destroy;
The laugh went round, and all was jest and joy.
What, is he mad? said they, or would he seek
Some lass, and with her wish to have a freak?
Still worse arrived:—his beauteous spouse complained;
A trial followed, and distractions reigned;
Her relatives supported well the cause,
And represented, that the MAN of LAWS,
Occasioned jars and matrimonial strife;

That he was mad, and she, a prudent wife,
The marriage was annulled, and she withdrew:
Retirement now the lady would pursue,
In Vavoureuse a prelate blessed the dame,
And, at Saint Croissant, she a nun became.

The Devil in Hell

HE surely must be wrong who loving fears;
And does not flee when beauty first appears.
Ye FAIR, with charms divine, I know your fame;
No more I'll burn my fingers in the flame.
From you a soft sensation seems to rise,
And, to the heart, advances through the eyes;
What there it causes I've no need to tell:
Some die of love, or languish in the spell.
Far better surely mortals here might do;
There's no occasion dangers to pursue.
By way of proof a charmer I will bring,
Whose beauty to a hermit gave the sting:
Thence, save the sin, which fully I except;
A very pleasant intercourse was kept;
Except the sin, again I must repeat,
My sentiments on this will never meet
The taste of him at Rome, who wine had swilled,
Till, to the throat, he thoroughly was filled,
And then exclaimed, is't not a sin to drink?
Such conduct horrid ever I shall think;
I wish to prove, e'en saints in fear should live;
The truth is clear:—our faults may Heav'n forgive;
If dread of punishment, from pow'rs divine,
Had led this friar in the proper line,

He never had the charming girl retained,
Who, young and artless, would your heart have gained.

HER name was Alibech, if I recollect;
Too innocent, deceptions to detect.
One day this lovely maiden having read,
How certain pious, holy saints were led,
The better to observe religious care,
To seek retirement in some lorn repair,
Where they, like Heav'nly Angels, moved around,
Some here, some there, were in concealment found,
Was quite delighted, strange as it may seem,
And presently she formed the frantick scheme,
Of imitating those her mind revered,
And to her plan most rigidly adhered.

WITH silent steps the innocent withdrew;
To mothers, sisters,—none she bade adieu.
Long time she walked through fields, and plain, and dale;
At length she gained a wood within a vale;
There met an aged man, who once might be,
Gay, airy, pleasing, blithe, gallant, and free,
But now a meagre skeleton was seen
The shadow only of what late he'd been:
Said she, good father, I have much desire
To be a saint: thither my hopes aspire;
I fain would merit reverence and prayer,
A festival have kept with anxious care;
What pleasure, ev'ry year, the palm in hand,
And, beaming round the head, a holy band,
Nice presents, flow'rs, and off'rings to receive

Your practice difficult must I believe?
Already I can fast for many days,
And soon should learn to follow all your ways.
Go, said the aged man, your plan resign;
I'd have you, as a friend, the state decline;
'Tis not so easy sanctity to meet,
That fasting should suffice the boon to greet.
Heav'n guards from ill the maids and wives who fast,
Or holiness would very seldom last.
'Tis requisite to practise other things;
These secrets are, which move by hidden springs;
A hermit, whom you'll find beneath yon' beech,

CAN, better far than I, their virtues teach;
Go, seek him, pray, make haste if you are sage;
I ne'er retain such birds within my cage.
This having said, at once he left the belle,
And wisely shut the door, and barred his cell:
Not trusting hair-cloth, fasting, age, nor gout;
With beauty, anchorites themselves should doubt.

OUR pensive fair soon found the person meant,
A man whose soul was on religion bent;
His name was Rustick, young and warm in prayer;
Such youthful hermits of deception share.
Her holy wish, the girl to him expressed,
A wish most fervent doubtless to be blessed,
And felt so strongly, Alibech had fear,
Some day the mark might on her fruit appear.

A SMILE her innocence from Rustick drew;

Said he, in me you little learning view;
But what I've got, I'll readily divide,
And nothing from your senses try to hide.

THE hermit surely would have acted right;
Such pupil to have sent away at sight.
He managed otherwise, as we shall state;
The consequences, let us now relate.

SINCE much he wished perfection to pursue;
He, to himself, exclaimed: what can'st thou do?
Watch, fast, and pray; wear hair-cloth too; but this
Is surely little that will lead to bliss;
All do as much, but with a FAIR to dwell,
And, never touch her, would be to excel;
'Twere triumph 'mong the Heav'nly Angels thought;
Let's merit it, and keep what here is brought;
If I resist a thing so sweet and kind,
I gain the end that pow'rs divine designed.

HE with him let the charming belle remain;
And confident he could at will abstain,
Both Satan and the flesh at once defied:
Two foes on mischief ready to decide.

BEHOLD our saints together in a hut;
Young Rustick, where a corner seemed to jut;
A bed of rushes for the novice placed,
Since sleeping on the floor had her debased,
Who, yet unused to hardships, much must feel:
'Twas best that these should on her senses steal.

A little fruit, and bread not over fine,
She had for supper:—water too for wine.
The hermit fasted; but the lady fed,
And ate with appetite her fruit and bread.

APART their place of rest, the maiden slept,
But something quite awake the other kept:
The Devil could by no means quiet rest,
Till he should get admitted as a guest.
He was received within the humble cell;
The friar's thoughts were on his smiling belle,
Her simple manners, fascinating grace,
Complexion, age; each feature he would trace;
The heaving bosom, and the beauteous charms;
That made him wish to clasp her in his arms.

BY passion moved, he bade at once adieu,
To hair-cloth, discipline, and fasting too;
Cried he, my saints are these; to them I'll pray;
From Alibech no longer he would stay,
But to her flew, and roused the girl from sleep:
Said he, so soon you should not silence keep,
It is not right:—there's something to be done,
Ere we suspend the converse we've begun:
'Tis proper that, to please the pow'rs divine;
We Satan instantly in Hell confine;
He was created for no other end;
To block him up let's ev'ry effort lend.

IMMEDIATELY within the bed he slid,
When, scarcely knowing what young Rustick did;

And, unaccustomed to the mystick scene,
She knew not what the anchorite could mean,
Nor this nor that but, partly by consent,
And partly force, yet wishing to prevent,
Though not presuming to resist his sway
To him 'mid pain and pleasure, she gave way,
Believing ev'ry thing was most exact,
And, what the saint performed, a gracious act,
By thus the Devil shutting up in Hell,
Where he was destined with his imps to dwell.

HENCEFORTH 'twas requisite, if saint she'd be;
From martyrdom she must not think to flee,
For friar Rustick little sought to please:
The lesson was not given quite at ease,
Which made the girl (not much improved in wit)
Exclaim, this Devil mischief will commit;
'Tis very plain, though strange it may appear
To hurt his prison e'en he'll persevere;
The injury now you clearly may perceive;
But, for the evil done, I shall not grieve:
Yet richly he deserves to be again
Shut up effectually in his domain.

IT shall be so, the anchorite replied;
Once more the mystick art was fully tried;
Such care he took, such charity was shown,
That Hell, by use, free with the Devil grown,
His presence pleasant always would have found;
Could Rustick equally have kept his ground.

CRIED Alibech, ‘tis very truly said,
No prison has so nice and soft a bed,
But presently the host will weary grow;
And here our pair soon discord seemed to show:
Hell, for the prisoner, in vain inquired;
Deaf was the fiend, and quietly retired;
Repeated calls of course must irksome prove:
The fair grew weary, when he would not move;
Her strong desire to be a saint declined;
And Rustick to get rid of her designed;
In this with him the belle agreed so well,
That secretly she left the hermit’s cell,
And home returned in haste the shortest way;
But what the fair could to her parents say,
Is what I fain would know, though truly yet;
The full particulars I ne’er could get.
‘Tis probable she made them understand,
Her heart was prompted by divine command;
To try to be a saint; that they believed,
Or seemingly for truth the tale received.
Perhaps the parents were not quite exact,
In narrowly examining the fact;
Though some suspicions doubtless might arise
About her Hell, they could not well disguise;
But ‘tis so formed that little can be seen,
And many jailors in it duped have been.

FOR Alibech great feasting was prepared,
When, through simplicity, the girl declared,
To those around, without the least restraint,
How she had acted to be made a saint.

You'd surely no occasion, they replied,
To go so far instruction to provide,
When at your house you might have had, with ease,
Like secret lectures, just as you should please.
Said one, my brother could the thing have done;
Another cried,—my cousin would have run
To do the same; or Neherbal, who's near,
No novice in the business would appear;
He seeks your hand, which you'll be wise to take
Before he learns—what might a diff'rence make.
She took the hint, and he the fair received;
A handsome fortune many fears relieved;
This joined to num'rous charms that had the belle;
He fancied pure a most suspicious Hell,
And freely used the blessings Hymen sends;
May Heav'n like joys bestow on all our friends!

Neighbour Peter's Mare

A CERTAIN pious rector (John his name),
But little preached, except when vintage came;
And then no preparation he required
On this he triumphed and was much admired.
Another point he handled very well,
Though oft'ner he'd thereon have liked to dwell,
And this the children of the present day,
So fully know, there's naught for me to say:
John to the senses things so clearly brought,
That much by wives and husbands he was sought,
Who held his knowledge of superior price,
And paid attention to his sage advice.
Around, whatever conscience he might find,
To soft delights and easy ways inclined,
In person he would rigidly attend,
And seek to act the confessor and friend;
Not e'en his curate would he trust with these;
But zealously he tried to give them ease,
And ev'ry where would due attention show,
Observing that divines should always know
Their flocks most thoroughly and visit round;
To give instruction and the truth expound.

AMONG the folks, to whom he visits paid,

Was neighbour Peter, one who used the spade;
A villager that God, in lieu of lands,
Had furnished only with a pair of hands,
To dig and delve, and by the mattock gain
Enough his wife and children to maintain.
Still youthful charms you in his spouse might trace;
The weather injured solely had her face,
But not the features which were perfect yet:
Some wish perhaps more blooming belles to get;
The rustick truly me would ne'er have pleased;
But such are oft by country parsons seized,
Who low amours and dishes coarse admire,
That palates more refined would not desire.

THE pastor John would often on her leer,
just as a cur, when store of bones are near,
That would good pickings for his teeth afford,
Attentively behold the precious hoard,
And seem uneasy; move his feet and tail;
Now prick his ears; then fear he can't prevail,
The eyes still fixed upon the bite in sight,
Which twenty times to these affords delight,
Ere to his longing jaws the boon arrives,
However anxiously the suitor strives.

SELF-TORMENTS solely parson John obtained;
By seeing her that o'er his senses reigned.
The village-wife was innocent of this,
And never dreamed of any thing amiss;
The pastor's mystick looks, nor flatt'ring ways;
Nor presents, aught in Magdalene could raise;

But nosegays made of thyme, and marj'ram too,
Were dropt on ground, or never kept in view;
A hundred little cares appeared as naught
'Twas Welch to her, and ne'er conveyed a thought.
A pleasant stratagem he now contrived,
From which, he hoped, success might be derived.

MOST clearly Peter was a heavy lout,
Yet truly I could never have a doubt,
That rashly he would ne'er himself commit,
Though folly 'twere from him to look for wit,
Or aught expect by questioning to find
'Yond this to reason, he was not designed.

THE rector to him said, thou'rt poor, my friend,
And hast not half enough for food to spend,
With other things that necessary prove,
If we below with comfort wish to move.
Some day I'll show thee how thou may'st procure
The means that will thy happiness insure,
And make thee feel contented as a king.
To me what present for it wilt thou bring?

ZOOKS! Peter answered, parson, I desire,
You'll me direct to do as you require;
My labour pray command; 'tis all I've got;
Our pig howe'er to you we can allot,
We want it not; and truly it has eat
More bran than thrice this vessel would complete;
The cow you'll take besides, from which my wife
A calf expects, to raise the means of life.

No, no, the pastor with a smile replied,
A recompense for this thou'lt not provide;
My neighbour to oblige is all I heed;
And now I'll tell thee how thou must proceed;
Thy spouse, by magick, I'll transform each day,
And turn her to a mare for cart or dray,
And then again restore her ev'ry night,
To human form to give thy heart delight.
From this to thee great profit will arise;
Thy ass, so slow is found, that when supplies,
It carries to the market, 'tis so late,
The hour is almost past ere at the gate,
And then thy cabbages, and herbs, and roots,
Provisions, provender, and wares and fruits,
Remain unsold, and home to spoil are brought,
Since rarely far from thence such things are sought.
But when thy wife's a mare, she'll faster go:
Strong, active, ev'ry way her worth she'll show,
And home will come without expense in meat:
No soup nor bread, but solely herbs she'll eat:

SAID Peter, parson, clearly you are wise;
From learning, what advantages arise!
Is this pray sold?—If I'd much money got,
To make the purchase I'd the cash allot.

CONTINUED John:—now I will thee instruct,
The proper manner, matters to conduct,
For thee to have a clever mare by day,
And still at night a charming wife survey;
Face, legs, and ev'ry thing shall reappear;

Come, see it done, and I'll perform it here;
Thou'lt then the method fully comprehend;
But hold thy tongue, or all will quickly end:
A single word the magick would dispel,
And, during life, no more with us 'twould dwell.
Keep close thy mouth and merely ope' thy eyes:
A glimpse alone to learn it will suffice;
This o'er, thyself shall practise it the same,
And all will follow as when first it came.

THE husband promised he would hold his tongue;
And John disliked deferring matters long.
Come, Magdalene, said he, you will undress;
To quit those Sunday-clothes, you'll acquiesce,
And put yourself in Nature's pure array
Well, well, proceed; with stays and sleeves away;
That's better still; now petticoats lay by;
How nicely with my orders you comply.

WHEN Magdalene was to the linen come,
Some marks of shame around her senses swum;
A wife to live and die was her desire,
Much rather than be seen in Eve's attire;
She vowed that, spite of what the priest disclosed;
She never would consent to be exposed.

SAID Peter, pretty work, upon my truth:—
Not let us see how you are made forsooth!
What silly scruples!—Are they in your creed?
You were not always led such scenes to heed:
Pray how d'ye manage when for fleas you seek?

'Tis strange, good sir, that she should be so weak;
What can you fear?—'tis folly time to waste;
He will not eat you: come, I say, make haste:
Have done with haggling; had you acted right,
Ere now the parson all had finished quite.

ON saying this, her garment off he took;
Put on his spectacles to overlook;
And parson John, without delay, began;
Said he (as o'er her person now he ran),
This part umbilical will make the mare
A noble breast, and strength at once declare:
Then further on the pastor placed his hand,
While, with the other, (as a magick wand,)
He set about transforming mounts of snow;
That in our climes a genial warmth bestow,
And semi-globes are called, while those that rise
In t'other hemisphere, of larger size,
Are seldom mentioned, through respect no doubt,
But these howe'er the parson, quite devout,
Would not neglect, and whatsoe'er he felt,
He always named, and on its beauties dwelt;
The ceremony this, it seems, required,
And fully ev'ry movement John admired.

PROCEEDINGS so minute gave Peter pain,
And as he could not see the rector gain
The slightest change, he prayed the pow'rs divine,
To give assistance to the priest's design;
But this was vain, since all the magick spell,
In metamorphosing the lady well,

Depended on the fixing of the tail;
Without this ornament the whole would fail.

TO set it on the parson hastened now,
When Neighbour Peter 'gan to knit his brow,
And bawled so loud, you might have heard him far:
No tail, said he, I'll have: there'll be a scar;
You put it on too low; but vain his cries,
The husband's diligence would not suffice,
For, spite of ev'ry effort, much was done,
And John completely his career had run,
If Peter had not pulled the rector's gown,
Who hastily replied, thou ninny, clown;
Did I not tell thee silence to observe,
And not a footstep from thy station swerve?
The whole is spoiled, insufferable elf!
And for it thou hast got to thank thyself.

THE husband, while the holy pastor spoke,
Appeared to grumble and his stars invoke.
The wife was in a rage, and 'gan to scold:
Said she to Peter, wretch that I behold!
Thou'lt be through life a prey to pain and grief,
Come not to me and bray and hope relief,
The worthy pastor would have us procured
The means that might much comfort have ensured.
Can he deserve such treatment to receive?
Good Mister John this goose I now would leave,
And ev'ry morning, while he gathers fruits,
Or plants, herbs, cabbages, and various roots,
Without averting him, pray, here repair,

You'll soon transform me to a charming mare.

No mare, replied the husband, I desire;
An ass for me is all that I require.

The Spectacles

I LATELY vowed to leave the nuns alone,
So oft their freaks have in my page been shown.
The subject may at length fatigue the mind;
My Muse the veil howe'er is still inclined,
Conspicuously to hold to publick view,
And, 'mong the sisters, scene and scene pursue.
Is this too much?—the nicest tricks they play;
Through soft amours oft artfully they stray,
And these in full I'd readily detail,
If I were sure the subject would not fail;
And that's impossible I must admit,
'Twould endless be, the tales appear so fit;
There's not a clerk so expeditious found,
Who could record the stories known around.
The sisters to forget, were I to try,
Suspicions might arise that, by and by,
I should return: some case might tempt my pen;
So oft I've overrun the convent-den,
Like one who always makes, from time to time,
The conversation with his feelings chime.
But let us to an end the subject bring,
And after this, of other matters sing.

IN former times was introduced a lad

Among the nuns, and like a maiden clad;
A charming girl by all he was believed;
Fifteen his age; no doubts were then conceived;
Coletta was the name the youth had brought,
And, till he got a beard, was sister thought.

THE period howsoe'er was well employed,
And from it Agnes profit had enjoyed;
What profit?—truly better had I said,
That sister Agnes by him was misled,
And store of ills received; misfortune dire
Obliged the nun more girdle to require,
And ultimately to produce (in spite
Of ev'ry wish to guard the fact from light)
A little creature that our hist'ries say,
Was found Coletta's features to display.

GREAT scandal quickly through the convent ran:
How could this child arrive?—the sisters 'gan
To laugh and ask, if in an evil hour,
The mushroom could have fallen with a show'r?
Or self-created was it not supposed?
Much rage the abbess presently disclosed;
To have her holy mansion thus disgraced!
Forthwith the culprit was in prison placed.

THE father to discover next they tried;
How could he enter, pass, escape, or hide;
The walls were high; the grate was double too;
Quite small the turning-box appeared to view,
And she who managed it was very old:—

Perhaps some youthful spark has been so bold,
Cried she who was superior to the rest,
To get admitted, like a maiden dressed,
And 'mong our flock (if rightly I surmise)
A wicked wolf is lurking in disguise.
Undress, I say, I'll verify the fact;
No other way remains for me to act.

THE lad disguised was terrified to death;
Each plan was dissipated with a breath;
The more he thought of means from thence to get,
The greater were the obstacles he met.
At length NECESSITY (the parent found
Of stratagems and wiles, so much renowned,)
Induced the youth . . . (I scarcely can proceed)
To tie . . . expression here I clearly need;
What word will decently express the thought?
What book has got it?—where should it be sought?
You've heard, in days of yore that human kind,
With windows in their bosoms were designed,
Through which 'twas easy all within to see,
And suited those of medical degree.

BUT if these windows useful were believed;
'Twas inconvenient in the heart perceived,
And women thoroughly disliked the scheme:—
They could not find the means to hide a dream.
Dame Nature howsoe'er contrived a plan:—
One lace she gave the woman, one the man,
Of equal length, and each enough no doubt,
By proper care to shut the ope throughout.

The woman much too thick her eyelets placed;
And consequently, ne'er was closely laced;
The fault was all her own: herself the cause;
The man as little merited applause,
For coarsely working, soon the hole was shut,
From which the remnant lace was left to jut;
In fact, on either side, whate'er was done,
The laces never equally would run,
And we are told, both sexes acted wrong:
The woman's was too short; the man's too long.

FROM this 'tis easy, it should seem to guess:
What by the youth was tied in this distress
The end of lace that by the men was left,
When nature ordered them to close the cleft:
With thread he fastened it so very well,
That all was flat as any nun or belle;
But thread or silk, you cannot find a string
To hold, what soon I fear will give a spring,
And get away, in spite of all you do;
Bring saints or angels such a scene to view,
As twenty nuns in similar array,
Strange creatures I should think them:—merely clay,
If they should at the sight unmoved remain;
I speak of nuns, howe'er, whose charms maintain
Superior rank, and like the Graces seem,
Delightful sisters! ev'ry way supreme.

THE prioress, this secret to disclose,
Appeared with spectacles upon her nose;
And twenty nuns around a dress displayed;

That convent mantua-makers never made,
Imagine to yourself what felt the youth,
'Mid this examination of the truth.
The nice proportions and the lily charms
Soon raised within his bosom dire alarms;
Like magick operated on the string,
And from it, what was tied, soon gave a spring;
Broke loose at once, just like a mettled steed,
That, having slipt its halter, flies with speed;
Against the abbess' nose with force it flew,
And spectacles from her proboscis threw.

THOUGH she had nearly fallen on the floor,
In thus attempting secrets to explore,
No jest she thought the accident, 'twas plain,
But would with force the discipline maintain.
A chapter instantly the lady held;
Long time upon the circumstance they dwelled.
The youthful wolf that caused the direful shock;
At length was given to the aged flock,
Who tied his hands and bound him to a tree
Face 'gainst the wood, that none his front might see;
And while the cruel troop, with rage inflamed,
Considered of rewards that vengeance framed;
While some the besoms from the kitchen brought;
And others, in the convent ars'nal sought
The various instruments the sisters used
To punish when obedience was refused;
Another double-locked, within a room.
The nuns of tender hearts and youthful bloom:—
By chance, a friend to sly gallants appeared,

And soon removed, what most our hero feared:
A miller mounted on his mule came by,
A tight-built active lad with piercing eye;
One much admired by all the girls around;
Played well at kayles:—a good companion found.
Aha! cried he, what's here?—a nice affair;
Young man, pray tell me who has placed thee there?
The sisters, say'st thou?—hast thou had thy fun,
And pleased thy fancy with a wanton nun?
Art satisfied?—and was she pretty too?
In truth, to judge by what appears to view,
Thou seemest thoroughly a wily wight,
That convent belles would relish morn and night.

ALAS! replied the other with a sigh,
In vain the nuns my virtue sought to try;
'Twas my misfortune:—patience heav'n bestow;
For worlds such wickedness I would not know.

THE miller laughed at what the other spoke;
Untied his hands, and ev'ry bandage broke.
Said he, thou ninny, scruples can'st thou find
To counteract, and prove to pleasure blind?
The business clearly should to me belong;
Our rector ne'er had thought such conduct wrong,
And never would have played the fool like this;
Fly, haste away, away; I'll thee dismiss,
First having nicely set me in thy place;
Like me thou wert not formed for soft embrace;
I'm stout and able:—quarter ne'er will ask;
Come ALL, these nuns, I'll execute the task,

And many pranks they'll see, unless a freak
Should happen any way the string to break.
The other never asked his wishes twice,
But tied him well, and left him in a trice.

WITH shoulders broad the miller you might see;
In Adam's birth-attire against the tree,
Await the coming of the aged band,
Who soon appeared, with tapers in the hand,
In solemn guise, and whips and scourges dire:
The virgin troop (as convent laws require)
In full procession moved around the Wight;
Without allowing time to catch his sight,
Or giving notice what they meant to do:
How now! cried he:—why won't you take a view?
Deceived you are; regard me well I pray;
I'm not the silly fool you had to-day,
Who woman hates, and scruples seeks to raise:
Employ but me, and soon I'll gain your praise;
I'll wonders execute; my strength appears;
And; if I fail, at once cut off my ears.
At certain pleasant play I'm clever found;
But as to whips—I never was renowned.

WHAT means the fellow? cried a toothless nun;
What would he tell us? Hast thou nothing done?
How!—Art thou not our brat-begetter?—speak;
So much the worse:—on thee our rage we'll wreak,
For him that's gone we'll make thee suffer now;
Once arms in hand, we never will allow
Such characters full punishment to miss;

The play that we desire is THIS and THIS;
Then whips and scourges round him 'gan to move,
And not a little troublesome to prove
The miller, writhing with the poignant smart,
Cried loudly:—I'll exert my utmost art,
Good ladies, to perform what is your due;
The more he bawled, the faster lashes flew.
This work so well the aged troop achieved,
He long remembered what his skin received.

WHILE thus the master chastisement had got;
His mule was feeding on the verdant spot.
But what became of this or that, at last,
I've never heard, and care not how it past.
'Tis quite enough to save the young gallant,
And more particulars we do not want.

MY readers, for a time, could they obtain
A dozen nuns like these, where beauties reign,
Would doubtless not be seen without their dress!
We do not always ev'ry wish express.

The Bucking-Tub

IF once in love, you'll soon invention find
And not to cunning tricks and freaks be blind;
The youngest 'prentice, when he feels the dart,
Grows wondrous shrewd, and studies wily art.
This passion never, we perceive, remains
In want from paucity of scheming brains.
The god of hearts so well exerts his force,
That he receives his dues as things of course.
A bucking-tub, of which a tale is told,
Will prove the case, and this I'll now unfold;
Particulars I heard some days ago,
From one who seemed each circumstance to know.

WITHIN a country town, no matter where,
Its appellation nothing would declare,
A cooper and his wife, whose name was Nan,
Kept house, and through some difficulties ran.
Though scanty were their means, LOVE thither flew;
And with him brought a friend to take a view;
'Twas Cuckoldom accompanied the boy,
Two gods most intimate, who like to toy,
And, never ceremonious, seek to please
Go where they will, still equally at ease;
'Tis all for them good lodging, fare, or bed;

And, hut or palace, pleasantly they tread.

IT happened then, a spark this fair caressed,
And, when he hoped most fully to be blessed,
When all was ready to complete the scene,
And on a point:—if naught should intervene
Not NAMED howe'er will quite enough suffice,
When suddenly the husband, by surprise,
Returned from drinking at an ale-house near,
just when, just when:—the rest is pretty clear.

THEY curst his coming; trouble o'er them spread;
Naught could be done but hide the lover's head;
Beneath a bucking-tub, in utmost haste,
Within the court, our gay gallant was placed.

THE husband, as he entered, loudly cried,
I've sold our bucking-tub. The wife replied,
What price, I pray?—Three crowns rejoined the man;
Then thou'rt a silly ass, said mistress Nan;
To-day, by my address, I've gained a crown,
And sold the same for twenty shillings down:
My bargain luckily the first was made;
The buyer, (who of flaws is much afraid)
Examines now if ev'ry part is tight;
He's in the tub to see if all be right.
What, blockhead, would'st thou do without thy wife?
Thou huntest taverns while she works for life;
But necessary 'tis for her to act,
When thou art out, or naught would be exact.
No pleasure ever yet received have I;

But take my word, to get it now I'll try.
Gallants are plenty; husbands should have wives;
That, like themselves, lead gay or sober lives.

I PRYTHEE softly, wife, the husband said;
Come, come, sir, leave the tub, there's naught to dread;
When you are out, I'll ev'ry quarter scrape,
Then try if water from it can escape;
I'll warrant it to be as good as nice,
And nothing can be better worth the price.

OUT came the lover; in the husband went;
Scraped here and there, and tried if any vent;
With candle in his hand looked round and round,
Not dreaming once that LOVE without was found.
But nothing he could see of what was done;
And while the cooper sought to overrun
The various parts, and by the tub was hid,
The gods already noticed thither slid;
A job was by the deities proposed,
That highly pleased the couple when disclosed;
A very diff'rent work from what within
The husband had, who scraped with horrid din,
And rubbed, and scrubbed, and beat so very well,
Fresh courage took our gay gallant and belle;
They now resumed the thread so sadly lost,
When, by the cooper's coming, all was crossed.

THE reader won't require to know the rest;
What passed perhaps may easily be guessed.
'Tis quite enough, my thesis I have proved;

The artful trick our pair with raptures moved.
Nor one nor t'other was a 'prentice new;
A lover be:—and wiles you'll soon pursue.

The Impossible Thing

A DEMON, blacker in his skin than heart,
So great a charm was prompted to impart;
To one in love, that he the lady gained,
And full possession in the end obtained:
The bargain was, the lover should enjoy
The belle he wished, and who had proved so coy.
Said Satan, soon I'll make her lend an ear,
In ev'ry thing more complaisant appear;
But then, instead of what thou might'st expect,
To be obedient and let me direct,
The devil, having thus obliged a friend,
He'll thy commands obey, thou may'st depend,
The very moment; and within the hour
Thy humble servant, who has got such pow'r,
Will ask for others, which at once thou'lt find;
Make no delay, for if thou art so blind,
Thou comprehend'st, thy body and thy soul
The lovely fair no longer shall control,
But Satan then upon them both shall seize,
And with them do-whatever he may please:
'Gainst this the spark had not a word to say;
'Twas pleasing to command, though not obey.

HE sallied forth the beauteous belle to seek,

And found her as he wished:—complying-meek;
Indulged in blisses, and most happy proved,
Save that the devil always round him moved.
Whatever rose within the whirl of thought
He now commanded:—quickly it was brought;
And when he ordered palaces to rise,
Or raging tempests to pervade the skies,
The devil instantly obeyed his will,
And what he asked was done with wondrous skill.

LARGE sums his purse received;—the devil went
just where commanded, and to Rome was sent,
From whence his highness store of pardons got;
No journey long, though distant was the spot,
But ev'ry thing with magick ease arose,
And all was soon accomplished that he chose.
So oft the spark was asked for orders new,
Which he was bound to give the fiend at view,
That soon his head most thoroughly was drained,
And to the fair our lover much complained,
Declared the truth, and ev'ry thing detailed,
How he was lost, if in commands he failed.

IS'T this, said she, that makes thee so forlorn?
Mere nothing!-quickly I'll remove the thorn;
When Satan comes, present his highness this,
Which I have here, and say:—You will not miss
To make it flat, and not its curl retain
On which she gave him, what with little pain
She drew from covert of the Cyprian grove,
The fairy labyrinth where pleasures rove,

Which formerly a duke so precious thought;
To raise a knightly order thence he sought,
Illustrious institution, noble plan,
More filled with gods and demi-gods than man.

THE lover to the crafty devil said:—
'Tis crooked this, you see, and I am led
To wish it otherwise; go, make it straight;
A perfect line: no turn, nor twist, nor plait.
Away to work, be quick, fly, hasten, run;
The demon fancied it could soon be done;
No time he lost, but set it in the press,
And tried to manage it with great success;
The massy hammer, kept beneath the deep,
Made no impression: he as well might sleep;
Howe'er he beat: whatever charm he used:—
'Twas still the same; obedience it refused.
His time and labour constantly were lost;
Vain proved each effort: mystick skill was crossed;
The wind, or rain, or fog, or frost, or snow,
Had no effect: still circular 'twould go.
The more he tried, the ringlet less inclined
To drop the curvature so closely twined.
How's this? said Satan, never have I seen
Such stubborn stuff wherever I have been;
The shades below no demon can produce,
That could divine what here would prove of use:
'Twould puzzle hell to break the curling spring,
And make a line direct of such a thing.

ONE morn the devil to the other went:

Said he, to give thee up I'll be content;
If solely thou wilt openly declare
What 'tis I hold, for truly I despair;
I'm victus I confess, and can't succeed:
No doubt the thing's impossible decreed.

FRIEND Satan, said the lover, you are wrong;
Despondency should not to you belong,
At least so soon:—what you desire to know
Is not the only one that's found to grow;
Still many more companions it has got,
And others could be taken from the spot.

The Picture

SOLICITED I've been to give a tale,
In which (though true, decorum must prevail),
The subject from a picture shall arise,
That by a curtain's kept from vulgar eyes.
My brain must furnish various features new:
What's delicate and smart produce to view;
By this expressed, and not by t'other said:
And all so clear, most easy to be read,
By ev'ry fool, without the aid of notes,
That idiot's bad indeed who never quotes.

CATULLUS tells us, ev'ry matron sage
Will peep most willingly (whate'er her age),
At that gigantick gift, which Juno made,
To Venus' fruit, in gardens oft displayed.
If any belle recede, and shun the sight,
Dissimulation she supposes right.

THIS principle allowed, why scruples make?
Why, less than eyes, should ears a license take?
But since 'tis so resolved I'll do my best,
And naught in open terms shall be expressed:
A veil shall over ev'ry charm be cast,
Of gauze indeed, and this from first to last,

So nicely done, that howsoever tost,
To none I trust will any thing be lost.
Who nicely thinks, and speaks with graceful ease;
Can current make just whatsoe'er he please;
For all will pass, as I have often known:
The word well chosen, pardon soon is shown,
The sex o'erlook the thing no more the same,
The thought remains, but 'tis without a name;
No blush is raised; no difficulty found;
Yet ev'ry body understands around.

AT present, much I need this useful art:
Why? you will ask; because, when I impart
Such wondrous circumstances, ev'ry belle,
Without reserve, will con them over well.
To this I answer: female ears are chaste,
Though roguish are their eyes, as well as taste.

BE that as 'twill, I certainly should like,
With freedom to explain, by terms oblique,
To belles, how this was broken:—that was down:
Assist me pray, ye NINE of high renown;
But you are maids, and strangers, we agree,
To LOVE'S soft scenes, not knowing A from B.
Remain then, Muses, never stir an inch,
But beg the god of verse, when at a pinch,
To help me out and kind assistance lend,
To choose expressions which will not offend,
Lest I some silly things should chance to say,
That might displeasure raise, and spoil my lay.
Enough, howe'er, we've on the subject said:

'Tis time we t'wards the painting should be led,
Which an adventure you will find contains,
That happened once in Cupid's famed domains.

IN former days, just by Cythera town
A monastery was, of some renown,
With nuns the queens of beauty filled the place,
And gay gallants you easily might trace.
The courtier, citizen, and parson too,
The doctor and the bachelor you'd view,
With eager steps:—all visits thither made;
And 'mong the latter, one (a pleasing blade)
Had free access: was thought a prudent friend,
Who might to sisters many comforts lend;
Was always closely shaved and nicely dressed;
And ev'ry thing he said was well expressed;
The breath of scandal, howsoever pat,
Ne'er lighted on his neat cravat nor hat.

TWO nuns alternatively, from the youth;
Experienced many services, in truth;
The one had recently a novice been;
Few months had passed since she complete was seen;
The other still the dress of novice wore;
The youngest's age was seventeen years, not more
Time doubtless very proper (to be plain)
Love's wily thesis fully to sustain:
The bachelor so well the fair had taught,
And they so earnestly the science sought,
That by experience both the art had learned,
And ev'ry thing most perfectly discerned.

THESE sisters eagerly had made one day
An assignation with the lover gay;
To have the entertainment quite complete,
They'd Bacchus, Ceres too, who Venus greet:
With perfect neatness all the meats were served,
And naught from grace and elegancy swerved;
The wines, the custards, jellies, creams, and ice:
The decorations, ev'ry thing was nice;
What pleasing objects and delights were viewed!
The room with sweetest flow'rs fair Flora strewed;
A sort of garden o'er the linen traced
Here lakes of love:—there names entwined were placed;
Magnificence like this the nuns admired,
And such amusements ardently desired.
Their beauty too incited to be free;
A thousand matters filled their souls with glee;
In height the belles were pretty much the same
Like alabaster fair; of perfect frame;
In num'rous corners Cupid nestling lay:
Beneath a stomacher he'd slyly play,
A veil or scapulary, this or that,
Where least the eye of day perceived he sat,
Unless a lover called to mystick bow'rs,
Where he might hearts entwine with chains of flow'rs;
A thousand times a day the urchin flew,
With open arms the sisters to pursue;
Their charms were such in ev'ry air and look,
Both (one by one) he for his mother took.

WITH anxious looks, the ladies thus prepared,
Expected him who all their kindness shared;

Now they bestowed abuse; next fondly praised:
Then of his conduct dark suspicions raised,
Conceived, a new amour him kept away:
What can it be, said one, that makes him stay?
Of honour an affair.—love—sickness—what?
Said t'other whether it be this or that,
If here again his face he ever show,
A pretty trick in turn we'll let him know.

WHILE thus the couple sought their plot to frame,
A convent porter with a burden came,
For her who kept the stores of ev'ry kind,
Depositary of the whole designed.
'Twas merely a pretence, as I am told:
The things were not required for young or old;
But she much appetite had got in truth,
Which made her have recourse to such a youth,
Who was regarded, in repasts like these,
A first rate cook that all prepared at ease.

THIS awkward, heavy lout mistook the cell;
By chance upon our ladies' room he fell,
And knocked with weighty hands: they ope'd the door.
And gave abuse, but soon their anger o'er,
The nuns conceived a treasure they had found,
And, laughing heartily, no longer frowned,
But both exclaimed at once: let's take this fool;
Of him we easily can make a tool;
As well as t'other, don't you think he'll do?
The eldest added:—let's our whim pursue;
'Tis well determined;—What were we to get,

That here we waited, and are waiting yet?
Fine words and phrases; nothing of the kind;
This wight 's as good, for what we have a mind,
As any bachelor or doctor wise
At all events, for present, he'll suffice.

SHE rightly judged; his height, form, simple air,
And ev'ry act, so clearly void of care,
Raised expectation; this was AEsop's man,
He never thought: 'twas all without a plan;
Both ate and drank, and, had he been at will,
Would matters far have pushed, though void of skill.

FAMILIAR grown, the fellow ready seemed,
To execute whate'er was proper deemed;
To serve the convent he was porter made,
And in their wishes nuns of course obeyed.

'TIS here begins the subject we've in view,
The scene that faithfully our painter drew;
Apollo, give me aid, assistance lend,
Enable me, I pray, to comprehend,
Why this mean stupid rustick sat at ease,
And left the sisters (Claudia, formed to please,
And lovely fair Theresa) all the care?
Had he not better done to give a chair?

I THINK I hear the god of verse reply:
Not quite so fast my friend, you may rely,
These matters never can the probe endure;
I understand you; Cupid, to be sure,

Is doubtless found a very roguish boy,
Who, though he please at times, will oft annoy;
I'm wrong a wicked whelp like this to take,
And, master of the ceremonies make.

NO sooner in a house the urchin gets,
But rules and laws he at defiance sets;
The place of reason whim at once assumes,
Breaks ev'ry obstacle, frets, rages, fumes.
With scenes like these will Cupid oft surprise,
And frantick passion sparkle in his eyes.

SOON on the floor was seen this boorish wight;
For, whether that the chair was rather slight,
Or that the composition of the clown
Was not, like that of geese, of softest down,
Or that Theresa, by her gay discourse,
Had penetrated to the mystick source,
The am'rous pulpit suddenly gave way,
And on the ground the rustick quickly lay.
The first attempt had clearly bad success,
And fair Theresa suffered you may guess.

YE censors keep from hence your eyes prophane;
See, honest hearts, how Claudia tried amain,
To take advantage of the dire mishap,
And all she could, with eagerness entrap;
For in the fall Theresa lost her hold;
The other pushed her:—further off she rolled;
And then, what she had quitted Claudia seized;
Theresa, like a demon quite displeased,

Endeavoured to recover what she'd lost:—
Again to take her seat, but she was crossed.
The sister in possession ne'er inclined
To cede a post so pleasant to her mind;
Theresa raised her hand to give a stroke;
And what of that?—if any thing provoke
When thus engaged, unheeded it remains
Small ills are soon forgot where pleasure reigns.

IN spite of rage apparent in the face;
Of her who in the scuffle lost her place,
The other followed up the road she took;
His course the rustick also ne'er forsook.
Theresa scolded; anger marked her eyes;
In Venus' games contentions oft arise;
Their violence no parallel has seen:—
In proof, remember Menelaus' queen.
Though here to take a part Bellona 's found,
Of cuirasses I see but few around;
When Venus closes with the god of Thrace,
Her armour then appears with ev'ry grace.
The FAIR will understand: enough is said;
When beauty's goddess is to combat led,
Her body-cuirass shows superior charms;
The Cyclops rarely forge such pleasing arms.
Had Vulcan graven on Achilles' shield
The picture we've described, more praise 'twould yield.

THE nun's adventure I in verse have told,
But not in colours, like the action, bold;
And as the story in the picture fails,

The latter seems to lose in my details.
The pen and brush express not quite the same;
Eyes are not ears, however we may aim.

ENTANGLED in the net, I long have left
The fair Theresa, of her throne bereft;
Howe'er, this sister had her turn we find,
So much to please, the porter was inclined,
That both were satisfied, and felt content;
Here ends our tale, and truly I lament,
That not a word about the feast is said,
Though I've no doubt, they freely drank and fed;
And this for reasons easily conceived:
The interlude gave rest that much relieved.
In fine, 'twas well throughout, except, in truth,
The hour of meeting settled with the youth,
Which much embarrasses I will avow,
For if he never came and made his bow,
The sisters had the means, when they might please,
Completely to console themselves at ease;
And if the spark appeared, the belles could hide
Both clown and chair, or any thing beside
The lover what he wanted soon possessed,
And was as usual treated with the best.

The Pack-Saddle

A FAMOUS painter, jealous of his wife;
Whose charms he valued more than fame or life,
When going on a journey used his art,
To paint an ASS upon a certain part,
(Umbilical, 'tis said) and like a seal:
Impressive token, nothing thence to steal.

A BROTHER brush, enamoured of the dame;
Now took advantage, and declared his flame:
The Ass effaced, but God knows how 'twas done;
Another soon howe'er he had begun,
And finished well, upon the very spot;
In painting, few more praises ever got;
But want of recollection made him place
A saddle, where before he none could trace.

THE husband, when returned, desired to look
At what he drew, when leave he lately took.
Yes, see my dear, the wily wife replied,
The Ass is witness, faithful I abide.
Zounds! said the painter, when he got a sight,—
What!—you'd persuade me ev'ry thing is right?
I wish the witness you display so well,
And him who saddled it, were both in Hell.

The Ear-Maker and the Mould-Mender

WHEN William went from home (a trader styled):
Six months his better half he left with child,
A simple, comely, modest, youthful dame,
Whose name was Alice; from Champaign she came.
Her neighbour Andrew visits now would pay;
With what intention, needless 'tis to say:
A master who but rarely spread his net,
But, first or last, with full success he met;
And cunning was the bird that 'scaped his snare;
Without surrendering a feather there.

QUITE raw was Alice; for his purpose fit;
Not overburdened with a store of wit;
Of this indeed she could not be accused,
And Cupid's wiles by her were never used;
Poor lady, all with her was honest part,
And naught she knew of stratagem or art.

HER husband then away, and she alone,
This neighbour came, and in a whining tone,
To her observed, when compliments were o'er:—
I'm all astonishment, and you deplore,
To find that neighbour William's gone from hence,

And left your child's completing in suspense,
Which now you bear within, and much I fear,
That when 'tis born you'll find it wants an ear.
Your looks sufficiently the fact proclaim,
For many instances I've known the same.
Good heav'ns! replied the lady in a fright;
What say you, pray?—the infant won't be right!
Shall I be mother to a one-eared child?
And know you no relief that's certain styled?
Oh yes, there is, rejoined the crafty knave,
From such mishap I can the baby save;
Yet solemnly I vow, for none but you
I'd undertake the toilsome job to do.
The ills of others, if I may be plain,
Except your husband's, never give me pain;
But him I'd serve for ever, while I've breath;
To do him good I'd e'en encounter death.
Now let us see, without more talk or fears,
If I know how to forge the bantling ears.
Remember, cried the wife, to make them like.
Leave that to me, said he, I'll justly strike.
Then he prepared for work; the dame gave way;
Not difficult she proved:—well pleased she lay;
Philosophy was never less required,
And Andrew's process much the fair admired,
Who, to his work extreme attention paid;
'Twas now a tendon; then a fold he made,
Or cartilage, of which he formed enough,
And all without complaining of the stuff.
To-morrow we will polish it, said he:
Then in perfection soon the whole will be;

And from repeating this so oft, you'll get
As perfect issue as was ever met.
I'm much obliged to you, the wife replied,
A friend is good in whom we may confide.

NEXT day, when tardy Time had marked the hour;
That Andrew hoped again to use his pow'r,
He was not plunged in sleep, but briskly flew,
His purpose with the charmer to pursue.
Said he, all other things aside I've laid,
This ear to finish, and to lend you aid.
And I, the dame replied, was on the eve,
To send and beg you not the job to leave;
Above stairs let us go:—away they ran,
And quickly recommenced as they began.
The work so oft was smoothed, that Alice showed
Some scruples lest the ear he had bestowed
Should do too much, and to the wily wight,
She said, so little you the labour slight,
'Twere well if ears no more than two appear;
Of that, rejoined the other, never fear;
I've guarded thoroughly against defects,
Mistake like that shall ne'er your senses vex.

THE ear howe'er was still in hand the same,
When from his journey home the husband came.
Saluted Alice, who with anxious look,
Exclaimed,—your work how finely you forsook,
And, but for neighbour Andrew's kindness here,
Our child would incomplete have been—an ear,
I could not let a thing remain like this,

And Andrew would not be to friends remiss,
But, worthy man, he left his thriving trade,
And for the babe a proper ear has made.

THE husband, not conceiving how his wife,
Could be so weak and ignorant of life,
The circumstances made her fully tell,
Repeat them o'er and on each action dwell.
Enraged at length, a pistol by the bed
He seized and swore at once he'd shoot her dead..
The belle with tears replied, howe'er she'd swerved,
Such cruel treatment never she deserved.
Her innocence, and simple, gentle way,
At length appeared his frantick rage to lay.
What injury, continued she, is done?
The strictest scrutiny I would not shun;
Your goods and money, ev'ry thing is right;
And Andrew told me, nothing he would slight;
That you would find much more than you could want;
And this I hope to me you'll freely grant;
If falsehood I advance, my life I'll lose;
Your equity, I trust, will me excuse.

A LITTLE cooled, then William thus replied,
We'll say no more; you have been drawn aside;
What passed you fancied acting for the best,
And I'll consent to put the thing at rest;
To nothing good such altercations tend;
I've but a word: to that attention lend;
Contrive to-morrow that I here entrap
This fellow who has caused your sad mishap;

You'll utter not a word of what I've said;
Be secret or at once I'll strike you dead.
Adroitly you must act: for instance say;
I'm on a second journey gone away;
A message or a letter to him send,
Soliciting that he'll on you attend,
That something you have got to let him know;—
To come, no doubt, the rascal won't be slow;
Amuse him then with converse most absurd,
But of the EAR remember,—not a word;
That's finished now, and nothing can require;
You'll carefully perform what I desire.
Poor innocent! the point she nicely hit;
Fear oft gives simpletons a sort of wit.

THE arch gallant arrived; the husband came
Ascended to the room where sat his dame;
Much noise he made, his coming to announce;
The lover, terrified, began to bounce;
Now here, now there, no shelter could he meet;
Between the bed and wall he put his feet,
And lay concealed, while William loudly knocked;
Fair Alice readily the door unlocked,
And, pointing with her hand, informed the spouse,
Where he might easily his rival rouse.

THE husband ev'ry way was armed so well,
He four such men as Andrew could repel;
In quest of succour howsoe'er he went:
To kill him surely William never meant,
But only take an ear, or what the Turks,

Those savage beasts, cut off from Nature's works;
Which doubtless must be infinitely worse
Infernal practice and continual curse.
'Twas this he whispered should be Andrew's doom,
When with his easy wife he left the room;
She nothing durst reply: the door he shut,
And our gallant 'gan presently to strut,
Around and round, believing all was right,
And William unacquainted with his plight.

THE latter having well the project weighed,
Now changed his plan, and other schemes surveyed;
Proposed within himself revenge to take,
With less parade:—less noise it then would make,
And better fruit the action would produce,
Than if he were apparently profuse.
Said he to Alice, go and seek his wife;
To her relate the whole that caused our strife;
Minutely all from first to last detail;
And then the better on her to prevail,
To hasten here, you'll hint that you have fears,
That Andrew risks the loss of—more than ears,
For I have punishment severe in view,
Which greatly she must wish I should not do;
But if an ear-maker, like this, is caught,
The worst of chastisement is always sought;
Such horrid things as scarcely can be said:
They make the hair to stand upon the head;
That he's upon the point of suff'ring straight,
And only for her presence things await;
That though she cannot all proceedings stay,

Perhaps she may some portion take away.
Go, bring her instantly, haste quickly, run;
And, if she comes, I'll pardon what's been done.

WITH joy to Andrew's house fair Alice went;
The wife to follow her appeared content;
Quite out of breath, alone she ran up stairs,
And, not perceiving him who shared her cares;
Believed he was imprisoned in a room;
And while with fear she trembled for his doom;
The master (having laid aside his arms)
Now came to compliment the lady's charms;
He gave the belle a chair, who looked most nice:—
Said he, ingratitude's the worst of vice;
To me your husband has been wondrous kind;
So many services has done I find,
That, ere you leave this house, I'd wish to make
A little return, and this you will partake.
When I was absent from my loving dear,
Obligingly he made her babe an ear.
The compliment of course I must admire;
Retaliation is what I desire,
And I've a thought:—your children all have got
The nose a little short, which is a blot;
A fault within the mould no doubt's the cause,
Which I can mend, and any other flaws.
The business now let's execute I pray,
On which the dame he took without delay,
And placed her near where Andrew hid his head,
Then 'gan to operate as he was led.

THE lady patiently his process bore,
And blessed her stars that Andrew's risk was o'er
That she had thus the dire return received,
And saved the man for whom her bosom grieved.
So much emotion William seemed to feel,
No grace he gave, but all performed with zeal;
Retaliated ev'ry way so well,
He measure gave for measure:—ell for ell.
How true the adage, that revenge is sweet!
The plan he followed clearly was discrete;
For since he wished his honour to repair:—
Of any better way I'm not aware.

THE whole without a murmur Andrew viewed,
And thanked kind Heav'n that nothing worse ensued;
One ear most readily he would have lost,
Could he be certain that would pay the cost.
He thought 'twould lucky be, could he get out,
For all considered, better 'twere no doubt,
Howe'er ridiculous the thing appears,
To have a pair of horns than lose his ears.

The River Scamander

I'M now disposed to give a pretty tale;
Love laughs at what I've sworn and will prevail;
Men, gods, and all, his mighty influence know,
And full obedience to the urchin show.
In future when I celebrate his flame,
Expressions not so warm will be my aim;
I would not willingly abuses plant,
But rather let my writings spirit want.
If in these verses I around should twirl,
Some wily knave and easy simple girl,
'Tis with intention in the breast to place;
On such occasions, dread of dire disgrace;
The mind to open, and the sex to set
Upon their guard 'gainst snares so often met.
Gross ignorance a thousand has misled,
For one that has been hurt by what I've said.

I'VE read that once, an orator renowned
In Greece, where arts superior then were found,
By law's severe decree, compelled to quit
His country, and to banishment submit,
Resolved that he a season would employ,
In visiting the site of ancient Troy.
His comrade, Cymon, with him thither went,

To view those ruins, we so oft lament.
A hamlet had been raised from Ilion's wall,
Ennobled by misfortune and its fall;
Where now mere names are Priam and his court;
Of all devouring Time the prey and sport.

O TROY! for me thy very name has got
Superior charms:—in story fruitful spot;
Thy famed remains I ne'er can hope to view,
That gods by labour raised, and gods o'erthrew;
Those fields where daring acts of valour shone;
So many fights were lost:—so many won.

BUT to resume my thread, and not extend
Too much the subjects which our plan suspend;
This Cymon, who's the hero of our tale,
When walking near the banks that form the dale
Through which Scamander's waters freely flow,
Observed a youthful charmer thither go,
To breathe the cool refreshing breeze around;
That on its verdant borders oft she'd found.
Her veil was floating, and her artless dress,
A shepherdess seemed clearly to express.
Tall, elegantly formed, with beauteous mien,
And ev'ry feature lovely to be seen,
Young Cymon felt emotion and surprise,
And thought 'twas Venus that had caught his eyes,
Who on the river's side her charms displayed,
Those wondrous treasures all perfection made.

A GROT was nigh, to which the simple fair,

Not dreaming ills, was anxious to repair;
The heat, some evil spirit, and the place,
Invited her the moment to embrace,
To bathe within the stream that near her ran;
And instantly her project she began.

THE spark concealed himself; each charm admired;
Now this, now that, now t'other feature fired;
A hundred beauties caught his eager sight;
And while his bosom felt supreme delight,
He turned his thoughts advantages to take,
And of the maiden's error something make;
Assumed the character, and dress; and air;
That should a wat'ry deity declare;
Within the gliding flood his vestments dipt:
A crown of rushes on his head he slipt;
Aquatick herbs and plants around he twined:
Then Mercury intreated to be kind,
And Cupid too, the wily god of hearts;
How could the innocent resist these arts?

AT length a foot so fair the belle exposed,
E'en Galatea never such disclosed;
The stream, that glided by, received the prize;
Her lilies she beheld with downcast eyes,
And, half ashamed, herself surveyed at ease,
While round the zephyrs wantoned in the breeze.

WHEN thus engaged, the lover near her drew;
At whose approach away the damsel flew,
And tried to hide within the rocky cell;

Cried Cymon, I beneath these waters dwell,
And o'er their course a sov'reign right maintain;
Be goddess of the flood, and with me reign;
Few rivers could with you like pow'rs divide;
My crystal's clear: in me you may confide;
My heart is pure; with flow'rs I'll deck the stream,
If worthy of yourself the flood you deem;
Too happy should this honour you bestow,
And with me, 'neath the current, freely go.
Your fair companions, ev'ry one I'll make
A nymph of fountains, hill, or grove, or lake;
My pow'r is great, extending far around
Where'er the eye can reach, 'tis fully found.

THE eloquence he used, her fears and dread;
Lest she might give offence by what she said,
In spite of bashfulness that bliss alloys,
Soon all concluded with celestial joys.
'Tis even said that Cupid lent supplies;
From superstition many things arise.

THE spark withdrew, delighted by success;
Return said he:—we'll mutually caress;
But secret prove: let none our union learn;
Concealment is to me of high concern;
To make it publick would improper be,
Till on Olympus' mount the gods we see,
In council met, to whom I'll state the case;
On this the new-made goddess left the place,
In ev'ry thing contented as a dove,
And fully witnessed by the god of love.

Two months had passed, and not a person knew
Their frequent meetings, pleasure to pursue.
O mortals! is it true, as we are told,
That ev'ry bliss at last is rendered cold?
The sly gallant, though not a word he said,
The grot to visit now was rarely led.

AT length a wedding much attention caught;
The lads and lasses of the hamlet sought,
To see the couple pass: the belle perceived
The very man for whom her bosom heaved,
And loudly cried, behold Scamander's flood!
Which raised surprise; soon numbers round her stood,
Astonishment expressed, but still the fair,
Whate'er was asked, would nothing more declare,
Than, in the spacious, blue, ethereal sky,
Her marriage would be soon, they might rely.
A laugh prevailed; for what was to be done?
The god with hasty steps away had run,
And none with stones pursued his rapid flight:
The deity was quickly ought of sight.

WERE this to happen now, Scamander's stream
Would not so easily preserve esteem;
But crimes like these (whoever was abused),
In former days, were easily excused.
With time our maxims change, and what was then,
Though wrong at present, may prevail agen.
Scamander's spouse some raillery received;
But in the end she fully was relieved:
A lover e'en superior thought her charms,

(His taste was such) and took her to his arms.
The gods can nothing spoil! but should they cause
A belle to lose a portion of applause,
A handsome fortune give, and you'll behold,
That ev'ry thing can be repaired by gold.

A Confidant Without Knowing it; or The Stratagem

NO master sage, nor orator I know,
Who can success, like gentle Cupid show;
His ways and arguments are pleasing smiles,
Engaging looks, soft tears, and winning wiles.
Wars in his empire will at times arise,
And, in the field, his standard meet the eyes;
Now stealing secretly, with skilful lure.
He penetrates to hearts supposed secure,
O'erleaps the ramparts that protect around,
And citadels reduces, most renowned.

I DARE engage, two fortresses besiege
Leave one to Mars, and t'other to this liege.
And though the god of war should numbers bring,
With all the arms that can his thunders fling,
Before the fort he'll vainly waste his time,
While Cupid, unattended, in shall climb,
Obtain possession perfectly at ease,
And grant conditions just as he shall please.

I NOW propose to give a fav'rite tale:—
The god of Love was never known to fail,
In finding stratagems, as I have read,

And many have I seen most nicely spread.

THE young Aminta was Gerontes' wife,
With whom she lived, it seems, a wretched life.
Far better she deserved than what she had,
For he was jealous, and his temper bad:
An aged hunks, while she was in the hour
When hearts, that never felt LOVE'S mighty pow'r,
Are presently by tender objects caught,
Which ne'er before had entered in the thought.

WHEN first Aminta saw young Cleon's face,
A lad possessing all engaging grace,
Much prudence then she ev'ry way displayed,
E'en more perhaps than necessary made.
For though we may suppose the lovely fair,
Would ev'ry effort use to 'scape the snare,
Yet when the god of soft persuasion takes
The fatal moment, havock soon he makes,
In vain his duty, any thing opposed,
If once the tender sentiment's disclosed.
Aminta consolation had in view
'Twas that alone the passion from her drew,
A meeting innocent, to vent her tears,
And, to a feeling friend, express her fears.
'Tis represented thus I cannot doubt;
But sight of meat brings appetite about;
And if you would avoid the tempting bit,
'Tis better far at table not to sit.

AMINTA hoped to render Cleon kind;

Poor innocent! as yet to dangers blind,
These conversations she was led to deem,
Mere friendly ways that raised sincere esteem;
And this alone she ardently desired,
Without supposing more would be required,
Or any thing improper be the case:
She'd rather die than suffer such disgrace.
'Twas difficult the business to commence;
A letter 's often lost, or gives offence,
And many serious accidents arrive:
To have a confidant 'twere better strive;
But where could such a female friend be found?
Gerontes dreaded was by all around.
I've said already, Cupid will obtain,
One way or t'other, what he wants to gain;
And this will show the observation just
The maxim's such as you may always trust.

A FEMALE relative young Cleon had,
A peevish prude, who looked upon the lad,
As one she had a right to rule and scold;
Her name was Mistress Alice: sour and old.

ONE summer's day, Aminta to her said:
I cannot think how 'tis, your cousin's led,
(Though quite indifferent he is to me,
And doubtless such will ever prove to be)
With various fond attentions, to pretend,
He loves me—much beyond a common friend.
My window oft he passes day and night;
I cannot move a step, but he's in sight,

And in a moment at my heels appears;
Notes, letters full of soft expressions, dears,
To me are sent by one I will not name,
For known to you, she would be thought to blame:
Pray put an end to such a wild pursuit
It nothing can produce but wretched fruit;
My husband may take fire at things like these;
And as to Cleon.—me he'll never please;
I'll thank you to inform him what I say;
Such steps are useless: folly they betray.

MUCH praise Aminta from the dame received;
Who promised that the conduct, which aggrieved;
To Cleon she would mention, as desired,
And reprimand him, as the fault required:
So well would scold him, that she might be sure,
From him in future she would be secure.

THE foll'wing day our youth to Alice came;
To pay a visit solely was his aim;
She told him what Aminta had declared,
And, in her lecture, words by no means spared.
The lad, surprised, on oath the whole denied,
And vowed to gain her love, he never tried.
Old Alice called her cousin, imp of Hell;
Said she, in all that's wicked, you excel;
You will not all your base designs confess;
The oaths are false on which you lay such stress,
And punishment most richly you deserve;
But false or true, from this I will not swerve,
That you should recollect, Aminta 's chaste,

And never will submit to be disgraced;
Renounce her from this hour; no more pursue:—
That easily, said Cleon, I can do;
Away he went: the case considered o'er;
But still the myst'ry he could not explore.

THREE days had scarcely passed: Aminta came,
To pay a visit to our ancient dame;
Cried she I fear, you have not seen as yet,
This youth, who worse and worse appears to get.
Rage, Mistress Alice, instantly o'erspread,
And ev'ry thing that's vile she of him said.

NO sooner had Aminta gone away,
But she for Cleon sent without delay.
He presently appeared; yet to detail
How Alice stormed, I certainly should fail;
Unless an iron tongue I could obtain:
All Hell was ransacked epithets to gain;
And Lucifer and Beelzebub were used:
No mortal ever was so much abused.

QUITE terrified, poor lad, he scarcely knew;
Her fury was so great, what best to do;
If he allowed that he had acted wrong,
'Twould wound his conscience and defile his tongue.
He home repaired, and turning in his mind
What he had heard, at length his thoughts inclined,
To fancy that Aminta was disposed,
To play some cunning trick, which, not disclosed,
Would operate to bring her wish about;

I see, said he, the scheme I should not doubt;
It surely is my duty kind to be:
Methinks I hear her freely say to me,
O Cleon! show affection, I am yours;
I love her too, for beauty that secures;
And while her seraph charms my bosom fire;
I equally the stratagem admire.
Most freely howsoe'er I will confess,
At first I was so dull, I could not guess
At what she aimed, but now the object's plain:
Aminta o'er my heart desires to reign.

THIS minute, if I durst, I'd thither go,
And, full of confidence, declare my woe,
The subtle flame that burns without controul;
What hurt to paint feelings of my soul?
From balance of accounts 'twill both exempt:
'Tis better far to love than show contempt.
But should the husband find me in the house?—
Ne'er think of that, and try the hunks to chouse.

THEIR course had hardly run three other days,
When fair Aminta, studious still of ways
To have her wish, again to Alice came,
To give dear Cleon notice of her flame.
My home, cried she, 'tis requisite I leave:
To ruin me, your cousin, I perceive,
Is still resolved, for presents now he sends;
But he mistakes, and blindly wealth expends;
I'm clearly not the woman he suspects:
See here, what jewels rare to please the sex!

Nice rubies, diamonds too, but what is more,
My portrait I have found among the store,
Which must have been from memory designed,
Since only with my husband that you'll find.

WHEN I arose, this person known to you,
Whose name I must conceal (to honour true),
Arrived and brought me what I just have shown;
The whole should at your cousin's head be thrown;
And were he present:—but I'll curb my rage;
Allow me to proceed, and you engage
To hear the rest:—he word has also sent,
That as to-day he knew my husband went
On business to his cottage in the wood,
Where he would sleep the night, he understood,
No sooner should the servants be in bed,
And Morpheus' robe be o'er their senses spread,
But to my dressing room he would repair:—
What can he hope, such project to declare?
A meeting place indeed!—he must be mad;
Were I not fearful 'twould affliction add
To my old husband, I would set a watch,
Who, at the entrance, should the villain catch;
Or put him instantly to shame and flight;
This said, she presently was out of sight.

AN hour had passed when Cleon came anew;
The jewels at him in a moment flew;
And scarcely Mistress Alice could refrain,
From wreaking further vengeance on the swain.
Is this your plan? cried she; but what is worse,

I find you still desire a greater curse;
And then she told him all Aminta said,
When last to visit her the fair was led.

HIMSELF most fully warned the youth now thought;
I loved, cried he, 'tis true; but that is naught,
Since nothing from the belle I must expect:
In future her completely I'll neglect.
That is the line, said Alice, you should take;
The lad howe'er was fully now awake,
And thoroughly resolved to seek the dame,
Whose cunning wiles had set him in a flame.

THE midnight hour the clock no sooner told;
Than Cleon ran the myst'ry to unfold,
And to the spot repaired, which he supposed,
Aminta meant, from what had been disclosed;
The place was well described, and there he found;
Awaiting at the door, this belle renowned,
Without attendants: sleep their eyes o'erspread:
Behind thick clouds the very stars had fled:
As all had been expected, in he went,
Most thoroughly they both appeared content;
Few words were used: in haste the pair withdrew,
Where ev'ry wish at ease they might pursue.
The smart gallant at once her beauty praised;
His admiration presently was raised;
Sweet kindness followed; charms were oft admired;
And all was managed as their hearts desired.

SAID youthful Cleon, now you'll tell me why

This stratagem you were induced to try?
For such before in love was never seen;
'Tis excellent, and worthy Beauty's queen.
A lovely blush o'erspread Aminta's face,
And gave her lily-cheeks superior grace.
He praised her person, artifice, and wit,
And did whate'er the moments would admit.

The Clyster

IF truth give pleasure, surely we should try;
To found our tales on what we can rely;
Th' experiment repeatedly I've made,
And seen how much realities persuade:
They draw attention: confidence awake;
Fictitious names however we should take,
And then the rest detail without disguise:
'Tis thus I mean to manage my supplies.

IT happened then near Mans, a Normand town,
For sapient people always of renown,
A maid not long ago a lover had
Brisk, pleasing, ev'ry way a handsome lad;
The down as yet was scarcely on his chin;
The girl was such as many wished to win:
Had charms and fortune, all that was desired,
And by the Mansian sparks was much admired;
Around they swarmed, but vain was all their art
Too much our youth possessed the damsel's heart.

THE parents, in their wisdom, meant the fair
Should marry one who was a wealthy heir;
But she contrived to manage matters well;
In spite of ev'ry thing which might repel,

(I know not how) at length he had access;
Though whether through indulgence or address,
It matters not: perhaps his noble blood
Might work a change when fully understood:
The LUCKY, ev'ry thing contrives to please;
The rest can nothing but misfortune seize.

THE lover had success; the parents thought
His merit such as prudence would have sought;
What more to wish?—the miser's hoarded store:
The golden age's wealth is now no more,
A silly shadow, phantom of the brain;
O happy time! I see indeed with pain,
Thou wilt return:—in MAINE thou shalt arise;
Thy innocence, we fondly may surmise,
Had seconded our lover's ardent flame,
And hastened his possession of the dame.

THE slowness usually in parents found,
Induced the girl, whose heart by LOVE was bound;
To celebrate the Hymeneal scene,
As in the statutes of Cythera's queen.
Our legendary writers this define
A present contract, where they nothing sign;
The thing is common;—marriage made in haste:
LOVE'S perparation: Hymen's bit for taste.

NOT much examination Cupid made,
As parent, lawyer, priest, he lent his aid,
And soon concluded matters as desired;
The Mansian wisdom no ways was required.

OUR spark was satisfied, and with his belle,
Passed nights so happy, nothing could excel;
'Twere easy to explain;—the double keys,
And gifts designed the chambermaid to please,
Made all secure, and ev'ry joy abound;
The soft delights with secrecy were crowned.

IT happened that our fair one evening said,
To her who of each infant step had led,
But of the present secret nothing knew:—
I feel unwell; pray tell me what to do.
The other answered, you my dear must take
A remedy that easily I'll make,
A clyster you shall have to-morrow morn:
By me most willingly it will be borne.

WHEN midnight came the sly gallant appeared,
Unluckily no doubt, but he revered
The moments that so pleasantly were passed,
Which always seemed, he thought, to glide too fast;
Relief he sought, for ev'ry one below
Is destined torments more or less to know.
He not a word was told of things designed,
And just as our gallant to sleep inclined,
As oft's the case at length with lovers true,
Quite open bright Aurora's portals flew,
And with a smile the aged dame arrived;
The apparatus properly contrived,
Was in her hand, she hastened to the bed,
And took the side that to the stripling led.

OUR lady fair was instantly confused,
Or she precaution properly had used,
'Twas easy to have kept a steady face,
And 'neath the clothes the other's head to place.
Pass presently beyond the hidden swain,
And t'other side with rapid motion gain,
A thing quite natural, we should suppose;
But fears o'erpow'red; the frightened damsel chose
To hide herself, then whispered her gallant,
What mighty terrors made her bosom pant.
The youth was sage, and coolly undertook
To offer for her:—t'other 'gan to look,
With spectacles on nose: soon all went right;
Adieu, she cried, and then withdrew from sight.
Heav'n guard her steps, and all conduct away,
Whose presence secret friendships would betray:

SHOULD this be thought a silly, idle tale;
(And that opinion may perhaps prevail)
To censure me, enough will surely try,
For criticks are severe, and these will cry,
Your lady like a simpleton escaped;
Her character you better might have shaped;
Which makes us doubt the truth of what is told:
Naught in your prologue like it we behold.

'TWERE sueless to reply: 'twould endless prove:
No arguments such censurers could move;
On men like these, devoid of sense or taste,
In vain might Cicero his rhet'rick waste.
Sufficient 'tis for me, that what is here,

I got from those who ev'ry-where appear
The friends of truth:—let others say the same;
What more would they expect should be my aim?

The Indiscreet Confessions

FAMED Paris ne'er within its walls had got,
Such magick charms as were Aminta's lot,
Youth, beauty, temper, fortune, she possessed,
And all that should a husband render blessed,
The mother still retained her 'neath the wing;
Her father's riches well might lovers bring;
Whate'er his daughter wished, he would provide,
Amusements, jewels, dress, and much beside.

BLITHE Damon for her having felt the dart,
The belle received the offer of his heart;
So well he managed and expressed his flame.
That soon her lord and master he became,
By Hymen's right divine, you may conceive,
And nothing short of it you should believe.

A YEAR had passed, and still our charming pair,
Were always pleased, and blisses seemed to share;
(The honeymoon appeared but just began)
And hopes were entertained to have a son,
When Damon on the subject chanced to touch:
In truth, said he, my soul is troubled much;
There is a fact, my dear, to you I'll tell:
I wish sincerely (since I love so well)

That for another, I had never known
Such fond affection as to you I've shown;
And none but you had entered in my breast,
So worthy ev'ry way to be caressed.
I have howe'er experienced other flame;
The fault's acknowledged: I confess my shame.
'Twas in a wood; the nymph was young and nice,
And Cupid only near to give advice;
So well he managed:—or so ill, you'll say;
A little girl I've living at this day.

WHAT, cried Aminta, now to you I'll state;
What happened once to be your spouse's fate;
I was at home alone, to say the truth,
When thither came by chance a sprightly youth.
The lad was handsome, with engaging mien;
I felt his worth:—my nature is serene;
In short so many things were our employ,
I've still upon my hands a little boy.

THESE words no sooner had escaped the belle,
Than Damon into jealous torments fell;
With rage he left the room; and on his way,
A large pack-saddle near his footsteps lay,
Which on his back he put, then cried aloud,
I'm saddled! see; round quickly came a crowd;
The father, mother, all the servants ran;
The neighbours too; the husband then began
To state the circumstance that gave him pain;
And fully all the folly to explain.

THE reader must not fail to keep in mind;
Aminta's parents were both rich and kind,
And having only her to be their heir,
The aged couple let the youthful pair,
With all their train, within the house reside,
And tranquilly the moments seemed to glide.

THU mother fondly to her daughter flew;
The father followed, keeping her in view;
The dame went in, but he remained without:
To listen he designed beyond a doubt;
The door was on the jar; the sage drew near;
In short, to all they said, he lent an ear;
The lady thus he heard reproach her child:
You're clearly wrong; most silly may be styled;
I've many simpletons and ninnies seen;
But such as you before there ne'er has been:
Who'd have believed you indiscreet like this?
Who forced you to reveal what was amiss?
What obligation to divulge the fact?
More girls than one have failed to be exact;
The Devil's crafty; folks are wicked too;
But that is no excuse, however true;
In convents all of us should be immured,
Till perfectly by Hymen's bands secured.

E'EN I who speak, alas! have troubles met;
Within my bosom oft I feel regret;
Three children ere my marriage I had got;
Have I your father told this secret blot?
Have we together been less happy found?

The list'ner had no sooner heard the sound,
But like a man distracted off he flew;
The saddle's girth, which hazard near him threw;
He took and fastened tightly 'bout his waist,
Then bawled around and round with anxious haste;
I'm girth'd! d'ye see, completely taken in;
The people stared, an 'gan to laugh and grin.
Though each was conscious, if the truth were known;
The ridicule in turn might be his own.

BOTH husbands madly ran from cross to square,
And with their foolish clamours rent the air;
I'm saddled, hooted one; I'm girth'd, said this;
The latter some perhaps will doubt, and hiss;
Such things however should not be disbelieved
For instance, recollect (what's well received),
When Roland learned the pleasures and the charms;
His rival, in the grot, had in his arms,
With fist he gave his horse so hard a blow,
It sunk at once to realms of poignant woe.
Might he not, training, round the hapless beast,
From weight of saddle have its back released,
And putting it upon his own, have cried,
I'm saddled, I'm girth'd, and much beside;
(No matter this or that, since each is good,)
Which Echo would repeat from hill to wood?
You see that truth may be discovered here;
That's not enough; its object should appear;
And that I'll show as further we proceed;
Your full attention I of course shall need.

THE happy Damon clearly seems to me,
As poor a thing as any we shall see;
His confidence would soon have spoiled the whole,
To leave a belle like this without control!
Her simplicity I much admire:—
Confess herself to spouse, as if a friar!
What silliness! imprudence is a word,
Which here to use would truly be absurd.
To my discourse two heads alone remain;
The marriage vow you always should maintain;
Its faith the pair should ever keep in view:
The path of honour steadily pursue.
If some mishap howe'er should chance to glide;
And make you limp on one or t'other side,
Endeavour, of the fault, to make the best,
And keep the secret locked within your breast;
Your own consideration never lose;
Untruth 'tis pardonable then to use.

NO doubt my pages nice advice supply;
Is't what I've followed?—No, you may rely!

The Contract

THE husband's dire mishap, and silly maid,
In ev'ry age, have proved the fable's aid;
The fertile subject never will be dry:
'Tis inexhaustible, you may rely.
No man's exempt from evils such as these:—
Who thinks himself secure, but little sees.
One laughs at sly intrigues who, ere 'tis long,
May, in his turn, be sneered at by the throng:
With such vicissitudes, to be cast down,
Appears rank nonsense worthy Folly's crown.
He, whose adventures I'm about to write,
In his mischances,—found what gave delight.

A CERTAIN Citizen, with fortune large,
When settled with a handsome wife in charge,
Not long attended for the marriage fruit:
The lady soon put matters 'yond dispute;
Produced a girl at first, and then a boy,
To fill th' expecting parent's breast with joy.

THE son, when grown of size, a tutor had,
No pedant rude, with Greek and Latin mad,
But young and smart, a master too of arts,
Particularly learned in what imparts,

The gentle flame, the pleasing poignant pang,
That Ovid formerly so sweetly sang.
Some knowledge of good company he'd got;
A charming voice and manner were his lot;
And if we may disclose the mystick truth,
'Twas Cupid who preceptor made the youth.
He with the brother solely took a place,
That better he the sister's charms might trace;
And under this disguise he fully gained
What he desired, so well his part he feigned:
An able master, or a lover true,
To teach or sigh, whichever was in view,
So thoroughly he could attention get,
Success alike in ev'ry thing he met.

IN little time the boy could construe well
The odes of Horace:—Virgil's fable tell;
And she whose beauty caught the tutor's eyes,
A perfect mistress got of heaving sighs.
So oft she practised what the master taught,
Her stomach feeble grew, whate'er was sought;
And strange suspicions of the cause arose,
Which Time at length was driven to disclose.

MOST terribly the father raged and swore;
Our learned master, frightened, left the door,
The lady wished to take the youth for life;
The spark desired to make the girl his wife;
Both had the Hymeneal knot in view,
And mutual soft affection fondly knew.
At present love is little more than name:

In matrimony, gold's the only aim.
The belle was rich, while he had nothing got;
For him 'twas great:—for her a narrow lot.

O DIRE corruption, age of wretched ways!
What strange caprice such management displays!
Shall we permit this fatal pow'r to reign?
Base int'rest's impulse: hideous modern stain;
The curse of ev'ry tender soft delight,
That charms the soul and fascinates the sight.

BUT truce to moral; let's our tale resume;
The daughter scared; the father in a fume;
What could be done the evil to repair,
And hide the sad misfortune of the fair?
What method seek?—They married her in haste;
But not to him who had the belle debased,
For reasons I've sufficiently detailed;
To gain her hand a certain wight prevailed,
Who store of riches relished far above
The charms of beauty, warmed with fondest love.
Save this the man might well enough be thought:
In family and wealth just what was sought;
But whether fool or not, I cannot trace,
Since he was unacquainted with the case;
And if he'd known it, was the bargain bad?
Full twenty thousand pounds he with her had
A sprightly youthful wife to ease his care,
And with him ev'ry luxury to share.

HOW many tempted by the golden ore,

Have taken wives whose slips they know before;
And this good man the lady chaste believed,
So truly well she managed and deceived.
But when four months had passed, the fair-one showed.
How very much she to her lessons owed;
A little girl arrived: the husband stared
Cried he, what father of a child declared!
The time's too short: four months! I'm taken in!
A family should not so soon begin.

AWAY he to the lady's father flew,
And of his shame a horrid picture drew;
Proposed to be divorced: much rage disclosed;
The parent smiled and said, pray be composed;
Speak not so loud: we may be overheard,
And privacy is much to be preferred.
A son-in-law, like you, I once appeared,
And similar misfortune justly feared;
Complaint I made, and mentioned a divorce;
Of heat and rage the ordinary course.

THE father of my wife, who's now no more,
(Heav'n guard his soul, the loss I oft deplore,)
A prudent honest man as any round,
To calm my mind, a nice specifick found;
The pill was rather bitter, I admit;
But gilding made it for the stomach fit,
Which he knew how to manage very well:
No doctor in it him could e'er excel;
To satisfy my scruples he displayed
A CONTRACT (duly stamped and ably made),

Four thousand to secure, which he had got,
On similar occasion for a blot;
His lady's father gave it to efface
Domestick diff'rences and like disgrace:
With this my spouse's fortune he increased;
And instantly my dire complaining ceased.
From family to family the deed
Should pass, 'twill often prove a useful meed;
I kept it for the purpose:—do the same
Your daughter, married, may have equal blame.
On this the son-in-law the bond received,
And, with a bow, departed much relieved.

MAY Heav'n preserve from trouble those who find,
At cheaper rate, to be consoled inclined.

The Quid Pro Quo; or The Mistakes

DAME FORTUNE often loves a laugh to raise,
And, playing off her tricks and roguish ways,
Instead of giving us what we desire,
Mere quid pro quo permits us to acquire.
I've found her gambols such from first to last,
And judge the future by experience past.
Fair Cloris and myself felt mutual flame;
And, when a year had run, the sprightly dame
Prepared to grant me, if I may be plain,
Some slight concessions that would ease my pain.
This was her aim; but whatsoe'er in view,
'Tis opportunity we should pursue;
The lover, who's discreet, will moments seize;
And ev'ry effort then will tend to please.

ONE eve I went this charming fair to see;
The husband happened (luckily for me)
To be abroad; but just as it was night
The master came, not doubting all was right;
No Cloris howsoe'er was in the way;
A servant girl, of disposition gay,
Well known to me, with pretty smiling face,
'Tis said, was led to take her lady's place.

The mistress' loss for once was thus repaid;
The barter mutual:—wife against the maid.

WITH many tales like this the books abound;
But able hands are necessary found,
To place the incidents, arrange the whole,
That nothing may be forced nor feel control.
The urchin blind, who sees enough to lay
His num'rous snares, such tricks will often play.
The CRADLE in Boccace excels the most,
As to myself I do not mean to boast,
But fear, a thousand places, spite of toil,
By him made excellent, my labours spoil.
'Tis time howe'er with preface to have done,
And show, by some new turn, or piece of fun,
(While easy numbers from my pencil flow,)
Of Fortune and of Love the quid pro quo.
In proof, we'll state what happened at Marseilles:
The story is so true, no doubt prevails.

THERE Clidamant, whose proper name my verse,
Prom high respect, refuses to rehearse,
Lived much at ease: not one a wife had got,
Throughout the realm, who was so nice a lot,
Her virtues, temper, and seraphick charms,
Should have secured the husband to her arms;
But he was not to constancy inclined;
The devil's crafty; snares has often twined
Around and round, with ev'ry subtle art,
When love of novelty he would impart.

THE lady had a maid, whose form and size,
Height, easy manners, action, lips, and eyes,
Were thought to be so very like her own,
That one from t'other scarcely could be known;
The mistress was the prettiest of the two;
But, in a mask where much escapes the view,
'Twas very difficult a choice to make,
And feel no doubts which better 'twere to take.

THE Marseillesian husband, rather gay,
With mistress Alice was disposed to play;
(For such was called the maid we just have named;)
To show coquettish airs the latter aimed,
And met his wishes with reproof severe;
But to his plan the lover would adhere,
And promised her at length a pretty sum:
A hundred crowns, if to his room she'd come.
To pay the girl with kindness such as this,
In my opinion, was not much amiss.
At that rate what should be the mistress' price?
Perhaps still less: she might not be so nice.
But I mistake; the lady was so coy,
No spark, whatever art he could employ,
How cleverly soe'er he laid the snare,
Would have succeeded, spite of ev'ry care.
Nor presents nor attentions would have swayed;
Should I have mentioned presents as an aid?
Alas! no longer these are days of old!
By Love both nymph and shepherdess are sold;
He sets the price of many beauties rare;
This was a god;—now nothing but a mayor.

O ALTERED times! O customs how depraved!
At first fair Alice frowardly behaved;
But in the sequel 'gan to change her way,
And said, her mistress, as the foll'wing day,
A certain remedy to take designed;
That, in the morning then, if so inclined,
They could at leisure in the cavern meet;—
The plan was pleasing: all appeared discreet.

THE servant, having to her mistress said,
What projects were in view: what nets were spread;
The females, 'tween themselves, a plot contrived,
Of Quid pro quo, against the hour arrived.
The husband of the trick was ne'er aware,
So much the mistress had her servant's air;
But if he had, what then? no harm of course;
She might have lectured him with double force.

NEXT day but one, gay Clidamant, whose joy
Appeared so great, 'twas free from all alloy,
By hazard met a friend, to whom he told
(Most indiscreetly) what to him was sold;
How Cupid favoured what he most required,
And freely granted all he had desired.
Though large the blessing, yet he grudged the cost;
The sum gave pain: a hundred crowns were lost!
The friend proposed they should at once decide,
The charge and pleasure 'tween them to divide.
Our husband thought his purse not over strong,
That saving fifty crowns would not be wrong.
But then, on t'other hand, to lend the fair,

In ev'ry view had got an awkward air;
Would she, as was proposed, consent to two?
To keep things secret would their lips be true?
Or was it fair to sacrifice her charms,
And lay her open thus to dire alarms?

THE friend this difficulty soon removed,
And represented that the cavern proved
So very dark, the girl would be deceived;
With one more shrewd the trick might be achieved.
Sufficient howsoever it would be,
If they by turns, and silent, could agree
To meet the belle, and leave to Love the rest,
From whom they hoped assistance if distressed.
Such silence to observe no hurt could do,
And Alice would suppose, a prudent view
Retained the tongue, since walls have often ears,
And, being mum, expressive was of fears.

WHEN thus the two gallants their plan had laid,
And ev'ry promised pleasure fully weighed,
They to the husband's mansion made their way,
Where yet the wife between the bed-clothes lay.
The servant girl was near her mistress found;
Her dress was plain: no finery around;
In short, 'twas such that, when the moment came;
To fail the meeting could not be her aim.

THE friends disputed which the lead should take,
And strong pretentions both appeared to make;
The husband, honours home would not allow:

Such compliments were out of fashion now.
To settle this, at length three dice they took;
The friend was highest placed in Fortune's book.
The both together to the cavern flew,
And for the servant soon impatient grew;
But Alice never came, and in her room
The mistress, softly treading 'mid the gloom,
The necessary signal gently gave,
On which she entered presently the cave,
And this so suddenly, no time was found
To make remarks on change or errors round,
Or any diff'rence 'tween the friend and spouse;
In short, before suspicions 'gan to rouse,
Or alteration lent the senses aid:—
To LOVE, a sacrifice was fully made.
The lucky wight more pleasure would have felt,
If sensible he'd been with whom he dealt:
The mistress rather more of beauty had,
And QUALITY of course must something add.

THIS scene just ended, t'other actor came,
Whose prompt arrival much surprised the dame,
For, as a husband, Clidamant had ne'er
Such ardour shown, he seemed beyond his sphere.
The lady to the girl imputed this,
And thought, to hint it, would not be amiss.

THE entertainment o'er, away they went
To quit the dark abode they were intent.
The partner in amour repaired above;
But when the husband saw his wedded love

Ascend the stairs, and she the friend perceived,
We well may judge how bosoms beat and heaved.

THE master of the house conceived it best
To keep the whole a secret in his breast.
But to discover ALL, his lovely rib
Appeared disposed, though wives can often fib;
The silliest of the throng (or high or low),
Most perfectly the science seem to know.

SOME will pretend that Alice, in her heart
Was sorry she had acted such a part,
And not a better method sought to gain
The money which had caused her master's pain;
Lamented much the case, and tried to please
By ev'ry means that might his trouble ease.
But this is merely with design to make
The tale a more impressive feature take.

TWO questions may agitate around;
The one, if 'mong the brotherhood renowned,
The husband, who thus felt disgraced,
Should (with the usual ornaments) be placed?
But I no grounds for such conclusion see:
Both friend and wife were from suspicion free;
Of one another they had never thought,
Though in the mystick scene together brought.
The other is:—Should she, who was misused,
Have sought revenge for being so abused?
Though this sufficiently I have maintained,
The lady inconsolable remained.

HEAV'N guard the FAIR, who meet with ills like these,
And nothing can their wounded minds appease:
I many know howe'er, who would but laugh,
And treat such accidents as light as chaff.
But I have done: no more of that or this;
May ev'ry belle receive her lot of bliss!

The Dress-Maker

A CLOISTERED nun had a lover
Dwelling in the neighb'ring town;
Both racked their brains to discover
How they best their love might crown.
The swain to pass the convent-door!—
No easy matter!—Thus they swore,
And wished it light.—I ne'er knew a nun
In such a pass to be outdone:—
In woman's clothes the youth must dress,
And gain admission. I confess
The ruse has oft been tried before,
But it succeeded as of yore.
Together in a close barred cell
The lovers were, and sewed all day,
Nor heeded how time flew away.—
"What's that I hear? Refection bell!
"'Tis time to part. Adieu!—Farewell!—
"How's this?" exclaimed the abbess, "why
"The last at table?"—"Madam, I
"Have had my dress-maker."—"The rent
"On which you've both been so intent
"Is hard to stop, for the whole day
"To sew and mend, you made her stay;
"Much work indeed you've had to do!

"—Madam, 't would last the whole night through,
"When in our task we find enjoyment
"There is no end of the employment."

The Gascon

I AM always inclined to suspect
The best story under the sun
As soon as by chance I detect
That teller and hero are one.

WE'RE all of us prone to conceit,
And like to proclaim our own glory,
But our purpose we're apt to defeat
As actors in chief of our story.

TO prove the truth of what I state
Let me an anecdote relate:
A Gascon with his comrade sat
At tavern drinking. This and that
He vaunted with assertion pat.
From gasconade to gasconade
Passed to the conquests he had made
In love. A buxom country maid,
Who served the wine, with due attention
Lent patient ear to each invention,
And pressed her hands against her side
Her bursting merriment to hide.
To hear our Gascon talk, no Sue
Nor Poll in town but that he knew;

With each he'd passed a blissful night
More to their own than his delight.
This one he loved for she was fair,
That for her glossy ebon hair.
One miss, to tame his cruel rigour,
Had brought him gifts.—She owned his vigour
In short it wanted but his gaze
To set each trembling heart ablaze.
His strength surpassed his luck,—the test—
In one short night ten times he'd blessed
A dame who gratefully expressed
Her thanks with corresponding zest.
At this the maid burst forth, "What more?
"I never heard such lies before!
"Content were I if at that sport
"I had what that poor dame was short."

The Pitcher

THE simple Jane was sent to bring
Fresh water from the neighb'ring spring;
The matter pressed, no time to waste,
Jane took her jug, and ran in haste
The well to reach, but in her flurry
(The more the speed the worse the hurry),
Tripped on a rolling stone, and broke
Her precious pitcher,—ah! no joke!
Nay, grave mishap! 'twere better far
To break her neck than such a jar!
Her dame would beat and soundly rate her,
No way could Jane propitiate her.
Without a sou new jug to buy!
'Twere better far for her to die!
O'erwhelmed by grief and cruel fears
Unhappy Jane burst into tears
"I can't go home without the delf,"
Sobbed Jane, "I'd rather kill myself;
"So here am I resolved to die."
A friendly neighbour passing by
O'erheard our damsel's lamentation;
And kindly offered consolation:
"If death, sweet maiden, be thy bent,
"I'll aid thee in thy sad intent."

Throwing her down, he drew his dirk,
And plunged it in the maid,—a work
You'll say was cruel,—not so Jane,
Who even seemed to like the pain,
And hoped to be thus stabbed again.
Amid the weary world's alarms,
For some e'en death will have its charms;
"If this, my friend, is how you kill,
"Of breaking jugs I'll have my fill!"

To Promise is One Thing
To Keep it, Another

JOHN courts Perrette; but all in vain;
Love's sweetest oaths, and tears, and sighs
All potent spells her heart to gain
The ardent lover vainly tries:
Fruitless his arts to make her waver,
She will not grant the smallest favour:
A ruse our youth resolved to try
The cruel air to mollify:—
Holding his fingers ten outspread
To Perrette's gaze, and with no dread
"So often," said he, "can I prove,
"My sweet Perrette, how warm my love."
When lover's last avowals fail
To melt the maiden's coy suspicions
A lover's sign will oft prevail
To win the way to soft concessions:
Half won she takes the tempting bait;
Smiles on him, draws her lover nearer,
With heart no longer obdurate
She teaches him no more to fear her—
A pinch,—a kiss,—a kindling eye,—
Her melting glances,—nothing said.—
John ceases not his suit to ply

Till his first finger's debt is paid.
A second, third and fourth he gains,
Takes breath, and e'en a fifth maintains.
But who could long such contest wage?
Not I, although of fitting age,
Nor John himself, for here he stopped,
And further effort sudden dropped.
Perrette, whose appetite increased
just as her lover's vigour ceased,
In her fond reckoning defeated,
Considered she was greatly cheated—
If duty, well discharged, such blame
Deserve; for many a highborn dame
Would be content with such deceit.
But Perrette, as already told,
Out of her count, began to scold
And call poor John an arrant cheat
For promising and not performing.
John calmly listened to her storming,
And well content with work well done,
Thinking his laurels fairly won,
Cooly replied, on taking leave:
"No cause I see to fume and grieve;
"Or for such trifle to dispute;
"To promise and to execute
"Are not the same, be it confessed,
"Suffice it to have done one's best;
"With time I'll yet discharge what's due;
"Meanwhile, my sweet Perrette, adieu!"

The Nightingale

NO easy matter 'tis to hold,
Against its owner's will, the fleece
Who troubled by the itching smart
Of Cupid's irritating dart,
Eager awaits some Jason bold
To grant release.
E'en dragon huge, or flaming steer,
When Jason's loved will cause no fear.

DUENNAS, grating, bolt and lock,
All obstacles can naught avail;
Constraint is but a stumbling block;
For youthful ardour must prevail.
Girls are precocious nowadays,
Look at the men with ardent gaze,
And longings' an infinity;
Trim misses but just in their teens
By day and night devise the means
To dull with subtlety to sleep
The Argus vainly set to keep
In safety their virginity.
Sighs, smiles, false tears, they'll fain employ
An artless lover to decoy.
I'll say no more, but leave to you,

Friend reader, to pronounce if true
What I've asserted when you have heard
How artful Kitty, caged her bird.

IN a small town in Italy,
The name of which I do not know,
Young Kitty dwelt, gay, pretty, free,
Varambon's child.—Boccacio
Omits her mother's name, which not
To you or me imports a jot.
At fourteen years our Kitty's charms
Were all that could be wished—plump arms,
A swelling bosom; on her cheeks
Roses' and lilies' mingled streaks,
A sparkling eye—all these, you know,
Speak well for what is found below.
With such advantages as these
No virgin sure could fail to please,
Or lack a lover; nor did Kate;
But little time she had to wait;
One soon appeared to seal her fate.
Young Richard saw her, loved her, wooed her—
What swain I ask could have withstood her?
Soft words, caresses, tender glances,
The battery of love's advances,
Soon lit up in the maiden's breast
The flame which his own heart possessed,
Soon growing to a burning fire
Of love and mutual desire.
Desire for what? My reader knows,
Or if he does not may suppose,

And not be very wond'rous wise.
When youthful lovers mingle sighs,
Believe me, friend, I am not wrong,
For one thing only do they long.
One check deferred our lover's bliss,
A thing quite natural, 'twas this:
The mother loved so well her child
That, fearful she might be beguiled,
She would not let her out of sight,
A single minute, day or night.
At mother's apron string all day
Kate whiled the weary hours away,
And shared her bed all night. Such love
In parents we must all approve,
Though Catherine, I must confess,
In place of so much tenderness
More liberty would have preferred.
To little girls maternal care
In such excess is right and fair,
But for a lass of fourteen years,
For whom one need have no such fears,
Solicitude is quite absurd,
And only bores her. Kitty could
No moment steal, do what she would,
To see her Richard. Sorely vexed
She was, and he still more perplexed.
In spite of all he might devise
A squeeze, a kiss, quick talk of eyes
Was all he could obtain, no more.
Bread butterless, a sanded floor,
It seemed no better. Joy like this

Could not suffice, more sterling bliss
Our lovers wished, nor would stop short
Till they'd obtained the thing they sought.
And thus it came about. One day
By chance they met, alone, away
From jealous parents. "What's the use;"
Said Richard, "of all our affection?
"Of love it is a rank abuse,
"And yields me nothing but dejection
"I see you without seeing you,
"Must always look another way,
"And if we meet I dare not stay,
"Must ev'ry inclination smother.
"I can't believe your love is true;
"I'll never own you really kind
"Unless some certain means you find
"For us to meet without your mother."
Kate answered: "Were it not too plain
"How warm my love, another strain
"I would employ. In converse vain
"Let us not waste our moments few;
"But think what it were best to do."
"If you will please me," Robert said,
"You must contrive to change your bed,
"And have it placed—well, let me see—
"Moved to the outer gallery,
"Where you will be alone and free.
"We there can meet and chat at leisure
"While others sleep, nor need we fear,
"Of merry tales I have a treasure
"To tell, but cannot tell them here."

Kate smiled at this for she knew well
What sort of tales he had to tell;
But promised she would do her best
And soon accomplish his request.
It was not easy, you'll admit,
But love lends foolish maidens wit;
And this is how she managed it.
The whole night long she kept awake,
Snored, sighed and kicked, as one possessed,
That parents both could get not rest,
So much she made the settle shake.
This is not strange. A longing girl,
With thoughts of sweetheart in her head,
In bed all night will sleepless twirl.
A flea is in her ear, 'tis said.
The morning broke. Of fleas and heat
Kitty complained. "Let me entreat,
"O mother, I may put my bed
"Out in the gallery," she said,
"'Tis cooler there, and Philomel
"Who warbles in the neigh'bring dell
"Will solace me." Ready consent
The simple mother gave, and went
To seek her spouse. "Our Kate, my dear,
"Will change her bed that she may hear
"The nightingale, and sleep more cool."
"Wife," said the good man, "You're a fool,
"And Kate too with her nightingale;
"Don't tell me such a foolish tale.
"She must remain. No doubt to-night
"Will fresher be. I sleep all right

"In spite of heat, and so can she.
"Is she more delicate than me?"
Incensed was Kate by this denial
After so promising a trial,
Nor would be beat, but firmly swore
To give more trouble than before.
That night again no wink she slept
But groaned and fretted, sighed and wept,
Upon her couch so tossed and turned,
The anxious mother quite concerned
Again her husband sought. "Our Kate
"To me seems greatly changed of late.
"You are unkind," she said to him,
"To thwart her simple, girlish whim.
"Why may she not her bed exchange,
"In naught will it the house derange?
"Placed in the passage she's as near
"To us as were she lying here.
"You do not love your child, and will
"With your unkindness make her ill."
"Pray cease," the husband cried, "to scold
"And take your whim. I ne'er could hold
"My own against a screaming wife;
"You'll drive me mad, upon my life.
"Her belly-full our Kate may get
"Of nightingale or of linnet."
The thing was settled. Kate obeyed,
And in a trice her bed was made,
And lover signalled. Who shall say
How long to both appeared that day,
That tedious day! But night arrived

And Richard too; he had contrived
By ladder, and a servant's aid,
To reach the chamber of the maid.
To tell how often they embraced,
How changed in form their tenderness,
Would lead to nothing but a waste
Of time, my readers will confess.
The longest, most abstruse discourse
Would lack precision, want the force
Their youthful ardour to portray.
To understand there's but one way—
Experience. The nightingale
Sang all night long his pleasing tale,
And though he made but little noise,
The lass was satisfied. Her joys
So exquisite that she averred
The other nightingale, the bird
Who warbles to the woods his bliss,
Was but an ass compared with this.
But nature could not long maintain
Of efforts such as these the strain;
Their forces spent, the lovers twain
In fond embrace fell fast asleep
Just as the dawn began to peep:
The father as he left his bed
By curiosity was led
To learn if Kitty soundly slept,
And softly to the passage crept.
"I'll see the influence," he said,
"Of nightingale and change of bed."
With bated breath, upon tip toes,

Close to the couch he cautious goes
Where Kitty lay in calm repose.
Excessive heat had made all clothes
Unbearable. The sleeping pair
Had cast them off, and lay as bare
As our first happy parents were
In Paradise. But in the place
Of apple, in her willing hand
Kate firmly grasp the magic wand
Which served to found the human race,
The which to name were a disgrace,
Though dames the most refined employ it;
Desire it, and much enjoy it,
If good Catullus tells us true.
The father scarce believed his view,
But keeping in his bosom pent
His anger, to his wife he went,
And said, "Get up, and come with me.
"At present I can plainly see
"Why Kate had such anxiety
"To hear the nightingale, for she
"To catch the bird so well has planned
"That now she holds him in her hand."
The mother almost wept for glee.
"A nightingale, oh! let me see.
"How large is he, and can he sing,
"And will he breed, the pretty thing?
"How did she catch him, clever child?"
Despite his grief the good man smiled.
"Much more than you expect you'll see.
"But hold your tongue, and come with me;

"For if your chattering is heard,
"Away will fly the timid bird;
"And you will spoil our daughter's game."
Who was surprised? It was the dame.
Her anger burst into a flame
As she the nightingale espied
Which Kitty held; she could have cried,
And scolded, called her nasty slut,
And brazen hussey, bitch, and—but
Her husband stopped her. "What's the use
"Of all your scolding and abuse?
"The mischief's done, in vain may you
"From now till doomsday fret and stew,
"Misfortune done you can't undo,
"But something may be done to mend:
"For notary this instant send,
"Bid holy priest and mayor attend.
"For their good offices I wait
"To set this nasty matter straight."
As he discoursed, Richard awoke,
And seeing that the sun had broke,
These troubled words to Kitty spoke
"Alas, my love, 'tis broad day light,
"How can I now effect my flight?"
"All will go well," rejoined the sire,
"I will not grumble, my just ire
"Were useless here; you have committed
"A wrong of which to be acquitted,
"Richard, there is one only way,
"My child you wed without delay.
"She's well brought up, young, full of health

"If fortune has not granted wealth,
"Her beauty you do not deny,
"So wed her, or prepare to die."
To hesitate in such a case
Would surely have been out of place
The girl he loved to take to wife,
Or in his prime to lose his life,
The point in truth needs no debate,
Nor did our Richard hesitate.
Besides, the most supreme delight
Of life he'd tasted one short night,
But one, in lovely Kitty's arms;
Could he so soon resign her charms!
While Richard, pleased with his escape
From what he feared an awkward scrape,
Was dreaming of his happy choice,
Our Kitty, by her father's voice
Awakened, from her hand let go
The cause of all her joy and woe,
And round her naked beauties wound
The sheet picked up from off the ground:
Meanwhile the notary appears
To put an end to all their fears.
They wrote, they signed, the sealed—and thus
The wedding ended free from fuss.
They left the happy couple there.
His satisfaction to declare,
Thus spoke their father to the pair:
"Take courage, children, have no care;
"The nightingale in cage is pent,
"May sing now to his heart's content."

Epitaph of La Fontaine Made by Himself

JOHN, as he came, so went away,
Consuming capital and pay,
Holding superfluous riches cheap;
The trick of spending time he knew,
Dividing it in portions two,
For idling one, and one for sleep.

THE END

www.ingramcontent.com/pod-product-compliance
Lightning Source LLC
Chambersburg PA
CBHW030342310726
48979CB00001B/151

* 9 7 8 1 8 4 9 0 2 3 8 3 2 *